Scott Walter

The Poetical Works of Sir Walter Scott, Bart.

The lord of the isles. Vol. X

Scott Walter

The Poetical Works of Sir Walter Scott, Bart.
The lord of the isles. Vol. X

ISBN/EAN: 9783337394004

Printed in Europe, USA, Canada, Australia, Japan

Cover: Foto ©Andreas Hilbeck / pixelio.de

More available books at **www.hansebooks.com**

THE

POETICAL WORKS

OF

SIR WALTER SCOTT, BART.

VOL X.

THE LORD OF THE ISLES.
OCCASIONAL PIECES.

EDINBURGH:

ADAM AND CHARLES BLACK.

1861.

CONTENTS

OCCASIONAL PIECES NOT CONTAINED IN ANY FORMER EDITION OF
SIR WALTER SCOTT'S POETICAL WORKS.

NOTICE.

[THE composition of " The Lord of the Isles," as we now have it in the Author's MS., seems to have been begun at Abbotsford, in the Autumn of 1814, and it ended at Edinburgh, the 16th of December. Some part of Canto I. had probably been committed to writing in a rougher form earlier in the year. The original Quarto appeared on the 2d of January, 1815.

It may be mentioned, that those parts of this poem which were written at Abbotsford, were composed almost all in the presence of Sir Walter Scott's family, and many in that of casual visitors also : the original cottage which he then occupied not affording him any means of retirement. Neither conversation nor music seemed to disturb him.

In this volume are included some occasional pieces not printed in any preceding edition of the Author's Works.]

INTRODUCTION

TO

THE LORD OF THE ISLES.

INTRODUCTION

TO

THE LORD OF THE ISLES.

I could hardly have chosen a subject more
popular in Scotland, than any thing connected
with the Bruce's history, unless I had attempted
that of Wallace. But I am decidedly of opinion,
that a popular, or what is called a *taking* title,
though well qualified to ensure the publishers
against loss, and clear their shelves of the original impression, is rather apt to be hazardous than
otherwise to the reputation of the author. He
who attempts a subject of distinguished popularity, has not the privilege of awakening the
enthusiasm of his audience ; on the contrary, it
is already awakened, and glows, it may be, more

ardently than that of the author himself. In
this case, the warmth of the author is inferior to
that of the party whom he addresses, who has,
therefore, little chance of being, in Bayes's
phrase, "elevated and surprised" by what he
has thought of with more enthusiasm than the
writer. The sense of this risk, joined to the
consciousness of striving against wind and tide,
made the task of composing the proposed Poem
somewhat heavy and hopeless ; but, like the
prize-fighter in "As You Like it," I was to
wrestle for my reputation, and not neglect any
advantage. In a most agreeable pleasure-voyage,
which I have tried to commemorate in the Introduction to the new edition of the "Pirate," I
visited, in social and friendly company,[1] the
coasts and islands of Scotland, and made myself
acquainted with the localities of which I meant
to treat. But this voyage, which was in every
other effect so delightful, was in its conclusion
saddened by one of those strokes of fate which

[1] [See a note to the lines superscribed "Pharos loquitur,"
included in this volume; and see also "Fragments of a Tour in
the Hebrides," &c. printed in the Edinburgh Annual Register for
1812.]

so often mingle themselves with our pleasures. The accomplished and excellent person who had recommended to me the subject for "The Lay of the Last Minstrel," and to whom I proposed to inscribe what I already suspected might be the close of my poetical labours, was unexpectedly removed from the world, which she seemed only to have visited for purposes of kindness and benevolence. It is needless to say how the author's feelings, or the composition of his trifling work, were affected by a circumstance which occasioned so many tears and so much sorrow.[1] True it is, that "The Lord of the Isles" was concluded, unwillingly and in haste, under the painful feeling of one who has a task which must be finished, rather than with the ardour of one who endeavours to perform that task well. Although the Poem cannot be said to have made a favourable impression on the public, the sale of fifteen thousand copies enabled the author to retreat from the field with the honours of war.

[1] [Harriet, Duchess of Buccleuch, died 24th August, 1814. Sir Walter Scott received the mournful intelligence while visiting the Giant's Causeway, and immediately returned home.]

In the meantime, what was necessarily to be considered as a failure, was much reconciled to my feelings by the success attending my attempt in another species of composition. " Waverley " had, under strict incognito, taken its flight from the press, just before I set out upon the voyage already mentioned ; it had now made its way to popularity, and the success of that work and the volumes which followed, was sufficient to have satisfied a greater appetite for applause than I have at any time possessed.[1]

I may as well add in this place, that, being much urged by my intimate friend, now unhappily no more, William Erskine, (a Scottish judge, by the title of Lord Kinedder,) I agreed to write the little romantic tale called the " Bridal of Triermain ;" but it was on the condition, that he should make no serious effort to disown the composition, if report should lay it at his door. As he was more than suspected of a taste for poetry, and as I took care, in several places, to mix something which might resemble (as far as was in my power) my friend's feeling and man-

---

[1] [The first edition of Waverley appeared in July 1814.]

ner, the train easily caught, and two large editions were sold. A third being called for, Lord Kinedder became unwilling to aid any longer a deception which was going farther than he expected or desired, and the real author's name was given. Upon another occasion, I sent up another of these trifles, which, like schoolboys' kites, served to shew how the wind of popular taste was setting. The manner was supposed to be that of a rude minstrel, or Scald, in opposition to the " Bridal of Triermain," which was designed to belong rather to the Italian school. This new fugitive piece was called " Harold the Dauntless ; "[1] and I am still astonished at my having committed the gross error of selecting the very name which Lord Byron had made so famous. It encountered rather an odd fate. My ingenious friend, Mr James Hogg, had published, about the same time, a work called the " Poetic Mirror," containing imitations of the principal living poets.[2] There was in it a very good imi-

---

[1] [" Harold the Dauntless " was first published in a small 12mo volume, December, 1816.]

[2] [Mr Hogg's " Poetic Mirror " appeared in October, 1816.]

tation of my own style, which bore such a resemblance to " Harold the Dauntless," that there was no discovering the original from the imitation ; and I believe that many who took the trouble of thinking upon the subject, were rather of opinion that my ingenious friend was the true, and not the fictitious Simon Pure.   Since this period, which was in the year 1816, the Author has not been an intruder on the public by any poetical work of importance.

W. S.

ABBOTSFORD, April, 1830

THE

LORD OF THE ISLES.

A POEM.

IN SIX CANTOS.

ADVERTISEMENT.

The scene of this poem lies, at first, in the Castle of Artornish, on the coast of Argyleshire; and, afterwards, in the Islands of Skye and Arran, and upon the coast of Ayrshire. Finally, it is laid near Stirling. The story opens in the spring of the year 1307, when Bruce, who had been driven out of Scotland by the English, and the Barons who adhered to that foreign interest, returned from the Island of Rachrin on the coast of Ireland, again to assert his claims to the Scottish crown. Many of the personages and incidents introduced are of historical celebrity. The authorities used are chiefly those of the venerable Lord Hailes, as well entitled to be called the restorer of Scottish history, as Bruce the restorer of Scottish monarchy; and of Archdeacon Barbour, a correct edition of whose Metrical History of Robert Bruce[1] will soon, I trust, appear, under the care of my learned friend, the Rev. Dr Jamieson.

Abbotsford, 10th December, 1814.[2]

[1] [The work alluded to appeared in 1820, under the title of " The Bruce and Wallace." 2 vols. 4to.]

[2] ["Here is another genuine lay of the great Minstrel, with all his characteristic faults, beauties, and irregularities. The same glow of colouring—the same energy of narration—the same am-

plitude of description, are conspicuous here, which distinguish all his other productions :—with the same still more characteristic disdain of puny graces and small originalities—the true poetical hardihood, in the strength of which he urges on his Pegasus fearlessly through dense and rare, and aiming gallantly at the great ends of truth and effect, stoops but rarely to study the means by which they are to be attained—avails himself, without scruple, of common sentiments and common images whereever they seem fitted for his purposes—and is original by the very boldness of his borrowing, and impressive by his disregard of epigram and emphasis.

" Though bearing all these marks of the master's hand, the work before us does not come up, in interest, to the Lady of the Lake, or even to Marmion. There is less connected story—and, what there is, is less skilfully complicated and disentangled, and less diversified with change of scene, or variety of character. In the scantiness of the narrative, and the broken and discontinuous order of the events, as well as the inartificial insertion of detached descriptions and morsels of ethical reflection, it bears more resemblance to the earliest of the author's greater productions ; and suggests a comparison, perhaps not altogether to his advantage, with the structure and execution of the Lay of the Last Minstrel :—for though there is probably more force and substance in the latter parts of the present work, it is certainly inferior to that enchanting performance in delicacy and sweetness, and even—is it to be wondered at, after four such publications ?—in originality.

" The title of ' The Lord of the Isles,' has been adopted, we presume, to match that of ' The Lady of the Lake ;' but there is no analogy in the stories—nor does the title, on this occasion, correspond very exactly with the contents. It is no unusual misfortune, indeed, for the author of a modern Epic to have his hero turn out but a secondary personage, in the gradual unfolding of the story, while some unruly underling runs off with the whole glory and interest of the poem. But here the author, we conceive, must have been aware of the misnomer from the beginning ; the true, and indeed the ostensible hero being, from tho very first, no less a person than King Robert Bruce."—*Edinburgh Review*, No. xlviii. 1815.]

[" If it be possible for a poet to bestow upon his writings a superfluous degree of care and correction, it may also be possible, we should suppose, to bestow too little. Whether this be the case in the poem before us, is a point upon which Mr Scott can possibly form a much more competent judgment than ourselves ; we can only say, that without possessing greater beauties than its predecessors, it has certain violations of propriety, both in the language and in the composition of the story, of which the former efforts of his muse afforded neither so many nor such striking examples.

" We have not now any quarrel with Mr Scott on account of the measure which he has chosen; still less on account of his subjects : we believe that they are both of them not only pleasing in themselves, but well adapted to each other and to the bent of his peculiar genius. On the contrary, it is because we admire his genius, and are partial to the subjects which he delights in, that we so much regret he should leave room for any difference of opinion respecting them, merely from not bestowing upon his publications that common degree of labour and meditation which we cannot help saying it is scarcely decorous to withhold."—*Quarterly Review*, No. xxvi. July, 1815.]

LORD OF THE ISLES.

CANTO FIRST.

.

THE

LORD OF THE ISLES.

CANTO FIRST.

~~~~~~~

Autumn departs—but still his mantle's fold
Rests on the groves of noble Somerville,
Beneath a shroud of russet dropp'd with gold
Tweed and his tributaries mingle still ;
Hoarser the wind, and deeper sounds the rill,
Yet lingering notes of silvan music swell,
The deep-toned cushat, and the readbreast shrill ;
And yet some tints of summer splendour tell
When the broad sun sinks down on Ettrick's western
    fell.

1 [John, fifteenth Lord Somerville, illustrious for his patriotic
devotion to the science of agriculture, resided frequently in his
beautiful villa called the Pavilion, situated on the Tweed over
against Melrose, and was an intimate friend and most daily
companion of the poet, from whose windows at Abbotsford his
lordship's plantations formed a prominent object. Lord S. died
in 1819.]

Autumn departs—from Gala's fields[1] no more
Come rural sounds our kindred banks to cheer;
Blent with the stream, and gale that wafts it o'er,
No more the distant reaper's mirth we hear.
The last blithe shout hath died upon our ear,
And harvest-home hath hush'd the clanging wain,
On the waste hill no forms of life appear,
Save where, sad laggard of the autumnal train,
Some age-struck wanderer gleans few ears of scat-
ter'd grain.

Deem'st thou these sadden'd scenes have pleasure
still,
Lovest thou through Autumn's fading realms to
stray,
To see the heath-flower wither'd on the hill,
To listen to the wood's expiring lay,
To note the red leaf shivering on the spray,
To mark the last bright tints the mountain stain,
On the waste fields to trace the gleaner's way,
And moralize on mortal joy and pain?—
O! if such scenes thou lovest, scorn not the minstrel
strain.

No! do not scorn, although its hoarser note
Scarce with the cushat's homely song can vie,

---

[1] [The river Gala, famous in song, flows into the Tweed a few
hundred yards below Abbotsford; but probably the word *Gala*
here stands for the poet's neighbour and kinsman, and much
attached friend; John Scott, Esq. of Gala.]

Though faint its beauties as the tints remote
That gleam through mist in autumn's evening sky,
And few as leaves that tremble, sear and dry,
When wild November hath his bugle wound;
Nor mock my toil—a lonely gleaner I,[1]
Through fields time-wasted, on sad inquest bound,
Where happier bards of yore have richer harvest
    found.

So shalt thou list, and haply not unmoved,
To a wild tale of Albyn's warrior day;
In distant lands, by the rough West reproved,
Still live some relics of the ancient lay.
For, when on Coolin's hills the lights decay,
With such the Seer of Skye[2] the eve beguiles;
'Tis known amid the pathless wastes of Reay,
In Harries known, and in Iona's piles,
Where rest from mortal coil the Mighty of the Isles.

[1] [MS.——"an humble gleaner I."]
[2] [MS.——"the aged of Skye."]

I.

" Wake, Maid of Lorn!" the Minstrels sung.
Thy rugged halls, Artornish! rung,[1]
And the dark seas, thy towers that lave,
Heaved on the beach a softer wave,
As mid the tuneful choir to keep
The diapason of the Deep.
Lull'd were the winds on Inninmore,
And green Loch-Alline's woodland shore,
As if wild woods and waves had pleasure
In listing to the lovely measure.
And ne'er to symphony more sweet
Gave mountain echoes[2] answer meet,
Since, met from mainland and from isle,
Ross, Arran, Ilay, and Argyle,
Each minstrel's tributary lay
Paid homge to the festal day.
Dull and dishonour'd were the bard,
Worthless of guerdon and regard,
Deaf to the hope of minstrel fame,
Or lady's smiles, his noblest aim, •
Who on that morn's resistless call
Were silent in Artornish hall.

[1] [See Appendix, Note A.]
[2] [MS.—" *Made* mountain echoes," &c.]

II.

" Wake, Maid of Lorn !" 'twas thus they sung,
And yet more proud the descant rung,
" Wake, Maid of Lorn ! high right is ours,
To charm dull sleep[1] from Beauty's bowers ;
Earth, Ocean, Air, have nought so shy
But owns the power of minstrelsy.
In Lettermore the timid deer
Will pause, the harp's wild chime to hear ;
Rude Heiskar's seal through surges dark
Will long pursue the minstrel's bark ;[2]
To list his notes, the eagle proud
Will poise him on Ben-Cailliach's cloud ;
Then let not Maiden's ear disdain
The summons of the minstrel train,
But, while our harps wild music make,
Edith of Lorn, awake, awake !

III.

" O wake, while Dawn, with dewy shine,
Wakes Nature's charms to vie with thine !

---

[1] [MS.————————"*for* right is ours
      To summon sleep," &c.]

[2] The seal displays a taste for music, which could scarcely be
expected from his habits and local predilections. They will long
follow a boat in which any musical instrument is played, and
even a tune simply whistled has attractions for them. The Dean
of the Isles says of Heiskar, a small uninhabited rock, about
twelve (Scottish) miles from the Isle of Uist, that an infinite .
slaughter of seals takes place there.

She bids the mottled thrush rejoice
To mate thy melody of voice ;
The dew that on the violet lies
Mocks the dark lustre of thine eyes ;
But, Edith, wake, and all we see
Of sweet and fair shall yield to thee !"—
" She comes not yet," grey Ferrand cried ;
" Brethren, let softer spell be tried,
Those notes prolong'd, that soothing theme,
Which best may mix with Beauty's dream,
And whisper, with their silvery tone,
The hope she loves, yet fears to own."
He spoke, and on the harp-strings died
The strains of flattery and of pride ;
More soft, more low, more tender fell
The lay of love he bade them tell.

IV.

" Wake, Maid of Lorn ! the moments fly,
 Which yet that maiden-name allow ;
Wake, Maiden, wake ! the hour is nigh,
 When Love shall claim a plighted vow.
By Fear, thy bosom's fluttering guest,
 By Hope, that soon shall fears remove,
We bid thee break the bonds of rest,
 And wake thee at the call of Love !

" Wake, Edith, wake ! in yonder bay
 Lies many a galley gaily mann'd,

We hear the merry pibrochs play,
    We see the streamers' silken band.
What Chieftain's praise these pibrochs swell,
    What crest is on these banners wove,
The harp, the minstrel, dare not tell—
    The riddle must be read by Love."

V.

Retired her maiden train among,
Edith of Lorn received the song,[1]
But tamed the minstrel's pride had been
That had her cold demeanour seen;
For not upon her cheek awoke
The glow of pride when Flattery spoke,
Nor could their tenderest numbers bring
One sigh responsive to the string.
As vainly had her maidens vied
In skill to deck the princely bride.
Her locks, in dark-brown length array'd,
Cathleen of Ulne, 'twas thine to braid;
Young Eva with meet reverence drew
On the light foot the silken shoe,
While on the ancle's slender round
Those strings of pearl fair Bertha wound,
That, bleach'd Lochryan's depths within,
Seem'd dusky still on Edith's skin.

---

[1] [MS.—"Retired amid her menial train,
    Edith of Lorn received the strain."

But Einion, of experience old,
Had weightiest task—the mantle's fold
In many an artful plait she tied,
To shew the form it seem'd to hide,
Till on the floor descending roll'd[1]
Its waves of crimson blent with gold.

VI.

O! lives there now so cold a maid,
Who thus in beauty's pomp array'd,
In beauty's proudest pitch of power,
And conquest won—the bridal hour—
With every charm that wins the heart,
By nature given, enhanced by Art,
Could yet the fair reflection view,
In the bright mirror pictured true,
And not one dimple on her cheek
A tell-tale consciousness bespeak?—
Lives still such maid?—Fair damsels, say,
For further vouches not my lay,
Save that such lived in Britain's isle,
When Lorn's bright Edith scorn'd to smile.

VII.

But Morag, to whose fostering care
Proud Lorn had given his daughter fair,

---

[1] [MS.—" The train upon the pavement } flow'd."
        Then to the floor descending }

Morag, who saw a mother's aid[1]
By all a daughter's love repaid,
(Strict was that bond—most kind of all—
Inviolate in Highland hall—)
Grey Morag sate a space apart,
In Edith's eyes to read her heart.
In vain the attendants' fond appeal
To Morag's skill, to Morag's zeal;
She mark'd her child receive their care,
Cold as the image sculptured fair,
(Form of some sainted patroness,)
Which cloister'd maids combine to dress;
She mark'd—and knew her nursling's heart
In the vain pomp took little part.
Wistful a while she gazed—then press'd
The maiden to her anxious breast
In finish'd loveliness—and led
To where a turret's airy head,
Slender and steep, and battled round,
O'erlook'd, dark Mull! thy mighty Sound,[2]

---

[1] [MS.—"But Morag, who the maid had press'd,
        An infant, to her fostering breast,
        And seen a mother's early aid," &c.]

[2] The Sound of Mull, which divides that island from the continent of Scotland, is one of the most striking scenes which the Hebrides afford to the traveller. Sailing from Oban to Aros, or Tobermory, through a narrow channel, yet deep enough to bear vessels of the largest burden, he has on his left the bold and mountainous shores of Mull; on the right those of that district of Argyleshire, called Morven, or Morvern, successively indented by

Where thwarting tides, with mingled roar,
Part thy swarth hills from Morven's shore.

VIII.

"Daughter," she said, "these seas behold,
Round twice a hundred islands roll'd,
From Hirt, that hears their northern roar,
To the green Ilay's fertile shore ;[1]

deep salt-water lochs, running up many miles inland. To the south-eastward arise a prodigious range of mountains, among which Cruachan Ben is preeminent. And to the north-east is the no less huge and picturesque range of the Ardnamurchan hills. Many ruinous castles, situated generally upon cliffs overhanging the ocean, add interest to the scene. Those of Donolly and Dunstaffnage are first passed, then that of Duart, formerly belonging to the chief of the warlike and powerful sept of Macleans, and the scene of Miss Baillie's beautiful tragedy, entitled the Family Legend. Still passing on to the northward, Artornish and Aros become visible upon the opposite shores ; and, lastly, Mingarry, and other ruins of less distinguished note. In fine weather, a grand and more impressive scene, both from its natural beauties, and associations with ancient history and tradition, can hardly be imagined. When the weather is rough, the passage is both difficult and dangerous, from the narrowness of the channel, and in part from the number of inland lakes, out of which sally forth a number of conflicting and thwarting tides, making the navigation perilous to open boats. The sudden flaws and gusts of wind which issue without a moment's warning from the mountain glens, are equally formidable So that in unsettled weather, a stranger, if not much accustomed to the sea, may sometimes add to the other sublime sensations excited by the scene, that feeling of dignity which arises from a sense of danger.

[1] The number of the western isles of Scotland exceeds two hundred, of which St Kilda is the most northerly, anciently called

Or mainland turn, where many a tower
Owns thy bold brother's feudal power,[1]
Each on its own dark cape reclined,
And listening to its own wild wind,

Hirth, or Hirt, probably from " earth," being in fact the whole
globe to its inhabitants. Ilay, which now belongs almost entirely
to Walter Campbell, Esq. of Shawfield, is by far the most fertile
of the Hebrides, and has been greatly improved under the spirited and sagacious management of the present proprietor. This
was in ancient times the principal abode of the Lords of the
Isles, being, if not the largest, the most important island of their
archipelago. In Martin's time, some relics of their grandeur
were yet extant. " Loch-Finlagan, about three miles in circum-
ference, affords salmon, trouts, and eels : this lake lies in the
centre of the isle. The Isle Finlagan, from which this lake hath
its name, is in it. It's famous for being once the court in which
the great Mac-Donald, King of the Isles, had his residence ; his
houses, chapel, &c. are now ruinous. His guards de corps, called Lucht-tach, kept guard on the lakeside nearest to the isle ;
the walls of their houses are still to be seen there. The high
court of judicature, consisting of fourteen, sat always here ; and
there was an appeal to them from all the courts in the isles :
the eleventh share of the sum in debate was due to the principal
judge. There was a big stone of seven foot square, in which
there was a deep impression made to receive the feet of Mac-
Donald ; for he was crowned King of the Isles standing in this
stone, and swore that he would continue his vassals in the possession of their lands, and do exact justice to all his subjects ; and
then his father's sword was put into his hand. The Bishop of
Argyle and seven priests anointed him king, in presence of all
the heads of the tribes in the isles and continent, and were his
vassals ; at which time the orator rehearsed a catalogue of his
ancestors," &c.—MARTIN'S *Account of the Western Isles*, 8vo,
London, 1716, p. 240, 1.

[1] [MS.————" father's feudal power."]

From where Mingarry, sternly placed,
O'erawes the woodland and the waste,[1]
To where Dunstaffnage hears the raging
Of Connal with his rocks engaging.
Think'st thou, amid this ample round,
A single brow but thine has frown'd,
To sadden this auspicious morn,
That bids the daughter of high Lorn
Impledge her spousal faith to wed
The heir of mighty Somerled?[2]

---

[1] [See Appendix, Note B.]

[2] Somerled was thane of Argyle and Lord of the Isles, about the middle of the 12th century. He seems to have exercised his authority in both capacities, independent of the crown of Scotland, against which he often stood in hostility. He made various incursions upon the western lowlands during the reign of Malcolm IV., and seems to have made peace with him upon the terms of an independent prince, about the year 1157. In 1164, he resumed the war against Malcolm, and invaded Scotland with a large, but probably a tumultuary army, collected in the Isles, in the mainland of Argyleshire, and in the neighbouring provinces of Ireland. He was defeated and slain in an engagement with a very inferior force, near Renfrew. His son Gillicolane fell in the same battle. This mighty chieftain married a daughter of Olaus, King of Man. From him our genealogists deduce two dynasties, distinguished in the stormy history of the middle ages; the Lords of the Isles descended from his elder son Ronald,—and the Lords of Lorn, who took their sirname of M'Dougal, as descended of his second son Dougal. That Somerled's territories upon the mainland, and upon the islands, should have been divided between his two sons, instead of passing to the elder exclusively, may illustrate the uncertainty of descent among the great Highland families, which we shall presently notice.

Ronald, from many a hero sprung,
The fair, the valiant, and the young,
LORD OF THE ISLES, whose lofty name[1]
A thousand bards have given to fame,
The mate of monarchs, and allied
On equal terms with England's pride.—
From chieftain's tower to bondsman's cot,
Who hears the tale,[2] and triumphs not?
The damsel dons her best attire,
The shepherd lights his beltane fire,
Joy, joy! each warder's horn hath sung,
Joy, joy! each matin bell hath rung;
The holy priest says grateful mass,
Loud shouts each hardy galla-glass,
No mountain den holds outcast boor,
Of heart so dull, of soul so poor,
But he hath flung his task aside,
And claim'd this morn for holy-tide;
Yet, empress of this joyful day,
Edith is sad while all are gay."—

IX.

Proud Edith's soul came to her eye,
Resentment check'd the struggling sigh,
Her hurrying hand indignant dried
The burning tears of injured pride—

[1] [See Appendix, Note C.]
[2] [MS.—" The news."]

" Morag, forbear! or lend thy praise
To swell yon hireling harpers' lays ;
Make to yon maids thy boast of power,
That they may waste a wondering hour,
Telling of banners proudly borne,
Of pealing bell and bugle-horn,
Or, theme more dear, of robes of price,
Crownlets and gauds of rare device.
But thou, experienced as thou art,
Think'st thou with these to cheat the heart,
That, bound in strong affection's chain,
Looks for return and looks in vain ?
No ! sum thine Edith's wretched lot
In these brief words—He loves her not !

X.

" Debate it not—too long I strove
To call his cold observance love,
All blinded by the league that styled
Edith of Lorn,—while yet a child,
She tripp'd the heath by Morag's side,—
The brave Lord Ronald's destined bride.
Ere yet I saw him, while afar
His broadsword blazed in Scotland's war,
Train'd to believe our fates the same,
My bosom throbb'd when Ronald's name
Came gracing Fame's heroic tale,
Like perfume on the summer gale.

What pilgrim sought our halls, nor told
Of Ronald's deeds in battle bold ;
Who touch'd the harp to heroes' praise,
But his achievements swell'd the lays?
Even Morag—not a tale of fame
Was hers but closed with Ronald's name.
He came ! and all that had been told
Of his high worth seem'd poor and cold,
Tame, lifeless, void of energy,
Unjust to Ronald and to me !

XI.

" Since then, what thought had Edith's heart
And gave not plighted love its part !—   •
And what requital?[1] cold delay—
Excuse that shunn'd the spousal day.—
It dawns, and Ronald is not here !
Hunts he Bentalla's nimble deer,[2]
Or loiters he in secret dell
To bid some lighter love farewell,
And swear, that though he may not scorn
A daughter of the House of Lorn,[3]
Yet, when these formal rites are o'er,
Again they meet, to part no more?"

---

[1] [MS.—"When, from that hour, had Edith's heart
   A thought, and Ronald, lack'd his part !
   And what her guerdon ?"]
[2] [MS.—"And on its dawn the bridegroom lags;—
   Hunts he Bentalla's nimble stags."]
[3] [See Appendix, Note D.]

XII.

—" Hush, daughter, hush ! thy doubts remove,
More nobly think of Ronald's love.
Look, where beneath the castle gray
His fleet unmoor from Aros bay !
See'st not each galley's topmast bend,
As on the yards the sails ascend ?
Hiding the dark-blue land they rise,
Like the white clouds on April skies ;
The shouting vassals man the oars,
Behind them sink Mull's mountain shores,
Onward their merry course they keep,
Through whistling breeze and foaming deep.
And mark the headmost, seaward cast,
Stoop to the freshening gale her mast,
As if she veil'd its banner'd pride,
To greet afar her prince's bride !
Thy Ronald comes, and while in speed
His galley mates the flying steed,
He chides her sloth !—Fair Edith sigh'd,
Blush'd, sadly smiled, and thus replied :—

XIII.

" Sweet thought, but vain !—No, Morag ! mark,
Type of his course, yon lonely bark,
That oft hath shifted helm and sail,
To win its way against the gale.
Since peep of morn, my vacant eyes
Have view'd by fits the course she tries ;[1] ·

[1] [MS.—" Since dawn of morn, with vacant eyes
        Young Eva view'd the course she tries."]

Now, though the darkening scud comes on,
And dawn's fair promises be gone,
And though the weary crew may see
Our sheltering haven on their lee,
Still closer to the rising wind
They strive her shivering sail to bind,
Still nearer to the shelves' dread verge [1]
At every tack her course they urge,
As if they fear'd Artornish more
Than adverse winds and breakers' roar."

XIV.

Sooth spoke the Maid.—Amid the tide
  The skiff she mark'd lay tossing sore,
And shifted oft her stooping side,
  In weary tack from shore to shore.
  Yet on her destined course no more
    She gain'd, of forward way,
  Than what a minstrel may compare
  To the poor meed which peasants share,
    Who toil the livelong day;
  And such the risk her pilot braves,
    That oft, before she wore,
  Her boltsprit kiss'd the broken waves,
  Where in white foam the ocean raves
    Upon the shelving shore.

[1] [MS.———" the breakers' verge."]

Yet, to their destined purpose true,
Undaunted toil'd her hardy crew,
   Nor look'd where shelter lay,
Nor for Artornish Castle drew,
   Nor steer'd for Aros bay.

XV.

Thus while they strove with wind and seas,
Borne onward by the willing breeze,
   Lord Ronald's fleet swept by,
Streamer'd with silk, and trick'd with gold,
Mann'd with the noble and the bold
   Of Island chivalry.
Around their prows the ocean roars,
And chafes beneath their thousand oars,
   Yet bears them on their way :
So chafes[1] the war-horse in his might,
That fieldward bears some valiant knight,[2]
Champs, till both bit and boss are white,
   But, foaming, must obey.
On each gay deck they might behold
Lances of steel and crests of gold,
And hauberks with their burnish'd fold,
   That shimmer'd fair and free ;
And each proud galley, as she pass'd,
To the wild cadence of the blast

---

[1] [MS.—" So fumes," &c.]
[2] [MS.—" That bears to fight some valiant knight."]

Gave wilder minstrelsy.
Full many a shrill triumphant note
Saline and Scallastle bade float
    Their misty shores around;
And Morven's echoes answer'd well,
And Duart heard the distant swell
    Come down the darksome Sound.

XVI.

So bore they on with mirth and pride,
And if that labouring bark they spied,
    'Twas with such idle eye
As nobles cast on lowly boor,
When, toiling in his task obscure,
    They pass him careless by.[1]
Let them sweep on with heedless eyes!
But, had they known what mighty prize
    In that frail vessel lay,
The famish'd wolf, that prowls the wold,
Had scatheless pass'd the unguarded fold,
Ere, drifting by these galleys bold,
    Unchallenged were her way![2]
And thou, Lord Ronald, sweep thou on,
With mirth, and pride, and minstrel tone!

---

1 [MS.—" As the gay nobles give the boor,
    When, toiling in his task obscure,
        Their greatness passes by."]
2 [MS.—" She held unchallenged way."]

But had'st thou known who sailed so nigh,
Far other glance were in thine eye!
Far other flush were on thy brow,
That, shaded by the bonnet, now
Assumes but ill the blithesome cheer
Of bridegroom when the bride is near!

XVII.

Yes, sweep they on!—We will not leave,
For them that triumph, those who grieve.
　　With that armada gay
Be laughter loud and jocund shout,
And bards to cheer the wassail rout,
　　With tale, romance, and lay;[1]
And of wild mirth each clamorous art,
Which, if it cannot cheer the heart,
May stupify and stun its smart,
　　For one loud busy day.
Yes, sweep thee on!—But with that skiff
　　Abides the minstrel tale,
Where there was dread of surge and cliff,
Labour that strain'd each sinew stiff,
　　And one sad Maiden's wail.

XVIII.

All day with fruitless strife they toil'd,
With eve the ebbing currents boil'd

---

[1] [MS.—"With mirth, song, tale, and lay."]

More fierce from strait and lake ;
And midway through the channel met
Conflicting tides that foam and fret,
And high their mingled billows jet,
As spears, that, in the battle set,
    Spring upward as they break.
Then, too, the lights of eve were past,[1]
And louder sung the western blast
    On rocks of Inninmore ;
Rent was the sail, and strain'd the mast,
And many a leak was gaping fast,
And the pale steersman stood aghast,
    And gave the conflict o'er.

XIX.

'Twas then that One, whose lofty look
Nor labour dull'd nor terror shook,
    Thus to the Leader spoke :—
" Brother, how hopest thou to abide
The fury of this wilder'd tide,
Or how avoid the rock's rude side,
    Until the day has broke ?
Didst thou not mark the vessel reel,
With quivering planks, and groaning keel,
    At the last billow's shock ?
Yet how of better counsel tell,
Though here thou see'st poor Isabel

---

[1] [MS.—" Then, too, the clouds were sinking fast."]

Half dead with want and fear;
For look on sea, or look on land,
Or yon dark sky, on every hand
    Despair and death are near.
For her alone I grieve—on me
Danger sits light by land and sea,
    I follow where thou wilt;
Either to bide the tempest's lour,
Or wend to yon unfriendly tower,
Or rush amid their naval power,[1]
With war-cry wake their wassail-hour,
    And die with hand on hilt."—

XX.

That elder Leader's calm reply
    In steady voice was given,
" In man's most dark extremity
    Oft succour dawns from Heaven.
Edward, trim thou the shatter'd sail,
The helm be mine, and down the gale
    Let our free course be driven;
So shall we 'scape the western bay,
The hostile fleet, the unequal fray,
So safely hold our vessel's way
    Beneath the Castle wall;
For if a hope of safety rest,
'Tis on the sacred name of guest,

---

[1] [MS.——— ' the hostile power.'']

Who seeks for shelter, storm distress'd,
    Within a chieftain's hall.
If not—it best beseems our worth,
Our name, our right, our lofty birth,
    By noble hands to fall."

XXI.

The helm, to his strong arm consign'd,
Gave the reef'd sail to meet the wind,
    And on her alter'd way,
Fierce bounding, forward sprung the ship,
Like greyhound starting from the slip
    To seize his flying prey.
Awaked before the rushing prow,
The mimic fires of ocean glow,
    Those lightnings of the wave;[1]

---

[1] The phenomenon called by sailors Sea-fire, is one of the most beautiful and interesting which is witnessed in the Hebrides. At times the ocean appears entirely illuminated around the vessel, and a long train of lambent coruscations are perpetually bursting upon the sides of the vessel, or pursuing her wake through the darkness. These phosphoric appearances, concerning the origin of which naturalists are not agreed in opinion, seem to be called into action by the rapid motion of the ship through the water, and are probably owing to the water being saturated with fish-spawn, or other animal substances. They remind one strongly of the description of the sea-snakes in Mr Coleridge's wild but highly poetical ballad of the Ancient Mariner :—

> " Beyond the shadow of the ship
>   I watch'd the water-snakes,
> They moved in tracks of shining white,
> And when they rear'd, the elvish light
>   Fell off in hoary flakes."

Wild sparkles crest the broken tides,
And, flashing round, the vessel's sides[1]
   With elvish lustre lave.
While, far behind, their livid light
To the dark billows of the night
   A gloomy splendour gave,
It seems as if old Ocean shakes
From his dark brow the lucid[2] flakes
   In envious pageantry,
To match the meteor light that streaks
   Grim Hecla's midnight sky.

XXII.

Nor lack'd they steadier light to keep
Their course upon the darken'd deep ;—
Artornish, on her frowning steep
   'Twixt cloud and ocean hung,
Glanced with a thousand lights of glee,
And landward far, and far to sea,
   Her festal radiance flung.[3]

---

[1] [MS.—" And, *bursting* round the vessel's sides.
      A livid lustre gave."]

[2] [MS.—" Livid."]

[3] [" The description of the vessel's approach to the Castle
through the tempestuous and sparkling waters, and the contrast
of the gloomy aspect of the billows with the glittering splendour
of Artornish,

      " 'Twixt cloud and ocean hung,'

sending her radiance abroad through the terrors of the night, and
mingling at intervals the shouts of her revelry with the wilder ca-

By that blithe beacon-light they steer'd,
   Whose lustre mingled well
With the pale beam that now appear'd,
As the cold moon her head uprear'd
   Above the eastern fell.

XXIII.

Thus guided, on their course they bore,
Until they near'd the mainland shore,
When frequent on the hollow blast
Wild shouts of merriment were cast,
And wind and wave and sea-birds' cry
With wassail sounds in concert vie,[1]
Like funeral shrieks with revelry,
   Or like the battle-shout
By peasants heard from cliffs on high,
When Triumph, Rage, and Agony,
   Madden the fight and rout.
Now nearer yet, through mist and storm
Dimly arose the Castle's form,
   And deepen'd[2] shadow made,
Far lengthen'd on the main below,
Where, dancing in reflected glow,

---

dence of the blast, is one of the happiest instances of Mr Scott's
felicity in awful and magnificent scenery."—*Critical Review.*]

   [1] [MS.—" The wind, the wave, the sea-bird's cry,
      In melancholy concert vie."]

  [2] [MS.—" Dark-some."]

A hundred torches play'd,
Spangling the wave with lights as vain
As pleasures in this vale of pain,
       That dazzle as they fade.[1]

XXIV.

Beneath the Castle's sheltering lee,
They staid their course in quiet sea.
Hewn in the rock, a passage there
Sought the dark fortress by a stair,
       So straight, so high, so steep,
With peasant's staff one valiant hand
Might well the dizzy pass have mann'd,
'Gainst hundreds arm'd with spear and brand,
       And plunged them in the deep.[2] .

---

[1] ["Mr Scott, we observed in the newspapers, was engaged
during last summer in a maritime expedition; and, accordingly,
the most striking novelty in the present poem is the extent and
variety of the sea pieces with which it abounds. One of the first
we meet with is the picture of the distresses of the King's little
bark, and her darkling run to the shelter of Artornish Castle."—
Edinburgh Review, 1815.]

[2] The fortress of a Hebridean chief was almost always on the
sea-shore, for the facility of communication which the ocean
afforded. Nothing can be more wild than the situations which
they chose, and the devices by which the architects endeavoured
to defend them. Narrow stairs and arched vaults were the usual
mode of access; and the drawbridge appears at Dunstaffnage
and elsewhere, to have fallen from the gate of the building to
the top of such a staircase; so that any one advancing with hostile purpose, found himself in a state of exposed and precarious
elevation, with a gulf between him and the object of his attack.

His bugle then the helmsman wound ;
Loud answer'd every echo round,
   From turret, rock, and bay,
The postern's hinges crash and groan,
And soon the warder's cresset shone
On those rude steps of slippery stone,
   To light the upward way.

These fortresses were guarded with equal care. The duty of the watch devolved chiefly upon an officer called the Cockman, who had the charge of challenging all who approached the castle. The very ancient family of Mac-Niel of Barra kept this attendant at their castle about a hundred years ago. Martin gives the following account of the difficulty which attended his procuring entrance there:—" The little island Kismul lies about a quarter of a mile from the south of this Isle (Barra); it is the seat of Mackneil of Barra; there is a stone wall round it two stories high, reaching the sea; and within the wall there is an old tower and an hall, with other houses about it. There is a little magazine in the tower, to which no stranger has access. I saw the officer called the Cockman, and an old cock he is; when I bid him ferry me over the water to the island, he told me that he was but an inferior officer, his business being to attend in the tower: but if (says he) the constable, who then stood on the wall, will give you access, I'll ferry you over. I desired him to procure me the constable's permission, and I would reward him; but having waited some hours for the constable's answer, and not receiving any, I was obliged to return without seeing this famous fort. Mackneil and his lady being absent, was the cause of this difficulty, and of my not seeing the place. I was told some weeks after, that the constable was very apprehensive of some design I might have in viewing the fort, and thereby to expose it to the conquest of a foreign power; of which I supposed there was no great cause of fear."

"Thrice welcome, holy Sire!" he said;
"Full long the spousal train have staid,
    And, vex'd at thy delay,
Fear'd lest, amidst these wildering seas,
The darksome night and freshening breeze
    Had driven thy bark astray."—

XXV.

"Warder," the younger stranger[1] said,
"Thine erring guess some mirth had made
In mirthful hour; but nights like these,
When the rough winds wake western seas,
Brook not of glee. We crave some aid
And needful shelter for this maid
    Until the break of day;
For, to ourselves, the deck's rude plank
Is easy as the mossy bank
    That's breathed upon by May.
And for our storm-toss'd skiff we seek
Short shelter in this leeward creek,
Prompt when the dawn the east shall streak
    Again to bear away."—
Answered the Warder, "In what name
Assert ye hospitable claim?
    Whence come, or whither bound?
Hath Erin seen your parting sails?

---

[1] [MS.—"That younger leader."]

Or come ye on Norweyan gales?
And seek ye England's fertile vales,
    Or Scotland's mountain ground?"—

XXVI.

" Warriors—for other title none
For some brief space we list to own,
Bound by a vow—warriors are we;
In strife by land, and storm by sea,
    We have been known to fame;
And these brief words have import dear,
When sounded in a noble ear,
To harbour safe, and friendly cheer,
    That gives us rightful claim.
Grant us the trivial boon we seek,
And we in other realms will speak
    Fair of your courtesy;
Deny—and be your niggard Hold
Scorn'd by the noble and the bold,
Shunn'd by the pilgrim on the wold,
And wanderer on the lea!"—

XXVII.

" Bold stranger, no—'gainst claim like thine,
No bolt revolves by hand of mine,[1]
Though urged in tone that more express'd
A monarch than a suppliant guest.

1 [MS.———" 'gainst claim like yours,
    No bolt ere closed our castle doors."]

Be what ye will, Artornish Hall
On this glad eve is free to all.
Though ye had drawn a hostile sword
'Gainst our ally, great England's Lord,
Or mail upon your shoulders borne,
To battle with the Lord of Lorn,
Or, outlaw'd, dwelt by greenwood tree
With the fierce Knight of Ellerslie,[1]
Or aided even the murderous strife,
When Comyn fell beneath the knife
Of that fell homicide The Bruce,[2]
This night had been a term of truce.—
Ho, vassals! give these guests your care,
And show the narrow postern stair."

XXVIII.

To land these two bold brethren leapt,
(The weary crew their vessel kept,)
And, lighted by the torches' flare,
That seaward flung their smoky glare,
The younger knight that maiden bare
    Half lifeless up the rock ;
On his strong shoulder lean'd her head,
And down her long dark tresses shed,
As the wild vine in tendrils spread,
    Droops from the mountain oak.

---

[1] [Sir William Wallace.]
[2] [See Appendix, Note G.]

Him follow'd close that elder Lord,
And in his hand a sheathed sword,
　　Such as few arms could wield ;
But when he boun'd him to such task,
Well could it cleave the strongest casque,
　　And rend the surest shield.[1]

XXIX.

The raised portcullis' arch they pass,
The wicket with its bars of brass,
　　The entrance long and low,[2]
Flank'd at each turn by loop-holes strait,
Where bowmen might in ambush wait,
(If force or fraud should burst the gate,)
　　To gall an entering foe.
But every jealous post of ward
Was now defenceless and unbarr'd,
　　And all the passage free
To one low-brow'd and vaulted room,
Where squire and yeoman, page and groom,
　　Plied their loud revelry.

XXX.

And " Rest ye here," the Warder bade,
" Till to our Lord your suit is said.—

---

i [MS.—" Well could it cleave the gilded casque,
　　And rend the trustiest shield."]
2 [MS.—" The entrance vaulted low."]

And, comrades, gaze not on the maid,
And on these men who ask our aid,
    As if ye ne'er had seen
A damsel tired of midnight bark,
Or wanderers of a moulding stark,[1]
    And bearing martial mien."
But not for Eachin's reproof
Would page or vassal stand aloof,
    But crowded on to stare,
As men of courtesy untaught,
Till fiery Edward roughly caught,
    From one the foremost there,[2]
His chequer'd plaid, and in its shroud,
To hide her from the vulgar crowd,
    Involved his sister fair.
His brother, as the clansman bent
His sullen brow in discontent,
    Made brief and stern excuse ;—
" Vassal, were thine the cloak of pall
That decks thy Lord in bridal hall,
    'Twere honour'd by her use."

XXXI.

Proud was his tone, but calm ; his eye
Had that compelling dignity,

---

[1] [MS.—" Or warlike men of moulding stark."]
[2] [MS.—" Till that hot Edward fiercely caught
    From one, the boldest there."]

His mien that bearing haught and high,
　　Which common spirits fear ;[1]
Needed nor word nor signal more,
Nod, wink, and laughter, all were o'er ;
Upon each other back they bore,
　　And gazed like startled deer.
But now appear'd the Seneschal,
Commission'd by his lord to call
The strangers to the Baron's hall,
　　Where feasted fair and free
That Island Prince in nuptial tide,
With Edith there his lovely bride,
And her bold brother by her side,
And many a chief, the flower and pride
　　Of Western land and sea.[2]

Here pause we, gentles, for a space ;
And, if our tale hath won your grace,

[1] [" Still sways their souls with that commanding art
　　That dazzles, leads, yet chills the vulgar heart.
　　What is that spell, that thus his lawless train
　　Confess and envy, yet oppose in vain ?
　　What should it be, that thus their faith can bind ?
　　The power of Thought—the magic of the Mind !
　　Link'd with success, assumed and kept with skill,
　　That moulds another's weakness to its will ;
　　Wields with their hands, but, still to these unknown,
　　Makes even their mightiest deeds appear his own.
　　Such hath it been—shall be—beneath the sun
　　The many still must labour for the one !
　　'Tis Nature's doom."—BYRON's *Corsair.*]
[2] [MS.—" Of mountain chivalry."]

Grant us brief patience, and again
We will renew the minstrel strain.[1]

[1] [" The first Canto is full of business and description, and the
scenes are such as Mr Scott's muse generally excels in. The
scene between Edith and her nurse is spirited, and contains
many very pleasing lines. The description of Lord Ronald's
fleet, and of the bark endeavouring to make her way against the
wind, more particularly of the last, is executed with extraordinary beauty and fidelity."—*Quarterly Review.*]

LORD OF THE ISLES.

CANTO SECOND.

THE

LORD OF THE ISLES.

CANTO SECOND.

Fill the bright goblet, spread the festive board!
Summon the gay, the noble, and the fair!
Through the loud hall in joyous concert pour'd,
Let mirth and music sound the dirge of Care!
But ask thou not if Happiness be there,
If the loud laugh disguise convulsive throe,
Or if the brow the heart's true livery wear;
Lift not the festal mask!—enough to know,
No scene of mortal life but teems with mortal woe.[1]

II.

With beakers' clang, with harpers' lay,
With all that olden time deem'd gay,.
The Island Chieftain feasted high;
But there was in his troubled eye

---

[1] [" Even in laughter the heart is sorrowful; and the end of
that mirth is heaviness."—*Proverbs*, xiv. 13.]

A gloomy fire, and on his brow
Now sudden flush'd, and faded now,
Emotions such as draw their birth
From deeper source than festal mirth.
By fits he paused, and harper's strain
And jester's tale went round in vain,
Or fell but on his idle ear .   ·   .
Like distant sounds which dreamers hear.
Then would he rouse him, and employ
Each art to aid the clamorous joy,[1]
 And call for pledge and lay,
And, for brief space, of all the crowd,
As he was loudest of the loud,
 Seem gayest of the gay.[2]

III.

Yet nought amiss the bridal throng
Mark'd in brief mirth, or musing long;
The vacant brow, the unlistening ear,
They gave to thoughts of raptures near,
And his fierce starts of sudden glee
Seem'd bursts of bridegroom's ecstasy.
Nor thus alone misjudged the crowd,
Since lofty Lorn, suspicious, proud,[3]

---

[1] [MS.————————" and give birth
  To jest, to wassail, and to mirth."]
[2] [MS.—" Would seem the loudest of the loud.
  And gayest of the gay."]
[3] [MS.—" Since Lorn, the proudest of the proud."]

And jealous of his honour'd line,
And that keen knight, De Argentine,[1]
(From England sent on errand high,
The western league more firm to tie,)[2]

---

[1] [MS.—" And since the keen De Argentine."]

[2] Sir Egidius, or Giles de Argentine, was one of the most accomplished knights of the period. He had served in the wars of Henry of Luxemburg with such high reputation, that he was, in popular estimation, the third worthy of the age. Those to whom fame assigned precedence over him were, Henry of Luxemburg himself, and Robert Bruce. Argentine had warred in Palestine, encountered thrice with the Saracens, and had slain two antagonists in each engagement :—an easy matter, he said, for one Christian knight to slay two Pagan dogs. His death corresponded with his high character. With Aymer de Valence, Earl of Pembroke, he was appointed to attend immediately upon the person of Edward II. at Bannockburn. When the day was utterly lost they forced the king from the field. De Argentine saw the king safe from immediate danger, and then took his leave of him : "God be with you, sir," he said, " it is not my wont to fly." So saying, he turned his horse, cried his war-cry, plunged into the midst of the combatants, and was slain. Baston, a rhyming monk who had been brought by Edward to celebrate his expected triumph, and who was compelled by the victors to compose a poem on his defeat, mentions with some feeling the death of Sir Giles de Argentine :

Nobilis Argenten, pugil inclyte, dulcis Egidi,
Vix scieram mentem cum te succumbere vidi.

" The first line mentions the three chief requisites of a true knight, noble birth, valour, and courteousness. Few Leonine couplets can be produced that have so much sentiment. I wish that I could have collected more ample memorials concerning a character altogether different from modern manners. Sir Giles d'Argentine was a hero of romance in real life." So observes the excellent Lord Hailes.

Both deem'd in Ronald's mood to find
A lover's transport-troubled mind.
But one sad heart, one tearful eye,
Pierced deeper through the mystery,
And watch'd, with agony and fear,
Her wayward bridegroom's varied cheer.

IV.

She watch'd—yet fear'd to meet his glance,
And he shunn'd hers;—till when by chance
They met, the point of foeman's lance
  Had given a milder pang!
Beneath the intolerable smart
He writhed;—then sternly mann'd his heart
To play his hard but destined part,
  And from the table sprang.
" Fill me the mighty cup!" he said,
" Erst own'd by royal Somerled:[1]
Fill it, till on the studded brim
In burning gold the bubbles swim,
And every gem of varied shine
Glow doubly bright in rosy wine!
 To you, brave lord, and brother mine,
  Of Lorn, this pledge I drink—
 The union of Our House with thine,
  By this fair bridal-link!"—

---

[1] [See Appendix, Note E.]

V.

" Let it pass round !" quoth He of Lorn,
" And in good time—that winded horn
    Must of the Abbot tell;
The laggard monk is come at last."
Lord Ronald heard the bugle-blast,
And on the floor at random cast,
    The untasted goblet fell.
But when the warder in his ear
Tells other news, his blither cheer
    Returns like sun of May,
When through a thunder-cloud it beams !—
Lord of two hundred isles, he seems
    As glad of brief delay,
As some poor criminal might feel,
When from the gibbet or the wheel
    Respited for a day.

VI.

" Brother of Lorn," with hurried voice
He said, " And you, fair lords, rejoice !
    Here, to augment our glee,
Come wandering knights from travel far,
Well proved, they say, in strife of war,
    And tempest on the sea.—
Ho! give them at your board such place
As best their presences may grace,[1]
    And bid them welcome free !"

---

1 [MS.—"As may their presence fittest grace."]

With solemn step, and silver wand,
The Seneschal the presence scann'd
Of these strange guests;[1] and well he knew
How to assign their rank its due;[2]
   For though the costly furs
That erst had deck'd their caps were torn,
And their gay robes were over-worn,
   And soil'd their gilded spurs,
Yet such a high commanding grace
Was in their mien and in their face,

---

[1] [MS.—" With solemn pace, and silver rod,
The Seneschal the entrance show'd
To these strange guests."]

[2] The Sewer, to whom, rather than the Seneschal, the office of arranging the guests of an island chief appertained, was an officer of importance in the family of a Hebridean chief.—"Every family had commonly two stewards, which, in their language, were called Marischal Tach: the first of these served always at home, and was obliged to be versed in the pedigree of all the tribes in the isles, and in the highlands of Scotland; for it was his province to assign every man at table his seat according to his quality; and this was done without one word speaking, only by drawing a score with a white rod, which this Marischal had in his hand, before the person who was bid by him to sit down: and this was necessary to prevent disorder and contention; and though the Marischal might sometimes be mistaken, the master of the family incurred no censure by such an escape; but this custom has been laid aside of late. They had also cup-bearers, who always filled and carried the cup round the company, and he himself always drank of the first draught. They had likewise purse-masters, who kept their money. Both these officers had an hereditary right to their office in writing, and each of them had a town and land for his service: some of those rights I have seen fairly written on good parchment."—MARTIN'S *Western Isles.*

As suited best the princely dais,[1]
    And royal canopy;
And there he marshall'd them their place,
    First of that company.

VII.

Then lords and ladies spake aside,
And angry looks the error chide,[2]
That gave to guests unnamed, unknown,
A place so near their prince's throne;
    But Owen Erraught said,
" For forty years a seneschal,
To marshal guests in bower and hall
    Has been my honour'd trade.
Worship and birth to me are known,
By look, by bearing, and by tone,
Not by furr'd robe, or broider'd zone;
    And 'gainst an oaken bough
I'll gage my silver wand of state,
That these three strangers oft have sate
    In higher place than now."—[3]

---

[1] *Dais*—the great hall-table—elevated a step or two above the rest of the room.

[2] [MS.—" Aside then lords and ladies spake,
And ushers censured the mistake."]

[3] [" The first entry of the illustrious strangers into the Castle of the Celtic chief, is in the accustomed and peculiar style of *the poet of chivalry.*"—JEFFREY.]

VIII.

" I, too," the aged Ferrand said,
" Am qualified by minstrel trade[1]
  Of rank and place to tell ;—
Mark'd ye the younger stranger's eye,
My mates, how quick, how keen, how high,
  How fierce its flashes fell,
Glancing among the noble rout[2]
As if to seek the noblest out,
Because the owner might not brook
On any save his peers to look ?
  And yet it moves me more,
That steady, calm, majestic brow,
With which the elder chief even now
  Scann'd the gay presence o'er,
Like being of superior kind,
In whose high-toned impartial mind
Degrees of mortal rank and state
Seem objects of indifferent weight.
  The lady too—though closely tied
  The mantle veil both face and eye.
  Her motions' grace it could not hide,
   Nor could[3] her form's fair symmetry."

---

1 [MS.—"' I, too,' old Ferraud said, and laugh'd,
  ' Am qualified by minstrel craft.' "]
2 [MS.————————" the festal rout."]
3 [MS.—" Nor hide," &c.]

IX.

Suspicious doubt and lordly scorn
Lour'd on the haughty front of Lorn.
From underneath his brows of pride,
The stranger guests he sternly eyed,
  And whisper'd closely what the ear
  Of Argentine alone might hear;
    Then question'd, high and brief,
If, in their voyage, aught they knew
Of the rebellious Scottish crew,
Who to Rath-Erin's shelter drew,
    With Carrick's outlaw'd Chief?[1]

[1] It must be remembered by all who have read the Scottish history, that after he had slain Comyn at Dumfries, and asserted his right to the Scottish crown, Robert Bruce was reduced to the greatest extremity by the English and their adherents. He was crowned at Scone by the general consent of the Scottish barons, but his authority endured but a short time. According to the phrase said to have been used by his wife, he was for that year " a summer king, but not a winter one." On the 29th March, 1306, he was crowned king at Scone. Upon the 19th June, in the same year, he was totally defeated at Methven, near Perth; and his most important adherents, with few exceptions, were either executed or compelled to embrace the English interest, for safety of their lives and fortunes. After this disaster, his life was that of an outlaw rather than a candidate for monarchy. He separated himself from the females of his retinue, whom he sent for safety to the Castle of Kildrummie, in Aberdeenshire, where they afterward became captives to England. From Aberdeenshire, Bruce retreated to the mountainous parts of Breadalbane, and approached the borders of Argyleshire. There, as mentioned in the Appendix, Note D, and more fully in Note F, he was defeated by the Lord of Lorn, who had assumed arms against him in re-

And if, their winter's exile o'er,
They harbour'd still by Ulster's shore,
Or launch'd their galleys on the main,
To vex their native land again?

X.

That younger stranger, fierce and high,
At once confronts the Chieftain's eye[1]

venge of the death of his relative, John the Red Comyn. Escaped from this peril, Bruce, with his few attendants, subsisted by hunting and fishing, until the weather compelled them to seek better sustenance and shelter than the Highland mountains afforded. With great difficulty they crossed, from Rowardennan probably, to the western banks of Lochlomond, partly in a miserable boat, and partly by swimming. The valiant and loyal Earl of Lennox, to whose territories they had now found their way, welcomed them with tears, but was unable to assist them to make an effectual head. The Lord of the Isles, then in possession of great part of Cantyre, received the fugitive monarch and future restorer of his country's independence, in his Castle of Dunnaverty, in that district. But treason, says Barbour, was so general, that the King durst not abide there. Accordingly, with the remnant of his followers, Bruce embarked for Rath-Erin, or Rachrine, the Recina of Ptolemy, a small island, lying almost opposite to the shores of Ballycastle, on the coast of Ireland. The islanders at first fled from their new and armed guests, but upon some explanation submitted themselves to Bruce's sovereignty. He resided among them until the approach of spring [1306,] when he again returned to Scotland, with the desperate resolution to reconquer his kingdom, or perish in the attempt. The progress of his success, from its commencement to its completion, forms the brightest period in Scottish history.

---

1 [MS.—"That younger stranger, not out-dared,
      Was prompt the haughty Chief to beard."]

With look of equal scorn;—
"Of rebels have we nought to show;
But if of Royal Bruce thou'dst know,
    I warn thee he has sworn,[1]
Ere thrice three days shall come and go,
His banner Scottish winds shall blow,
Despite each mean or mighty foe,
From England's every bill and bow,
    To Allaster of Lorn."
Kindled the mountain Chieftain's ire,
But Ronald quench'd the rising fire;
" Brother, it better suits the time
To chase the night with Ferrand's rhyme,
Than wake, 'midst mirth and wine, the jars
That flow from these unhappy wars."—[2]
" Content," said Lorn; and spoke apart
With Ferrand, master of his art,
    Then whisper'd Argentine,—
" The lay I named will carry smart
To these bold strangers' haughty heart,
    If right this guess of mine."
He ceased, and it was silence all,
Until the Minstrel waked the hall.[3]

---

[1] [MS.—" Men say that he has sworn."]

[2] [" The description of the bridal feast, in the second canto,
has several animated lines; but the real power and poetry of the
author do not appear to us to be called out until the occasion of
the Highland quarrel which follows the feast."—*Monthly Review*,
March, 1815.]

[3] [" In a very different style of excellence (from that of the

XI.

𝕿𝖍𝖊 𝕭𝖗𝖔𝖆𝖈𝖍 𝖔𝖋 𝕷𝖔𝖗𝖓.[1]

" Whence the broach of burning gold,
That clasps the Chieftain's mantle-fold,
Wrought and chased with rare device,
Studded fair with gems of price,[2]
On the varied tartans beaming,
As, through night's pale rainbow gleaming,
Fainter now, now seen afar,
Fitful shines the northern star?

first three stanzas) is the triumphant and insulting song of the
bard of Lorn, commemorating the pretended victory of his chief
over Robert Bruce, in one of their roncontres. Bruce, in truth,
had been set on by some of that clan, and had extricated himself
from a fearful overmatch by stupendous exertions. In the
strugle, however, the broach which fastened his royal mantle
had been torn off by the assailants; and it is on the subject of
this trophy that the Celtic poet pours forth this wild, rapid, and
spirited strain."—JEFFREY.]

[1] [See Appendix, Note F.]

[2] Great art and expense was bestowed upon the *fibula,* or
broach, which secured the plaid, when the wearer was a person
of importance. Martin mentions having seen a silver broach of
a hundred marks value. " It was broad as any ordinary pewter
plate, the whole curiously engraven with various animals, &c.
There was a lesser buckle, which was wore in the middle of the
larger, and above two ounces weight; it had in the centre a
large piece of crystal, or some finer stone, and this was set all
round with several finer stones of a lesser size."—*Western Islands.*
Pennant has given an engraving of such a broach as Martin
describes, and the workmanship of which is very elegant. It is
said to have belonged to the family of Lochbuy.—See PEN-
NANT'S *Tour,* vol. iii. p. 14.

" Gem!'ne'er wrought on highland mountain,
Did the fairy of the fountain,
Or the mermaid of the wave,
Frame thee in some coral cave?
Did in Iceland's darksome mine
Dwarf's swart hands thy metal twine?
Or, mortal-moulded, comest thou here,
From England's love, or France's fear?

XII.
Song continued.

" No!—thy splendours nothing tell
Foreign art or faëry spell.
Moulded thou for monarch's use,
By the overweening Bruce,
When the royal robe he tied
O'er a heart of wrath and pride;
Thence in triumph wert thou torn,
By the victor hand of Lorn!

" When the gem was won and lost,
Widely was the war-cry toss'd!
Rung aloud Bendourish fell,
Answer'd Douchart's sounding dell,
Fled the deer from wild Teyndrum,
When the homicide, o'ercome,
Hardly 'scaped with scathe and scorn,
Left the pledge with conquering Lorn!

XIII.

Song concluded.

" Vain was then the Douglas brand,[1]
Vain the Campbell's vaunted hand,
Vain Kirkpatrick's bloody dirk,[2]
Making sure of murder's work ;
Barendown fled fast away,
Fled the fiery De la Haye,[3]

[1] The gallant Sir James, called the Good Lord Douglas, the most faithful and valiant of Bruce's adherents, was wounded at the battle of Dalry. Sir Nigel, or Niel Campbell, was also in that unfortunate skirmish. He married Marjorie, sister to Robert Bruce, and was among his most faithful followers. In a manuscript account of the house of Argyle, supplied, it would seem, as materials for Archbishop Spottiswoode's History of the Church of Scotland, I find the following passage concerning Sir Niel Campbell :—" Moreover, when all the nobles in Scotland had left King Robert after his hard success, yet this noble knight was most faithful, and shrinked not, as it is to be seen in an indenture bearing these words :—*Memorandum quod cum ab incarnatione Domini* 1308 *conventum fuit et concordatum inter nobiles viros Dominum Alexandrum de Seatoun militem et Dominum Gilbertum de Haye militem et Dominum Nigellum Campbell militem apud monasterium de Cambuskenneth* 9° *Septembris qui tacta sancta eucharista, magnoque juramento facto, jurarunt se debere libertatem regni et Robertum nuper regem coronatum contra omnes mortales Francos Anglos Scotos defendere usque ad ultimum terminum vitæ ipsorum.* Their sealles are appended to the indenture in greene wax, togithir with the seal of Gulfrid, Abbot of Cambuskenneth."

[2] [See Appendix, Note G.]

[3] These knights are enumerated by Barbour among the small

When this broach, triumphant borne,
Beam'd upon the breast of Lorn.

" Farthest fled its former Lord,
Left his men to brand and cord,[1]
Bloody brand of Highland steel,
English gibbet, axe, and wheel.
Let him fly from coast to coast,
Dogg'd by Comyn's vengeful ghost,
While his spoils, in triumph worn,
Long shall grace victorious Lorn!"

XIV.

As glares the tiger on his foes,
Hemm'd in by hunters, spears, and bows,

number of Bruce's adherents, who remained in arms with him
after the battle of Methven.

> "With him was a bold baron,
> Schyr William the Baroundoun,
> — — —
> Schyr Gilbert de la Haye alsua."

There were more than one of the noble family of Hay engaged in
Bruce's cause ; but the principal was Gilbert de la Haye, Lord of
Errol, a stanch adherent to King Robert's interest, and whom
he rewarded by creating him hereditary Lord High Constable of
Scotland, a title which he used 16th March, 1308, where, in a
letter from the peers of Scotland to Philip the Fair of France,
he is designed *Gilbertus de Hay Constabularius Scotiœ.* He was
slain at the battle of Halidoun-hill. Hugh de la Haye, his brother, was made prisoner at the battle of Methven.

[MS.—" Left his followers to the sword."]

And, ere he bounds upon the ring,
Selects the object of his spring,—
Now on the bard, now on his Lord,
So Edward glared and grasp'd his sword—
But stern his brother spoke,—" Be still.
What! art thou yet so wild of will,
After high deeds and sufferings long,
To chafe thee for a menial's song ?—
Well hast thou framed, Old Man, thy strains,
To praise the hand that pays thy pains ; [1]

[1] The character of the Highland bards, however high in an earlier period of society, seems soon to have degenerated. The Irish affirm, that in their kindred tribes severe laws became necessary to restrain their avarice. In the Highlands they seem gradually to have sunk into contempt, as well as the orators, or men of speech, with whose office that of family poet was often united. —" The orators, in their language called Isdane, were in high esteem both in these islands and the continent : until within these forty years, they sat always among the nobles and chiefs of families in the streah, or circle. Their houses and little villages were sanctuaries, as well as churches, and they took place before doctors of physic. The orators, after the Druids were extinct, were brought in to preserve the genealogy of families, and to repeat the same at every succession of chiefs ; and upon the occasion of marriages and births, they made epithalamiums and panegyricks, which the poet or bard pronounced. The orators, by the force of their eloquence, had a powerful ascendant over the greatest men in their time; for if any orator did but ask the habit, arms, horse, or any other thing belonging to the greatest man in these islands, it was readily granted them, sometimes out of respect, and sometimes for fear of being exclaimed against by a satyre, which, in those days, was reckoned a great dishonour. But these gentlemen becoming insolent, lost ever since both the

Yet something might thy song have told
Of Lorn's three vassals, true and bold,
Who rent their Lord from Bruce's hold,
As underneath his knee he lay,
And died to save him in the fray.
I've heard the Bruce's cloak and clasp
Was clench'd within their dying grasp,
What time a hundred foemen more
Rush'd in and back the victor bore,[1]
Long after Lorn had left the strife,[2]
Full glad to 'scape with limb and life.—
Enough of this—And, Minstrel, hold,
As minstrel-hire, this chain of gold,

profit and esteem which was formerly due to their character;
for neither their panegyricks nor satyres are regarded to what
they have been, and they are now allowed but a small salary.
I must not omit to relate their way of study, which is very singular: They shut their doors and windows for a day's time,
and lie on their backs, with a stone upon their belly, and plads
about their heads, and their eyes being covered, they pump their
brains for rhetorical encomium or panegyrick; and indeed they
furnish such a style from this dark cell as is understood by very
few; and if they purchase a couple of horses as the reward of
their meditation, they think they have done a great matter.
The poet, or bard, had a title to the bridegroom's upper garb,
that is, the plad and bonnet; but now he is satisfyed with what
the bridegroom pleases to give him on such occasions."—MAR
TIN'S *Western Isles.*

   1 [The MS. has not this couplet.]

       2 [MS.—" When breathless Lorn had left the strife."]

For future lays a fair excuse,
To speak more nobly of the Bruce."—

XV.

"Now, by Columba's shrine, I swear,
And every saint that's buried there,
'Tis he himself!" Lorn sternly cries,
"And for my kinsman's death he dies."
As loudly Ronald calls—"Forbear!
Not in my sight while brand I wear,
O'ermatch'd by odds, shall warrior fall,
Or blood of stranger stain my hall!
This ancient fortress of my race
Shall be misfortune's resting-place,
Shelter and shield of the distress'd,
No slaughter-house for shipwreck'd guest."—
"Talk not to me," fierce Lorn replied,
"Of odds or match!—when Comyn died,
Three daggers clash'd within his side!
Talk not to me of sheltering hall,
The church of God saw Comyn fall!
On God's own altar stream'd his blood,
While o'er my prostrate kinsman stood,
The ruthless murderer—e'en as now—
With armed hand and scornful brow!—
Up, all who love me! blow on blow!
And lay the outlaw'd felons low!"

XVI.

Then up sprung many a mainland Lord,
Obedient to their Chieftain's word.
Barcaldine's arm is high in air,
And Kinloch-Alline's blade is bare,
Black Murthok's dirk has left its sheath,
And clench'd is Dermid's hand of death.
Their mutter'd threats of vengeance swell
Into a wild and warlike yell;
Onward they press with weapons high,
The affrighted females shriek and fly,
And, Scotland, then thy brightest ray
Had darken'd ere its noon of day,
But every chief of birth and fame,
That from the Isles of Ocean came,
At Ronald's side that hour withstood
Fierce Lorn's relentless thirst for blood.[1]

XVII.

Brave Torquil from Dunvegan high,
Lord of the misty hills of Skye,
Mac-Niel, wild Bara's ancient thane,
Duart, of bold Clan Gillian's strain,
Fergus, of Canna's castled bay,
Mac-Duffith, Lord of Colonsay,

---

[1] [For these four lines the MS. has,

"But stern the Island Lord withstood
The vengeful Chieftain's thirst of blood."]

Soon as they saw the broadswords glance,
With ready weapons rose at once,
More prompt, that many an ancient feud,
Full oft suppress'd, full oft renew'd,
Glow'd 'twixt the chieftains of Argyle,
And many a lord of ocean's isle.
Wild was the scene—each sword was bare,
Back stream'd each chieftain's shaggy hair,
In gloomy opposition set,
Eyes, hands, and brandish'd weapons met;
Blue gleaming o'er the social board,
Flash'd to the torches many a sword;
And soon those bridal lights may shine
On purple blood for rosy wine.

XVIII.

While thus for blows and death prepared,
Each heart was up,[1] each weapon bared,
Each foot advanced,—a surly pause
Still reverenced hospitable laws.
All menaced violence, but alike
Reluctant each the first to strike,
(For aye accursed in minstrel line
Is he who brawls 'mid song and wine,)
And, match'd in numbers and in might,
Doubtful and desperate seem'd the fight.

[1] [MS.—" While thus for blood and blows prepared
      Rais'd was each hand," &c.]

Thus threat and murmur died away,
Till on the crowded hall there lay
Such silence, as the deadly still,
Ere bursts the thunder on the hill.
With blade advanced, each Chieftain bold
Show'd like the Sworder's form of old,[1]
As wanting still the torch of life,
To wake the marble into strife.[2]

XIX.

That awful pause the stranger maid,
And Edith, seized to pray for aid.
As to De Argentine she clung,
Away her veil the stranger flung,
And, lovely 'mid her wild despair,
Fast stream'd her eyes, wide flow'd her hair.
" O thou, of knighthood once the flower,
Sure refuge in distressful hour,
Thou, who in Judah well hast fought
For our dear faith, and oft hast sought
Renown in knightly exercise,
When this poor hand has dealt the prize,
Say, can thy soul of honour brook
On the unequal strife to look,
When, butcher'd thus in peaceful hall,
Those once thy friends, my brethren, fall!"

[1] [MS.————" each Chieftain rude,
    Like that fam'd Swordsman's statue stood."]
[2] [MS.—" To waken him to deadly strife."]

To Argentine she turn'd her word,
But her eye sought the Island Lord.[1]
A flush like evening's setting flame
Glow'd on his cheek; his hardy frame,
As with a brief convulsion, shook:
With hurried voice and eager look,—
"Fear not," he said, "my Isabel!
What said I—Edith—all is well—
Nay, fear not—I will well provide
The safety of my lovely bride—
My bride?"—but there the accents clung
In tremor to his faltering tongue.

XX.

Now rose De Argentine, to claim
The prisoners in his sovereign's name,
To England's crown, who, vassals sworn,
'Gainst their liege lord had weapon borne—
(Such speech, I ween, was but to hide
His care their safety to provide;
For knight more true in thought and deed
Than Argentine ne'er spurr'd a steed)—
And Ronald, who his meaning guess'd,
Seem'd half to sanction the request.
This purpose fiery Torquil broke;—
" Somewhat we've heard of England's yoke,"

---

[1] [The MS. adds:—
   " With such a frantic fond appeal,
   As only lovers make and feel."]

He said, "and, in our islands, Fame
Hath whisper'd of a lawful claim,
That calls the Bruce fair Scotland's Lord,
Though dispossess'd by foreign sword.
This craves reflection—but though right
And just the charge of England's Knight,
Let England's crown her rebels seize
Where she has power;—in towers like these,
'Mid'st Scottish Chieftains summon'd here
To bridal mirth and bridal cheer,
Be sure, with no consent of mine,
Shall either Lorn or Argentine
With chains or violence, in our sight,
Oppress a brave and banish'd Knight."

XXI.

Then waked the wild debate again,
With brawling threat and clamour vain.
Vassals and menials, thronging in,
Lent their brute rage to swell the din;
When, far and wide, a bugle-clang
From the dark ocean upward rang.
   "The Abbot comes!" they cry at once,
   "The holy man, whose favour'd glance
      Hath sainted visions known;
   Angels have met him on the way,
   Beside the blessed martyrs' bay,
      And by Columba's stone,

His monks have heard their hymnings high
Sound from the summit of Dun-Y,
    To cheer his penance lone,
When at each cross, on girth and wold,[1]
(Their number thrice a hundred-fold,)
His prayer he made, his beads he told,
    With Aves many a one—
He comes our feuds to reconcile,
A sainted man from sainted isle;
We will his holy doom abide,
The Abbot shall our strife decide."[2]

XXII.

Scarcely this fair accord was o'er,[3]
When through the wide revolving door
    The black-stoled brethren wind;
Twelve sandall'd monks, who relics bore,
With many a torch-bearer before,
    And many a cross behind.[4]
Then sunk each fierce uplifted hand
And dagger bright and flashing brand

---

1 [MS.—" What time at every cross of old."]
2 [MS.—" We will his holy rede obey,
    The Abbot's voice shall end the fray."]
3 [MS.—" Scarce was this peaceful paction o'er."]
    4 [MS.—" Did slow procession wind;
    Twelve monks, who stole and mantle wore,
    And chalice, pyx, and relics bore,
      With many," &c.]

Dropp'd swiftly at the sight;
They vanish'd from the Churchman's eye,
As shooting stars, that glance and die,
    Dart from the vault of night.

XXIII.

The Abbot on the threshold stood,
And in his hand the holy rood;
Back on his shoulders flow'd his hood,
    The torch's glaring ray
Show'd, in its red and flashing light,
His wither'd cheek and amice white,
His blue eye glistening cold and bright,
    His tresses scant and gray.
" Fair Lords," he said, " Our Lady's love,
And peace be with you from above,
    And Benedicite!—
—But what means this? no peace is here!—
Do dirks unsheathed suit bridal cheer?
    Or are these naked brands
A seemly show for Churchman's sight,
When he comes summon'd to unite
Betrothed hearts and hands?"

XXIV.

Then, cloaking hate with fiery zeal,
Proud Lorn first answer'd the appeal;—
    "Thou comest, O holy Man,

True sons of blessed church to greet,[1]
But little deeming here to meet
   A wretch, beneath the ban
Of Pope and Church, for murder done
Even on the sacred altar-stone!—[2]
Well may'st thou wonder we should know
Such miscreant here, nor lay him low,[3]
Or dream of greeting, peace, or truce,
With excommunicated Bruce!
Yet will I grant, to end debate,
Thy sainted voice decide his fate.[4]

XXV.

Then Ronald pled the stranger's cause,
And knighthood's oath and honour's laws;[5]

---

[1] [The MS. here adds :—

     "Men bound in her communion sweet.
     And duteous to the Papal seat."]

[2] [MS.———" the blessed altar-stone."]

[3] [In place of the couplet which follows, the MS. has--

     "But promptly had my dagger's edge
     Aveng'd the guilt of sacrilege,
     Save for my new and kind ally,
     And Torquil, chief of stormy Skye,
     (In whose wild land there rests the seed,
     Men say, of ancient heathen creed,)
     Who would enforce me to a truce
     With excommunicated Bruce."]

[4] [The MS. adds:

     "Secure such foul offenders find
     No favour in a holy mind."]

[5] [The MS. has:

     "Alleged the best of honour's laws,

And Isabel on bended knee,
Brought pray'rs and tears to back the plea:
And Edith lent her generous aid,
And wept, and Lorn for mercy pray'd.[1]
" Hence," he exclaim'd, " degenerate maid !
Was't not enough to Ronald's bower
I brought thee, like a paramour,[2]
Or bond-maid at her master's gate,
His careless cold approach to wait ?—

The succour { due to claim'd by } storm-staid guest,
The refuge due to the distress'd,
The oath which binds each generous knight
Still to prevent unequal fight ;
And Isabel," &c.]

[1] [MS.—" And wept alike and knelt and pray'd."—The nine lines which intervene betwixt this and the concluding couplet of the stanza are not in the MS.]

[2] It was anciently customary in the Highlands to bring the bride to the house of the husband. Nay, in some cases the complaisance was stretched so far, that she remained there upon trial for a twelvemonth; and the bridegroom, even after this period of cohabitation, retained an option of refusing to fulfil his engagement. It is said that a desperate feud ensued between the clans of MacDonald of Sleate and Mac-Leod, owing to the former chief having availed himself of this license to send back to Dunvegan a sister, or daughter of the latter. Mac-Leod, resenting the indignity, observed, that since there was no wedding bonfire, there should be one to solemnize the divorce. Accordingly, he burned and laid waste the territories of MacDonald, who retaliated, and a deadly feud, with all its accompaniments, took place in form.

But the bold Lord of Cumberland,
The gallant Clifford, seeks thy hand;
His it shall be—Nay, no reply!
Hence! till those rebel eyes be dry."
With grief the Abbot heard and saw,
Yet nought relax'd his brow of awe.[1]

XXVI.

Then Argentine, in England's name,
So highly urged his sovereign's claim,[2]
He waked a spark, that, long suppress'd,
Had smoulder'd in Lord Ronald's breast;
And now, as from the flint the fire,
Flash'd forth at once his generous ire.
"Enough of noble blood," he said,
"By English Edward had been shed,

[1] [The MS. adds—

> " He raised the suppliants from the floor,
> And bade their sorrowing be o'er,
> And bade them give their weeping o'er,
> But in a tone that well explain'd
> How little grace their pray'rs had gain'd;
> For though he purposed true and well,
> Still stubborn and inflexible
> In what he deem'd his duty high,
> Was Abbot Ademar of Y."]

[2] [MS.—" For Bruce's custody made claim."—In place of the
two couplets which follow, the MS. has—

> " And Torquil, stout Dunvegan's Knight,
> As well defended Scotland's right.
> Enough of,' &c.]

Since matchless Wallace first had been
In mock'ry crown'd with wreaths of green.·
And done to death by felon hand,
For guarding well his father's land.
Where 's Nigel Bruce ? and De la Haye,
And valiant Seton—where are they ?

¹ Stow gives the following curious account of the trial and execution of this celebrated patriot:—"William Wallace, who had
oft-times set Scotland in great trouble, was taken and brought to
London, with great numbers of men and women wondering upon
him. He was lodged in the house of William Delect, a citizen of
London, in Fenchurch-street. On the morrow, being the eve of
St Bartholomew, he was brought on horseback to Westminster.
John Legrave and Jeffrey, knights, the mayor, sheriffs, and al-
dermen of London, and many others, both on horseback and on
foot, accompanying him; and in the great hall at Westminster, he
being placed on the south bench, crowned with laurel, for that he
had said in times past that he ought to bear a crown in that hall,
as it was commonly reported; and being appeached for a traitor
by Sir Peter Malorie, the king's justice, he answered, that he was
never traitor to the king of England; but for other things where-
of he was accused he confessed them; and was after headed and
quartered."—STOW, *Chr.* p. 209. There is something singularly
doubtful about the mode in which Wallace was taken. That he
was betrayed to the English is indubitable; and popular fame
charges Sir John Menteith with the indelible infamy. "Accursed,"
says Arnold Blair, "be the day of nativity of John de Menteith,
and may his name be struck out of the book of life." But John
de Menteith was all along a zealous favourer of the English interest, and was governor of Dumbarton Castle by commission from
Edward the First; and therefore, as the accurate Lord Hailes has
observed, could not be the friend and confidant of Wallace, as
tradition states him to be. The truth seems to be, that Menteith.
thoroughly engaged in the English interest, pursued Wallace

Where Somerville, the kind and free?
And Fraser, flower of chivalry?[1]
Have they not been on gibbet-bound,
Their quarters flung to hawk and hound,
And hold we here a cold debate,
To yield more victims to their fate?
What! can the English Leopard's mood
Never be gorged with northern blood?
Was not the life of Athole shed,
To soothe the tyrant's sicken'd bed?[2]

closely, and made him prisoner through the treachery of an attendant, whom Peter Langtoft calls Jack Short.

> " William Waleis is nomen that master was of theves,
> Tiding to the king is comen that robbery mischeives,
> Sir John of Menetest sued William so nigh,
> He tok him when he ween'd least, on night, his leman him by,
> That was through treason of *Jack Short* his man,
> He was the encheson that Sir John so him ran,
> Jack's brother had he slain, the Waleis that is said,
> The more Jack was fain to do William that braid."

From this it would appear that the infamy of seizing Wallace, must rest between a degenerate Scottish nobleman, the vassal of England, and a domestic, the obscure agent of his treachery: between Sir John Menteith, son of Walter, Earl of Menteith, and the traitor Jack Short.

[1] [See Appendix, Note II.]

[2] John de Strathbogie, Earl of Athole, had attempted to escape out of the kingdom, but a storm cast him upon the coast, when he was taken, sent to London, and executed, with circumstances of great barbarity, being first half strangled, then let down from the gallows while yet alive, barbarously dismembered, and his body burnt. It may surprise the reader to learn, that this was a *mitigated*

And must his word, till dying day,
Be nought but quarter, hang, and slay!—[1]
Thou frown'st, De Argentine,—My gage
Is prompt to prove the strife I wage."—

punishment; for in respect that his mother was a grand-daughter
of King John, by his natural son Richard, he was not drawn on a
sledge to execution, "that point was forgiven," and he made the
passage on horseback. Matthew of Westminster tells us that
King Edward, then extremely ill, received great ease from the
news that his relative was apprehended. "*Quo audito, Rex An-
gliæ, etsi gravissimo morbo tunc langueret, levius tamen tulit do-
lorem.*" To this singular expression the text alludes.

[1] This alludes to a passage in Barbour, singularly expressive
of the vindictive spirit of Edward I. The prisoners taken at the
castle of Kildrummie had surrendered upon condition that they
should be at King Edward's disposal. "But his will," says Barbour, "was always evil toward Scottishmen." The news of the
surrender of Kildrummie arrived when he was in his mortal
sickness at Burgh-upon-sands.

> " And when he to the death was near.
> The folk that at Kildromy wer
> Come with prisoners that they had tanc,
> And syne to the king are gane.
> And for to comfort him they tauld
> How they the castell to them yauld ;
> And how they till his will were brought,
> To do off that whatever he thought ;
> And ask'd what men should off them
> Then look'd he angryly them to,
> He said, grinning, ' HANOS AND DRAWA.'
> That was wonder of sic saws.
> That he, that to the death was near,
> Should answer upon sic maner.
> Forouten moaning and mercy ;
> How might he trust on him to cry,

XXVII.

" Nor deem," said stout Dunvegan's knight,[1]
" That thou shalt brave alone the fight !
By saints of isle and mainland both,
By Woden wild, (my grandsire's oath,)[2]
Let Rome and England do their worst,
Howe'er attainted or accursed,
If Bruce shall e'er find friends again,
Once more to brave a battle plain,
If Douglas couch again his lance,
Or Randolph dare another chance,
Old Torquil will not be to lack
With twice a thousand at his back.—
Nay, chafe not at my bearing bold,
Good Abbot ! for thou know'st of old,

That sooth-fastly dooms all thing
To have mercy for his crying,
Off him that, throw his felony,
Into sic point had no mercy ! "

There was much truth in the Leonine couplet, with which Matthew of Westminster concludes his encomium on the first Edward :

" Scotos Edwardus, dum vixit, suppeditavit,
Tenuit, afflixit, depressit, dilaniavit."

[1] [In the MS. this couplet is wanting, and, without breaking the stanza, Lord Ronald continues,

" By saints of isle," &c.]

[2] The MacLeods, and most other distinguished Hebridean families, were of Scandinavian extraction, and some were late or imperfect converts to Christianity. The family names of Torquil, Thormod, &c. are all Norwegian.

Torquil's rude thought and stubborn will
Smack of the wild Norwegian still;
Nor will I barter Freedom's cause
For England's wealth or Rome's applause."

XXVIII.

The Abbot seem'd with eye severe
The hardy Chieftain's speech to hear;
Then on King Robert turn'd the Monk,[1]
But twice his courage came and sunk,
Confronted with the hero's look;
Twice fell his eye, his accents shook;
At length, resolved in tone and brow,
Sternly he question'd him—" And thou,
Unhappy! what hast thou to plead,
Why I denounce not on thy deed
That awful doom which canons tell
Shuts paradise, and opens hell;
Anathema of power so dread,
It blends the living with the dead,
Bids each good angel soar away,
And every ill one claim his prey;
Expels thee from the church's care,
And deafens Heaven against thy prayer;
Arms every hand against thy life,
Bans all who aid thee in the strife,

---

[1] [MS.—" Then turn'd him on the Bruce the Monk."]

Nay, each whose succour, cold and scant,[1]
With meanest alms relieves thy want;
Haunts thee while living,—and, when dead,
Dwells on thy yet devoted head,
Rends Honour's scutcheon from thy hearse,
Stills o'er thy bier the holy verse,
And spurns thy corpse from hallow'd ground,
Flung like vile carrion to the hound;
Such is the dire and desperate doom
For sacrilege, decreed by Rome;
And such the well-deserved meed
Of thine unhallow'd, ruthless deed." —

XXIX.

"Abbot!" The Bruce replied, "thy charge
It boots not to dispute at large.
This much, howe'er, I bid thee know,
No selfish vengeance dealt the blow,
For Comyn died his country's foe.
Nor blame I friends whose ill-timed speed
Fulfilled my soon-repented deed,
Nor censure those from whose stern tongue
The dire anathema has rung.
I only blame mine own wild ire,
By Scotland's wrongs incensed to fire.
Heaven knows my purpose to atone,
Far as I may, the evil done,

[1] [MS.—" Nay, curses each whose succour scant."]

And hears a penitent's appeal
From papal curse and prelate's zeal.
My first and dearest task achieved,
Fair Scotland from her thrall relieved,
Shall many a priest in cope and stole
Say requiem for Red Comyn's soul,
While I the blessed cross advance,
And expiate this unhappy chance,
In Palestine, with sword and lance.[1]
But, while content the church should know
My conscience owns the debt I owe,[2]
Unto De Argentine and Lorn
The name of traitor I return,
Bid them defiance stern and high,[3]
And give them in their throats the lie!
These brief words spoke, I speak no more.
Do what thou wilt; my shrift is o'er."

XXX.

Like man by prodigy amazed,
Upon the King the Abbot gazed;
Then o'er his pallid features glance,
Convulsions of ecstatic trance.

---

[1] Bruce uniformly professed, and probably felt, compunction for
having violated the sanctuary of the church by the slaughter of
Comyn; and finally, in his last hours, in testimony of his faith,
penitence, and zeal, he requested James Lord Douglas to carry his
heart to Jerusalem, to be there deposited in the Holy Sepulchre.

[2] [The MS. adds:—" For this ill-timed and luckless blow."]

[3] [MS.——" bold and high."]

His breathing came more thick and fast,
And from his pale blue eyes were cast
Strange rays of wild and wandering light;
Uprise his locks of silver white,
Flush'd is his brow, through every vein
In azure tide the current strain,
And undistinguish'd accents broke
The awful silence ere he spoke.[1]

XXXI.

" De Bruce! I rose with purpose dread
To speak my curse upon thy head,[2]
And give thee as an outcast o'er
To him who burns to shed thy gore ;—

---

[1] [MS.—" Swell on his wither'd brow the veins,
  Each in its azure current strains,
  And interrupted tears express'd
  The tumult of his labouring breast."]

[2] So soon as the notice of Comyn's slaughter reached Rome,
Bruce and his adherents were excommunicated. It was published
first by the Archbishop of York, and renewed at different times,
particularly by Lambyrton, Bishop of St Andrews, in 1308; but
it does not appear to have answered the purpose which the
English monarch expected. Indeed, for reasons which it may
be difficult to trace, the thunders of Rome descended upon the
Scottish mountains with less effect than in more fertile coun-
tries. Probably the comparative poverty of the benefices occasioned that fewer foreign clergy settled in Scotland; and the interest of the native churchmen were linked with that of their
country. Many of the Scottish prelates, Lambyrton the primate
particularly, declared for Bruce, while he was yet under the ban
of the church, although he afterwards again changed sides.

But, like the Midianite of old,
Who stood on Zophim, heaven controll'd,[1]
I feel within mine aged breast
A power that will not be repress'd.[2]
It prompts my voice, it swells my veins,
It burns, it maddens, it constrains!—
De Bruce, thy sacrilegious blow
Hath at God's altar slain thy foe :
O'ermaster'd yet by high behest,
I bless thee, and thou shalt be bless'd !"
He spoke, and o'er the astonish'd throng
Was silence, awful, deep, and long.

XXXII.

Again that light has fired his eye,
Again his form swells bold and high,
The broken voice of age is gone,
'Tis vigorous manhood's lofty tone :—
" Thrice vanquish'd on the battle-plain,
Thy followers slaughter'd, fled, or ta'en,
A hunted wanderer on the wild,
On foreign shores a man exil'd,[3]
Disown'd, deserted, and distress'd,[4]
I bless thee, and thou shalt be bless'd !

---

1 [See the Book of NUMBERS, chap. xxiii. and xxiv.]
2 [See Appendix, Note I.]
3 [See Appendix, Note K.]
4 [" On this transcendent passage we shall only remark, of that

Bless'd in the hall and in the field,
Under the mantle as the shield.
Avenger of thy country's shame,
Restorer of her injured fame,
Bless'd in thy sceptre and thy sword,
De Bruce, fair Scotland's rightful Lord,
Bless'd in thy deeds and in thy fame,
What lengthen'd honours wait thy name!
In distant ages, sire to son
Shall tell thy tale of freedom won,
And teach his infants, in the use
Of earliest speech, to falter Bruce.
Go, then, triumphant! sweep along
Thy course, the theme of many a song!
The Power, whose dictates swell my breast,
Hath bless'd thee, and thou shalt be bless'd!—
Enough—my short-lived strength decays,
And sinks the momentary blaze.—
Heaven hath our destined purpose broke,
Not here must nuptial vow be spoke;[1]
Brethren, our errand here is o'er,
Our task discharged.—Unmoor, unmoor!"—

the gloomy part of the prophecy we hear nothing more through
the whole of the poem, and though the Abbot informs the King
that he shall be ' On foreign shores a man exiled,' the poet never
speaks of him but as resident in Scotland, up to the period of
the battle of Bannockburn."—*Critical Review.*]

[1] [The MS. has not this couplet.]

His priests received the exhausted Monk,
As breathless in their arms he sunk.
Punctual his orders to obey,
The train refused all longer stay,
Embark'd, raised sail, and bore away.[1]

[1] [" The conception and execution of these stanzas constitute
excellence which it would be difficult to match from any other
part of the poem. The surprise is grand and perfect. The monk,
struck with the heroism of Robert, foregoes the intended anathema, and breaks out into a prophetic annunciation of his final
triumph over all his enemies, and the veneration in which his
name will be held by posterity. These stanzas which conclude
the second canto, derive their chief title to encomium from the
emphatic felicity of their burden,

              ' I bless the, and thou shalt be bless'd ; '

in which few and simple words, following, as they do, a series of
predicated ills, there is an energy that instantaneously appeals
to the heart, and surpasses, all to nothing, the results of passages less happy in their application, though more laboured
and tortuous in their construction."— *Critical Review.*

" The story of the second canto exhibits fewer of Mr Scott's
characteristical beauties than of his characteristical faults. The
scene itself is not of a very edifying description ; nor is the want
of agreeableness in the subject compensated by any detached
merit in the details. Of the language and versification in many
parts, it is hardly possible to speak favourably. The same must
be said of the speeches which the different characters address to
each other. The rude vehemence which they display seems to
consist much more in the loudness and gesticulation with which
the speakers express themselves, than in the force and energy of
their sentiments, which, for the most part, are such as the bar-
barous chiefs, to whom they are attributed, might, without any
great premeditation, either as to the thought or language, have
actually uttered. To find language and sentiments proportion-

ed to characters of such extraordinary dimensions as the agents in the poems of Homer and Milton, is indeed an admirable effort of genius; but to make such as we meet with in the epic poetry of the present day, persons often below the middle size, and never very much above it, merely speak in *character*, is not likely to occasion either much difficulty to the poet, or much pleasure to the reader. As an example, we might adduce the speech of stout Dunvegan's knight, stanza xxvii., which is not the less wanting in taste, because it is natural and characteristic."—*Quarterly Review.*]

LORD OF THE ISLES.

CANTO THIRD.

.

LORD OF THE ISLES.

CANTO THIRD.

HAST thou not mark'd, when o'er thy startled head
Sudden and deep the thunder-peal has roll'd,
How, when its echoes fell, a silence dead
Sunk on the wood, the meadow, and the wold?
The rye-grass shakes not on the sod-built fold,
The rustling aspen's leaves are mute and still,[1]
The wall-flower waves not on the ruin'd hold,
Till, murmuring distant first, then near and shrill,
The savage whirlwind wakes, and sweeps the groaning hill!

II.

Artornish! such a silence sunk
Upon thy halls, when that grey Monk
His prophet speech had spoke;

---

[1] [MS.—" The rustling aspen bids his leaf be still."]

And his obedient brethren's sail
Was stretch'd to meet the southern gale
   Before a whisper woke.
Then murmuring sounds of doubt and fear,
Close pour'd in many an anxious ear,
   The solemn stillness broke ;
And still they gazed with eager guess,
Where, in an oriel's deep recess,
The Island Prince seem'd bent to press .
What Lorn, by his impatient cheer,
And gesture fierce, scarce deign'd to hear.

III.

Starting at length with frowning look,
His hand he clench'd, his head he shook,
   And sternly flung apart ;—
" And deem'st thou me so mean of mood,
As to forget the mortal feud,
And clasp the hand with blood imbrued [1]
   From my dear Kinsman's heart ?
Is this thy rede ?—a due return
For ancient league and friendship sworn !
But well our mountain proverb shows
The faith of Islesmen ebbs and flows.
Be it even so—believe, ere long,
He that now bears shall wreak the wrong.
Call Edith—call the Maid of Lorn !
My sister, slaves !—for further scorn,

---

[1] [MS.—" And clasp the bloody hand imbrued."]

Be sure nor she nor I will stay.—
Away, De Argentine, away!—
We nor ally nor brother know,[1]
In Bruce's friend, or England's foe."

IV.

But who the Chieftain's rage can tell,
When, sought from lowest dungeon cell
To highest tower the castle round,
No Lady Edith was there found!
He shouted, "Falsehood!—treachery!—
Revenge and blood!—a lordly meed
To him that will avenge the deed!
A Baron's lands!"—His frantic mood
Was scarcely by the news withstood,
That Morag shared his sister's flight,
And that, in hurry of the night,
'Scaped noteless, and without remark,
Two strangers sought the Abbot's bark.—
"Man every galley!—fly—pursue!
The priest his treachery shall rue!
Ay, and the time shall quickly come,
When we shall hear the thanks that Rome
Will pay his feigned prophecy!"
Such was fierce Lorn's indignant cry;[2]

[1] [MS.—" Nor brother we, nor ally know."]
[2] [The MS. has,

"Such was fierce Lorn's cry."

See a note on a line in the Lay of the Last Minstrel, *ante*, vol.
vi. p. 62.]

And Cormac Doil in haste obey'd,
Hoisted his sail, his anchor weigh'd,
(For, glad of each pretext for spoil,
A pirate sworn was Cormac Doil.)[1]
But others, lingering, spoke apart,—
" The maid has given her maiden heart
    To Ronald of the Isles,
And, fearful lest her brother's word
Bestow her on that English Lord,
    She seeks Iona's piles,
And wisely deems it best to dwell
A votaress in the holy cell,
Until these feuds so fierce and fell
    The Abbot reconciles."[2]

V.

As, impotent of ire, the hall
Echoed to Lorn's impatient call,

[1] A sort of persons common in the isles, as may be easily believed, until the introduction of civil polity. Witness the Dean
of the Isles' account of Ronay. "At the north end of Raarsay,
be half myle of sea frae it, layes ane ile callit Ronay, maire then
a myle in lengthe, full of wood and heddir, with ane havein for
heiland galoys in the middis of it, and the same havein is guid for
fostering of theives, ruggairs and reivairs, till a nail, upon the
peilling and spulzeing of poor pepill. This ile perteins to M'Gil-
lychallan of Raarsay by force, and to the bishope of the iles be
heritage."—SIR DONALD MONRO'S *Description of the Western
Islands of Scotland, Edinburgh,* 1805, p. 22.

[2] [MS.—" While friends shall labour fair and well
    These feuds to reconcile."]

" My horse, my mantle, and my train !
Let none who honours Lorn remain !"—
Courteous, but stern, a bold request
To Bruce De Argentine express'd.
" Lord Earl," he said,—" I cannot chuse
But yield such title to the Bruce,
Though name and earldom both are gone,
Since he braced rebel's armour on—
But, Earl or Serf—rude phrase was thine
Of late, and launch'd at Argentine ;
Such as compels me to demand
Redress of honour at thy hand.
We need not to each other tell,
That both can wield their weapons well ;
   Then do me but the soldier grace,
   This glove upon thy helm to place
      Where we may meet in fight ;
   And I will say, as still I've said,
   Though by ambition far misled,
      Thou art a noble knight."—

VI.

" And I," the princely Bruce replied,
"Might term it stain on knighthood's pride,
That the bright sword of Argentine
Should in a tyrant's quarrel shine ;
   But, for your brave request,
Be sure the honour'd pledge you gave
In every battle-field shall wave

Upon my helmet-crest;
Believe, that if my hasty tongue
Hath done thine honour causeless wrong,
    It shall be well redress'd.
Not dearer to my soul was glove,
Bestow'd in youth by lady's love,
    Than this which thou hast given!
Thus, then, my noble foe I greet;
Health and high fortune till we meet,
    And then—what pleases Heaven."

VII.

Thus parted they—for now, with sound
Like waves roll'd back from rocky ground,
    The friends of Lorn retire;
Each mainland chieftain, with his train,
Draws to his mountain towers again,
Pondering how mortal schemes prove vain,
    And mortal hopes expire.
But through the castle double guard,
By Ronald's charge, kept wakeful ward,
Wicket and gate were trebly barr'd,
    By beam and bolt and chain;
Then of the guests, in courteous sort,
He pray'd excuse for mirth broke short,
And bade them in Artornish fort
    In confidence remain.
Now torch and menial tendance led
Chieftain and knight to bower and bed,

And beads were told, and aves said,
    And soon they sunk away
Into such sleep, as wont to shed
Oblivion on the weary head,
    After a toilsome day.

VIII.

But soon uproused, the Monarch cried
To Edward slumbering by his side,
    " Awake, or sleep for aye !
Even now there jarr'd a secret door—
A taper-light gleams on the floor—
    Up, Edward, up, I say !
Some one glides in like midnight ghost—
Nay, strike not ! 'tis our noble Host."
Advancing then his taper's flame,
Ronald stept forth, and with him came
    Dunvegan's chief—each bent the knee
    To Bruce in sign of fealty,
        And proffer'd him his sword,
And hail'd him, in a monarch's style,
As king of mainland and of isle,
        And Scotland's rightful lord.
" And O," said Ronald, " Own'd of Heaven !
Say, is my erring youth forgiven,
By falsehood's arts from duty driven,
    Who rebel falchion drew,
Yet ever to thy deeds of fame,
Even while I strove against thy claim,

Paid homage just and true ? "—
" Alas ! dear youth, the unhappy time,"
Answer'd the Bruce, " must bear the crime,
   Since, guiltier far than you,
Even I "—he paused ; for Falkirk's woes
Upon his conscious soul arose.[1]

---

[1] I have followed the vulgar and inaccurate tradition, that Bruce fought against Wallace, and the array of Scotland, at the fatal battle of Falkirk. The story, which seems to have no better authority than that of Blind Harry, bears, that having made much slaughter during the engagement, he sat down to dine with the conquerors without washing the filthy witness from his hands.

> " Fasting he was, and had been in great need,
> Blooded were all his weapons and his weed ;
> Southeron lords scorn'd him in terms rude,
> And said, Behold yon Scot eats his own blood.
>
> " Then rued he sore, for reason bad be known,
> That blood and land alike should be his own ;
> With them he long was, ere he got away, .
> But contrair Scots he fought not from that day."

The account given by most of our historians, of the conversation between Bruce and Wallace over the Carron river, is equally apocryphal. There is full evidence that Bruce was not at that time on the English side, nor present at the battle of Falkirk ; nay, that he acted as a guardian of Scotland, along with John Comyn, in the name of Baliol, and in opposition to the English. He was the grandson of the competitor, with whom he has been sometimes confounded. Lord Hailes has well described, and in some degree apologized for, the earlier part of his life.— " His grandfather, the competitor, had patiently acquiesced in the award of Edward. His father, yielding to the times, had served

The Chieftain to his breast he press'd,
And in a sigh conceal'd the rest.

IX.

They proffer'd aid, by arms and might,
To repossess him in his right;
But well their counsels must be weigh'd,
Ere banners raised and musters made,
For English hire and Lorn's intrigues
Bound many chiefs in southern leagues.
In answer, Bruce his purpose bold
To his new vassals[1] frankly told.
" The winter worn in exile o'er,
I long'd for Carrick's kindred shore.
I thought upon my native Ayr,
And long'd to see the burly fare
That Clifford makes, whose lordly call
Now echoes through my father's hall.
But first my course to Arran led,
Where valiant Lennox gathers head,
And on the sea, by tempest toss'd,
Our barks dispersed, our purpose cross'd,

under the English banners. But young Bruce had more ambition, and a more restless spirit. In his earlier years he acted upon no regular plan. By turns the partisan of Edward, and the vicegerent of Baliol, he seems to have forgotten or stifled his pretensions to the crown. But his character developed itself by degrees, and in maturer age became firm and consistent."—*Annals of Scotland, p.* 290, *quarto, London,* 1776.

[1] [MS.—" Allies."]

Mine own, a hostile sail to shun,
Far from her destined course had run,
When that wise will, which masters ours,
Compell'd us to your friendly towers."

X.

Then Torquil spoke: "The time craves speed!
We must not linger in our deed,
But instant pray our Sovereign Liege,
To shun the perils of a siege.
The vengeful Lorn, with all his powers,
Lies but too near Artornish towers,
And England's light-armed vessels ride,
Not distant far, the waves of Clyde,
Prompt at these tidings to unmoor,
And sweep each strait, and guard each shore.
Then, till this fresh alarm pass by,
Secret and safe my Liege must lie
In the far bounds of friendly Skye,
Torquil thy pilot and thy guide."—
" Not so, brave Chieftain," Ronald cried;
" Myself will on my Sovereign wait,[1]
And raise in arms the men of Sleate,
Whilst thou, renown'd where chiefs debate,
Shalt sway their souls by counsel sage,
And awe them by thy locks of age."—

---

[1] [MS.—"' Myself thy pilot and thy guide.'—
        ' Not so, kind Torquil,' Ronald cried;
        ''Tis I will on my Sovereign wait.'"]

—" And if my words in weight shall fail,[1]
This ponderous sword shall turn the scale."—

XI.

" The scheme," said Bruce, " contents me well ;
Meantime, 'twere best that Isabel,
For safety, with my bark and crew,
Again to friendly Erin drew.
There Edward, too, shall with her wend,
In need to cheer her and defend,
And muster up each scatter'd friend."—[2]
Here seem'd it as Lord Ronald's ear
Would other counsel gladlier hear ;
But, all achieved as soon as plann'd,
Both barks, in secret arm'd and mann'd,
  From out the haven bore ;
On different voyage forth they ply,
This for the coast of winged Skye,
  And that for Erin's shore.

XII.

With Bruce and Ronald bides the tale.
To favouring winds they gave the sail,

---

[1] [The MS. has,
  " ' Aye,' said the Chief, ' or if they fail,
  This broadsword's weight shall turn the scale.' "
In altering this passage, the poet appears to have lost a link.—ED.]
[2] [The MS. adds:
  " Our bark's departure, too, will blind
  To our intent the foeman's mind."]

Till Mull's dark headlands scarce they knew,
And Ardnamurchan's hills were blue.[1]
But then the squalls blew close and hard,
And, fain to strike the galley's yard,
 And take them to the oar,
With these rude seas, in weary plight,
They strove the livelong day and night,
Nor till the dawning had a sight
 Of Skye's romantic shore.
Where Coolin stoops him to the west,
They saw upon his shiver'd crest
 The sun's arising gleam ;
But such the labour and delay,
Ere they were moor'd in Scavigh bay,
(For calmer haven compell'd to stay,)[2]
 He shot a western beam.
Then Ronald said, "If true mine eye,
These are the savage wilds that lie
North of Strathnardill and Dunskye;[3]
 No human foot comes here,
And, since these adverse breezes blow,
If my good liege love hunter's bow,
What hinders that on land we go,
 And strike a mountain-deer ?
Allan, my page, shall with us wend ;
A bow full deftly can he bend,

1 [MS.—"Till Mull's dark isle no more they knew,
 Nor Ardnamurchan's mountains blue."]
2 [MS.—"For favouring gales compell'd to stay."]
3 [See Appendix, Note L.]

And, if we meet a herd, may send
    A shaft shall mend our cheer."
Then each took bow and bolts in hand,
Their row-boat launch'd and leapt to land,
    And left their skiff and train,
Where a wild stream, with headlong shock,
Came brawling down its bed of rock,
    To mingle with the main.

XIII.

A while their route they silent made,
    As men who stalk for mountain-deer,
Till the good Bruce to Ronald said,
    " St Mary ! what a scene is here !
I've traversed many a mountain-strand,
Abroad and in my native land,
And it has been my lot to tread
Where safety more than pleasure lead ;
    Thus, many a waste I've wander'd o'er,
    Clombe many a crag, cross'd many a moor,
      But, by my halidome,
A scene so rude, so wild as this,
Yet so sublime in barrenness,
Ne'er did my wandering footsteps press,
    Where'er I happ'd to roam."

XIV.

No marvel thus the Monarch spake ;
    For rarely human eye has known

A scene so stern as that dread lake,
    With its dark ledge [1] of barren stone.
Seems that primeval earthquake's sway
Hath rent a strange and shatter'd way
    Through the rude bosom of the hill,
And that each naked precipice,
Sable ravine, and dark abyss,
    Tells of the outrage still.
The wildest glen, but this, can show
Some touch of Nature's genial glow;
On high Benmore green mosses grow,
And heath-bells bud in deep Glencroe, [2]
    And copse on Cruchan-Ben;
· But here,—above, around, below,
    On mountain or in glen,
Nor tree, nor shrub, nor plant, nor flower,
Nor aught of vegetative power,
    The weary eye may ken.
For all is rocks at random thrown,
Black waves, bare crags, and banks of stone,
    As if were here denied
The summer sun, the spring's sweet dew,
That clothe with many a varied hue
    The bleakest [3] mountain-side. [4]

---

[1] [MS.—"Dark banks."]

[2] [MS.—" And {dears have buds / heather-bells } in deep Glencoe."]

[3] [MS. " { Wildest / Barest } "]

[4] [The Quarterly Reviewer says, " This picture of barren deso-

XV.

And wilder, forward as they wound,
Were the proud cliffs and lake profound.
Huge terraces of granite black[1]
Afforded rude and cumber'd track ;
    For from the mountain hoar,[2]
Hurl'd headlong in some night of fear,
When yell'd the wolf and fled the deer,
    Loose crags had toppled o'er ;[3]
And some, chance-poised and balanced, lay,
So that a stripling arm might sway
    A mass no host could raise,
In Nature's rage at random thrown,
Yet trembling like the Druid's stone
    On its precarious base.
The evening mists, with ceaseless change,
Now clothed the mountains' lofty range,
    Now left their foreheads bare,
And round the skirts their mantle furl'd,

lation is admirably touched ;" and if the opinion of Mr Turner
be worth any thing, "No words could have given a truer picture
of this, one of the wildest of Nature's landscapes." Mr Turner
adds, however, that he dissents in one particular ; but for *one or
two* tufts of grass he must have broken his neck, having slipped
when trying to attain the best position for taking the view which
embellishes this volume.]

    1 [MS.—"And wilder, at each step they take,
        Turn the proud cliffs and yawing lake,
        Huge naked sheets of granite black." &c.]
    2 [MS.—"For from the mountain's crown."]
    3 [MS.—"Huge crags had toppled down."]

Or on the sable waters curl'd,
Or on the eddying breezes whirl'd,
   Dispersed in middle air.
And oft, condensed, at once they lower,[1]
When, brief and fierce, the mountain shower
   Pours like a torrent down,[2]
And when return the sun's glad beams,
Whiten'd with foam a thousand streams
   Leap from the mountain's crown.[3]

XVI.

" This lake," said Bruce, " whose barriers drear
Are precipices sharp and sheer,
Yielding no track for goat or deer,
   Save the black shelves we tread,
How term you its dark waves? and how
Yon northern mountain's pathless brow,
   And yonder peak of dread,
That to the evening sun uplifts
The griesly gulfs and slaty rifts,
   Which scam its shiver'd head?"—
" Coriskin call the dark lake's name,
Coolin the ridge, as bards proclaim,
From old Cuchullin, chief of fame.
But bards, familiar in our isles
Rather with Nature's frowns than smiles,

---

[1] [MS.—" Oft closing too, at once they lower."]
[2] [MS.—" Pour'd like a torrent dread."]
[3] [MS.—" Leap from the mountain's head."]

Full oft their careless humours please
By sportive names from scenes like these.
I would old Torquil were to show
His maidens with their breasts of snow,
Or that my noble Liege were nigh
To hear his Nurse sing lullaby !
(The Maids—tall cliffs with breakers white,
The Nurse—a torrent's roaring might,)
Or that your eye could see the mood
Of Corryvrekin's whirlpool rude,
When dons the Hag her whiten'd hood—
'Tis thus our islesmen's fancy frames,
For scenes so stern, fantastic names."

XVII.

Answer'd the Bruce, " And musing mind
Might here a graver moral find.
These mighty cliffs, that heave on high
Their naked brows to middle sky,
Indifferent to the sun or snow,
Where nought can fade, and nought can blow,
May they not mark a monarch's fate,—
Raised high 'mid storms of strife and state,
Beyond life's lowlier pleasures placed,
His soul a rock, his heart a waste ?[1]

---

[1] [" He who ascends to mountain-tops, shall find
The loftiest peaks most wrapt in clouds and snow ;
He who surpasses or subdues mankind,
Must look down on the hate of those below.

O'er hope and love and fear aloft
High rears his crowned head—But soft!
Look, underneath yon jutting crag
Are hunters and a slaughter'd stag.
Who may they be? But late you said
No steps these desert regions tread?"—

XVIII.

"So said I—and believed in sooth,"
Ronald replied, "I spoke the truth.
Yet now I spy, by yonder stone,
Five men—they mark us, and come on;
And by their badge on bonnet borne,
I guess them of the land of Lorn,
Foes to my Liege."—" So let it be;
I've faced worse odds than five to three—
—But the poor page can little aid;
Then be our battle thus array'd,
·If our free passage they contest;
Cope thou with two, I'll match the rest."—
" Not so, my Liege—for, by my life,
This sword shall meet the treble strife;
My strength, my skill in arms, more small,
And less the loss should Ronald fall.

Though high above the sun of glory glow,
 And far beneath the earth and ocean spread,
 Round him are icy rocks, and loudly blow
 Contending tempests on his naked head,
And thus reward the toils which to those summits led."
                    Childe Harold, Canto iii.]

But islesmen soon to soldiers grow,
Allan has sword as well as bow,
And were my Monarch's order given,
Two shafts should make our number even."—
" No ! not to save my life !" he said;
" Enough of blood rests on my head,
Too rashly spill'd—we soon shall know,
Whether they come as friend or foe."

XIX.

Nigh came the strangers, and more nigh ;—
Still less they pleased the Monarch's eye.
Men were they all of evil mien,
Down-look'd, unwilling to be seen ;[1]
They moved with half-resolved pace,
And bent on earth each gloomy face.
The foremost two were fair array'd,
With brogue and bonnet, trews and plaid,
And bore the arms of mountaineers,
Daggers and broadswords, bows and spears.
The three, that lagg'd small space behind,
Seem'd serfs of more degraded kind ;
Goat-skins or deer-hides o'er them cast,
Made a rude fence against the blast;
Their arms and feet and heads were bare,
Matted their beards, unshorn their hair :

[See Appendix, Note M.]

For arms, the caitiffs bore in hand,
A club, an axe, a rusty brand.

XX.

Onward, still mute, they kept the track ;—
" Tell who ye be, or else stand back,"
Said Bruce ; " In deserts when they meet,
Men pass not as in peaceful street."
Still, at his stern command, they stood,
And proffer'd greeting brief and rude,
But acted courtesy so ill,
As seem'd of fear, and not of will.
" Wanderers we are, as you may be :
Men hither driven by wind and sea,
Who, if you list to taste our cheer,
Will share with you this fallow deer."—
" If from the sea, where lies your bark ?"—
" Ten fathom deep in ocean dark !
Wreck'd yesternight : but we are men,
Who little sense of peril ken.
The shades come down—the day is shut—
Will you go with us to our hut ?"—
" Our vessel waits us in the bay ;¹
Thanks for your proffer—have good-day."—
" Was that your galley, then, which rode
Not far from shore when evening glow'd ?"——⁵

---

¹ [MS.—" Our boat and vessel cannot stay."]
² [MS.—" Deep in the bay when evening glow'd."]

" It was."—" Then spare your needless pain,
There will she now be sought in vain.
We saw her from the mountain head,
When with St George's blazon red
A southern vessel bore in sight,
And yours raised sail, and took to flight."

XXI.

" Now, by the rood, unwelcome news !"   ·
Thus with Lord Ronald communed Bruce ;
" Nor rests there light enough to show
If this their tale be true or no.
The men seem bred of churlish kind,
Yet mellow nuts have hardest rind ;
We will go with them—food and fire[1]
And sheltering roof our wants require.
Sure guard 'gainst treachery will we keep,
And watch by turns our comrades' sleep.—
Good fellows, thanks ; your guests we'll be,
And well will pay the courtesy.
Come, lead us where your lodging lies,—
—Nay, soft ! we mix not companies.—
Show us the path o'er crag and stone,[2]
And we will follow you ;—lead on."

XXII.

They reach'd the dreary cabin, made
Of sails against a rock display'd,

---

[1] [MS.—" Yet rugged brows have bosoms kind ;
        Wend we with them—for food and fire."]
[2] [MS.—" Wend you the first o'er stock and stone."]

And there, on entering,[1] found
A slender boy, whose form and mien
Ill suited with such savage scene,
In cap and cloak of velvet green,
    Low seated on the ground.
His garb was such as minstrels wear,
Dark was his hue, and dark his hair,
His youthful cheek was marr'd by care,
    His eyes in sorrow drown'd.
" Whence this poor boy?"—As Ronald spoke,
The voice his trance of anguish broke;
As if awaked from ghastly dream,
He raised his head with start and scream,
    And wildly gazed around;
Then to the wall his face he turn'd,
And his dark neck with blushes burn'd.

XXIII.

" Whose is the boy?" again he said.
" By chance of war a captive made;
He may be yours, if you should hold
That music has more charms than gold;
For, though from earliest childhood mute,
The lad can deftly touch the lute,
And on the rote and viol play,
And well can drive the time away
    For those who love such glee;
For me, the favouring breeze, when loud
It pipes upon the galley's shroud,

---

[1] [MS.—" Entrance."]

Makes blither melody."—[1]
" Hath he, then, sense of spoken sound ?"—
" Aye ; so his mother bade us know,
A crone in our late shipwreck drown'd,
    And hence the silly stripling's woe.
More of the youth I cannot say,
Our captive but since yesterday ;
When wind and weather wax'd so grim,
We little listed think of him.—
But why waste time in idle words ?
Sit to your cheer—unbelt your swords."
Sudden the captive turn'd his head,
And one quick glance to Ronald sped.
It was a keen and warning look,
And well the chief the signal took.

XXIV.

" Kind host," he said, " our needs require
A separate board and separate fire ;
For know, that on a pilgrimage
Wend I, my comrade, and this page.
And, sworn to vigil and to fast,
Long as this hallow'd task shall last,

---

[1] [MS.—"But on the clairshoch he can play,
        And help a weary night away,
            With those who love such glee.
        To me, the favouring breeze, when loud
        It pipes through on my galley's shroud,
            Makes better melody."]

We never doff the plaid or sword,
Or feast us at a stranger's board;[1]
And never share one common sleep,
But one must still his vigil keep.
Thus, for our separate use, good friend,
We'll hold this hut's remoter end."—
"A churlish vow," the eldest said,
"And hard, methinks, to be obey'd.
How say you, if, to wreak the scorn
That pays our kindness harsh return,
We should refuse to share our meal?"
"Then say we, that our swords are steel!
And our vow binds us not to fast,
Where gold or force may buy repast."
Their host's dark brow grew keen and fell,
His teeth are clench'd, his features swell;
Yet sunk the felon's moody ire
Before Lord Ronald's glance of fire,
Nor could his craven courage brook
The Monarch's calm and dauntless look.
With laugh constrain'd,—" Let every man
Follow the fashion of his clan!
Each to his separate quarters keep,
And feed or fast, or wake or sleep."

---

1 [MS.—"And we have sworn to { sainted } powers,
                              { holy }
    While lasts this hallow'd task of ours,
    Never to doff the plaid or sword,
    Nor feast us at a stranger's board."]

XXV.

Their fire at separate distance burns,
By turns they eat, keep guard by turns ;
For evil seem'd that old man's eye,
Dark and designing, fierce yet shy.
Still he avoided forward look,
But slow and circumspectly took
A circling, never-ceasing glance,
By doubt and cunning mark'd at once,
Which shot a mischief-boding ray,[1]
From under eyebrows shagg'd and gray.
The younger, too, who seem'd his son,
Had that dark look the timid shun ;
The half-clad serfs behind them sate,
And scowl'd a glare 'twixt fear and hate—
Till all, as darkness onward crept,
Couch'd down, and seem'd to sleep, or slept.
Nor he, that boy, whose powerless tongue
Must trust his eyes to wail his wrong,
A longer watch of sorrow made,
But stretch'd his limbs to slumber laid.[2]

XXVI.

Not in his dangerous host confides
The King, but wary watch provides.

---

[1] [MS.————————" an ill foreboding ray."]
[2] [MS.—" But seems in senseless slumber laid."]

Ronald keeps ward till midnight past,
Then wakes the King, young Allan last;
Thus rank'd, to give the youthful page
The rest required by tender age.
What is Lord Ronald's wakeful thought,
To chase the languor toil had brought?—
(For deem not that he deign'd to throw
Much care upon such coward foe,)—
He thinks of lovely Isabel,
When at her foeman's feet she fell,
Nor less when, placed in princely selle,
She glanced on him with favouring eyes,
At Woodstocke when he won the prize.
Nor, fair in joy, in sorrow fair,
In pride of place as 'mid despair,
Must she alone engross his care.
His thoughts to his betrothed bride,[1]
To Edith, turn—O how decide,
When here his love and heart are given,
And there his faith stands plight to Heaven!
No drowsy ward 'tis his to keep,
For seldom lovers long for sleep.
Till sung his midnight hymn the owl,
Answer'd the dog-fox with his howl,
Then waked the King—at his request,
Lord Ronald stretch'd himself to rest.

[1] [MS.—" Must she alone his musings share.
  They turn to his betrothed bride."]

XXVII.

What spell was good King Robert's, say,
To drive the weary night away?
His was the patriot's burning thought,
Of Freedom's battle bravely fought,
Of castles storm'd, of cities freed,
Of deep design and daring deed,
Of England's roses reft and torn,
And Scotland's cross in triumph worn,
Of rout and rally, war and truce,—
As heroes think, so thought the Bruce.
No marvel, 'mid such musings high,
Sleep shunn'd the monarch's thoughtful eye.
Now over Coolin's eastern head
The greyish light[1] begins to spread,
The otter to his cavern drew,
And clamour'd shrill the wakening mew;
Then watch'd the page—to needful rest
The King resign'd his anxious breast.

XXVIII.

To Allan's eyes was harder task,
The weary watch their safeties ask.
He trimm'd the fire, and gave to shine
With bickering light the splinter'd pine;
Then gazed awhile, where silent laid
Their hosts were shrouded by the plaid.

[1] [MS.—" The cold blue light."]

But little fear waked in his mind,
For he was bred of martial kind,
And, if to manhood he arrive,
May match the boldest knight alive.
Then thought he of his mother's tower,
His little sisters' greenwood bower,
How there the Easter-gambols pass,
And of Dan Joseph's lengthen'd mass.
But still before his weary eye
In rays prolong'd the blazes die—
Again he roused him—on the lake
Look'd forth, where now the twilight-flake
Of pale cold dawn began to wake.
On Coolin's cliffs the mist lay furl'd,
The morning breeze the lake had curl'd,
The short dark waves, heaved to the land,
With ceaseless plash kiss'd cliff or sand ;
It was a slumbrous sound—he turn'd
. To tales at which his youth had burn'd,
Of pilgrim's path by demon cross'd,
Of sprightly elf or yelling ghost,
Of the wild witch's baneful cot,
And mermaid's alabaster grot,
Who bathes her limbs in sunless well
Deep in Strathaird's enchanted cell.[1]

---

[1] Imagination can hardly conceive anything more beautiful than the extraordinary grotto discovered not many years since upon the estate of Alexander Mac-Allister, Esq. of Strathaird. It has

Thither in fancy rapt he flies,
And on his sight the vaults arise ;

since been much and deservedly celebrated, and a full account of
its beauties has been published by Dr Mac-Leay of Oban. The
general impression may perhaps be gathered from the following
extract from a journal, which, written under the feelings of the
moment, is likely to be more accurate than any attempt to recollect the impressions then received.—"The first entrance to
this celebrated cave is rude and unpromising ; but the light of
the torches, with which we were provided, was soon reflected
from the roof, floor, and walls, which seem as if they were sheeted
with marble, partly smooth, partly rough with frost-work and
rustic ornaments, and partly seeming to be wrought into statuary. The floor forms a steep and difficult ascent, and might
be fancifully compared to a sheet of water, which, while it rushed
whitening and foaming down a declivity, had been suddenly arrested and consolidated by the spell of an enchanter. Upon at-
taining the summit of this ascent, the cave opens into a splendid
gallery, adorned with the most dazzling crystallizations, and
finally descends with rapidity to the brink of a pool, of the most
limpid water, about four or five yards broad. There opens beyond
this pool a portal arch, formed by two columns of white spar, with
beautiful chasing upon the sides, which promises a continuation
of the cave. One of our sailors swam across, for there is no other
mode of passing, and informed us (as indeed we partly saw by the
light he carried) that the enchantment of Maccalister's cave terminates with this portal, a little beyond which there was only a
rude cavern, speedily choked with stones and earth. But the pool,
on the brink of which we stood, surrounded by the most fanciful
mouldings, in a substance resembling white marble, and distinguished by the depth and purity of its waters, might have been the
bathing grotto of a naiad. The groups of combined figures projecting, or embossed, by which the pool is surrounded, are exquisitely elegant and fanciful. A statuary might catch beautiful hints
from the singular and romantic disposition of those stalactites.

That hut's dark walls he sees no more,
His foot is on the marble floor,
And o'er his head the dazzling spars
Gleam like a firmament of stars !
—Hark ! hears he not the sea-nymph speak
Her anger in that thrilling shriek !—
No ! all too late, with Allan's dream
Mingled the captive's warning scream.[1]
As from the ground he strives to start,
A ruffian's dagger finds his heart !
Upward he casts his dizzy eyes, . . .
Murmurs his master's name . . . and dies ![2]

There is scarce a form, or group, on which active fancy may not
trace figures or grotesque ornaments, which have been gradually
moulded in this cavern by the dropping of the calcareous water
hardening into petrifactions. Many of those fine groups have
been injured by the senseless rage of appropriation of recent tour-
ists; and the grotto has lost, (I am informed,) through the smoke
of torches, something of that vivid silver tint which was originally one of its chief distinctions. But enough of beauty remains
to compensate for all that may be lost."—Mr Mac-Allister of
Strathaird has, with great propriety, built up the exterior entrance to this cave, in order that strangers may enter properly
attended by a guide, to prevent any repetition of the wanton and
selfish injury which this singular scene has already sustained.

1 [MS.————————" with empty dream,
   Mingled the captive's real scream "]

2 [" Young Allan's turn (to watch) comes last, which gives the
poet the opportunity of marking, in the most natural and happy
manner, that insensible transition from the reality of waking

XXIX.

Not so awoke the King! his hand
Snatch'd from the flame a knotted brand,
The nearest weapon of his wrath ;
With this he cross'd the murderer's path,
 And venged young Allan well !
The spatter'd brain and bubbling blood
Hiss'd on the half-extinguish'd wood,
 The miscreant gasp'd and fell !![1]
Nor rose in peace the Island Lord ;
One caitiff died upon his sword,
And one beneath his grasp lies prone,
In mortal grapple overthrown.
But while Lord Ronald's dagger drank
The life-blood from his panting flank,
The Father-ruffian of the band
Behind him rears a coward hand!
 —O for a moment's aid,
'Till Bruce, who deals no double blow,[2]
Dash to the earth another foe,
 Above his comrade laid !—

thoughts, to the fanciful visions of slumber, and that delusive
power of the imagination which so blends the confines of these
separate states, as to deceive and sport with the efforts even of
determined vigilance."—*British Critic, February,* 1815.]

 [1] [MS.—" What time the miscreant fell."]

 [2] [" On witnessing the disinterment of Bruce's remains at Dun-

And it is gain'd—the captive sprung
On the raised arm, and closely clung,
  And, ere he shook him loose,
The master'd felon press'd the ground,
And gasp'd beneath a mortal wound,
  While o'er him stands the Bruce.

XXX.

" Miscreant! while lasts thy flitting spark,
Give me to know the purpose dark,
That arm'd thy hand with murderous knife,
Against offenceless stranger's life ?"—
" No stranger thou!" with accent fell,
Murmur'd the wretch; " I know thee well;
And know thee for the foeman sworn
Of my high chief, the mighty Lorn."—
" Speak yet again, and speak the truth
For thy soul's sake!—from whence this youth ?
His country, birth, and name declare,
And thus one evil deed repair."—
—"Vex me no more! ... my blood runs cold ...
No more I know than I have told.

fermline, in 1822," says Sir Walter, "many people shed tears;
for there was the wasted skull, which once was the head that
thought so wisely and boldly for his country's deliverance; and
there was the dry bone, which had once been the sturdy arm
that killed Sir Henry De Bohun, between the two armies,
at a single blow, on the evening before the battle of Bannockburn."—*Tales of a Grandfather. First Series*, vol. i. p. 255.]

We found him in a bark we sought
With different purpose ... and I thought ".....
Fate cut him short; in blood and broil,
As he had lived, died Cormac Doil.

XXXI.

Then resting on his bloody blade,
The valiant Bruce to Ronald said,
"Now shame upon us both!—that boy
    Lifts his mute face to heaven,[1]
And clasps his hands, to testify
His gratitude to God on high,
    For strange deliverance given.
His speechless gesture thanks hath paid,
Which our free tongues have left unsaid!"
He raised the youth with kindly word,
But mark'd him shudder at the sword:
He cleansed it from its hue of death,
And plunged the weapon in its sheath.
"Alas, poor child! unfitting part
Fate doom'd, when with so soft a heart,
    And form so slight as thine,
She made thee first a pirate's slave,
Then, in his stead, a patron gave
    Of wayward lot like mine;
A landless prince, whose wandering life
Is but one scene of blood and strife—

---

[1] [MS.—"Holds up his speechless face to heaven."]

Yet scant of friends the Bruce shall be,
But he'll find resting-place for thee.—
Come, noble Ronald! o'er the dead
Enough thy generous grief is paid,
And well has Allan's fate been wroke;
Come, wend we hence—the day has broke.
Seek we our bark—I trust the tale
Was false that she had hoisted sail."

XXXII.

Yet, ere they left that charnel-cell,
The Island Lord bade sad farewell
To Allan:—"Who shall tell this tale,"
He said, "in halls of Donagaile!
Oh, who his widow'd mother tell,
That, ere his bloom, her fairest fell!—
Rest thee, poor youth! and trust my care
For mass and knell and funeral prayer;
While o'er those caitiffs, where they lie,
The wolf shall snarl, the raven cry!"
And now the eastern mountain's head
On the dark lake threw lustre red;
Bright gleams of gold and purple streak
Ravine and precipice and peak—
(So earthly power at distance shows;
Reveals his splendour, hides his woes.)
O'er sheets of granite, dark and broad,[1]
Rent and unequal, lay the road.

[1] [MS.—"Along the lake's rude margin slow,
   O'er terraces of granite black they go."]

In sad discourse the warriors wind,
And the mute captive moves behind.[1]

1 [MS.—" And the mute page moves slow behind."—

" This canto is full of beauties ; the first part of it, containing
the conference of the chiefs in Bruce's chamber, might perhaps
have been abridged, because the discussion of a mere matter of
business is unsuited for poetry ; but the remainder of the canto
is unobjectionable ; the scenery in which it is laid excites the
imagination ; and the cave scene affords many opportunities
for the poet, of which Mr Scott has very successfully availed
himself.   The description of Allan's watch is particularly pleasing ; indeed, the manner in which he is made to fall asleep,
mingling the scenes of which he was thinking, with the scene
around him, and then mingling with his dreams the captive's
sudden scream, is, we think, among the most happy passages
of the whole poem."—*Quarterly Review.*

" We scarcely know whether we could have selected a passage from the poem that will more fairly illustrate its general
merits and pervading blemishes than the one which we have
just quoted (stanzas xxxi. and xxxii.)   The same happy mixture
of moral remark and vivid painting of dramatic situations, frequently occurs, and is as frequently debased by prosaic expressions and couplets, and by every variety of ungrammatical
license, or even barbarism.   Our readers, in short, will immediately here discover the powerful hand that has so often presented them with descriptions calculated at once to exalt and
animate their thoughts, and to lower and deaden the language
which is their vehicle ; but, as we have before observed again
and again, we believe, Mr Scott is inaccessible even to the mild-
est and the most just reproof on this subject.   We really believe
that he *cannot* write correct English ; and we therefore dismiss
him as an *incurable*, with unfeigned compassion for this one
fault, and with the highest admiration of his many redeeming
virtues."—*Monthly Review.*]

THE
LORD OF THE ISLES.

CANTO FOURTH.

TUE

LORD OF THE ISLES.

CANTO FOURTH.

~~~~~~~

STRANGER! if e'er thine ardent step hath traced
The northern realms of ancient Caledon,
Where the proud Queen of Wilderness hath placed,
By lake and cataract, her lonely throne;
Sublime but sad delight thy soul hath known,
Gazing on pathless glen, and mountain high,
Listing where from the cliffs the torrents thrown
Mingle their echoes with the eagle's cry,
And with the sounding lake, and with the moaning
      sky.

Yes! 'twas sublime, but sad.—The loneliness
Loaded thy heart, the desert tired thine eye;
And strange and awful fears began to press
Thy bosom with a stern solemnity.
Then hast thou wish'd some woodman's cottage nigh,

Something that show'd of life, though low and mean;
Glad sight, its curling wreath of smoke to spy,
Glad sound, its cock's blithe carol would have been,
Or children whooping wild beneath the willows green.

Such are the scenes, where savage grandeur wakes
An awful thrill that softens into sighs;
Such feelings rouse them by dim Rannoch's lakes,
In dark Glencoe such gloomy raptures rise:
Or farther, where, beneath the northern skies,
Chides wild Loch-Eribol his caverns hoar—
But, be the minstrel judge, they yield the prize
Of desert dignity to that dread shore,
That sees grim Coolin rise, and hears Coriskin roar.[1]

II.

Through such wild scenes the champion pass'd,
When bold halloo and bugle-blast
Upon the breeze came loud and fast,
" There," said the Bruce, " rung Edward's horn!
What can have caused such brief return?
And see, brave Ronald,—see him dart
O'er stock and stone like hunted hart,

[1] [" That Mr Scott can *occasionally* clothe the grandeur of his thought in the majesty of expression, unobscured with the jargon of antiquated ballads, and unencumbered by the awkwardness of rugged expression, or harsh involution, we can with pleasure acknowledge; a finer specimen cannot perhaps be exhibited than in this passage."—*British Critic.*]

Precipitate, as is the use,
In war or sport, of Edward Bruce.
—He marks us, and his eager cry
Will tell his news ere he be nigh."

III.

Loud Edward shouts, " What make ye here,
Warring upon the mountain-deer
    When Scotland wants her King ?
A bark from Lennox cross'd our track,
With her in speed I hurried back,
    These joyful news to bring—
The Stuart stirs in Teviotdale,
And Douglas wakes his native vale ;
Thy storm-toss'd fleet hath won its way
With little loss to Brodick-Bay,
And Lennox, with a gallant band,
Waits but thy coming and command
To waft them o'er to Carrick strand.
There are blithe news!—but mark the close!
Edward, the deadliest of our foes,
As with his host he northward pass'd,
Hath on the Borders breathed his last."

IV.

Still stood the Bruce—his steady cheek
Was little wont his joy to speak,
    But then his colour rose:

" Now, Scotland! shortly shalt thou see,
With God's high will, thy children free,
    And vengeance on thy foes!
Yet to no sense of selfish wrongs,
Bear witness with me, Heaven, belongs
    My joy o'er Edward's bier;[1]

[1] The generosity which does justice to the character of an enemy, often marks Bruce's sentiments, as recorded by the faithful
Barbour.   He seldom mentions a fallen enemy without praising
such good qualities as he might possess.   I shall only take one
instance.   Shortly after Bruce landed in Carrick, in 1306, Sir
Ingram Bell, the English governor of Ayr, engaged a wealthy
yeoman, who had hitherto been a follower of Bruce, to undertake
the task of assassinating him.   The King learned this treachery,
as he is said to have done other secrets of the enemy, by means of
a female with whom he had an intrigue.   Shortly after he was
possessed of this information, Bruce, resorting to a small thicket
at a distance from his men, with only a single page to attend
him, met the traitor, accompanied by two of his sons.   They approached him with their wonted familiarity, but Bruce, taking
his page's bow and arrow, commanded them to keep at a distance.
As they still pressed forward with professions of zeal for his person and service, he, after a second warning, shot the father with the
arrow; and being assaulted successively by the two sons, despatched first one, who was armed with an axe, then as the other
charged him with a spear, avoided the thrust, struck the head
from the spear, and cleft the skull of the assassin with a blow of
his two-handed sword.

> " He rushed down of blood all red.
> And when the king saw they were dead,
> All three lying, he wiped his brand.
> With that his boy came fast running,
> And said, ' Our lord might lowyt * be,
> That granted you might and poweste †
> To fell the felony and the pride,
> Of three in so little tide.'

* *Landed.*
† *Power.*

I took my nighthood at his hand,
And lordship held of him, and land,
   And well may vouch it here,
That, blot the story from his page,
Of Scotland ruin'd in his rage,
You read a monarch brave and sage,
   And to his people dear."—
" Let London's burghers morn her Lord,
And Croydon monks his praise record,"
   The eager Edward said ;
" Eternal as his own, my hate
Surmounts the bounds of mortal fate,
   And dies not with the dead !
Such hate was his on Solway's strand,
When vengeance clench'd his palsied hand,
That pointed yet to Scotland's land,[1]
   As his last accents pray'd
Disgrace and curse upon his heir,
If he one Scottish head should spare,
Till stretch'd upon the bloody lair
   Each rebel corpse was laid !
Such hate was his, when his last breath
Renounced the peaceful house of Death,
And bade his bones to Scotland's coast
Be borne by his remorseless host,

The king said, ' So our lord me see,
They have been worthy men all three,
Had they not been full of treason :
But that made their confusion."—BARBOUR's *Bruce*, b. v. p. 152.

   [1] [See Appendix, Note N.]

As if his dead and stony eye
Could still enjoy her misery !
Such hate was his—dark, deadly, long ;
Mine,—as enduring, deep, and strong ! "—

V.

" Let women, Edward, war with words,
With curses monks, and men with swords :
Nor doubt of living foes, to sate
Deepest revenge and deadliest hate.[1]
Now, to the sea ! behold the beach,
And see the galleys' pendants stretch
Their fluttering length down favouring gale !
Aboard, aboard ! and hoist the sail.

[1] [" The Bruce was, unquestionably, of a temper never sur-
passed for its humanity, munificence, and nobleness; yet, to represent him sorrowing over the death of the first Plantagenet,
after the repeated and tremendous ills inflicted by that man on
Scotland—the patriot Wallace murdered by his order, as well as
the royal race of Wales, and the very brothers of The Bruce,
slaughtered by his command—to represent the just and generous Robert, we repeat, feeling an instant's compassion for the
sudden fate of a miscreant like this, is, we are compelled to say
it, so monstrous, and in a *Scottish* poet, so unnatural a violation
of truth and decency, not to say patriotism, that we are really
astonished that the author could have conceived the idea, much
more that he could suffer his pen to record it. This wretched
abasement on the part of The Bruce, is farther heightened by
the King's half-reprehension of Prince Edward's noble and stern
expression of undying hatred against his country's spoiler, and
his family's assassin."—*Critical Review.*]

Hold we our way for Arran first,
Where meet in arms our friends dispersed ;
Lennox the loyal, De la Haye,
And Boyd the bold in battle fray.
I long the hardy band to head,
And see once more my standard spread.—
Does noble Ronald share our course,
Or stay to raise his island force ?"—
" Come weal, come woe, by Bruce's side,"
Replied the Chief, " will Ronald bide.
And since two galleys yonder ride,
Be mine, so please my liege, dismiss'd
To wake to arms the clans of Uist,
And all who hear the Minche's roar,
On the Long Island's lonely shore.
The nearer Isles, with slight delay,
Ourselves may summon in our way ;
And soon on Arran's shore shall meet,
With Torquil's aid, a gallant fleet,
If aught avails their Chieftain's hest
Among the islesmen of the west."

VI.

Thus was their venturous council said.
But, ere their sails the galleys spread,
Coriskin dark and Coolin high
Echoed the dirge's doleful cry.
Along that sable lake pass'd slow,—
Fit scene for such a sight of woe,—

The sorrowing islesmen, as they bore
The murder'd Allan to the shore.
At every pause, with dismal shout,
Their coronach of grief rung out,
And ever, when they moved again,
The pipes resumed their clamorous strain.
And, with the pibroch's shrilling wail,
Mourn'd the young heir of Donagaile.
Round and around, from cliff and cave,
His answer stern old Coolin gave,
Till high upon his misty side
Languish'd the mournful notes, and died.
For never sounds, by mortal made,
Attain'd his high and haggard head,
That echoes but the tempest's moan,
Or the deep thunder's rending groan.

VII.

Merrily, merrily bounds the bark,
    She bounds before the gale,
The mountain breeze from Ben-na-darch
    Is joyous in her sail !
With fluttering sound like laughter hoarse,
    The cords and canvass strain,
The waves, divided by her force,
In rippling eddies chased her course,
    As if they laugh'd again.
Not down the breeze more blithely flew,
Skimming the wave, the light sea-mew,

Then the gay galley bore
Her course upon that favouring wind,
And Coolin's crest has sunk behind,
    And Slapin's cavern'd shore.[2]
'Twas then that warlike signals wake
Dunscaith's dark towers and Eisord's lake,
And soon, from Cavilgarrigh's head,
Thick wreaths of eddying smoke were spre.
A summons these of war and wrath
To the brave clans of Sleat and Strath,
    And, ready at the sight,
Each warrior to his weapon sprung,
And targe upon his shoulder flung,
    Impatient for the fight.
Mac-Kinnon's chief, in warfare gray,
Had charge to muster their array,
And guide their barks to Brodick-Bay.

VIII.

Signal of Ronald's high command,
A beacon gleam'd o'er sea and land,
From Canna's tower, that, steep and gray,
Like falcon-nest o'erhangs the bay.[3]

---

[1] [MS.————" mountain-shore."]

[2] The little island of Canna, or Cannay, adjoins to those of
Rum and Muick, with which it forms one parish. In a pretty
bay opening towards the east, there is a lofty and slender rock
detached from the shore. Upon the summit are the ruins of a
very small tower, scarcely accessible by a steep and precipitous

Seek not the giddy crag to climb,
To view the turret scathed by time ;
It is a task of doubt and fear
To aught but goat or mountain-deer.
  But rest thee on the silver beach,
  And let the aged herdsman teach
    His tale of former day ;
  His cur's wild clamour he shall chide,
  And for thy seat by ocean's side,
    His varied play display ;
  Then tell, how with their Chieftain came,
  In ancient times, a foreign dame
    To yonder[1] turret gray.[2]
Stern was her Lord's suspicious mind,
Who in so rude a jail confined
    So soft and fair a thrall !
And oft when moon on ocean slept,
That lovely lady sate and wept
    Upon the castle wall,
And turn'd her eye to southern climes,
And thought perchance of happier times,

path. Here it is said one of the kings, or Lord of the Isles, confined a beautiful lady, of whom he was jealous. The ruins are
of course haunted by her restless spirit, and many romantic
stories are told by the aged people of the island concerning her
fate in life, and her appearances after death.

1 [MS.—" To Oanna's turret gray."]

2 [" The stanzas which follow are, we think, touchingly beautiful, and breathe a sweet and melancholy tenderness, perfectly
suitable to the sad tale which they record."—*Critical Review.*]

And touch'd her lute by fits, and sung
Wild ditties in her native tongue
And still, when on the cliff and bay
Placid and pale the moonbeams play,
 And every breeze is mute,
Upon the lone Hebridean's ear
Steals a strange pleasure mix'd with fear,
While from that cliff he seems to hear
 The murmur of a lute,
And sounds, as of a captive lone,
That mourns her woes in tongue unknown.—
Strange is the tale—but all too long
Already hath it staid the song—
 Yet who may pass them by,
That crag and tower in ruins grey,[1]
Nor to their hapless tenant pay
 The tribute of a sigh !

IX.

Merrily, merrily bounds the bark
 O'er the broad ocean driven,
Her path by Ronin's mountains dark
 The steersman's hand hath given.
And Ronin's mountains dark have sent
 Their hunters to the shore,[2]

---

[1] [MS.—" That crag with crest of ruins gray."]

[2] Ronin (popularly called Rum, a name which a poet may be pardoned for avoiding if possible) is a very rough and mountain-

And each his ashen bow unbent,
   And gave his pastime o'er,
And at the Island Lord's command, .
For hunting spear took warrior's brand.
On Scooreigg next a warning light
Summon'd her warriors to the fight;
A numerous race, ere stern Macleod
O'er their bleak shores in vengeance strode,[1]
When all in vain the ocean-cave
Its refuge to his victims gave.
The Chief, relentless in his wrath,
With blazing heath blockades the path;
In dense and stifling volumes roll'd,
The vapour fill'd the cavern'd hold!

---

ous island, adjacent to those of Eigg and Cannay. There is almost
no arable ground upon it, so that, except in the plenty of the deer,
which of course are now nearly extirpated, it still deserves the
description bestowed by the archdean of the Isles, " Ronin, sixteen myle north-wast from the ile of Coll, lyes ane ile callit
Ronin Ile, of sixteen myle long, and six in bredthe in the narrow-
est, ane forest of heigh mountains, and abundance of little deir
in it, quhilk deir will never be slane donnewith, but the principal saittis man be in the height of the hill, because the deir will
be callit upwart ay be the tainchell, or without tynchel they will
pass upwart perforce.   In this ile will be gotten about Britane
als many wild nests upon the plane mure as men pleasis to gad-
der, and yet by resson the fowls hes few to start them except
deir. This ile lyes from the west to the eist in lenth, and pertains
to M'Kenabrey of Colla.   Many solan geese are in this ile."—
Monro's *Description of the Western Isles*, p. 18.

  [1] [See Appendix, Note O.]

The warrior-threat, the infant's plain,
The mother's screams, were heard in vain ;
The vengeful Chief maintains his fires,
Till in the vault[1] a tribe expires !
The bones which strew that cavern's gloom,
Too well attest their dismal doom.

X.

Merrily, merrily goes the bark[2]
   On a breeze from the northward free,
So shoots through the morning sky the lark
   Or the swan through the summer sea.
The shores of Mull on the eastward lay,
And Ulva dark and Colonsay,
And all the group of islets gay
That guard famed Staffa round.

[1] [MS.—" Till in their smoke," &c.]

[2] [" And so also ' merrily, merrily goes the bard,' in a succession of *merriment*, which, like Dogberry's tediousness, he finds it in his heart to bestow wholly and entirely on us, through page after page, or wave after wave of his voyage. We could almost be tempted to believe that he was on his return from Skye when he wrote this portion of his poem ;—from Skye, the depository of the ' mighty cup of Royal Somerled,' as well as of ' Rorie More's' comparatively modern ' horn'—and that, as he says himself of a minstrel who celebrated the hospitalities of Dunvegan-castle in that island, ' it is pretty plain, that when *this* tribute of poetical praise was bestowed, the horn of Rorie More had not been inactive.' "—*Monthly Review*. See Appendix, Note E.]

[3] [" Of the prominent beauties which abound in the poem, the most magnificent we consider to be the description of the cele-

Then all unknown its columns rose,
Where dark and undisturb'd repose[1]
    The cormorant had found,
And the shy seal had quiet home,
And welter'd in that wondrous dome,
Where, as to shame the temples deck'd
By skill of earthly architect,
Nature herself, it seem'd, would raise
A Minster to her Maker's praise ![2]

brated cave of Fingal, which is conceived in a mighty mind, and
is expressed in a strain of poetry, clear, simple, and sublime."—
British Critic.]

[1] [MS.—" Where niched, his undisturb'd repose."]

[2] It would be unpardonable to detain the reader upon a wonder
so often described, and yet so incapable of being understood by
description. This palace of Neptune is even grander upon a second than the first view. The stupendous columns which form
the sides of the cave, the depth and strength of the tide which
rolls its deep and heavy swell up to the extremity of the vault—
the variety of tints formed by white, crimson, and yellow stalactites, or petrifactions, which occupy the vacancies between the
base of the broken pillars which form the roof, and intersect
them with a rich, curious, and variegated chasing, occupying
each interstice—the corresponding variety below water, where
the ocean rolls over a dark-red or violet-coloured rock, from
which, as from a base, the basaltic columns arise—the tremendous noise of the swelling tide, mingling with the deep-toned
echoes of the vault,—are circumstances elsewhere unparalleled.

Nothing can be more interesting than the varied appearance
of the little archipelago of islets, of which Staffa is the most remarkable. This group, called in Gaelic Tresharnish, affords a
thousand varied views to the voyager, as they appear in different positions with reference to his course. The variety of their
shape contributes much to the beauty of these effects.

Not for a meaner use ascend
Her columns, or her arches bend;
Nor of a theme less solemn tells
That mighty surge that ebbs and swells,
And still, between each awful pause,
From the high vault an answer draws,
In varied tone prolong'd and high,
That mocks the organ's melody.
Nor doth its entrance front in vain
To old Iona's holy fane,
That Nature's voice might seem to say,
" Well hast thou done, frail child of clay!
Thy humble powers that stately shrine
Task'd high and hard—but witness mine!"[1]

XI.

Merrily, merrily goes the bark,
    Before the gale she bounds;
So darts the dolphin from the shark,
    Or the deer before the hounds.
They left Loch-Tua on their lee,
And they waken'd the men of the wild Tiree,
    And the Chief of the sandy Coll;

[1] [The MS. adds,
    " Which, when the ruins of thy pile
    Cumber the desolated isle,
    Firm and immutable shall stand,
    'Gainst winds, and waves, and spoiler's hand."]

They paused not at Columba's isle,
Though peal'd the bells from the holy pile
    With long and measured toll;[1]   •
No time for matin or for mass,
And the sounds of the holy summons pass
    Away on the billows' roll.
Lochbuie's fierce and warlike Lord
Their signal saw, and grasped his sword,
And verdant Ilay call'd her host,
And the clans of Jura's rugged coast
    Lord Ronald's call obey,
And Scarba's isle, whose tortured shore
Still rings to Corrievreken's roar,
    And lonely Colonsay;
—Scenes sung by him who sings no more!
His bright and brief[2] career is o'er,

---

[1] ["We were now treading that illustrious island, which was once the luminary of the Caledonian regions, whence savage clans and roving barbarians derived the benefits of knowledge, and the blessings of religion. To abstract the mind from all local emotion would be impossible, if it were endeavoured, and would be foolish, if it were possible. Whatever withdraws us from the power of our senses; whatever makes the past, the distant, or the future predominate over the present, advances us in the dignity of thinking beings. Far from me and from my friends be such frigid philosophy, as may conduct us indifferent and unmoved over any ground which has been dignified by wisdom, bravery, or virtue. That man is little to be envied, whose patriotism would not gain force upon the plain of Marathon, or whose piety would not grow warmer among the ruins of Iona."—JOHNSON.]

[2] [MS.—"His short but bright," &c.]

And mute his tuneful strains ,
Quench'd is his lamp of varied lore,
That loved the light of song to pour ;
A distant and a deadly shore
    Has LEYDEN's cold remains ![1]

XII.

Ever the breeze blows merrily,
But the galley ploughs no more the sea.
Lest, rounding wild Cantire, they meet
The southern foeman's watchful fleet,
    They held unwonted way ;—
Up Tarbat's western lake they bore,
Then dragg'd their bark the isthmus o'er,[2]
As far as Kilmaconnel's shore,
    Upon the eastern bay.
It was a wondrous sight to see
Topmast and pennon glitter free,
High raised above the greenwood tree,
As on dry land the galley moves,
By cliff and copse and alder groves.

---

[1] The ballad, entitled "Macphail of Colonsay, and the Mermaid of Corrievrekin," [See Border Minstrelsy, vol. iv. p. 285,] was composed by John Leyden, from a tradition which he found while making a tour through the Hebrides about 1801, soon before his fatal departure for India, where, after having made farther progress in Oriental literature than any man of letters who had embraced those studies, he died a martyr to his zeal for knowledge, in the island of Java, immediately after the landing of our forces near Batavia, in August, 1811.

[2] [See Appendix, Note P.]

Deep import from that selcouth sign,
Did many a mountain Seer divine,
For ancient legends told the Gael,
That when a royal bark should sail
    O'er Kilmaconnel moss,
Old Albyn should in fight prevail,
And every foe should faint and quail
    Before her silver Cross.

XIII.

Now launch'd once more, the inland sea
They furrow with fair augury,
    And steer for Arran's isle;
The sun, ere yet he sunk behind
Ben-Ghoil, "the Mountain of the Wind,"
Gave his grim peaks a greeting kind,
    And bade Loch Ranza smile.[1]
Thither their destined course they drew;
It seem'd the isle her monarch knew,

---

[1] Loch Ranza is a beautiful bay, on the northern extremity of
Arran, opening towards East Tarbat Loch. It is well described
by Pennant:—"The approach was magnificent; a fine bay in
front, about a mile deep, having a ruined castle near the lower
end, on a low far projecting neck of land, that forms another
harbour, with a narrow passage; but within has three fathom of
water, even at the lowest ebb. Beyond is a little plain watered
by a stream, and inhabited by the people of a small village. The
whole is environed with a theatre of mountains; and in the
background the serrated crags of Grianan-Athol soar above.—
PENNANT'S *Tour to the Western Isles*, p. 191-2. Ben-Ghaoil,
"the mountain of the winds," is generally known by its English,
and less poetical name, of Goatfield.

So brilliant was the landward view,
    The ocean so serene ;
Each puny wave in diamonds roll'd
O'er the calm deep, where hues of gold
    With azure strove and green.
The hill, the vale, the tree, the tower,
Glow'd with the tints of evening's hour,
    The beach was silver sheen,
The wind breathed soft as lover's sigh,
And, oft renew'd, seem'd oft to die,
    With breathless pause between.
O who, with speech of war and woes,
Would wish to break the soft repose
    Of such enchanting scene !

XIV.

Is it of war Lord Ronald speaks ?
The blush that dyes his manly cheeks,
The timid look, and downcast eye,
And faltering voice the theme deny.
    And good King Robert's brow express'd,
    He ponder'd o'er some high request,
        As doubtful to approve ;
    Yet in his eye and lip the while,
    Dwelt the half-pitying glance and smile,
    Which manhood's graver mood beguile,
        When lovers talk of love.
Anxious his suit Lord Ronald pled ;
—" And for my bride betrothed," he said,

"My Liege has heard the rumour spread
Of Edith from Artornish fled.
Too hard her fate—I claim no right[1]
To blame her for her hasty flight;
Be joy and happiness her lot!—
But she hath fled the bridal-knot,
And Lorn recall'd his promised plight,
In the assembled chieftain's sight.—
    When, to fulfil our fathers' band,
    I proffer'd all I could—my hand—
      I was repulsed with scorn;
    Mine honour I should ill assert,
    And worse the feelings of my heart,
    If I should play a suitor's part
      Again, to pleasure Lorn."—

XV.

"Young Lord," the Royal Bruce[2] replied,
"That question must the Church decide;
Yet seems it hard, since rumours state
Edith takes Clifford for her mate,
The very tie, which she hath broke,
To thee should still be binding yoke.
But, for my sister Isabel—
The mood of woman who can tell?
I guess the champion of the Rock,
Victorious in the tourney shock,

      [1] [MS.———"no tongue is mine
           To blame her," &c.]
      [2] [MS.—"The princely Bruce."]

That knight unknown, to whom the prize
She dealt,—had favour in her eyes;
But since our brother Nigel's fate,
Our ruin'd house and hapless state,
From worldly joy and hope estranged,
Much is the hapless mourner changed.
Perchance," here smiled the noble King,
" This tale may other musings bring.
Soon shall we know—yon mountains hide
The little convent of St Bride;
There, sent by Edward, she must stay,
Till fate shall give more prosperous day;[1]
And thither will I bear thy suit,
Nor will thine advocate be mute."

XVI.

As thus they talk'd in earnest mood,
That speechless boy beside them stood.
He stoop'd his head against the mast,
And bitter sobs came thick and fast,
A grief that would not be repress'd,
But seem'd to burst his youthful breast.
His hands, against his forehead held,
As if by force his tears repell'd,
But through his fingers, long and slight,
Fast trill'd the drops of crystal bright.
Edward, who walk'd the deck apart,
First spied this conflict of the heart.

---

[1] [MS.—" Thither, by Edward sent, she stays
        Till fate shall lend more prosperous days."]

Thoughtless as brave, with bluntness kind
He sought to cheer the sorrower's mind;
By force the slender hand he drew
From those poor eyes that stream'd with dew.
As in his hold the stripling strove,—
('Twas a rough grasp, though meant in love,)
Away his tears the warrior swept,
And bade shame on him that he wept.[1]
" I would to Heaven, thy helpless tongue
Could tell me who hath wrought thee wrong!
For, were he of our crew the best,
The insult went not unredress'd.
Come, cheer thee; thou art now of age
To be a warrior's gallant page;
Thou shalt be mine!—a palfrey fair
O'er hill and holt my boy shall bear,
To hold my bow in hunting grove,
Or speed on errand to my love;
For well I wot thou wilt not tell
The temple where my wishes dwell."

XVII.

Bruce interposed,—" Gay Edward, no,
This is no youth to hold thy bow,
To fill thy goblet, or to bear
Thy message light to lighter fair.
Thou art a patron all too wild
And thoughtless, for this orphan child.

[1] [MS.—" And as away the tears he swept,
He bade shame on him that he wept."]

See'st thou not how apart he steals,
Keeps lonely couch, and lonely meals?
Fitter by far in yon calm cell
To tend our sister Isabel,
With father Augustin to share
The peaceful change of convent prayer,
Than wander wild adventures through,
With such a wreckless guide as you."—
"Thanks, brother!" Edward answer'd gay,
" For the high laud thy words convey!
But we may learn some future day,
If thou or I can this poor boy
Protect the best, or best employ.
Meanwhile, our vessel nears the strand;
Launch we the boat, and seek the land."

XVIII.

To land King Robert lightly sprung,
And thrice aloud his bugle rung
With note prolong'd and varied strain,
Till bold Ben-ghoil replied again.
Good Douglas then, and De la Haye,
Had in a glen a hart at bay,
And Lennox cheer'd the laggard hounds,
When waked that horn the greenwood bounds.
" It is the foe!" cried Boyd, who came
In breathless haste with eye on flame,—
" It is the foe!—Each valiant lord
Fling by his bow, and grasp his sword! "—

" Not so," replied the good Lord James,
" That blast no English bugle claims.
Oft have I heard it fire the fight,
Cheer the pursuit, or stop the flight.
Dead were my heart, and deaf mine ear,
If Bruce should call, nor Douglas hear!
Each to Loch Ranza's margin spring;
That blast was winded by the King!"[1]

[1] The passage in Barbour, describing the landing of Bruce.
and his being recognised by Douglas and those of his followers
who had preceded him, by the sound of his horn, is in the original
singularly simple and affecting.—The king arrived in Arran with
thirty-three small row-boats. He interrogated a female if there
had arrived any warlike men of late in that country. " Surely,
sir," she replied, " I can tell you of many who lately came hither,
discomfited the English governor, and blockaded his castle of
Brodick. They maintain themselves in a wood at no great distance." The king, truly conceiving that this must be Douglas
and his followers, who had lately set forth to try their fortune
in Arran, desired the woman to conduct him to the wood. She
obeyed.

> " The king then blew his horn on high;
> And gert his men that were him by,
> Hold them still, and all privy;
> And syne again his horne blew he.
> James of Dowglas heard him blow,
> And at the last alone gan know,
> And said, ' Soothly yon is the king;
> I know long while since his blowing.'
> The third time therewithall he blew,
> And then Sir Robert Boid it knew;
> And said, ' Yon is the king, but dread,
> Go we forth till him, better speed.'
> Then went they till the king in hye,
> And him inclined courteously.

XIX.

Fast to their mates the tidings spread,
And fast to shore the warriors sped.
Bursting from glen and greenwood tree,
High waked their loyal jubilee!
Around the royal Bruce they crowd,
And clasp'd his hands, and wept aloud.
Veterans of early fields were there,
Whose helmets press'd their hoary hair,
Whose swords and axes bore a stain
From life-blood of the red-hair'd Dane;[1]
And boys, whose hands scarce brook'd to wield
The heavy sword or bossy shield.
Men too were there, that bore the scars
Impress'd in Albyn's woful wars,
At Falkirk's fierce and fatal fight,
Teyndrum's dread rout and Methven's flight;
The might of Douglas there was seen,
There Lennox with his graceful mien;
Kirkpatrick, Closeburn's dreaded Knight;
The Lindsay, fiery, fierce, and light;

And blithly welcomed them the king,
And was joyful of their meeting,
And kissed them; and speared * syne   * *Asked.*
How they had fared in hunting?
And they him told all, but lesing;†   † *Without lying.*
Syne land they God of their meeting.
Syne with the king till his harbourye
Went both joyfu' and jolly."

          BARBOUR's *Bruce*, Book v. p. 115, 116.

1 [MS.—"Impress'd by life-blood of the Dane."]

The Heir of murder'd De la Haye,
And Boyd the grave, and Seton gay.
Around their King regain'd they press'd,
Wept, shouted, clasp'd him to their breast,
And young and old, and serf and lord,
And he who ne'er unsheathed a sword,
And he in many a peril tried,
Alike resolved the brunt to bide,
And live or die by Bruce's side!

XX.

Oh, War! thou hast thy fierce delight,
Thy gleams of joy, intensely bright!
Such gleams, as from thy polish'd shield
Fly dazzling o'er the battle-field!
Such transports wake, severe and high,
Amid the pealing conquest-cry;
Scarce less, when, after battle lost,
Muster the remnants of a host,
And as each comrade's name they tell,
Who in the well-fought conflict fell,
Knitting stern brow o'er flashing eye,
Vow to avenge them or to die!—
Warriors!—and where are warriors found,
If not on martial Britain's ground?[1]
And who, when waked with note of fire,
Love more than they the British lyre?

_____

[1] [MS.—" If not on Britain's warlike ground."]

Know ye not,—hearts to honour dear!
That joy, deep-thrilling, stern, severe,
At which the heartstrings vibrate high,
And wake the fountains of the eye?[1]
And blame ye, then, the Bruce, if trace
Of tear is on his manly face,
When, scanty relics of the train
That hail'd at Scone his early reign,
This patriot band around him hung,
And to his knees and bosom clung?—
Blame ye the Bruce?—his brother blamed,
But shared the weakness, while ashamed,
With haughty laugh his head he turn'd,
And dash'd away the tear he scorn'd.[2]

[1] [" Ours are the tears, though few, sincerely shed,
When Ocean shrouds and sepulchres our dead,
For us, even banquets fond regret supply
In the red cup that crowns our memory;
And the brief epitaph in danger's day,
When those who win at length divide the prey,
And cry, Remembrance saddening o'er each brow,
How had the brave who fell exulted now!"
BYRON'S *Corsair.*]

[2] The kind, and yet fiery character of Edward Bruce, is well painted by Barbour, in the account of his behaviour after the battle of Bannockburn. Sir Walter Ross, one of the very few Scottish nobles who fell in that battle, was so dearly beloved by Edward, that he wished the victory had been lost, so Ross had lived.

" Out-taken him, men has not seen
Where he for any men made moaning."

And here the venerable Archdeacon intimates a piece of scandal. Sir Edward Bruce, it seems, loved Ross's sister, *par amours*, to the neglect of his own lady, sister to David de Strathbogie, Earl

XXI.

'Tis morning, and the Convent bell
Long time had ceased its matin knell,
    Within thy walls, Saint Bride!
An aged Sister sought the cell
Assign'd to Lady Isabel,
    And hurriedly she cried,
" Haste, gentle Lady, haste—there waits
A noble stranger at the gates;
Saint Bride's poor vot'ress ne'er has seen
A Knight of such a princely mien;
His errand, as he bade me tell,
Is with the Lady Isabel."
The princess rose,—for on her knee
Low bent she told her rosary,—[1]

of Athole. This criminal passion had evil consequences; for, in resentment of the affront done to his sister, Athole attacked the guard which Bruce had left at Cambuskenneth, during the battle of Bannockburn, to protect his magazine of provisions, and slew Sir William Keith the commander. For which treason he was forfeited.

In like manner, when in a sally from Carrickfergus, Neil Fleming, and the guards whom he commanded, had fallen, after the protracted resistance which saved the rest of Edward Bruce's army, he made such moan as surprised his followers:

> "Sic moan he made men had ferly, *   * *Wonder.*
> For he was not customably
> Wont for to moan men any thing,
> Nor would not bear men make moaning."

Such are the nice traits of character so often lost in general history.

[1] [" Mr Scott, we have said, contradicts himself. How will he explain the following facts to his reader's satisfaction? The *third* canto informs us that Isabel accompanies Edward to Ireland,

" Let him by thee his purpose teach ;
I may not give a stranger speech."—
" Saint Bride forefend, thou royal Maid !"
The portress cross'd herself, and said,—
" Not to be prioress might I
Debate his will, his suit deny."—
" Has earthly show then, simple fool,
Power o'er a sister of thy rule,
And art thou, like the worldly train,
Subdued by splendours light and vain ? "—

XXII.

" No, Lady ! in old eyes like mine,
Gauds have no glitter, gems no shine ;
Nor grace his rank attendants vain,
One youthful page is all his train.
It is the form, the eye, the word,
The bearing of that stranger Lord ;
His stature, manly, bold, and tall,
Built like a castle's battled wall,
Yet moulded in such just degrees,
His giant strength seems lightsome ease.
Close as the tendrils of the vine
His locks upon his forehead twine,

there to remain till the termination of the war; and in the *fourth*
canto, the second day after her departure, we discover the princess counting her beads and reading homilies in the Cloister of
St Bride, in the Island of Arran !   We humbly beseech the
' Mighty Minstrel ' to clear up this matter."—*Critical Review.*]

Jet-black, save where some touch of gray
Has ta'en the youthful hue away.
Weather and war their rougher trace
Have left on that majestic face;—
But 'tis his dignity of eye!
There, if a suppliant, would I fly,
Secure, 'mid danger, wrongs, and grief,
Of sympathy, redress, relief—
That glance, if guilty, would I dread
More than the doom that spoke me dead!"—
"Enough, enough," the princess cried,
"'Tis Scotland's hope, her joy, her pride!
To meaner front was ne'er assign'd
Such mastery o'er the common mind—
Bestow'd thy high designs to aid,
How long, O Heaven! how long delay'd!—
Haste, Mona, haste, to introduce
My darling brother, Royal Bruce!"

XXIII.

They met like friends who part in pain,
And meet in doubtful hope again.
But when subdued[1] that fitful swell,
The Bruce survey'd the humble cell;—
"And this is thine, poor Isabel!—
That pallet-couch, and naked wall,
For room of state, and bed of pall;

---

[1] [MS.—"But when subsides," &c.]

For costly robes and jewels rare,
A string of beads and zone of hair ;
And for the trumpet's sprightly call
To sport or banquet, grove or hall,
The bell's grim voice divides thy care,
'Twixt hours of penitence and prayer !—
O ill for thee, my royal claim
From the First David's sainted name !
O woe for thee, that while he sought
His right, thy brother feebly fought !"—

XXIV.

" Now lay these vain regrets aside,
And be the unshaken Bruce !" she cried.
" For more I glory to have shared
The woes thy venturous spirit dared,
When raising first thy valiant band
In rescue of thy native land,
Than had fair Fortune set me down   .
The partner of an empire's crown.
And grieve not that on Pleasure's stream
No more I drive in giddy dream,
For Heaven the erring pilot knew,
And from the gulf the vessel drew,
Tried me with judgments stern and great,
My house's ruin, thy defeat,
Poor Nigel's death, till, tamed, I own,
My hopes are fixed on Heaven alone ;

Nor e'er shall earthly prospects win
My heart to this vain world of sin."—

XXV.

" Nay, Isabel, for such stern choice,
First wilt thou wait thy brother's voice;
Then ponder if in convent scene
No softer thoughts might intervene—
Say they were of that unknown Knight,
Victor in Woodstock's tourney-fight—
Nay, if his name such blush you owe,
Victorious o'er a fairer foe !"
Truly his penetrating eye
Hath caught that blush's passing dye,—
Like the last beam of evening thrown
On a white cloud,—just seen and gone.[1]

[1] [We would bow with veneration to the powerful and rugged
genius of Scott. We would style him above all others, Homer
and Shakspeare excepted, the Poet of Nature—of Nature in all
her varied beauties, in all her wildest haunts. No appearance,
however minute, in the scenes around him, escapes his penetrating eye; they are all marked with the nicest discrimination;
are introduced with the happiest effect. Hence, in his similes,
both the genius and the judgment of the poet are peculiarly conspicuous; his accurate observation of the appearances of nature,
which others have neglected, imparts an originality to those al-
lusions, of which the reader immediately recognises the aptness
and propriety; and only wonders that what must have been so
often witnessed, should have been so uniformly passed unregard-
ed by. Such is the simile applied to the transient blush observed
by Bruce on the countenance of Isabel upon his mention of
Ronald."—*British Critic.*]

Soon with calm cheek and steady eye,
The princess made composed reply :—
" I guess my brother's meaning well ;
For not so silent is the cell,
But we have heard the islesmen all
Arm in thy cause at Ronald's call,
And mine eye proves that Knight unknown[1]
And the brave Island Lord are one.—
Had then his suit been earlier made,
In his own name, with thee to aid,
(But that his plighted faith forbade,)[2]
I know not . . . . . . But thy page so near?—
This is no tale for menial's ear."

XXVI.

Still stood that page, as far apart
    As the small cell would space afford ;
With dizzy eye and bursting heart,
    He leant his weight on Bruce's sword,
The monarch's mantle too he bore,[3]
And drew the fold his visage o'er.
" Fear not for him—in murderous strife,"
Said Bruce, " his warning saved my life ;[4]
Full seldom parts he from my side,
And in this silence I confide,

---

[1] [MS.—"And well I judge that knight unknown."]

[2] [MS.—"But that his $\left\{ \begin{array}{c} \text{earlier} \\ \text{former} \end{array} \right\}$ plight forbade."]

[3] [MS.—" The monarch's brand and cloak he bore."

[4] [MS.—"Answered the Bruce, ' he saved my life.' "]

Since he can tell no tale again.
He is a boy of gentle strain,
And I have purposed he shall dwell
In Augustine the chaplain's cell,
And wait on thee my Isabel.—
Mind not his tears ; I've seen them flow,
As in the thaw dissolves the snow.
'Tis a kind youth, but fanciful,
Unfit against the tide to pull,
And those that with the Bruce would sail,
Must learn to strive with stream and gale.—
But forward, gentle Isabel—
My answer for Lord Ronald tell."—

XXVII.

" This answer be to Ronald given—
The heart he asks is fix'd on heaven.[1]
My love was like a summer flower
That wither'd in the wintry hour,
Born but of vanity and pride,
And with these sunny visions died.
If further press his suit—then say,
He should his plighted troth obey,
Troth plighted both with ring and word,
And sworn on crucifix and sword.—

---

[1] [The MS. has—
        " Isabel's thoughts are fix'd on heav'n ;"
and the two couplets which follow are interpolated on the blank
page.]

Oh, shame thee, Robert! I have seen
Thou hast a woman's guardian been!
Even in extremity's dread hour,
When press'd on thee the Southern power,
And safety, to all human sight,
Was only found in rapid flight,
Thou heard'st a wretched female plain
In agony of travail-pain,
And thou didst bid thy little band
Upon the instant turn and stand,
And dare the worst the foe might do,
Rather than, like a knight untrue,
Leave to pursuers merciless
A woman in her last distress.—[1]

[1] [This incident, which illustrates so happily the chivalrous
generosity of Bruce's character, is one of the many simple and
natural traits recorded by Barbour. It occurred during the expedition which Bruce made to Ireland, to support the pretensions
of his brother Edward to the throne of that kingdom. Bruce
was about to retreat, and his host was arrayed for moving.

" The king has heard a woman cry,	
He asked what that was in hy.[1]	[1] *Haste.*
' It is the layndar,[2] sir,' sai ane,	[2] *Laundress.*
' That her child-ill[3] right now has ta en :	[3] *Child-bed.*
And must leave now behind us here,	
Therefore she makes an evil cheer.'[4]	[4] *Stop.*
The king said, ' Certes,[5] it were pity	[5] *Certainly.*
That she in that point left should be,	
For certes I trow there is no man	
That he no will rue[6] a woman than.'	[6] *Pity.*
His hosts all there arrested be,	
And gert[7] a tent soon stintit[8] be,	[7] *Caused.* [8] *Pitched.*

And wilt thou now deny thine aid
To an oppress'd and injured maid,
Even plead for Ronald's perfidy,
And press his fickle faith on me?—
So witness Heaven, as true I vow,
Had I those earthly feelings now,
Which could my former bosom move
Ere taught to set its hopes above,
I'd spurn each proffer he could bring,
Till at my feet he laid the ring,
The ring and spousal contract both,
And fair acquittal of his oath,
By her who brooks his perjured scorn,
The ill-requited Maid of Lorn!"

XXVIII.

With sudden impulse forward sprung
The page, and on her neck he hung;
Then, recollected instantly,
His head he stoop'd, and bent his knee,

And gert her gang in hastily.
And other women to be her by
While she was delivered he bade;
And syne forth on his ways rade.
And how she forth should carried be,
Or he forth fure,* ordained he.   * *Moved.*
This was a full great courtesy,
That swilk a king and so mighty,
Gert his men dwell on this manner,
But for a poor lavender."

BARBOUR's *Bruce*, Book xvi. pp. 39, 40.

Kiss'd twice the hand of Isabel,
Arose, and sudden left the cell.—
The princess, loosen'd from his hold,
Blush'd angry at his bearing bold ;
  But good King Robert cried,
" Chafe not—by signs he speaks his mind,
He heard the plan my care design'd,
  Nor could his transports hide.—
But, sister, now bethink thee well ;
No easy choice the convent cell ;
Trust, I shall play no tyrant part,
Either to force thy hand or heart,
Or suffer that Lord Ronald scorn,
Or wrong for thee, the Maid of Lorn.
But think,—not long the time has been,
That thou wert wont to sigh unseen,
And wouldst the ditties best approve,
That told some lay of hapless love.
Now are thy wishes in thy power,
And thou art bent on cloister bower !
O ! if our Edward knew the change,
How would his busy satire range,
With many a sarcasm varied still
On woman's wish and woman's will !"—

XXIX.

" Brother, I well believe," she said,
" Even so would Edward's part be play'd.

Kindly in heart, in word severe,
A foe to thought, and grief, and fear,
He holds his humour uncontroll'd ;
But thou art of another mould.
Say then to Ronald, as I say,
Unless before my feet he lay
The ring which bound the faith he swore,
By Edith freely yielded o'er,
He moves his suit to me no more.
Nor do I promise, even if now
He stood absolved of spousal vow,
That I would change my purpose made,
To shelter me in holy shade.—
Brother, for little space, farewell !
To other duties warns the bell."—

XXX.

" Lost to the world," King Robert said,
When he had left the royal maid,
" Lost to the world by lot severe,
O what a gem lies buried here,
Nipp'd by misfortune's cruel frost,
The buds of fair affection lost !—[1]
But what have I with love to do ?
Far sterner cares my lot pursue.

[1] [The MS. here adds :—
" She yields one shade of empty hope ;
But well I guess her wily scope
Is to elude Lord Ronald's plea,
And still my importunity."]

—Pent in this isle we may not lie,
Nor would it long our wants supply.
Right opposite, the mainland towers
Of my own Turnberry court our powers—
—Might not my father's beadsman hoar,
Cuthbert, who dwells upon the shore,
Kindle a signal-flame, to show
The time propitious for the blow ?
It shall be so—some friend shall bear
Our mandate with despatch and care ;
—Edward shall find the messenger.
That fortress ours, the island fleet
May on the coast of Carrick meet.—
O Scotland ! shall it e'er be mine
To wreak thy wrongs in battle-line,
To raise my victor-head, and see
Thy hills, thy dales, thy people free,—
That glance of bliss is all I crave,
Betwixt my labours and my grave !"
Then down the hill he slowly went,
Oft pausing on the steep descent,
And reach'd the spot where his bold train
Held rustic camp upon the plain.[2]

---

¹ [This and the twelve succeeding lines are interpolated on
the blank page of the MS.]

² [" The fourth canto cannot be very greatly praised. It contains, indeed, many pleasing passages ; but the merit which they
possess is too much detached from the general interest of the
poem. The only business is Bruce's arrival at the isle of Arran.

The voyage is certainly described with spirit ; but the remainder of the canto is rather tedious, and might, without any considerable inconvenience, have been left a good deal to the reader's imagination.   Mr Scott ought to reserve, as much as possible, the interlocutory parts of his narrative, for occasions which admit of high and animated sentiment, or the display of powerful emotions, because this is almost the only poetical beauty of which speeches are susceptible.   But to fill up three-fourths of a canto with a lover's asking a brother in a quiet and friendly manner for permission to address his sister in marriage, and a brother's asking his sister whether she has any objections, is, we think, somewhat injudicious."— *Quarterly Review.*]

THE

LORD OF THE ISLES.

CANTO FIFTH.

LORD OF THE ISLES. '

CANTO FIFTH.

~~~~~~~~

On fair Loch-Ranza stream'd the early day,
Thin wreaths of cottage-smoke are upward curl'd
From the lone hamlet, which her inland bay
And circling mountains sever from the world.
And there the fisherman his sail unfurl'd,
The goat-herd drove his kids to steep Ben-Ghoil,
Before the hut the dame her spindle twirl'd,
Courting the sunbeam as she plied her toil,—
For, wake where'er he may, Man wakes to care and
  coil.

But other duties call'd each convent maid,
Roused by the summons of the moss-grown bell;
Sung were the matins, and the mass was said,
And every sister sought her separate cell,
Such was the rule, her rosary to tell.

And Isabel has knelt in lonely prayer;
The sunbeam, through the narrow lattice, fell
Upon the snowy neck and long dark hair,
As stoop'd her gentle head in meek devotion there.

II.

She raised her eyes, that duty done,
When glanced upon the pavement-stone,
Gemm'd and enchased, a golden ring,
Bound to a scroll with silken string,[1]
With few brief words inscribed to tell,
" This for the Lady Isabel."
Within, the writing farther bore,—
" 'Twas with this ring his plight he swore,
With this his promise I restore ;
To her who can the heart command,
Well may I yield the plighted hand.
And O! for better fortune born,
Grudge not a passing sigh to mourn
Her who was Edith once of Lorn!"
One single flash of glad surprise
Just glanced from Isabel's dark eyes,
But vanish'd in the blush of shame,
That, as its penance, instant came.
" O thought unworthy of my race !
Selfish, ungenerous, mean, and base,

---

1 [MS.————" a ring of gold,
       A scroll around the jewel roll'd.
       Had few brief words," &c.]

A moment's throb of joy to own,[1]
That rose upon her hopes o'erthrown!—
Thou pledge of vows too well believed,
Of man ingrate and maid deceived,
Think not thy lustre here shall gain
Another heart to hope in vain!
For thou shalt rest, thou tempting gaud,
Where worldly thoughts are overawed,
And worldly splendours sink debased."
Then by the cross the ring she placed.

III.

Next rose the thought,—its owner far,
How came it here through bolt and bar?—
But the dim lattice is ajar.—
She looks abroad—the morning dew
A light short step had brush'd anew,
    And there were foot-prints seen
On the carved buttress rising still,
Till on the mossy window-sill
    Their track effaced the green.
The ivy twigs were torn and fray'd,
As if some climber's steps to aid.—
But who the hardy messenger,
Whose venturous path these signs infer?—
" Strange doubts are mine!—Mona, draw nigh;
—Nought 'scapes old Mona's curious eye—

---

[1] [MS.—" A single throb of joy to own."]

What strangers, gentle mother, say,
Have sought these holy walls to-day ?"—
" None, Lady, none of note or name;
Only your brother's foot-page came,
At peep of dawn—I pray'd him pass
To chapel where they said the mass;
But like an arrow he shot by,
And tears seem'd bursting from his eye."

IV.

The truth at once on Isabel.
As darted by a sunbeam fell.—
" 'Tis Edith's self!¹—her speechless woe,
Her form, her looks, the secret show!
—Instant, good Mona, to the bay,
And to my royal brother say,
I do conjure him seek my cell,
With that mute page he loves so well."—
" What! know'st thou not his warlike host
At break of day has left our coast?²
My old eyes saw them from the tower.
At eve they couch'd in greenwood bower,
At dawn a bugle-signal, made
By their bold Lord, their ranks array'd;
Up sprung the spears through bush and tree,
No time for benedicite!

---

¹ [MS.—'Tis she herself."]
² [MS.—" What! know'st thou not in sudden haste
    The warriors from our woods have pass'd."]

Like deer, that, rousing from their lair,
Just shake the dewdrops from their hair,
And toss their armed crests aloft,
Such matins theirs!"—"Good mother, soft—
Where does my brother bend his way?"—[1]
"As I have heard, for Brodick-Bay,
Across the isle—of barks a score
Lie there, 'tis said, to waft them o'er,
On sudden news, to Carrick-shore."—
"If such their purpose, deep the need,"
Said anxious Isabel, "of speed!
Call Father Augustine, good dame."
The nun obey'd, the Father came.

V.

"Kind Father, hie without delay,
Across the hills to Brodick-Bay.
This message to the Bruce be given;
I pray him, by his hopes of Heaven,
That, till he speak with me, he stay!
Or, if his haste brook no delay,
That he deliver, on my suit,
Into thy charge that stripling mute.
Thus prays his sister Isabel,
For causes more than she may tell—
Away, good Father!—and take heed,
That life and death are on thy speed."

---

[1] [MS.—" Canst tell where they have bent their way?"]

His cowl the good old priest did on,
Took his piked staff and sandall'd shoon,
And like a palmer bent by eld,
O'er moss and moor his journey held.[1]

VI.

Heavy and dull the foot of age,
And rugged was the pilgrimage;
But none was there beside, whose care
Might such important message bear.
Through birchen copse he wander'd slow,
Stunted and sapless, thin and low;
By many a mountain stream he pass'd,
From the tall cliffs in tumult cast,
Dashing to foam their waters dun,
And sparkling in the summer sun.
Round his grey head the wild curlew
In many a fearless circle flew.
O'er chasms he pass'd, where fractures wide
Craved wary eye and ample stride;[2]

---

[1] [MS.—" And cross the island took his way,
       O'er hill and holt, to Brodick-Bay."]

[2] The interior of the island of Arran abounds with beautiful
highland scenery. The hills, being very rocky and precipitous,
afford some cataracts of great height, though of inconsiderable
breadth. There is one pass over the river Machrai, renowned for
the dilemma of a poor woman, who, being tempted by the narrowness of the ravine to step across, succeeded in making the first
movement, but took fright when it became necessary to move the
other foot, and remained in a posture equally ludicrous and dan-

He cross'd his brow beside the stone,
Where Druids erst heard victims groan,[1]
And at the cairns upon the wild,
O'er many a heathen hero piled,[2]
He breathed a timid prayer for those
Who died ere Shiloh's sun arose.
Beside Macfarlane's Cross he staid,
There told his hours within the shade,
And at the stream his thirst allay'd.
Thence onward journeying slowly still,
As evening closed he reach'd the hill,
Where, rising through the woodland green,
Old Brodick's gothic towers were seen,
From Hastings, late their English lord,
Douglas had won them by the sword.[3]

gerous, until some chance passenger assisted her to extricate
herself. It is said she remained there some hours.

> 1 [MS.—" He cross'd him by the Druid's stone,
> That heard of yore the victim's groan."]

[1] The isle of Arran, like those of Man and Anglesea, abounds
with many relics of heathen, and probably Druidical, superstition.
There are high erect columns of unhewn stone, the most early of
all monuments, the circles of rude stones, commonly entitled
Druidical, and the cairns or sepulchral piles, within which are
usually found urns enclosing ashes. Much doubt necessarily
rests upon the history of such monuments, nor is it possible to
consider them as exclusively Celtic, or Druidical. By much the
finest circles of standing stones, excepting Stonehege, are those
of Stenhouse, at Stennis, in the island of Pomona, the principal
isle of the Orcades. These, of course, are neither Celtic nor
Druidical ; and we are assured that many circles of the kind occur both in Sweden and Norway.

[3] Brodick or Brathwick Castle, in the Isle of Arran, is an an-

The sun that sunk behind the isle,
Now tinged them with a parting smile.

VII.

But though the beams of light decay,
'Twas bustle all in Brodick-Bay.
The Bruce's followers crowd the shore,
And boats and barges some unmoor,
Some raise the sail, some seize the oar ;
Their eyes oft turn'd where glimmer'd far
What might have seem'd an early star.

cient fortress, near an open roadstead called Brodick-Bay, and
not far distant from a tolerable harbour, closed in by the island
of Lamlash. This important place had been assailed a short
time before Bruce's arrival in the island. James Lord Douglas,
who accompanied Bruce to his retreat in Rachrine, seems, in the
spring of 1306, to have tired of his abode there, and set out accordingly, in the phrase of the times, to see what adventure God
would send him. Sir Robert Boyd accompanied him; and his
knowledge of the localities of Arran appears to have directed
his course thither. They landed in the island privately, and appear to have laid an ambush for Sir John Hastings, the English
governor of Brodwick, and surprised a considerable supply of
arms and provisions, and nearly took the castle itself. Indeed,
that they actually did so, has been generally averred by historians, although it does not appear from the narrative of Barbour. On the contrary, it would seem that they took shelter
within a fortification of the ancient inhabitants, a rampart called
Tor an Schian. When they were joined by Bruce, it seems probable that they had gained Brodick Castle. At least tradition
says, that from the battlements of the tower he saw the supposed signal-fire on Turnberry-nook....The castle is now much
modernized, but has a dignified appearance, being surrounded
by flourishing plantations.

On heaven's blue arch, save that its light
Was all too flickering, fierce, and bright.
   Far distant in the south, the ray
   Shone pale amid retiring day,
      But as, on Carrick shore,
   Dim seen in outline faintly blue,
   The shades of evening closer drew,[1]
      It kindled more and more.
The monk's slow steps now press the sands,
And now amid a scene he stands,
   Full strange to churchman's eye;
Warriors, who, arming for the fight,
Rivet and clasp their harness light,
And twinkling spears, and axes bright,
   And helmets flashing high.
   Oft, too, with unaccustom'd ears,
   A language much unmeet he hears,[2]

---

[1] [MS.—" The shades of even more closely drew,
It brighten'd more and more.
Now print his sandall'd feet the sands,
And now amid," &c.]

[2] Barbour, with great simplicity, gives an anecdote, from which
it would seem that the vice of profane swearing, afterwards too
general among the Scottish nation, was, at this time, confined
to military men. As Douglas, after Bruce's return to Scotland,
was roving about the mountainous country of Tweeddale, near
the water of Line, he chanced to hear some persons in a farm-
house say *" the devil."* Concluding from this hardy expression,
that the house contained warlike guests, he immediately assailed
it, and had the good fortune to make prisoners Thomas Randolph, afterwards the famous Earl of Murray, and Alexander

While, hastening all on board,
As stormy as the swelling surge
That mix'd its roar, the leaders urge
Their followers to the ocean verge,
          With many a haughty word.

VIII.

Through that wild throng the Father pass'd,
And reach'd the Royal Bruce at last.
He leant against a stranded boat,
That the approaching tide must float,
And counted every rippling wave,
As higher yet her sides they lave,
And oft the distant fire he eyed,
And closer yet his hauberk tied,
And loosen'd in its sheath his brand.
Edward and Lennox were at hand,
Douglas and Ronald had the care
The soldiers to the barks to share.—
The monk approach'd and homage paid;
" And art thou come," King Robert said,
" So far to bless us ere we part?"—
—" My Liege, and with a loyal heart!— ·
But other charge I have to tell,"—
And spoke the hest of Isabel.

Stuart, Lord Bonkle. Both were then in the English interest,
and had come into that country with the purpose of driving out
Douglas. They afterwards ranked among Bruce's most zealous
adherents.

—"Now by Saint Giles," the monarch cried,
"This moves me much!—this morning tide,
I sent the stripling to Saint Bride,
With my commandment there to bide."—
—"Thither he came the portress show'd,
But there, my Liege, made brief abode."—

IX.

"'Twas I," said Edward, "found employ
Of nobler import for the boy.
Deep pondering in my anxious mind,
A fitting messenger to find,
To bear thy written mandate o'er.
To Cuthbert on the Carrick shore,
I chanced, at early dawn, to pass
The chapel gate to snatch a mass.
I found the stripling on a tomb
Low-seated, weeping for the doom
That gave his youth to convent gloom.
I told my purpose, and his eyes
Flash'd joyful at the glad surprise.
He bounded to the skiff, the sail
Was spread before a prosperous gale,
And well my charge he hath obey'd;
For, see! the ruddy signal made,
That Clifford, with his merry-men all,
Guards carelessly our father's hall."—[1]

[1] [The MS. reads:
      " Keeps careless guard in Turnberry hall."
See Appendix, Note Q.]

X.

"O wild of thought, and hard of heart!"
Answer'd the Monarch, "on a part
Of such deep danger to employ
A mute, an orphan, and a boy[1]
Unfit for flight, unfit for strife,
Without a tongue to plead for life!
Now, were my right restored by Heaven,
Edward, my crown I would have given,
Ere, thrust on such adventure wild,
I peril'd thus the helpless child."—
—Offended half, and half submiss,
"Brother and Liege, of blame like this,"
Edward replied, "I little dream'd.
A stranger messenger, I deem'd,
Might safest seek the beadsman's cell,
Where all thy squires are known so well.
Noteless his presence, sharp his sense,
His imperfection his defence.
If seen, none can his errand guess;
If ta'en, his words no tale express—
Methinks, too, yonder beacon's shine
Might expiate greater fault than mine."—
"Rash," said King Robert, "was the deed—
But it is done—Embark with speed!—
Good Father, say to Isabel
How this unhappy chance befell;

---

[1] [MS.—" Said Robert, ' to assign a part
   Of such deep peril, to employ
   A mute, a stranger, and a boy?'"]

If well we thrive on yonder shore,
Soon shall my care her page restore.
Our greeting to our sister bear,
And think of us in mass and prayer."—

XI.

" Aye !"—said the Priest, " while this poor hand
Can chalice raise or cross command,
While my old voice has accents' use,
Can Augustine forget the Bruce !"
Then to his side Lord Ronald press'd,
And whisper'd, " Bear thou this request,
That when by Bruce's side I fight,
For Scotland's crown and freedom's right,
The princess grace her knight to bear
Some token of her favouring care ;
It shall be shown where England's best
May shrink to see it on my crest.
And for the boy—since weightier care
For royal Bruce the times prepare,
The helpless youth is Ronald's charge,
His couch my plaid, his fence my targe."
He ceased; for many an eager hand
Had urged the barges from the strand.
Their number was a score and ten,
They bore thrice threescore chosen men.
With such small force did Bruce at last
The die for death or empire cast !

XII.

Now on the darkening main afloat,
Ready and mann'd rocks every boat;
Beneath their oars the ocean's might
Was dash'd to sparks of glimmering light.
Faint and more faint, as off they bore,
Their armour glanced against the shore,
And, mingled with the dashing tide,
Their murmuring voices distant died.—
"God speed them!" said the Priest, as dark
On distant billows glides each bark;
"O Heaven! when swords for freedom shine,
And monarch's right, the cause is thine!
Edge doubly every patriot blow!
Beat down the banners of the foe!
And be it to the nations known,
That Victory is from God alone!"[1]
As up the hill his path he drew,
He turn'd his blessings to renew,
Oft turn'd, till on the darken'd coast
All traces of their course were lost;
Then slowly bent to Brodick tower,
To shelter for the evening hour.

XIII.

In night the fairy prospects sink,
Where Cumray's isles with verdant link

[1] [MS.——"is thine alone!"]

Close the fair entrance of the Clyde;
The woods of Bute, no more descried,
Are gone[1]—and on the placid sea
The rowers ply their task with glee,
While hands that knightly lances bore
Impatient aid the labouring oar.
The half-faced moon shone dim and pale,
And glanced against the whiten'd sail;
But on that ruddy beacon-light
Each steersman kept the helm aright,
And oft, for such the King's command,
That all at once might reach the strand,
From boat to boat loud shout and hail
Warn'd them to crowd or slacken sail.
South and by west the armada bore,
And near at length the Carrick shore.
As less and less the distance grows,
High and more high the beacon rose;
The light, that seem'd a twinkling star,
Now blazed portentous, fierce, and far.
Dark-red the heaven above it glow'd,
Dark-red the sea beneath it flow'd,
Red rose the rocks on ocean's brim,
In blood-red light her islets swim;
Wild scream the dazzled sea-fowl gave,
Dropp'd from their crags on plashing wave.[2]

[MS.—" Have sunk."]
[MS.—" And from their crags plash'd in the wave."]

The deer to distant covert drew,
The black-cock deem'd it day, and crew.
Like some tall castle given to flame,
O'er half the land the lustre came.
" Now, good my Liege, and brother sage,
What think ye of mine elfin page ?"—
" Row on !" the noble King replied,
" We'll learn the truth whate'er betide ;
Yet sure the beedsman and the child
Could ne'er have waked that beacon wild."

XIV.

With that the boats approach'd the land,[1]
But Edward's grounded on the sand ;
The eager knight leap'd in the sea
Waist-deep, and first on shore was he,
Though every barge's hardy band
Contended which should gain the land,
When that strange light, which, seen afar,
Seem'd steady as the polar star,
Now, like a prophet's[2] fiery chair,
Seem'd travelling the realms of air.
Wide o'er the sky the splendour glows,
As that portentous meteor rose ;
Helm, axe, and falchion glitter'd bright,
And in the red and dusky light

---

[1] [MS.—"With that the barges near'd the land."]
[2] [MS.—" A wizard's."]

His comrade's face each warrior saw,
Nor marvell'd it was pale with awe.
Then high in air the beams were lost,
And darkness sunk upon the coast.—
Ronald to Heaven a prayer address'd,
And Douglas cross'd his dauntless breast;
" Saint James protect us !" Lennox cried,
But reckless Edward spoke aside,
" Deem'st thou, Kirkpatrick, in that flame
Red Comyn's angry spirit came,
Or would thy dauntless heart endure
Once more to make assurance sure ?"—
" Hush !" said the Bruce ; " we soon shall know,
If this be sorcerer's empty show,[1]
Or stratagem of southern foe.
The moon shines out—upon the sand
Let every leader rank his band."

XV.

Faintly the moon's pale beams supply
That ruddy light's unnatural dye ;
The dubious cold reflection lay
On the wet sands and quiet bay.
Beneath the rocks King Robert drew
His scatter'd files to order due,
Till shield compact and serried spear
In the cool light shone blue and clear.

[1] [MS.—" 'Gallants be hush'd ; we soon shall know,'
       Said Bruce, ' if this be sorcerer's show.' "]

Then down a path that sought the tide,
That speechless page was seen to glide ;
He knelt him lowly[1] on the sand,
And gave a scroll to Robert's hand.
" A torch," the Monarch cried, " What, ho !
Now shall we Cuthbert's tidings know."
But evil news the letters bare,
The Clifford's force was strong and ware,[2]
Augmented, too, that very morn,
By mountaineers who came with Lorn.
Long harrow'd by oppressor's hand,
Courage and faith had fled the land,
And over Carrick, dark and deep,
Had sunk dejection's iron sleep.—
Cuthbert had seen that beacon-flame,
Unwitting from what source it came.
Doubtful of perilous event,
Edward's mute messenger he sent,
If Bruce deceived should venture o'er,
To warn him from the fatal shore.

XVI.

As round the torch the leaders crowd,
Bruce read these chilling news aloud.
" What council, nobles, have we now ?—
To ambush us in greenwood bough,
And take the chance which fate may send
To bring our enterprise to end,

---

1 [MS.———" on the moisten'd sand."]
2 [MS.—" That Clifford's force in watch were ware."]

Or shall we turn us to the main
As exiles, and embark again?"—
Answer'd fierce Edward, " Hap what may,
In Carrick, Carrick's Lord must stay.
I would not minstrels told the tale,
Wildfire or meteor¹ made us quail."
Answer'd the Douglas, " If my liege
May win yon walls by storm or siege,
Then were each brave and patriot heart
Kindled of new for loyal part."—²
Answer'd Lord Ronald, " Not for shame
Would I that aged Torquil came,
And found, for all our empty boast,
Without a blow we fled the coast.
I will not credit that this land,
So famed for warlike heart and hand,
The nurse of Wallace and of Bruce,
Will long with tyrants hold a truce."—
" Prove we our fate—the brunt we'll bide!
So Boyd and Haye and Lennox cried ;
So said, so vow'd, the leaders all ;
So Bruce resolved : " And in my hall
Since the bold Southern make their home,
The hour of payment soon shall come,³

---

¹ [MS.—" A wildfire meteor," &c.]
² [MS.————" to play their part."]
³ [MS.—" Since Clifford needs will make his home,
       The hour of reckoning soon shall come."]

When with a rough and rugged host
Clifford may reckon[1] to his cost.
Meantime, through well-known bosk and dell,
I'll lead where we may shelter well."

XVII.

Now ask you whence that wondrous light,
Whose fairy glow beguiled their sight ?—
It ne'er was known[2]—yet grey-hair'd eld
A superstitious credence held,

[1] [MS.—"The Knight shall reckon," &c.]

[2] The following are the words of an ingenious correspondent, to whom I am obliged for much information respecting Turnberry and its neighbourhood. "The only tradition now remembered of the landing of Robert the Bruce in Carrick, relates to the fire seen by him from the Isle of Arran. It is still generally reported, and religiously believed by many, that this fire was really the work of supernatural power, unassisted by the hand of any mortal being; and it is said, that, for several centuries, the flame rose yearly on the same hour of the same night of the year, on which the king first saw it from the turrets of Brodick castle; and some go so far as to say, that if the exact time were known, it would be still seen. That this superstitious notion is very ancient, is evident from the place where the fire is said to have appeared, being called the Bogles' Brae, beyond the remembrance of man. In support of this curious belief, it is said that the practice of burning heath for the improvement of land was then unknown; that a spunkie (Jack o' lanthorn) could not have been seen across the breadth of the Forth of Clyde, between Ayrshire and Arran; and that the courier of Bruce was his kinsman, and never suspected of treachery."—Letter from Mr Joseph Train, of Newton Stuart, author of an ingenious Collection of Poems, illustrative of many ancient Traditions in Galloway and Ayrshire, Edinburgh, 1814. [Mr Train made a journey into

That never did a mortal hand
Wake its broad glare on Carrick strand ;
Nay, and that on the self-same night
When Bruce cross'd o'er, still gleams the light.
Yearly it gleams o'er mount and moor,
And glittering wave and crimson'd shore—
But whether beam celestial, lent
By Heaven to aid the King's descent,
Or fire hell-kindled from beneath,
To lure him to defeat and death,
Or were it but some meteor strange,
Of such as oft through midnight range,
Startling the traveller late and lone,[1]
I know not—and it ne'er was known.

XVIII.

Now up the rocky pass they drew,
And Ronald, to his promise true,
Still made his arm the stripling's stay,
To aid him on the rugged way.
" Now cheer thee, simple Amadine !
Why throbs that silly heart of thine ?"—

Ayrshire at Sir Walter Scott's request, on purpose to collect
accurate information for the Notes to this poem ; and the reader
will find more of the fruits of his labours in the Appendix,
Note R. This is the same gentleman whose friendly assistance
is so often acknowledged in the Notes and Introductions of the
Waverley Novels.]

1 [MS.—" Such as through midnight ether range.
Affrightening oft the traveller lone."]

—That name the pirates to their slave
(In Gaelic 'tis the Changeling) gave—
" Dost thou not rest thee on my arm ?
Do not my plaid-folds hold thee warm ?
Hath not the·wild bull's treble hide
This targe for thee and me supplied ?
Is not Clan-Colla's sword of steel ?
And, trembler,. canst thou terror feel ?
Cheer thee, and still that throbbing heart ;
From Ronald's guard thou shalt not part."
—O ! many a shaft, at random sent,
Finds mark the archer little meant !
And many a word, at random spoken,
May soothe or wound a heart that's broken !
Half sooth'd, half grieved, half terrified,
Close drew the page to Ronald's side ;
A wild delirious thrill of joy
Was in that hour of agony,
As up the steepy pass he strove,
Fear, toil, and sorrow, lost in love !

XIX.

The barrier of that iron shore,
The rock's steep ledge, is now climb'd o'er ;
And from the castle's distant wall,
From tower to tower the warders call :
The sound swings over land and sea,[1]
And marks a watchful enemy.—

---

1 [MS.—" Sounds sadly over land and sea."]

They gain'd the Chase, a wide domain
Left for the Castle's silvan reign,
(Seek not the scene—the axe, the plough,
The boor's dull fence, have marr'd it now,)[1]
But then, soft swept in velvet green
The plain with many a glade between,
Whose tangled alleys far invade
The depth of the brown forest shade.
Here the tall fern obscured the lawn,
Fair shelter for the sportive fawn;
There, tufted close with copsewood green,
Was many a swelling hillock seen;

---

[1] The Castle of Turnberry, on the coast of Ayrshire, was the property of Robert Bruce, in right of his mother. Lord Hailes mentions the following remarkable circumstance concerning the mode in which he became proprietor of it :—" Martha, Countess of Carrick in her own right, the wife of Robert Bruce, Lord of Annandale, bare him a son, afterwards Robert I. (11th July, 1274.) The circumstances of her marriage were singular : happening to meet Robert Bruce in her domains, she became enamoured of him, and with some violence led him to her castle of Turnberry. A few days after she married him, without the knowledge of the relations of either party, and without the requisite consent of the king. The king instantly seized her castle and whole estates: She afterwards atoned by a fine for her feudal delinquency. Little did Alexander foresee, that, from this union, the restorer of the Scottish monarchy was to arise."—*Annals of Scotland*, vol. ii. p. 180. The same obliging correspondent, whom I have quoted in the preceding note, gives me the following account of the present state of the ruins of Turnberry :—" Turnberry Point is a rock projecting into the sea; the top of it is about eighteen feet above high-water mark. Upon this rock was built the castle. There is about twenty-five feet high of

And all around was verdure meet
For pressure of the fairies' feet.
The glossy holly loved the park,
The yew-tree lent its shadow dark,[1]
And many an old oak, worn and bare,
With all its shiver'd boughs, was there.
Lovely between, the moonbeams fell
On lawn and hillock, glade and dell.
The gallant Monarch sigh'd to see
These glades so loved in childhood free,

the wall next to the sea yet standing. Upon the land-side the wall is only about four feet high; the length has been sixty feet, and the breadth forty-five: It was surrounded by a ditch, but that is now nearly filled up. The top of the ruin, rising between forty and fifty feet above the water, has a majestic appearance from the sea. There is not much local tradition in the vicinity connected with Bruce or his history. In front, however, of the rock, upon which stands Culzean Castle, is the mouth of a romantic cavern, called the Cove of Colean, in which it is said Bruce and his followers concealed themselves immediately after landing, till they arranged matters for their farther enterprises. Burns mentions it in the poem of Hallowe'en. The only place to the south of Turnberry worth mentioning, with reference to Bruce's history, is the Weary Nuik, a little romantic green hill, where he and his party are said to have rested, after assaulting the castle."

Around the Castle of Turnberry was a level plain of about two miles in extent, forming the castle park. There could be nothing, I am informed, more beautiful than the copsewood and verdure of this extensive meadow, before it was invaded by the ploughshare.

[1] [MS.—" The dark-green holly loved the down,
The yew-tree lent its shadow brown."]

Bethinking that, as outlaw now,
He ranged beneath the forest bough.[1]

XX.

Fast o er the moonlight Chase they sped.
Well knew the band that measured tread,
When, in retreat or in advance,
The serried warriors move at once;
And evil were the luck, if dawn
Descried them on the open lawn.
Copses they traverse, brooks they cross,
Strain up the bank and o'er the moss.
From the exhausted page's brow[2]
Cold drops of toil are streaming now;
With effort faint[3] and lengthen'd pause,
His weary step the stripling draws.
" Nay, droop not yet!"[4] the warrior said;
" Come, let me give thee ease and aid !
Strong are mine arms, and little care
A weight so slight as thine to bear.—
What ! wilt thou not ?—capricious boy !—
Then thine own limbs and strength employ.

---

[1] [" Their moonlight muster on the beach, after the sudden
extinction of this portentous flame, and their midnight march
through the paternal fields of their royal leader, also display
much beautiful painting, (stanzas 15 and 19.) After the castle
is won, the same strain is pursued."—JEFFREY.]

[2] [MS.—" From Amadine's exhausted brow."]
[3] [MS.—" And double toil," &c.]
[4] [MS.—" Nay, *fear* not yet," &c.]

Pass but this night, and pass thy care,
I'll place thee with a lady fair,
Where thou shalt tune thy lute to tell
How Ronald loves fair Isabel !"
Worn out, dishearten'd and dismay'd,
Here Amadine let go the plaid ;
His trembling limbs their aid refuse,[1]
He sunk among the midnight dews ![2]

XXI.

What may be done ?—the night is gone—
The Bruce's band moves swiftly on—
Eternal shame, if at the brunt
Lord Ronald grace not battle's front !—
" See yonder oak, within whose trunk
Decay a darken'd cell hath sunk ;
Enter, and rest thee there a space,
Wrap in my plaid thy limbs, thy face.[3]
I will not be, believe me, far ;
But must not quit the ranks of war.

---

[1] [MS.———— " his weight refuse."]

[2] [" This canto is not distinguished by many passages of extraordinary merit ; as it is, however, full of business, and comparatively free from those long rhyming dialogues which are so frequent in the poem, it is upon the whole spirited and pleasing. The scene in which Ronald is described sheltering Edith under his plaid, for the love which he bears to Isabel, is, we think, more poetically conceived than any other in the whole poem, and contains some touches of great pathos and beauty."— *Quarterly Review.*]

[3] [MS.—" And mantle in my plaid thy face."]

Well will I mark the bosky bourne,
And soon, to guard thee hence, return.—
Nay, weep not so, thou simple boy!
But sleep in peace, and wake in joy."
In silvan lodging close bestow'd,[1]
He placed the page, and onward strode
With strength put forth, o'er moss and brook,
And soon the marching band o'ertook.

XXII.

Thus strangely left, long sobb'd and wept
The page, till, wearied out, he slept—
A rough voice waked his dream—" Nay, here,
Here by this thicket, pass'd the deer—
Beneath that oak old Ryno staid—
What have we here?—a Scottish plaid,
And in its folds a stripling laid?—
Come forth! thy name and business tell!—
What, silent?—then I guess thee well,
The spy that sought old Cuthbert's cell,
Wafted from Arran yester morn—
Come, comrades, we will straight return.
Our Lord may choose the rack should teach
To this young lurcher use of speech.
Thy bow-string, till I bind him fast."—
" Nay, but he weeps and stands aghast;

---

[1] [MS.—" In silvan castle warm bestow'd,
He left the page."]

Unbound we'll lead him, fear it not ;
'Tis a fair stripling, though a Scot."
The hunters to the castle sped,
And there the hapless captive led.

XXIII.

Stout Clifford in the castle-court
Prepared him for the morning sport ;
And now with Lorn held deep discourse,
Now gave command for hound and horse.[1]
War-steeds and palfreys paw'd the ground,
And many a deer-dog howl'd around.
To Amadine, Lorn's well-known word
Replying to that Southern Lord,
Mix'd with this clanging din, might seem
The phantasm of a fever'd dream.
The tone upon his ringing ears
Came like the sounds which fancy hears,
When in rude waves or roaring winds
Some words of woe the muser finds,
Until more loudly and more near,
Their speech arrests the page's ear.[2]

---

[1] [MS.—"And now with Lorn he spoke aside,
        And now to squire and yeoman cried.
        War-horse and palfrey," &c.]
[2] [MS.———————" or roaring wind,
        Some words of woe his musings find,
        Till spoke more loudly and more near,
        These words arrest the page's ear."]

XXIV.

"And was she thus," said Clifford, "lost?
The priest should rue it to his cost !
What says the monk ?"—"The holy Sire
Owns, that in masquer's quaint attire,
She sought his skiff, disguised, unknown
To all except to him alone.
But, says the priest, a bark from Lorn[1]
Laid them aboard that very morn,
And pirates seized her for their prey.
He proffer'd ransom-gold to pay,
And they agreed—but ere told o'er,
The winds blow loud, the billows roar;
They sever'd, and they met no more.
He deems—such tempest vex'd the coast—
Ship, crew, and fugitive, were lost.
So let it be, with the disgrace
And scandal of her lofty race![2]
Thrice better she had ne'er been born,
Than brought her infamy on Lorn !"

---

[1] [MS.—" To all save to himself alone.
        Then, says he, that a bark from Lorn
        Laid him aboard," &c.]

[2] [In place of the couplet which follows, the MS. has:
        " For, stood she there, and should refuse
        The choice my better purpose views,
        I'd spurn her like a bond-maid tame,
        Lost to { resentment and to } shame."]
                { each sense of pride and }

XXV.

Lord Clifford now the captive spied ;—
" Whom, Herbert, hast thou there ?" he cried.
" A spy we seized within the Chase,
A hollow oak his lurking place."—[1]
" What tidings can the youth afford ?"—
" He plays the mute."—" Then noose a cord—
Unless brave Lorn reverse the doom
For his plaid's sake."—" Clan-Colla's loom,"
Said Lorn, whose careless glances trace
Rather the vesture than the face,
" Clan-Colla's dames such tartans twine ;
Wearer nor plaid claims care of mine.
Give him, if my advice you crave,
His own scathed oak ;[2] and let him wave
In air, unless, by terror wrung,
A frank confession find his tongue.—[3]
Nor shall he die without his rite ;
—Thou, Angus Roy, attend the sight,
And give Clan-Colla's dirge thy breath,
As they convey him to his death."—
" O brother ! cruel to the last !"
Through the poor captive's bosom pass'd

---

[1] [MS.—" A spy, whom, guided by our hound,
      Lurking conceal'd this morn we found."]
[2] [MS.—" Yon scathed oak."]
[3] [MS.————" by terror wrung
     To speech, confession finds his tongue."]

The thought, but, to his purpose true,
He said not, though he sigh'd, " Adieu!"

XXVI.

And will he keep his purpose still,
In sight of that last closing ill,[1]
When one poor breath, one single word,
May freedom, safety, life, afford ?
Can he resist the instinctive call,
For life that bids us barter all ?—
Love, strong as death, his heart hath steel'd,
His nerves hath strung—he will not yield !
Since that poor breath, that little word,
May yield Lord Ronald to the sword.—[2]
Clan-Colla's dirge is pealing wide,
The griesly headsman 's by his side ;
Along the greenwood Chase they bend,
And now their march has ghastly end !
That old and shatter'd oak beneath,
They destine for the place of death.[3]
—What thoughts are his, while all in vain
His eye for aid explores the plain ?
What thoughts, while, with a dizzy ear,
He hears the death-prayer mutter'd near ?

[1] [MS.————" last human ill."]
[2] [MS.—" Since that one word, that little breath,
        May speak Lord Ronald's doom of death."]
[3] [MS.—" Beneath that shatter'd old oak-tree,
        Design'd the slaughter-place to be."]

And must he die such death accurst,
Or will that bosom-secret burst?
Cold on his brow breaks terror's dew,
His trembling lips are livid blue;
The agony of parting life
Has nought to match that moment's strife!

XXVII.

But other witnesses are nigh,
Who mock at fear, and death defy!
Soon as the dire lament was play'd,
It waked the lurking ambuscade.
The Island Lord look'd forth, and spied
The cause, and loud in fury cried,[1]
" By Heaven they lead the page to die,
And mock me in his agony!
They shall abye it!"—On his arm
Bruce laid strong grasp, " They shall not harm
A ringlet of the stripling's hair;
But, till I give the word, forbear.
—Douglas, lead fifty of our force
Up yonder hollow water-course,
And couch the midway on the wold,
Between the flyers and their hold:
A spear above the copse display'd
Be signal of the ambush made.

[1] [MS.—" Soon as the due lament was play'd,
     The Island Lord in fury said,
     'By Heaven they lead,'" &c.]

—Edward, with forty spearmen, straight
Through yonder copse approach the gate,
And, when thou hear'st the battle-din,
Rush forward, and the passage win,
Secure the drawbridge—storm the port,
And man and guard the castle-court.—
The rest move slowly forth with me,
In shelter of the forest-tree,
Till Douglas at his post I see."

XXVIII.

Like war-horse eager to rush on,
Compell'd to wait the signal blown,[1]
Hid, and scarce hid, by greenwood bough,
Trembling with rage, stands Ronald now,
And in his grasp his sword gleams blue,
Soon to be dyed with deadlier hue.—
Meanwhile the Bruce, with steady eye,
Sees the dark[2] death-train moving by,
And heedful measures oft the space,
The Douglas and his band must trace,
Ere they can reach their destined ground.
Now sinks the dirge's wailing sound,
Now cluster round the direful tree
That slow and solemn company,
While hymn mistuned and mutter'd prayer
The victim for his fate prepare.—

---

[1] [MS.—" Yet waiting for the trumpet tone."]
[2] [MS.—" Sees the slow death-train."]

What glances o'er the greenwood shade?
The spear that marks the ambuscade!—
" Now, noble Chief! I leave thee loose ;
Upon them, Ronald!" said the Bruce.

XXIX.

" The Bruce, the Bruce!" to well-known cry
His native rocks and woods reply.
" The Bruce, the Bruce!" in that dread word
The knell of hundred deaths was heard.
The astonish'd Southern gazed at first,
Where the wild tempest was to burst,
That waked in that presaging name.
Before, behind, around it came!
Half-arm'd, surprised, on every side
Hemm'd in, hew'd down, they bled and died.
Deep in the ring the Bruce engaged,
And fierce Clan-Colla's broadsword raged!
Full soon the few who fought were sped,
Nor better was their lot who fled,
And met, 'mid terror's wild career,
The Douglas's redoubted spear!
Two hundred yeomen on that morn
The castle left, and none return.

XXX.

Not on their flight press'd Ronald's brand,
A gentler duty claim'd his hand.

He raised the page, where on the plain
His fear had sunk him with the slain:
And twice, that morn, surprise well near
Betray'd the secret kept by fear;
Once, when, with life returning, came
To the boy's lip Lord Ronald's name,
And hardly recollection[1] drown'd
The accents in a murmuring sound;
And once, when scarce he could resist
The Chieftain's care to loose the vest,
Drawn tightly o'er his labouring breast.
But then the Bruce's bugle blew,
For martial work was yet to do.

XXXI.

A harder task fierce Edward waits.
Ere signal given, the castle gates
    His fury had assail'd;[2]
Such was his wonted reckless mood,
Yet desperate valour oft made good,
Even by its daring, venture rude,
    Where prudence might have fail'd.
Upon the bridge his strength he threw,[3]
And struck the iron chain in two,

---

[1] [MS.—" And scarce his recollection," &c.]
[2] [MS.—" A harder task fierce Edward waits,
    Whose ire assail'd the castle gates."]
[3] [MS.—" Where sober thought had fail'd.
    Upon the bridge *himself* he threw."]

By which its planks arose;
The warder next his axe's edge[1]
Struck down upon the threshold ledge,
'Twixt door and post a ghastly wedge!
    The gate they may not close.
Well fought the Southern in the fray,
Clifford and Lorn fought well that day,
But stubborn Edward forced his way[2]
    Against a hundred foes.
Loud came the cry, " The Bruce, the Bruce!"
No hope or in defence or truce,
    Fresh combatants pour in;
Mad with success, and drunk with gore,
They drive the struggling foe before,
    And ward on ward they win.
Unsparing was the vengeful sword,
And limbs were lopp'd and life-blood pour'd,
The cry of death and conflict roar'd,
    And fearful was the din!
The startling horses plunged and flung,
Clamour'd the dogs till turrets rung,
    Nor sunk the fearful cry,

---

[1] [MS.—" His axe was steel of temper'd edge.
            That truth the warder well might pledge,
            He sunk upon the threshold ledge!
                The gate," &c.]
[2] [MS.—" Well fought the English yeoman then,
            And Lorn and Clifford play'd the men,
            But Edward mann'd the pass he won
                Against," &c.]

Till not a foeman was there found
Alive, save those who on the ground
   Groan'd in their agony![1]

XXXII.

The valiant Clifford is no more;[2]
On Ronald's broadsword stream'd his gore.
But better hap had he of Lorn,
Who, by the foeman backward borne,
Yet gain'd with slender train the port,
Where lay his bark beneath the fort,
   And cut the cable loose.[3]
Short were his shrift in that debate,
That hour of fury and of fate,
   If Lorn encounter'd Bruce![4]

[1] [The concluding stanza of "The Siege of Corinth" contains an obvious, though, no doubt, an unconscious imitation of the preceding nine lines, magnificently expanded through an extent of about thirty couplets:—

> "All the living things that heard
> That deadly earth-shock disappear'd;
> The wild birds flew, the wild dogs fled,
> And howling left the unburied dead;
> The camels from their keepers broke;
> The distant steer forsook the yoke—
> The nearer steed plunged o'er the plain,
> And burst his girth, and tore his rein," &c.]

[In point of fact, Clifford fell at Bannockburn.]

[2] [MS.—" And swiftly hoisted sail."]

[3] [MS.—" Short were his shrift, if in that hour
> Of fate, of fury, and of power,
>   He 'counter'd Edward Bruce!"]

Then long and loud the victor shout
From turret and from tower rung out,
  The rugged vaults replied;
And from the donjon tower on high
The men of Carrick may descry
Saint Andrew's cross, in blazonry
  Of silver, waving wide!

XXXIII.

The Bruce hath won his father's hall![1]
—"Welcome, brave friends and comrades all,
  Welcome to mirth and joy!
The first, the last, is welcome here,
From lord and chieftain, prince and peer,
  To this poor speechless boy.
Great God! once more my sire's abode
Is mine—behold the floor I trode
  In tottering infancy!
And there[2] the vaulted arch, whose sound
Echoed my joyous shout and bound
In boyhood, and that rung around
  To youth's unthinking glee!
O first, to thee, all-gracious Heaven,
Then to my friends, my thanks be given!"—
He paused a space, his brow he cross'd—
Then on the board his sword he toss'd,

[1] [See Appendix, Note R.]
[2] [MS.—" And see the vaulted arch," &c.]

Yet steaming hot; with Southern gore
From hilt to point 'twas crimson'd o'er.

XXXIV.

" Bring here," he said, " the mazers four,
My noble fathers loved of yore.[1]
Thrice let them circle round the board,
The pledge, fair Scotland's rights restored!
And he whose lip shall touch the wine,
Without a vow as true as mine,
To hold both lands and life at nought,
Until her freedom shall be bought,—
Be brand of a disloyal Scot,
And lasting infamy his lot![2]
Sit, gentle friends! our hour of glee
Is brief, we'll spend it joyously!
Blithest of all the sun's bright beams,
When betwixt storm and storm he gleams.
Well is our country's work begun,
But more, far more, must yet be done.
Speed messengers the country through;
Arouse old friends, and gather new;[3]

[1] [See Appendix, Note S.]

[2] [MS.—" Be lasting infamy his lot,
And brand of a disloyal Scot!"]

[3] As soon as it was known in Kyle, says ancient tradition, that
Robert Bruce had landed in Carrick, with the intention of reco-
vering the crown of Scotland, the Laird of Craigie, and forty-
eight men in his immediate neighbourhood, declared in favour
of their legitimate prince. Bruce granted them a tract of land,

Warn Lanark's knights to gird their mail,
Rouse the brave sons of Teviotdale,
Let Ettrick's archers sharp their darts,
The fairest forms, the truest hearts![1]

still retained by the freemen of Newton to this day. The original
charter was lost when the pestilence was raging at Ayr; but it
was renewed by one of the Jameses, and is dated at Faulkland.
The freemen of Newton were formerly officers by rotation. The
Provost of Ayr at one time was a freeman of Newton, and it
happened to be his turn, while provost in Ayr, to be officer in
Newton, both of which offices he discharged at the same time.

[1] The forest of Selkirk, or Ettrick, at this period, occupied all
the district which retains that denomination, and embraced the
neighbouring dales of Tweeddale, and at least the Upper Ward
of Clydesdale. All that tract was probably as waste us it is
mountainous, and covered with the remains of the ancient Caledonian Forest, which is supposed to have stretched from Cheviot
Hills as far as Hamilton, and to have comprehended even a part
of Ayrshire. At the fatal battle of Falkirk, Sir John Stewart
of Bonkill, brother to the Steward of Scotland, commanded the
archers of Selkirk Forest, who fell around the dead body of their
leader. The English historians have commemorated the tall
and stately persons, as well as the unswerving faith, of these
foresters. Nor has their interesting fall escaped the notice of
an elegant modern poetess, whose subject led her to treat of
that calamitous engagement.

> " The glance of the morn had sparkled bright
> On their plumage green and their actions light ;
> The bugle was strung at each hunter's side, ▪.
> As they had been bound to the chase to ride ;
> But the bugle is mute, and the shafts are spent,
> The arm unnerved and the bow unbent,
> And the tired forester is laid
> Far, far from the clustering greenwood shade !
> Sore have they toil'd—they are fallen asleep,
> And their slumber is heavy, and dull, and deep !

Call all, call all! from Reedswair-Path,
To the wild confines of Cape-Wrath;
Wide let the news through Scotland ring,
The Northern Eagle claps his wing!"

When over their bones the grass shall wave,
When the wild winds over their tombs shall rave,
Memory shall lean on their graves, and tell
How Selkirk's hunters bold around old Stewart fell! "
                    WALLACE, *or the Fight of Falkirk*, [by Miss HOLFORD,]
                        Lond. 4to, 1809, pp. 170, 1.

LORD OF THE ISLES.

CANTO SIXTH.

THE

LORD OF THE ISLES.

CANTO SIXTH.

O WHO, that shared them, ever shall forget[1]
The emotions of the spirit-rousing time,
When breathless in the mart the couriers met,
Early and late, at evening and at prime;
When the loud cannon and the merry chime
Hail'd news on news, as field on field was won,[2]
When Hope, long doubtful, soar'd at length sublime,
And our glad eyes, awake as day begun,
Watch'd Joy's broad banner rise, to meet the rising
        sun![3]

[1] [MS.—" Hast thou forgot—No! who can e'er forget."]
[2] [" Who can avoid conjuring up the idea of men with broad
sheets of foolscap scored with victories rolled round their hats,
and horns blowing loud defiance in each other's mouth, from the
top to the bottom of Pall-Mall, or the Haymarket, when he reads
such a passage? We actually hear the Park and Tower guns.
and the clattering of ten thousand bells, as we read, and stop
our ears from the close and sudden intrusion of the clamours of
some hot and *hornfisted* patriot, blowing ourselves, as well as
Bonaparte, to the devil! And what has all this to do with
Bannockburn?"—*Monthly Review.*]
[3] [MS.—" Watch'd Joy's broad banner rise, watch'd Triumph's flashing
        gun."]

O these were hours, when thrilling joy repaid
A long, long course of darkness, doubts, and
  fears!
The heart-sick faintness of the hope delay'd,
The waste, the woe, the bloodshed, and the tears.
That track'd with terror twenty rolling years,
All was forgot in that blithe jubilee!
Her downcast eye even pale Affliction rears,
To sigh a thankful prayer, amid the glee,
That hail'd the Despot's fall, and peace and liberty!

Such news o'er Scotland's hills triumphant rode,
When 'gainst the invaders turn'd the battle's scale,
When Bruce's banner had victorious flow'd
O'er Loudoun's mountain, and in Ury's vale;[1]
When English blood oft deluged Douglas-dale,[2]

---

[1] The first important advantage gained by Bruce, after landing at Turnberry, was over Aymer de Valence, Earl of Pembroke, the same by whom he had been defeated near Methven. They met, as has been said, by appointment, at Loudonhill, in the west of Scotland. Pembroke sustained a defeat; and from that time Bruce was at the head of a considerable flying army. Yet he was subsequently obliged to retreat into Aberdeenshire, and was there assailed by Comyn, Earl of Buchan, desirous to avenge the death of his relative, the Red Comyn, and supported by a body of English troops under Philip de Moubray. Bruce was ill at the time of a scrofulous disorder, but took horse to meet his enemies, although obliged to be supported on either side. He was victorious, and it is said that the agitation of his spirits restored his health.

[2] [See Appendix, Note T.]

And fiery Edward routed stout St John,[1]
When Randolph's warcry swell'd the southern gale,[2]
And many a fortress, town, and tower, was won,
And Fame still sounded forth fresh deeds of glory
  done.

[1] " John de St John, with 15,000 horsemen, had advanced to
oppose the inroad of the Scots. By a forced march he endeavoured to surprise them, but intelligence of his motions was
timeously received. The courage of Edward Bruce, approaching
to temerity, frequently enabled him to achieve what men of
more judicious valour would never have attempted. He ordered
the infantry, and the meaner sort of his army, to intrench themselves in strong narrow ground. He himself, with fifty horsemen well harnessed, issued forth under cover of a thick mist,
surprised the English on their march, attacked and dispersed
them."—DALRYMPLE'S *Annals of Scotland, quarto, Edinburgh,*
1779, p. 25.

[2] Thomas Randolph, Bruce's sister's son, a renowned Scottish
chief, was in the early part of his life not more remarkable for
consistency than Bruce himself. He espoused his uncle's party
when Bruce first assumed the crown, and was made prisoner at
the fatal battle of Methven, in which his relative's hopes appeared to be ruined. Randolph accordingly not only submitted to
the English, but took an active part against Bruce, appeared in
arms against him, and in the skirmish where he was so closely
pursued by the bloodhound, it is said his nephew took his standard with his own hand. But Randolph was afterwards made
prisoner by Douglas in Tweeddale, and brought before King
Robert. Some harsh language was exchanged between the uncle
and nephew, and the latter was committed for a time to close
custody. Afterwards, however, they were reconciled, and Randolph was created Earl of Moray about 1312. After this period
he eminently distinguished himself, first by the surprise of
Edinburgh Castle, and afterwards by many similar enterprises,
conducted with equal courage and ability.

II.

Blithe tidings flew from baron's tower,
.To peasant's cot, to forest-bower,
And waked the solitary cell,
Where lone Saint Bride's recluses dwell.
Princess no more, fair Isabel,
 A vot'ress of the order now,
Say, did the rule that bid thee wear
Dim veil and woollen scapulare,
And reft thy locks of dark-brown hair,
 ' That stern and rigid vow,
Did it condemn the transport high,
Which glisten'd in thy watery eye,
When minstrel or when palmer told
Each fresh exploit of Bruce the bold?—
And whose the lovely form, that shares
Thy anxious hopes, thy fears, thy prayers?
No sister she of convent shade;
So say these locks in lengthen'd braid,
So say the blushes and the sighs,
The tremors that unbidden rise,
When, mingled with the Bruce's fame,
The brave Lord Ronald's praises came.

III.

Believe, his father's castle won,
And his bold enterprise begun,
That Bruce's earliest cares restore
The speechless page to Arran's shore:

Nor think that long the quaint disguise
Conceal'd her from a sister's eyes;
And sister-like in love they dwell
In that lone convent's silent cell.
There Bruce's slow assent allows
Fair Isabel the veil and vows;
And there, her sex's dress regain'd,
The lovely maid of Lorn remain'd,
Unnamed, unknown, while Scotland far
Resounded with the din of war;
And many a month, and many a day,
In calm seclusion wore away.

IV.

These days, these months, to years had worn,
When tidings of high weight were borne
 To that lone island's shore;
Of all the Scottish conquests made
By the first Edward's ruthless blade,
 His son retain'd no more,
Northward of Tweed, but Stirling's towers,
Beleaguer'd by King Robert's powers;
 And they took term of truce,[1]

---

[1] When a long train of success, actively improved by Robert
Bruce, had made him master of almost all Scotland, Stirling
Castle continued to hold out. The care of the blockade was
committed by the king to his brother Edward, who concluded a
treaty with Sir Philip Mowbray, the governor, that he should
surrender the fortress, if it were not succoured by the King of
England before St John the Baptist's day. The King severely

If England's King should not relieve
The siege ere John the Baptist's eve,
    To yield them to the Bruce.
England was roused—on every side
Courier and post and herald hied,
    To summon prince and peer,
At Berwick-bounds to meet their Liege,·
Prepared to raise fair Stirling's siege,
    With buckler, brand, and spear.
The term was nigh—they muster'd fast,
By beacon and by bugle-blast
    Forth marshall'd for the field ;

blamed his brother for the impolicy of a treaty, which gave time
to the King of England to advance to the relief of the castle
with all his assembled forces, and obliged himself either to meet
them in battle with an inferior force, or to retreat with dishonour. " Let all England come," answered the reckless Edward
" we will fight them were they more." The consequence was,
of course, that each kingdom mustered its strength for the expected battle ; and as the space agreed upon reached from Lent
to Midsummer, full time was allowed for that purpose.

1 There is printed in Rymer's Fœdera the summons issued
upon this occasion to the sheriff of York; and he mentions eighteen other persons to whom similar ordinances were issued. It
seems to respect the infantry alone, for it is entitled, *De pediti-
bus ad recussum Castri de Stryvelin a Scotis obsessi, properare faci-
cndis.* This circumstance is also clear from the reasoning of the
writ, which states: " We have understood that our Scottish enemies and rebels are endeavouring to collect as strong a force as
possible of infantry, in strong and marshy grounds, where the
approach of cavalry would be difficult, between us and the castle
of Stirling."—It then sets forth Mowbray's agreement to surrender the castle, if not relieved before St John the Baptist's
day, and the king's determination, with divine grace, to raise the

There rode each knight of noble name,
There England's hardy archers came,
The land they trode seem'd all on flame,
    With banner, blade, and shield !
And not famed England's powers alone,
Renown'd in arms, the summons own ;
    For Neustria's knights obey'd,
Gascogne hath lent her horsemen good,
And Cambria, but of late subdued,
Sent forth her mountain-multitude,²

siege. " Therefore," the summons further bears, " to remove
our said enemies and rebels from such places as above mentioned,
it is necessary for us to have a strong force of infantry fit for
arms." And accordingly the sheriff of York is commanded to
equip and send forth a body of four thousand infantry, to be
assembled at Werk, upon the tenth day of June first, under pain
of the royal displeasure, &c.

¹ [The MS. has not this line.]

² Edward the First, with the usual policy of a conqueror, employed the Welsh, whom he had subdued, to assist him in his
Scottish wars, for which their habits, as mountaineers, particularly fitted them. But this policy was not without its risks
Previous to the battle of Falkirk, the Welsh quarrelled with
the English men-at-arms, and after bloodshed on both parts,
separated themselves from his army, and the feud between them,
at so dangerous and critical a juncture, was reconciled with difficulty. Edward II. followed his father's example in this particular, and with no better success. They could not be brought
to exert themselves in the cause of their conquerors. But they
had an indifferent reward for their forbearance. Without arms,
and clad only in scanty dresses of linen cloth, they appeared
naked in the eyes even of the Scottish peasantry ; and after the
rout of Bannockburn, were massacred by them in great numbers, as they retired in confusion towards their own country.
They were under command of Sir Maurice de Berkeley.

And Connoght pour'd from waste and wood
Her hundred tribes, whose sceptre rude
   Dark Eth O'Connor sway'd.[1]

V.

Right to devoted Caledon
The storm of war rolls slowly on,[2]
   With menace deep and dread;
So the dark clouds, with gathering power,
Suspend awhile the threaten'd shower,
Till every peak and summit lower
   Round the pale pilgrim's head.
Not with such pilgrim's startled eye
King Robert mark'd the tempest nigh!
   Resolved the brunt to bide,
His royal summons warn'd the land,
That all who own'd their King's command
Should instant take the spear and brand,[3]
   To combat at his side.
O who may tell the sons of fame,
That at King Robert's bidding came,
   To battle for the right!
From Cheviot to the shores of Ross,
From Solway-Sands to Marshal's-Moss,[4]
   All boun'd them for the fight.

[1] [See Appendix. Note U.]
   [2] [MS.—" The gathering storm of war rolls on."]
   [3] [MS.—" Should instant belt them with the brand."]
   [4] [MS.—" From Solway's sands to wild Cape Wrath,
      From Ilay's Rinns to Colbrand's Path."]

Such news the royal courier tells,
Who came to rouse dark Arran's dells;
But farther tidings must the ear
Of Isabel in secret hear.
These in her cloister walk, next morn,
Thus shared she with the Maid of Lorn.

VI.

" My Edith, can I tell how dear
Our intercourse of hearts sincere
  Hath been to Isabel ?—
Judge then the sorrow of my heart,
When I must say the words, We part !
  The cheerless convent-cell
Was not, sweet maiden, made for thee ;
Go thou where thy vocation free
  · On happier fortunes fell.
Nor, Edith, judge thyself betray'd,
Though Robert knows that Lorn's high Maid
And his poor silent page were one.
Versed in the fickle heart of man,[1]
Earnest and anxious hath he look'd
How Ronald's heart the message brook'd
That gave him, with her last farewell,
The charge of Sister Isabel,
To think upon that better right,
And keep the faith his promise plight.

[1] [MS.—" And his mute page were one.
   For, versant in the heart of man."]

Forgive him for thy sister's sake,
At first if vain repinings wake—[1]
   Long since that mood is gone:
Now dwells he on thy juster claims,
And oft his breach of faith he blames—
   Forgive him for thine own!"—

VII.

"No! never to Lord Ronald's bower
Will I again as paramour"——
"Nay, hush thee, too impatient maid,
Until my final tale be said!—
The good King Robert would engage
Edith once more his elfin page,
By her own heart, and her own eye,
Her lover's penitence to try—
Safe in his royal charge, and free,
Should such thy final purpose be,
Again unknown to seek the cell,
And live and die with Isabel."
Thus spoke the maid—King Robert's eye
Might have some glance of policy;
Dunstaffnage had the monarch ta'en,
And Lorn had own'd King Robert's reign;[3]
Her brother had to England fled,
And there in banishment was dead;

---

[1] [MS.—"If brief and vain repinings wake."]
[2] [MS.—"Her lover's alter'd mood to try."]
[3] [MS.—"Her aged sire had own'd his reign."]

Ample, through exile, death, and flight,
O'er tower and land was Edith's right;
This ample right o'er tower and land
Were safe in Ronald's faithful hand.

VIII.

Embarrass'd eye and blushing cheek
Pleasure and shame, and fear bespeak!
Yet much the reasoning Edith made:
" Her sister's faith she must upbraid,
Who gave such secret, dark and dear,
In council to another's ear.
Why should she leave the peaceful cell?—
How should she part with Isabel?—
How wear that strange attire agen?—
How risk herself 'midst martial men?—
And how be guarded on the way?—
At least she might entreat delay."
Kind Isabel, with secret smile,
Saw and forgave the maiden's wile,
Reluctant to be thought to move
At the first call of truant love.[1]

---

[1] The MS. here presents, *erased*—

> " But all was overruled—a band
> From Arran's mountains left the land;
> Their chief, MacLouis, had the care
> The speechless Amadine to bear
> To Bruce, with { honour } as behoved
>   { reverence }
> To page the monarch dearly loved."

With one verbal alteration these lines occur hereafter—the poet

IX.

Oh, blame her not!—when zephyrs wake,
The aspen's trembling leaves must shake;
When beams the sun through April's shower,
It needs must bloom, the violet flower;
And Love, howe'er the maiden strive,
Must with reviving hope revive!
A thousand soft excuses came,
To plead his cause 'gainst virgin shame.
Pledged by their sires in earliest youth,
He had her plighted faith and truth—
Then, 'twas her Liege's strict command,
And she, beneath his royal hand,
A ward in person and in land:—
And, last, she was resolved to stay
Only brief space—one little day—
Close hidden in her safe disguise
From all, but most from Ronald's eyes—
But once to see him more!—nor blame
Her wish—to hear him name her name!—
Then, to bear back to solitude
The thought, he had his falsehood rued!
But Isabel, who long had seen
Her pallid cheek and pensive mien,
And well herself the cause might know,
Though innocent, of Edith's woe,

having postponed them, in order to apologize more at length for
Edith's acquiescence in an arrangement, not certainly at first
sight over delicate.]

Joy'd, generous, that revolving time
Gave means to expiate the crime.
High glow'd her bosom as she said,
" Well shall her sufferings be repaid !"
Now came the parting hour—a band
From Arran's mountains left the land ;
Their chief, Fitz-Louis,[1] had the care
The speechless Amadine to bear
To Bruce, with honour, as behoved
To page the monarch dearly loved.

X.

The King had deem'd the maiden bright
Should reach him long before the fight,
But storms and fate her course delay :
It was on eve of battle-day,
When o'er the Gillie's-hill she rode.
The landscape like a furnace glow'd,
And far as e'er the eye was borne,
The lances waved like autumn-corn.

---

[1] Fitz-Louis, or Mac-Louis, otherwise called Fullarton, is a
family of ancient descent in the Isle of Arran. They are said
to be of French origin, as the name intimates. They attached
themselves to Bruce upon his first landing; and Fergus Mac-
Louis, or Fullarton, received from the grateful monarch a
charter, dated 26th November, in the second year of his reign
(1307), for the lands of Kilmichel, and others, which still remain
in this very ancient and respectable family

In battles four beneath their eye,[1]
The forces of King Robert lie.[2]
And one below the hill was laid,[3]
Reserved for rescue and for aid ;
And three, advanced, form'd vaward-line,
'Twixt Bannock's brook and Ninian's shrine.
Detach'd was each, yet each so nigh
As well might mutual aid supply.
Beyond, the Southern host appears,[4]
A boundless wilderness of spears,

[1] [MS.—" Nearest and plainest to the eye."]

[2] [See Appendix, Note V.]

[3] [MS.—" One close beneath the hill was laid."]

[4] Upon the 23d June, 1314, the alarm reached the Scottish
army of the approach of the enemy. Douglas and the Marshal
were sent to reconnoitre with a body of cavalry;

> " And soon the great host have they seen,
> Where shields shining were so sheen,
> And basinets burnished bright,
> That gave against the sun great light.
> They saw so fele * brawdyne † baners,   * *Many.* † *Displayed.*
> Standards and pennons and spears,
> And so fele knights upon steeds,
> All flaming in their weeds.
> And so fele bataills, and so broad,
> And too so great room as they rode,
> That the maist host, and the stoutest
> Of Christendom, and the greatest,
> Should be abaysit for to see
> Their foes into such quantity."

The Bruce, vol. ii. p. 111.

The two Scottish commanders were cautious in the account

Whose verge or rear the anxious eye
Strove far, but strove in vain, to spy.
Thick flashing in the evening beam,
Glaives, lances, bills, and banners gleam ;
And where the heaven join'd with the hill,
Was distant armour flashing still,
So wide, so far, the boundless host
Seem'd in the blue horizon lost.

XI.

Down from the hill the maiden pass'd
At the wild show of war aghast ;
And traversed first the rearward host,
Reserved for aid where needed most.
The men of Carrick and of Ayr,
Lennox and Lanark too, were there,
 And all the western land ;
With these the valiant of the Isles
Beneath their chieftains rank'd their files,[1]
 In many a plaided band.
There, in the centre, proudly raised,
The Bruce's royal standard blazed,
And there Lord Ronald's banner bore
A galley driven by sail and oar.

which they brought back to their camp. To the king in private
they told the formidable state of the enemy; but in public reported that the English were indeed a numerous host, but ill
commanded and worse disciplined.

 [1] [See Appendix, Note W.]

A wild, yet pleasing contrast, made
Warriors in mail and plate array'd,
With the plumed bonnet and the plaid
    By these Hebrideans worn;
But O! unseen for three long years,
Dear was the garb of mountaineers
To the fair maid of Lorn!
For one she look'd—but he was far
Busied amid the ranks of war—
Yet with affection's troubled eye
She mark'd his banner boldly fly,
Gave on the countless foe a glance,
And thought on battle's desperate chance.

XII.

To centre of the vaward line
Fitz-Louis guided Amadine.[1]
Arm'd all on foot, that host appears
A serried mass of glimmering spears.
There stood the Marcher's warlike band,
The warriors there of Lodon's land;
Ettrick and Liddell bent the yew,
A band of archers fierce, though few;
The men of Nith and Annan's vale,
And the bold Spears of Teviotdale;
The dauntless Douglas these obey,
And the young Stuart's gentle sway.

---

[1] [MS.—"Her guard conducted Amadine."]

North-eastward by Saint Ninian's shrine,
Beneath fierce Randolph's charge, combine
The warriors whom the hardy North
From Tay to Sutherland sent forth.
The rest of Scotland's war-array
With Edward Bruce to westward lay,
Where Bannock, with his broken bank
And deep ravine, protects their flank.
Behind them, screen'd by sheltering wood,
The gallant Keith, Lord Marshal, stood :
His men-at-arms bear mace and lance,
And plumes that wave, and helms that glance.
Thus fair divided by the King,
Centre, and right, and left-ward wing,
Composed his front; nor distant far
Was strong reserve to aid the war.
And 'twas to front of this array,
Her guide and Edith made their way.

XIII.

Here must they pause; for, in advance
As far as one might pitch a lance,
The Monarch rode along the van,[1]
The foe's approaching force to scan,
His line to marshal and to range,
And ranks to square, and fronts to change.
Alone he rode—from head to heel
Sheathed in his ready arms of steel;

[1] [See Appendix, Note X.]

Nor mounted yet on war-horse wight,
But, till more near the shock of fight,
Reining a palfrey low and light.
A diadem of gold was set
Above his bright steel basinet,
And clasp'd within its glittering twine
Was seen the glove of Argentine;
Truncheon or leading staff he lacks,
Bearing, instead, a battle-axe.
He ranged his soldiers for the fight,
Accoutred thus, in open sight
Of either host.—Three bowshots far,
Paused the deep front of England's war,
And rested on their arms awhile,
To close and rank their warlike file,
And hold high council, if that night
Should view the strife, or dawning light.

XIV.

O gay, yet fearful[1] to behold,
Flashing with steel and rough with gold,
    And bristled o'er with bills and spears,
With plumes and pennons waving fair,
Was that bright battle-front! for there
    Rode England's King and peers:
And who, that saw that monarch ride,
His kingdom battled by his side,

---

[1] [MS.—"O { fair, bright, } yet fearful," &c.]

Could then his direful doom foretell!—
Fair was his seat in knightly selle,
And in his sprightly eye was set
Some spark of the Plantagenet.
Though light and wandering was his glance,
It flash'd at sight of shield and lance.
" Know'st thou," he said, " De Argentine,
Yon knight who marshals thus their line?"—
" The tokens on his helmet tell
The Bruce, my Liege : I know him well."—
" And shall the audacious traitor brave
The presence where our banners wave?"—
" So please my Liege," said Argentine,
 " Were he but horsed on steed like mine,
To give him fair and knightly chance,
I would adventure forth my lance."—
" In battle-day," the King replied,
" Nice tourney rules are set aside.
—Still must the rebel dare our wrath?
Set on him—sweep him from our path !"
And, at King Edward's signal, soon
Dash'd from the ranks Sir Henry Boune.

XV.

Of Hereford's high blood [1] he came,
A race renown'd for knightly fame.
He burn'd before his Monarch's eye
To do some deed of chivalry.

---

[1] [MS.—" Princely blood," &c.]

He spurr'd his steed, he couch'd his lance,
And darted on the Bruce at once.
—As motionless as rocks, that bide
The wrath of the advancing tide,
The Bruce stood fast.—Each breast beat high,
And dazzled was each gazing eye—
The heart had hardly time to think,
The eyelid scarce had time to wink,[1]
While on the King, like flash of flame,
Spurr'd to full speed the war-horse came!
The partridge may the falcon mock,
If that slight palfrey stand the shock—
But, swerving from the Knight's career,
Just as they met, Bruce shunn'd the spear.[2]
Onward the baffled warrior bore
His course—but soon his course was o'er!—
High in his stirrups stood the King,
And gave his battle-axe the swing.
Right on De Boune, the whiles he pass'd,
Fell that stern dint—the first—the last!—
Such strength upon the blow was put,
The helmet crash'd like hazel-nut;
The axe-shaft, with its brazen clasp,
Was shiver'd to the gauntlet grasp.

[1] [MS.—" The heart took hardly time to think,
          The eyelid scarce had space to wink."]
[2] [MS.—" Just as they closed in full career,
          Bruce swerved the palfrey from the spear."]

Springs from the blow the startled horse,
Drops to the plain the lifeless corse;
—First of that fatal field, how soon,
How sudden, fell the fierce De Boune!

XVI.

One pitying glance the Monarch sped,
Where on the field his foe lay dead;
Then gently turn'd his palfrey's head,
And, pacing back his sober way,
Slowly he gain'd his own array.
There round their King the leaders crowd,
And blame his recklessness aloud,
That risk'd 'gainst each adventurous spear
A life so valued and so dear.
His broken weapon's shaft survey'd
The King, and careless answer made,—
" My loss may pay my folly's tax;
I've broke my trusty battle axe."
'Twas then Fitz-Louis, bending low,
Did Isabel's commission show;
Edith, disguised, at distance stands,
And hides her blushes with her hands.
The monarch's brow has changed its hue,
Away the gory axe he threw,
While to the seeming page he drew,
    Clearing war's terrors from his eye.
·Her hand with gentle ease he took,
With such a kind protecting look,

As to a weak and timid boy
Might speak, that elder brother's care
And elder brother's love were there.

XVII.

" Fear not," he said, " young Amadine !"
Then whisper'd, " Still that name be thine.
Fate plays her wonted fantasy,[1]
Kind Amadine, with thee and me,
And sends thee here in doubtful hour.
But soon we are beyond her power ;
For on this chosen battle-plain,
Victor or vanquish'd, I remain.
Do thou to yonder hill repair;
The followers of our host are there,
And all who may not weapons bear.—
Fitz-Louis, have him in thy care.—
Joyful we meet, if all go well ;
If not, in Arran's holy cell
Thou must take part with Isabel ;
For brave Lord Ronald, too, hath sworn,
Not to regain the Maid of Lorn,
(The bliss on earth he covets most,)
Would he forsake his battle-post,
Or shun the fortune that may fall
To Bruce, to Scotland, and to all.—
But, hark ! some news these trumpets tell ;
Forgive my haste—farewell—farewell."—

---

[1] [MS. ————" her wonted pranks, I see."]

And in a lower voice he said,
" Be of good cheer—farewell, sweet maid !"—

XVIII.

" What train of dust, with trumpet-sound
And glimmering spears, is wheeling round
Our leftward flank ?"[1]—the Monarch cried,
To Moray's Earl who rode beside.
" Lo ! round thy station pass the foes ![2]
Randolph, thy wreath has lost a rose."
The Earl his visor closed, and said,
" My wreath shall bloom, or life shall fade.—
Follow, my household !"—And they go
Like lightning on the advancing foe.
" My Liege," said noble Douglas then,
" Earl Randolph has but one to ten :[3]
Let me go forth his band to aid !"—
—" Stir not.   The error he hath made,
Let him amend it as he may ;
I will not weaken mine array."
Then loudly rose the conflict-cry,
And Douglas's brave heart swell'd high,—
" My Liege," he said, " with patient ear
I must not Moray's death-knell hear !"—
" Then go—but speed thee back again."—
Forth sprung the Douglas with his train :

[1] [See Appendix, Note Y.]

[2] [MS.—" Lo ! {round / through} thy post have pass'd the foes."]

[3] [MS.—" Earl Randolph's strength is one to ten."]

But, when they won a rising hill,
He bade his followers hold them still.—
" See, see ! the routed Southern fly !
The Earl hath won the victory.
Lo ! where yon steeds run masterless,
His banner towers above the press.
Rein up ; our presence would impair
The fame we come too late to share."
Back to the host the Douglas rode,
And soon glad tidings are abroad,[1]
That, Dayncourt by stout Randolph slain,
His followers fled with loosen'd rein.—
That skirmish closed the busy day,
And couch'd in battle's prompt array,
Each army on their weapons lay.

XIX.

It was a night of lovely June,
High rode in cloudless blue the moon,
　　Demayet smiled beneath her ray;
Old Stirling's towers arose in light,
And, twined in links of silver bright,
　　Her winding river lay.[2]
Ah, gentle planet ! other sight
Shall greet thee, next returning night,

---

[1] [MS.—" Back to his post the Douglas rode,
　　　And soon the tidings are abroad."]
[2] [The MS. here interposes the couplet.—
　　　"Glancing by fits from hostile line,
　　　Armour and lance return'd the shine."]

Of broken arms and banners tore,
And marshes dark with human gore,
And piles of slaughter'd men and horse,
And Forth that floats the frequent corse,
And many a wounded wretch to plain
Beneath thy silver light in vain!
But now, from England's host, the cry
Thou hear'st of wassail revelry,
While from the Scottish legions pass
The murmur'd prayer, the early mass!—
Here, numbers had presumption given;
There, bands o'ermatch'd sought aid from Heaven.

XX.

On Gillie's-hill, whose height commands
The battle-field, fair Edith stands,
With serf and page unfit for war,
To eye the conflict from afar.
O! with what doubtful agony
She sees the dawning tint the sky!—
Now on the Ochils gleams the sun,
And glistens now Demayet dun;
   Is it the lark that carols shrill,
     Is it the bittern's early hum?
   No!—distant, but increasing still,
   The trumpet's sound swells up the hill,
     With the deep murmur of the drum.
Responsive from the Scottish host,

Pipe-clang and bugle-sound were toss'd,[1]
His breast and brow each soldier cross'd,
   And started from the ground ;
Arm'd and array'd for instant fight,
Rose archer, spearman, squire and knight,
And in the pomp of battle bright
   The dread battalia frown'd.[2]

[1] There is an old tradition, that the well-known Scottish tune of " Hey, tutti taitti," was Bruce's march at the battle of Bannockburn. The late Mr Ritson, no granter of propositions, doubts whether the Scots had any martial music, quotes Froissart's account of each soldier in the host bearing a little horn, on which, at the onset, they would make such a horrible noise, as if all the devils of hell had been among them. He observes, that these horns are the only music mentioned by Barbour, and concludes, that it must remain a moot point whether Bruce's army were cheered by the sound even of a solitary bagpipe.— *Historical Essay prefixed to Ritson's Scottish Songs.* It may be observed in passing, that the Scottish of this period certainly observed some musical cadence, even in winding their horns, since Bruce was at once recognised by his followers from his mode of blowing. See Note X. on canto iv. But the tradition, true or false, has been the means of securing to Scotland one of the finest lyrics in the language, the celebrated war-song of Burns,—" Scots, whä hae wi' Wallace bled."

[2] [" Although Mr Scott retains that necessary and characteristic portion of his peculiar and well-known manner, he is free, we think, from any faulty self-imitation ; and the battle of Bannockburn will remain for ever as a monument of the fertile poetical powers of a writer, who had before so greatly excelled in this species of description."—*Monthly Review.*

" The battle, we think, is not comparable to the battle in Marmion, though nothing can be finer than the scene of contrasted repose and thoughtful anxiety by which it is introduced, (stanzas xix. xx. xxi.)"—JEFFREY.]

XXI.

Now onward, and in open view,
The countless ranks of England drew,*

---

* Upon the 24th of June, the English army advanced to the
attack. The narrowness of the Scottish front, and the nature
of the ground, did not permit them to have the full advantage of
their numbers, nor is it very easy to find out what was their
proposed order of battle. The vanguard, however, appeared a
distinct body, consisting of archers and spearmen on foot, and
commanded, as already said, by the Earls of Gloucester and Hereford. Barbour, in one place, mentions that they formed nine
BATTLES, or divisions; but from the following passage, it appears that there was no room or space for them to extend themselves, so that, except the vanguard, the whole army appeared
to form one solid and compact body :—

> "The English men, on either party,
> That as angels shone brightly,
> Were not arrayed on such manner :
> For all their battles samyn [1] were
> In a schiltrum.[2] But whether it was
> Through the great straitness of the place
> That they were in, to bide fighting ;
> Or that it was for abaysing ; [3]
> I wote not. But in a schiltrum
> It seemed they were all and some :

---

[1] Together.

[2] *Schiltrum.*—This word has been variously limited or extended in its significa-
tion. In general, it seems to imply a large body of men drawn up very closely
together. But it has been limited to imply a round or circular body of men so
drawn up. I cannot understand it with this limitation in the present case. The
schiltrum of the Scottish army at Falkirk was undoubtedly of a circular form,
in order to resist the attacks of the English cavalry, on whatever quarter they
might be charged. But it does not appear how, or why, the English, advancing
to the attack at Bannockburn, should have arrayed themselves in a circular
form. It seems more probable, that, by *Schiltrum* in the present case, Barbour
means to express an irregular mass into which the English army was com-
pressed by the unwieldiness of its numbers, and the carelessness or ignorance of
its leaders.

[3] Frightening.

Dark rolling like the ocean-tide,
When the rough west hath chafed his pride,
And his deep roar sends challenge wide
　　To all that bars his way !
In front the gallant archers trode,
The men-at-arms behind them rode,
And midmost of the phalanx broad
　　The Monarch held his sway.
Beside him many a war-horse fumes,
Around him waves a sea of plumes,
Where many a knight in battle known,
And some who spurs had first braced on,
And deem'd that fight should see them won,
　　King Edward's hests obey.
De Argentine attends his side,
With stout De Valence, Pembroke's pride,
Selected champions from the train,
To wait upon his bridle-rein.
Upon the Scottish foe he gazed—
—At once, before his sight amazed,
　　Sunk banner, spear, and shield ;

> Out ta'en the vaward anerly.[1]
> That right with a great company,
> Be them selwyn, arrayed were.
> Who had been by, might have seen there
> That folk ourtake a mekill feild
> On breadth, where many a shining shield,
> And many a burnished bright armour,
> And many a man of great valour,
> Might in that great schiltrum be seen ;
> And many a bright banner and sheen."
>
> 　　　　　　　　Barbour's *Bruce*, vol. ii. p. 137

　[1] Alone.

Each weapon-point is downward sent,
Each warrior to the ground is bent.
" The rebels, Argentine, repent !
        For pardon they have kneel'd."—[1]
" Aye !—but they bend to other powers,
And other pardon sue than ours !
See where yon bare-foot Abbot stands,
And blesses them with lifted hands ![2]
Upon the spot where they have kneel'd,
These men will die, or win the field."—
—" Then prove we if they die or win !
Bid Gloster's Earl the fight begin."

XXII.

Earl Gilbert waved his truncheon high,
    Just as the Northern ranks arose,
Signal for England's archery
    To halt and bend their bows.

---

[1] [MS.—" Do Argentine ! the cowards repent !
        For mercy they have kneel'd."]

[2] " Maurice, abbot of Inchaffray, placing himself on an eminence, celebrated mass in sight of the Scottish army. He then
passed along the front, bare-footed, and bearing a crucifix in his
hands, and exhorting the Scots in few and forcible words, to
combat for their rights and their liberty. The Scots kneeled
down. 'They yield,' cried Edward ; 'see, they implore mercy.'
—'They do,' answered Ingelram de Umfraville, 'but not ours.
On that field they will be victorious, or die.' "—. *Annals of Scotland,* vol. ii. p. 47.

Then stepp'd each yeoman forth a pace,
Glanced at the intervening space,
    And raised his left hand high ;
To the right ear the cords they bring—[1]
—At once ten thousand bow-strings ring,
    Ten thousand arrows fly !
Nor paused on the devoted Scot
The ceaseless fury of their shot ;
    As fiercely and as fast,
Forth whistling came the grey-goose wing
As the wild hailstones pelt and ring
    Adown December's blast.
Nor mountain targe of tough bull-hide,
Nor lowland mail, that storm may bide ;
Woe, woe to Scotland's banner'd pride,
    If the fell shower may last !
Upon the right, behind the wood,
Each by his steed dismounted, stood
    The Scottish chivalry ;—
—With foot in stirrup, hand on mane,
Fierce Edward Bruce can scarce restrain
His own keen heart, his eager train,
Until the archers gain'd the plain ;
    Then, " Mount, ye gallants free !"
He cried ; and, vaulting from the ground,
His saddle every horseman found.

---

[1] [MS.—" Drew to his ear the silken string."]

On high their glittering crests[1] they toss,
As springs the wild-fire from the moss ;
The shield hangs down on every breast,
Each ready lance is in the rest,
  And loud shouts Edward Bruce,—
" Forth, Marshal, on the peasant foe !
We'll tame the terrors of their bow,
  And cut the bow-string loose !"[2]

XXIII.

Then spurs were dash'd in chargers' flanks,
They rush'd among the archer ranks.
No spears were there the shock to let,
No stakes to turn the charge were set,
And how shall yeoman's armour slight
Stand the long lance and mace of might ?
Or what may their short swords avail,
'Gainst barbed horse and shirt of mail ?
Amid their ranks the chargers sprung,
High o'er their heads the weapons swung,
And shriek and groan and vengeful shout
Give note of triumph and of rout !
Awhile, with stubborn hardihood,
Their English hearts the strife made good.
Borne down at length on every side,
Compell'd to flight they scatter wide.—

[1] [MS.—" Their brandish'd spears."]
[2] [See Appendix, Note Z.]

Let stags of Sherwood leap for glee,
And bound the deer of Dallom-Lee !
The broken bows of Bannock's shore
Shall in the greenwood ring no more !
Round Wakefield's merry may-pole now,
The maids may twine the summer bough,
May northward look with longing glance,
For those that wont to lead the dance,
For the blithe archers look in vain !
Broken, dispersed, in flight o'erta'en,
Pierced through, trod down, by thousands slain,
They cumber Bannock's bloody plain.

XXIV.

The King with scorn beheld their flight.
" Are these," he said, "our yeomen wight ?
Each braggart churl could boast before,
Twelve Scottish lives his baldric bore ! " [1]

---

[1] Roger Ascham quotes a similar Scottish proverb, " whereby
they give the whole praise of shooting honestly to Englishmen,
saying thus, ' that every English archer beareth under his girdle
twenty-four Scottes.'   Indeed Toxophilus says before, and truly,
of the Scottish nation, ' The Scottes surely be good men of warre
in theyre owne feates as can be; but as for shootinge, they can
neither use it to any profite, nor yet challenge it for any praise.' "
—*Works of Ascham, edited by Bennet,* 4to, p. 110.
    It is said, I trust incorrectly, by an ancient English historian,
that the " good Lord James of Douglas " dreaded the superiority
of the English archers so much, that when he made any of them
prisoner, he gave him the option of losing the forefinger of his
right hand, or his right eye, either species of mutilation render-

Fitter to plunder chase or park,
Than make a manly foe[1] their mark.—
Forward, each gentleman and knight!
Let gentle blood show generous might,
And chivalry redeem the fight!"
To rightward of the wild affray,
The field show'd fair and level way;
    But, in mid-space, the Bruce's care
Had bored the ground with many a pit,
With turf and brushwood hidden yet,[2]
    That form'd a ghastly snare.
Rushing, ten thousand horsemen came,
With spears in rest, and hearts on flame,
    That panted for the shock!
With blazing crests and banners spread,
And trumpet-clang and clamour dread,
The wide plain thunder'd to their tread,
    As far as Stirling rock.
Down! down! in headlong overthrow,
Horseman and horse, the foremost go,[3]
    Wild floundering on the field!

---

ing him incapable to use the bow.   I have mislaid the reference
to this singular passage.

1 [MS.—" An armed foe."]

2 [MS.—" With many a pit the ground to bore,
    With turf and brushwood coverd o'er,
      Had form'd," &c.]

3 It is generally alleged by historians, that the English men-at-
arms fell into the hidden snare which Bruce had prepared for
them. Barbour does not mention the circumstance. According
to his account, Randolph, seeing the slaughter made by the

The first are in destruction's gorge,
Their followers wildly o'er them urge;—
The knightly helm and shield,
The mail, the acton, and the spear,
Strong hand, high heart, are useless here!
Loud from the mass confused the cry
Of dying warriors swells on high,
And steeds that shriek in agony![1]
They came like mountain-torrent red,
That thunders o'er its rocky bed;
They broke like that same torrent's wave.[2]
When swallow'd by a darksome cave.

cavalry on the right wing among the archers, advanced courageously against the main body of the English, and entered into
close combat with them. Douglas and Stuart, who commanded
the Scottish centre, led their division also to the charge, and the
battle becoming general along the whole line, was obstinately
maintained on both sides for a long space of time; the Scottish
archers doing great execution among the English men-at-arms,
after the bowmen of England were dispersed.

[1] I have been told that this line requires an explanatory note;
and, indeed, those who witness the silent patience with which
horses submit to the most cruel usage, may be permitted to
doubt, that, in moments of sudden or intolerable anguish, they
utter a most melancholy cry. Lord Erskine, in a speech made
in the House of Lords, upon a bill for enforcing humanity towards animals, noticed this remarkable fact, in language which
I will not mutilate by attempting to repeat it. It was my fortune, upon one occasion, to hear a horse, in a moment of agony,
utter a thrilling scream, which I still consider the most melancholy sound I over heard.

[2] [The MS. has

    " When plunging down some darksome cave.'"

Billows on billows burst and boil,
Maintaining still the stern turmoil,
And to their wild and tortured groan
Each adds new terrors of his own!

XXV.

Too strong in courage and in might
Was England yet, to yield the fight.
 Her noblest all are here;
Names that to fear were never known,
Bold Norfolk's Earl De Brotherton,
 And Oxford's famed De Vere.
There Gloster plied the bloody sword,
And Berkley, Grey, and Hereford,
 Bottetourt and Sanzavere,
Ross, Montague, and Mauley, came,[1]
And Courtenay's pride, and Percy's fame—
Names known too well[2] in Scotland's war,
At Falkirk, Methven, and Dunbar,

Billow on billow rushing on,
Follows the path the first had gone."

It is impossible not to recollect our author's own lines —

 " As Bracklinn's chasm, so black and steep,
  Receives her roaring linn,
 As the dark caverns of the deep
  Suck the wild whirlpool in ;
 So did the deep and darksome pass
 Devour the battle's mingled mass."
    Lady of the Lake, Canto vi. stanza .9.]

1 [MS.—" Ross, Tybtot, Neville, Mauley, came."]
2 [MS. —" Names known of yore," &c.,

Blazed broader yet in after years,
At Cressy red and fell Poitiers.
Pembroke with these, and Argentine,
Brought up the rearward battle-line.
With caution o'er the ground they tread,
Slippery with blood and piled with dead,
Till hand to hand in battle set,
The bills with spears and axes met,
And, closing dark on every side,
Raged the full contest far and wide.
Then was the strength of Douglas tried,
Then proved was Randolph's generous pride,
And well did Stuart's actions grace
The sire of Scotland's royal race !
    Firmly they kept their ground ;
As firmly England onward press'd,
And down went many a noble crest,
And rent was many a valiant breast,
    And Slaughter revell'd round.

XXVI.

Unflinching foot[1] 'gainst foot was set,
Unceasing blow by blow was met ;
    The groans of those who fell
Were drown'd amid the shriller clang,
That from the blades and harness rang,
    And in the battle-yell.

---

1 [MS.—" Unshifting .oot," &c.]

Yet fast they fell, unheard, forgot,
Both Southern fierce, and hardy Scot;
And O! amid that waste of life,
What various motives fired the strife!
The aspiring Noble bled for fame,
The Patriot for his country's claim;
This Knight his youthful strength to prove,
And that to win his lady's love;
Some fought from ruffian thirst of blood,
From habit some, or hardihood.
But ruffian stern, and soldier good,
 The noble and the slave,
From various cause the same wild road,
On the same bloody morning, trode,
 To that dark inn, the Grave![1]

XXVII.

The tug of strife to flag begins,
Though neither loses yet nor wins.[2]

[1] [" All these, life's rambling journey done,
Have found their home, the grave."—
        Cowper

[2] [" The dramatic, and even Shakspearian spirit of much of this battle must, we think, strike and delight the reader. We pass over much alternate, and much stubborn and 'unflinching' contest—

 ' The tug of strife to flag begins,
 Though neither loses yet nor wins;'

but the description of it, as we have ventured to prophesy, will last for ever.

" It will be as unnecessary for the sake of our readers, as it

High rides the sun, thick rolls the dust,[1]
And feebler speeds the blow and thrust.
Douglas leans on his war-sword now,
And Randolph wipes his bloody brow;
Nor less had toil'd each Southern knight,
From morn till mid-day in the fight.
Strong Egremont for air must gasp,
Beauchamp undoes his vizor-clasp,
And Montague must quit his spear,
And sinks thy falchion, bold De Vere!
The blows of Berkley fall less fast,
And gallant Pembroke's bugle-blast
   Hath lost its lively tone;
Sinks, Argentine, thy battle-word,
And Percy's shout was fainter heard,
   " My merry-men, fight on!"

would be useless for the sake of the author, to point out *many* of the obvious defects of these splendid passages, or of others in the poem. Such a line as
    ' The tug of strife to flag begins,'
must wound every ear that has the least pretension to judge of poetry; and no one, we should think, can miss the ridiculous point of such a couplet as the subjoined—
    ' Each heart had caught the patriot spark,
    Old man and stripling, *priest and clerk.*'"
                      Monthly Review.]

   [1] [" The adventures of the day are versified rather too literally from the contemporary chronicles. The following passage, however, is emphatic; and exemplifies what this author has so often exemplified, the power of well-chosen and well-arranged names, to excite lofty emotions, with little aid either from sentiment or description."—JEFFREY.]

XXVIII.

Bruce, with the pilot's wary eye,
The slackening[1] of the storm could spy.
  " One effort more, and Scotland's free !
  Lord of the Isles, my trust in thee
    Is firm as Ailsa Rock ;
Rush on with Highland sword and targe,
I, with my Carrick spearmen, charge ;[2]
    Now, forward to the shock !"[3]
At once the spears were forward thrown,
Against the sun the broadswords shone ;
The pibroch lent its maddening tone,
And loud King Robert's voice was known—
" Carrick, press on—they fail, they fail !
Press on, brave sons of Innisgail,
    The foe is fainting fast !

---

[1] [MS.—" The sinking," &c.]

[2] When the engagement between the main bodies had lasted some time, Bruce made a decisive movement, by bringing up the Scottish reserve. It is traditionally said, that at this crisis, he addressed the Lord of the Isles in a phrase used as a motto by some of his descendants, " My trust is constant in thee." Barbour intimates, that the reserve " assembled on one field," that is, on the same line with the Scottish forces already engaged ; which leads Lord Hailes to conjecture that the Scottish ranks must have been much thinned by slaughter, since, in that circumscribed ground, there was room for the reserve to fall into the line. But the advance of the Scottish cavalry must have contributed a good deal to form the vacancy occupied by the reserve.

[3] [MS.—" Then hurry to the shock !"]

Each strike for parent, child, and wife,
For Scotland, liberty, and life,—
    The battle cannot last !"

XXIX.

The fresh and desperate onset bore
The foes three furlongs back and more,
Leaving their noblest in their gore.
    Alone, De Argentine
Yet bears on high his red-cross shield,
Gathers the relics of the field,
Renews the ranks where they have reel'd,
    And still makes good the line.
Brief strife, but fierce, his efforts raise,
A bright but momentary blaze.
Fair Edith heard the Southern shout,
Beheld them turning from the rout,
Heard the wild call their trumpets sent,
In notes 'twixt triumph and lament.
That rallying force, combined anew,
Appear'd in her distracted view,
    To hem the Islesmen round ;
"O God ! the combat they renew,
    And is no rescue found !
And ye that look thus tamely on,
And see your native land o'erthrown,
O ! are your hearts of flesh or stone ?" [1]

    [1] [MS.————" of lead or stone."]

XXX.

The multitude that watch'd afar,
Rejected from the ranks of war,
Had not unmoved beheld the fight,
When strove the Bruce for Scotland's right;
Each heart had caught the patriot spark,
Old man and stripling, priest and clerk,
Bondsman and serf; even female hand
Stretch'd to the hatchet or the brand;
But, when mute Amadine they heard
Give to their zeal his signal-word,
A frenzy fired the throng;
" Portents and miracles impeach
Our sloth—the dumb our duties teach—
And he that gives the mute his speech,
Can bid the weak be strong.
To us, as to our lords, are given
A native earth, a promised heaven;
To us, as to our lords, belongs[1]
The vengeance for our nation's wrongs;
The choice, 'twixt death or freedom, warms
Our breasts as theirs—To arms, to arms!"
To arms they flew,—axe, club, or spear,—
And mimic ensigns high they rear,[2]
And, like a banner'd host afar,
Bear down on England's wearied war.

[1] [MS.—" To us, as well as them, belongs."]
[2] [See Appendix, Note A 2.]

XXXI.

Already scatter'd o'er the plain,
Reproof, command, and counsel vain,
The rearward squadrons fled amain,
    Or made but doubtful stay;—[1]
But when they mark'd the seeming show
Of fresh and fierce and marshall'd foe,
    The boldest broke array.
O give their hapless prince his due![2]
In vain the royal Edward threw
    His person 'mid the spears,
Cried "Fight!" to terror and despair,
Menaced, and wept, and tore his hair,[3]
    And cursed their caitiff fears;
Till Pembroke turned his bridle rein,
And forced him from the fatal plain.
With them rode Argentine, until
They gain'd the summit of the hill,
But quitted there the train:—
" In yonder field a gage I left,—
I must not live of fame bereft;
    I needs must turn again.
Speed hence, my Liege, for on your trace
The fiery Douglas takes the chase,
    I know his banner well.

---

[1] [MS.—" And rode in bands away."]
[2] [See Appendix, Note B 2.]
[3] [MS.—" And bade them hope amid despair."]

God send my Sovereign joy and bliss,
And many a happier field than this!—
 Once more, my Liege, farewell."

XXXII.

Again he faced the battle-field,—
Wildly they fly, are slain, or yield.[1]
"Now then," he said, and couch'd his spear,
"My course is run; the goal is near;
One effort more, one brave career,
  Must close this race of mine."
Then in his stirrups rising high,
He shouted loud his battle-cry,
 "Saint James for Argentine!"
And, of the bold pursuers, four
The gallant knight from saddle bore;
But not unharm'd—a lance's point
Has found his breastplate's loosen'd joint,
 An axe has razed his crest;
Yet still on Colonsay's fierce lord,
Who press'd the chase with gory sword,
 He rode with spear in rest,
And through his bloody tartans bor'ed,
 And through his gallant breast.
Nail'd to the earth, the mountaineer
Yet writhed him up against the spear,
 And swung his broadsword roud!

---

[1] [The MS. has not the seven lines which follow.]

--Stirrup, steel-boot, and cuish gave way,
Beneath that blow's tremendous sway,
    The blood gush'd from the wound;
And the grim Lord of Colonsay
    Hath turn'd him on the ground,
And laugh'd in death-pang, that his blade
The mortal thrust so well repaid.

XXXIII.

Now toil'd the Bruce, the battle done,
To use his conquest boldly won;[1]
And gave command for horse and spear
To press the Southern's scatter'd rear,
Nor let his broken force combine,
—When the war-cry of Argentine
    Fell faintly on his ear;
"Save, save his life," he cried, "O save
The kind, the noble, and the brave!"
The squadrons round free passage gave,
    The wounded knight drew near;
He raised his red-cross shield no more,
Helm, cuish, and breastplate stream'd with gore,
Yet, as he saw the King advance,
He strove even then to couch his lance—
    The effort was in vain!
The spur-stroke fail'd to rouse the horse;
Wounded and weary, in mid course

---

[1] [MS.—" Now toil'd the Bruce as leaders ought,
    To use his conquest boldly bought."]

He stumbled on the plain.
Then foremost was the generous Bruce
To raise his head, his helm to loose ;—
    " Lord Earl, the day is thine !
My Sovereign's charge, and adverse fate,
Have made our meeting all too late :
    Yet this may Argentine,
As boon from ancient comrade, crave—
A Christian's mass, a soldier's grave."

XXXIV.

Bruce press'd his dying hand—its grasp
Kindly replied ; but, in his clasp,
    It stiffen'd and grew cold—
" And, O farewell !" the victor cried,
" Of chivalry the flower and pride,
    The arm in battle bold,
The courteous mien, the noble race,
The stainless faith, the manly face !—
Bid Ninian's convent light their shrine,
For late-wake of De Argentine.
O'er better knight on death-bier laid,
Torch never gleam'd nor mass was said !"

XXXV.

Nor for De Argentine alone,
Through Ninian's church these torches shone,
And rose the death-prayer's awful tone.[1]

---

[1] [See Appendix, Note C 2.]

That yellow lustre glimmer'd pale,
On broken plate and bloodied mail,
Rent crest and shatter'd coronet,
Of Baron, Earl, and Bannaret;
And the best names that England knew,
Claim'd in the death-prayer dismal due.[1]
　　Yet mourn not, Land of Fame!
Though ne'er the leopards on thy shield
Retreated from so sad a field,
　　Since Norman William came.
Oft may thine annals justly boast
Of battles stern by Scotland lost;
　　Grudge not her victory,
When for her freeborn rights she strove;
Rights dear to all who freedom love,[2]
　　To none so dear as thee![3]

[1] [MS.—" And the best names that England owns
　　　　Swell the sad death-prayer's dismal tones."]
[2] [MS.—" When for her rights her sword was bare,
　　　　Rights dear to all who freedom share."
[3] [" The fictitious part of the story is, on the whole, the least interesting—though we think that the author has hazarded rather too little embellishment in recording the adventures of the Bruce. There are many places, at least, in which he has evidently given an air of heaviness and flatness to his narration, by adhering too closely to the authentic history; and has lowered down the tone of his poetry to the tame level of the rude chroniclers by whom the incidents were originally recorded. There is a more serious and general fault, however, in the conduct of all this part of the story,—and that is, that it is not sufficiently national—and breathes nothing either of that animosity towards England, or that exultation over her defeat, which must have animated all Scotland at the period to which he refers; and ought, conse-

XXXVI.

Turn we to Bruce, whose curious ear
Must from Fitz-Louis tidings hear;
With him, a hundred voices tell
Of prodigy and miracle,
    " For the mute page had spoke."—
" Page !" said Fitz-Louis, " rather say,
An angel sent from realms of day,
    To burst the English yoke.
I saw his plume and bonnet drop,
When hurrying from the mountain top;

quently, to have been the ruling passion of his poem. Mr Scott,
however, not only dwells fondly on the valour and generosity of
the invaders, but actually makes an elaborate apology to the
English for having ventured to select for his theme a story which
records their disasters. We hope this extreme courtesy is not
intended merely to appease critics, and attract readers in the
southern part of the island,—and yet it is difficult to see for what
other purposes it could be assumed. Mr Scott certainly need
not have been afraid either of exciting rebellion among his countrymen, or of bringing his own liberality and loyalty into question, although, in speaking of the events of that remote period,
where an overbearing conqueror was overthrown in a lawless
attempt to subdue an independent kingdom, he had given full
expression to the hatred and exultation which must have prevailed among the victors, and are indeed the only passions which
can be supposed to be excited by the story of their exploits. It
is not natural, and we are sure it is not poetical, to represent the
agents in such tremendous scenes as calm and indulgent judges
of the motives or merits of their opponents; and, by lending such
a character to the leaders of his host, the author has actually
lessened the interest of the mighty fight of Bannockburn, to
that which might be supposed to belong to a well-regulated
tournament among friendly rivals."—JEFFREY.]

A lovely brow, dark locks that wave
To his bright eyes new lustre gave,
A step as light upon the green,
As if his pinions waved unseen !"—
" Spoke he with none ?"—" With none—one word
Burst when he saw the Island Lord,[1]
Returning from the battle-field."—
" What answer made the Chief?"—" He kneel'd,
Durst not look up, but mutter'd low,
Some mingled sounds that none might know,[2]
And greeted him 'twixt joy and fear,
  As being of superior sphere."

XXXVII.

Even upon Bannock's bloody plain,
Heap'd then with thousands of the slain,
'Mid victor monarch's musings high,
Mirth laugh'd in good King Robert's eye.
" And bore he such angelic air,
Such noble front, such waving hair ?
Hath Ronald kneel'd to him ?" he said,
" Then must we call the church to aid—
Our will be to the Abbot known,
Ere these strange news are wider blown,

---

[1] [MS.—" Excepted to the Island Lord,
        When turning," &c.]
[2] [MS.—" Some mingled sounds of joy and woe."]

To Cambuskenneth straight ye pass,
And deck the church for solemn mass,[1]
To pay for high deliverance given,
A nation's thanks to gracious Heaven.
Let him array, besides, such state,
As should on princes' nuptials wait.
Ourself the cause, through fortune's spite,
That once broke short that spousal rite,
Ourself will grace, with early morn,
The bridal of the Maid of Lorn."[2]

[1] [The MS. adds :—
    " That priests and choir, with morning beams,
    Prepare, with reverence as beseems,
    To pay," &c.]

[2] [" Bruce issues orders for the celebration of the nuptials ;
whether they were ever solemnized, it is impossible to say. As
critics, we should certainly have forbidden the banns ; because,
although it is conceivable that the mere lapse of time might not
have eradicated the passion of Edith, yet how such a circumstance alone, without even the assistance of an interview, could
have created one in the bosom of Ronald, is altogether incon-
ceivable. He must have proposed to marry her merely from
compassion, or for the sake of her lands ; and, upon either sup-
position, it would have comported with the delicacy of Edith to
refuse his proffered hand."—*Quarterly Review.*

" *To Mr James Ballantyne.*—Dear Sir,—You have now the
whole affair, excepting two or three concluding stanzas. As
your taste for bride's cake may induce you to desire to know
more of the wedding, I will save you some criticism by saying,
I have settled to stop short as above.—Witness my hand.

                            " W. S."]

CONCLUSION.

~~~~~~~~~

Go forth, my Song, upon thy venturous way ;
Go boldly forth ; nor yet thy master blame,
Who chose no patron for his humble lay,
And graced thy numbers with no friendly name,
Whose partial zeal might smooth thy path to fame.
There was—and O ! how many sorrows crowd
Into these two brief words !—*there was* a claim
By generous friendship given—had fate allow'd,
It well had bid thee rank the proudest of the proud!

All angel now—yet little less than all,
While still a pilgrim in our world below !
What 'vails it us that patience to recall,
Which hid its own to soothe all other woe ;
What 'vails to tell, how Virtue's purest glow
Shone yet more lovely in a form so fair :[1]

---

[1] [The reader is referred to Mr Hogg's " Pilgrims of the Sun "
for some beautiful lines, and a highly-interesting note, on the
death of the Duchess of Buccleuch.   See *ante*, p. 7.]

And, least of all, what 'vails the world should know,
That one poor garland, twined to deck thy hair,
Is hung upon thy hearse, to droop and wither there ![1]

---

[1] [The *Edinburgh Reviewer* (Mr Jeffrey) says, "The story of the Lord of the Isles, in so far as it is fictitious, is palpably deficient both in interest and probability; and, in so far as it is founded on historical truth, seems to us to be objectionable, both for want of incident, and want of variety and connection in the incidents that occur. There is a romantic grandeur, however, in the scenery, and a sort of savage greatness and rude antiquity in many of the characters and events, which relieves the insipidity of the narrative, and atones for many defects in the execution."

After giving copious citations from what he considers as "the better parts of the poem," the critic says, "to give a complete and impartial idea of it, we ought to subjoin some from its more faulty passages. But this is but an irksome task at all times, and, with such an author as Mr Scott, is both invidious and unnecessary. His faults are nearly as notorious as his beauties; and we have announced in the outset, that they are equally conspicuous in this as in his other productions. There are innumerable harsh lines and uncouth expressions,—passages of a coarse and heavy diction,—and details of uninteresting minuteness and oppressive explanation. It is needless, after this, to quote such couplets as

> ' A damsel tired of midnight bark,
> Or wanderers of a moulding stark,'—

or—

> ' 'Tis a kind youth, but fanciful,
> Unfit against the tide to pull ;'—

or to recite the many weary pages which contain the colloquies of Isabel and Edith, and set forth the unintelligible reasons of their unreasonable conduct. The concerns of these two young ladies, indeed, form the heaviest part of the poem. The mawkish generosity of the one, and the piteous fidelity of the other, are equally oppressive to the reader, and do not tend at all to put him in good humour with Lord Ronald,—who, though the beloved of both, and the nominal hero of the work, is certainly as far as possible from an interesting person. The lovers of poetry have a particular aversion to the inconstancy of other lovers,—and especially to that sort of inconstancy which is liable to the suspicion of being partly inspired by worldly ambition, and partly abjured from considerations of a still meaner selfishness. We suspect, therefore, that they will have but little indulgence for the fickleness of the Lord of the Isles, who breaks the troth he had pledged to the heiress of Lorn, as soon as he sees a chance of succeeding with the King's sister, and comes back to the slighted bride, when his royal mistress takes the vows in a convent, and the heiress gets into possession of her lands, by the forfeiture of her brother. These characters, and this story, form the great blemish of the poem ; but it has rather less fire and flow and facility, we think, on the whole, than some of the author's other performances."

The *Monthly Reviewer* thus assails the title of the poem :—
" The Lord of the Isles himself, *selon les règles* of Mr Scott's compositions, *being* the hero, is *not* the first person in the poem. The attendant here is always in white muslin, and Tilburina herself in white linen. Still, among the *Deutero-protoi* (or *second best*) of the author, Lord Ronald holds a respectable rank. He is not so mere a magic-lantern figure, once seen in bower and once in field, as Lord Cranstoun : he far exceeds that tame rabbit boiled to rags, without onion or other sauce, De Wilton ; and although he certainly falls infinitely short of that accomplished swimmer Malcolm Græme, yet he rises proportionably above the red-haired Redmond. Lord Ronald, indeed, bating his intended marriage with one woman while he loves another, is a very noble fellow ; and, were he not so totally eclipsed by ' The Bruce,' he would have served very well to give a title to any octosyllabic epic, were it even as vigorous and poetical as the present. Nevertheless, it would have been just as proper to call Virgil's divine poem ' The *Anchiseid*,' as it is to call this

'The Lord of the Isles.' To all intents and purposes the aforesaid quarto *is*, and ought to *be*, ' *The Bruce.*' "

The *Monthly Reviewer* thus concludes his article : " In some
detached passages, the present poem may challenge any of Mr
Scott's compositions ; and perhaps in the Abbot's involuntary
blessing it excels any single part of any one of them. The battle,
too, and many dispersed lines besides, have transcendent merit.
In point of fable, however, it has not the grace and elegance of
' The Lady of the Lake,' nor the general clearness and vivacity
of its narrative ; nor the unexpected happiness of its catastrophe;
and still less does it aspire to the praise of the complicated, but
very proper and well-managed story of ' Rokeby.' It has nothing
so pathetic as ' The Cypress Wreath ;' nothing so sweetly touch-
ing as the last evening scene at Rokeby, before it is broken by
Bertram ; nothing (with the exception of the Abbot) so awfully
melancholy as much of Mortham's history, or so powerful as Bertram's farewell to Edmund. It vies, as we have already said,
with ' Marmion,' in the generally favourite part of that poem ; but
what has it (with the exception before stated) equal to the im-
murement of Constance ? On the whole, however, we prefer it to
' Marmion ;' which, in spite of much merit, always had a sort of
noisy royal-circus air with it ; a *clap-trappery*, if we may venture
on such a word. ' Marmion,' in short, has become quite identified
with Mr Braham in our minds ; and we are therefore not perhaps unbiassed judges of its perfections. Finally, we do not
hesitate to place ' The Lord of the Isles ' below both of Mr
Scott's remaining longer works ; and as to ' The Lay of the Last
Minstrel,' for numerous commonplaces and separate beauties,
that poem, we believe, still constitutes one of the highest steps,
if not the very highest, in the ladder of the author's reputation.
The characters of the present tale (with the exception of ' The
Bruce,' who is vividly painted from history, and of some minor
sketches) are certainly, in point of invention, of the most *novel*,
that is, of the most Minerva-press description ; and, as to the
language and versification, the poem is in its general course as
inferior to ' Rokeby ' (by much the most correct and the least
justly appreciated of the author's works) as it is in the construction and conduct of its fable. It supplies whole pages of the

most prosaic narrative; but, as we conclude by recollecting, it displays also whole pages of the noblest poetry."

The *British Critic* says: "No poem of Mr Scott has yet appeared with fairer claims to the public attention. If it have less pathos than the Lady of the Lake, or less display of character than Marmion, it surpasses them both in grandeur of conception, and dignity of versification. It is in every respect decidedly superior to Rokeby; and though it may not reach The Lay of the Last Minstrel in a few splendid passages, it is far more perfect as a whole. The fame of Mr Scott, among those who are capable of distinguishing the rich ore of poetry from the dross which surrounds it, will receive no small advancement by this last effort of his genius. We discover in it a brilliancy in detached expressions, and a power of language in the combination of images, which has never yet appeared in any of his previous publications.

"We would also believe that as his strength has increased, so his glaring errors have been diminished. But so embedded and engrained are these in the gems of his excellence, that no blindness can overlook, no art can divide or destroy their connexion. They must be tried together at the ordeal of time, and descend unseparated to posterity. Could Mr Scott but 'endow his purposes with words'—could he but decorate the justice and the splendour of his conceptions with more unalloyed aptness of expression, and more uniform strength and harmony of numbers, he would claim a place in the highest rank among the poets of natural feeling and natural imagery. Even as it is, with all his faults, we love him still; and *when he shall cease to write, we shall find it difficult to supply his place with a better.*"

The *Quarterly Reviewer*, after giving his outline of the story of The Lord of the Isles, thus proceeds:—"In whatever point of view it be regarded, whether with reference to the incidents it contains, or the agents by whom it is carried on, we think that one less calculated to keep alive the interest and curiosity of the reader could not easily have been conceived. Of the characters, we cannot say much; they are not conceived with any great

degree of originality, nor delineated with any particular spirit.
Neither are we disposed to criticise with minuteness the in
cidents of the story; but we conceive that the whole poem, consi-
dering it as a narrative poem, is projected upon wrong principles.

" The story is obviously composed of two independent plots,
connected with each other merely by the accidental circumstances of time and place.   The liberation of Scotland by Bruce
has not naturally any more connexion with the loves of Ronald
and the Maid of Lorn, than with those of Dido and Æneas ; nor
are we able to conceive any possible motive which should have
induced Mr Scott to weave them as he has done into the same
narrative, except the desire of combining the advantages of a
heroical, with what we may call, for want of an appropriate
word, an *ethical* subject ; an attempt which we feel assured he
never would have made, had he duly weighed the very different
principles upon which these dissimilar sorts of poetry are founded.   Thus, had Mr Scott introduced the loves of Ronald and
the Maid of Lorn as an episode of an epic poem upon the subject of the battle of Bannockburn, its want of connexion with
the main action might have been excused, in favour of its intrin-
sic merit; but, by a great singularity of judgment, he has introduced the battle of Bannockburn as an episode, in the loves of
Ronald and the Maid of Lorn.   To say nothing of the obvious
preposterousness of such a design, abstractedly considered, the
effect of it has, we think, decidedly been to destroy that interest which either of them might separately have created ; or if
any interest remain respecting the fate of the ill-requited Edith,
it is because at no moment of the poem do we feel the slightest
degree of it respecting the enterprise of Bruce.

" The many beautiful passages which we have extracted from
the poem, combined with the brief remarks subjoined to each
canto, will sufficiently shew, that although the Lord of the Isles
is not likely to add very much to the reputation of Mr Scott,
yet this must be imputed rather to the greatness of his previous
reputation, than to the absolute inferiority of the poem itself.
Unfortunately, its merits are merely incidental, while its defects are mixed up with the very elements of the poem.   But it
is not in the power of Mr Scott to write with tameness; be the

subject what it will, (and he could not easily have chosen one more impracticable,) he impresses upon whatever scenes he describes, so much movement and activity,—he infuses into his narrative such a flow of life, and, if we may so express ourselves, of animal spirits, that without satisfying the judgment, or moving the feelings, or elevating the mind, or even very greatly interesting the curiosity, he is able to seize upon, and, as it were, exhilarate the imagination of his readers, in a manner which is often truly unaccountable. This quality Mr Scott possesses in an admirable degree; and supposing that he had no other object in view than to convince the world of the great poetical powers with which he is gifted, the poem before us would be quite sufficient for his purpose. But this is of very inferior importance to the public; what they want is a good poem, and, as experience has shown, this can only be constructed upon a solid foundation of taste and judgment and meditation."

APPENDIX

THE LORD OF THE ISLES.

APPENDIX.

NOTE A.

Thy rugged halls, Artornish! rung.—P. 22.

THE ruins of the Castle of Artornish are situated upon a promontory, on the Morven, or mainland side of the Sound of Mull, a name given to the deep arm of the sea which divides that island from the continent. The situation is wild and romantic in the highest degree, having on the one hand a high and precipitous chain of rocks overhanging the sea, and on the other the narrow entrance to the beautiful salt-water lake, called Loch Alline, which is in many places finely fringed with copsewood. The ruins of Artornish are not now very considerable, and consist chiefly of the remains of an old keep, or tower, with fragments of outward defences. But, in former days, it was a place of great consequence, being one of the principal strongholds which the Lords of the Isles, during the period of their stormy independence, possessed upon the mainland of Argyleshire. Here they assembled what popular tradition calls their parliaments, meaning, I suppose, their *cour plénière*, or assembly of feudal and patriarchal vassals and dependents. From this Castle of Artornish, upon the 19th day of October, 1461, John de Yla, designing himself Earl of Ross and Lord of the Isles, granted, in the style of an independent sovereign, a commission to his trusty and well-beloved cousins, Ronald of the Isles, and Duncan, Arch-dean of the Isles, for empowering them to enter into a treaty with the most excellent Prince Edward, by the grace of God, King of France and England, and Lord of Ireland. Edward IV., on his part, named Laurence, Bishop of Durham, the Earl of Worcester, the Prior of St John's, Lord Wenlock, and Mr Robert Stillington, keeper of the privy seal, his deputies and commissioners, to confer with those named by the Lord of the Isles. The conference terminated in a treaty, by which the Lord of the Isles agreed to become a vassal to the crown of England, and to assist Edward IV. and James Earl of Douglas, then in banishment, in subduing the realm of Scotland.

The first article provides, that John de Isle, Earl of Ross, with his son Donald Balloch, and his grandson John de Isle, with all their subjects, men, people, and inhabitants, become vassals and liegemen to Edward IV. of England, and assist him in his wars in Scotland or Ireland; and then follow the allowances to be made to the Lord of the Isles, in recompense of his military service, and the provisions for dividing such conquests as their united arms should make upon the mainland of Scotland among the confederates. These appear such curious illustrations of the period, that they are here subjoined:

"*Item*, The seid John Erle of Rosse shall, from the seid fest of Whittesontyde next comyng, yerely, durying his lyf, have and take, for fees and wages in tyme of peas, of the seid most high and Christien prince c. marc sterlyng of Englysh money; and in tyme of werre, as long as he shall entende with his myght and power in the said werres, in manner and fourme abovesaid, he shall have wages of cc. lb. sterlyng of English money yearly; and after the rate of the tyme that he shall be occupied in the seid werres.

" *Item*, The seid Donald shall, from the seid feste of Whittesontyde, have and take, during his lyf, yerly, in tyme of peas, for his fees and wages, xx l. sterlyng of Englysh money; and, when he shall be occupied and intend to the werre, with his myght and power, and in manner and fourme aboveseid, he shall have and take, for his wages yearly, xl l. sterlynge of Englysh money; or for the rate of the tyme of werre——

"*Item*, The seid John, sonn and heire apparant of the said Donald, shall have and take, yerely, from the seid fest, for his fees and wages, in the tyme of peas, x l. sterlynge of Englysh money;

and for tyme of werre, and his intendyng thereto, in manner and fourme aboveseid, he shall have, for his fees and wages, yearly xx L sterlynge of Englysh money; or after the rate of the tyme that he shall be occupied in the werre: And the seid John, th' Erle Donald and John, and eche of them, shall have good and suffi-ciaunt paiment of the seid fees and wages, as wel for tyme of peas as of werre, accordyng to thees articules and appoyntements. *Item*, it is appointed, accorded, concluded, and finally determined, that, if it so be that hereafter the seid reaume of Scotlande, or the more part thereof, be conquered, subdued, and brought to the obeissance of the seid most high and Christien prince, and his heires, or suc-cessoures, of the seid Lionell, in fourme aboveseid descendyng, be the assistance, helpe, and aide of the seid John Erle of Rosse, and Donald, and of James Erle of Douglas, then, the seid fees and wages for the tyme of peas cessying, the same erles and Donald shall have, by the graunte of the same most Christien prince, all the possessions of the seid reaume beyonde Scottishe soe, they to be departed equally betwix them: eche of them, his heires and suc-cessours, to holde his parte of the seid most Christien prince, his heires and successours, for evermore, in right of his croune of England, by homage and feaute to be done therefore.

"*Item*, If so be that, by th' aide and assistence of the seid James Erle of Douglas, the saide reaume of Scotlande be conquered and subdued as above, then he shall have, enjoie, and inherite all his own possessions, landes, and inheritaunce, on this syde the Scot-tish see; that is to saye, betwixt the seid Scottishe see and Eng-lande, such he hath rejoiced and be possessed of before this; there to holde them of the seid most high and Christien prince, his heires, and successours, as is abovesaid, for evermore, in right of the coroune of Englonde, as weel the seid Erle of Douglas, as his heires and successours, by homage and feaute to be done there-fore."—RYMER's *Fœdera Conventiones Literæ et cujuscunque generis Acta Publica*, fol. vol. v. 1741.

Such was the treaty of Artornish; but it does not appear that the allies ever made any very active effort to realize their ambi-tious designs. It will serve to shew both the power of these re-guli, and their independence upon the crown of Scotland.

It is only farther necessary to say of the Castle of Artornish, that it is almost opposite to the Bay of Aros, in the Island of Mull, where there was another castle, the occasional residence of the Lord of the Isles.

NOTE B.

—— *Mingarry sternly placed,*
   O'erawes the woodland and the waste.—P. 30.

The Castle of Mingarry is situated on the sea-coast of the district of Ardnamurchan. The ruins, which are tolerably entire, are surrounded by a very high wall, forming a kind of polygon, for the purpose of adapting itself to the projecting angles of a precipice overhanging the sea, on which the castle stands. It was anciently the residence of the Mac-Ians, a clan of Mac-Donalds, descended from Ian, or John, a grandson of Angus Og, Lord of the Isles. The last time that Mingarry was of military importance, occurs in the celebrated Leabhar dearg, or Red-book of Clanronald, a MS. renowned in the Ossianic controversy.   Allaster Mac-Donald, commonly called Colquitto, who commanded the Irish auxiliaries, sent over by the Earl of Antrim during the great civil war to the assistance of Montrose, began his enterprise in 1644, by taking the castles of Kinloch-Alline, and Mingarry, the last of which made considerable resistance, as might, from the strength of the situation, be expected.   In the meanwhile, Allaster Mac-Donald's ships, which had brought him over, were attacked in Loch Eisord, in Skye, by an armament sent round by the covenanting parliament, and his own vessel was taken.   This circumstance is said chiefly to have induced him to continue in Scotland, where there seemed little prospect of raising an army in behalf of the king.   He had no sooner moved eastward to join Montrose, a junction which he effected in the braes of Athole, than the Marquis of Argyle besieged the castle of Mingarry, but without success.   Among other warriors and chiefs whom Argyle summoned to his camp to assist upon this occasion, was John of Moidart, the Captain of Clanronald.

Clanronald appeared ; but, far from yielding effectual assistance to Argyle, he took the opportunity of being in arms to lay waste the district of Sunart, then belonging to the adherents of Argyle, and sent part of the spoil to relieve the Castle of Mingarry. Thus the castle was maintained until relieved by Allaster Mac-Donald (Colquitto), who had been detached for the purpose by Montrose. These particulars are hardly worth mentioning, were they not connected with the memorable successes of Montrose, related by an eyewitness, and hitherto unknown to Scottish historians.

NOTE C.

Lord of the Isles.—P. 31.

The representative of this independent principality, for such it seems to have been, though acknowledging occasionally the pre-eminence of the Scottish crown, was, at the period of the poem, Angus, called Angus Og; but the name has been, *euphoniæ gratia,* exchanged for that of Ronald, which frequently occurs in the genealogy. Angus was a protector of Robert Bruce, whom he received in his Castle of Dunnaverty, during the time of his greatest distress. As I shall be equally liable to censure for attempting to decide a controversy which has long existed between three distinguished chieftains of this family, who have long disputed the representation of the Lord of the Isles, or for leaving a question of such importance altogether untouched, I choose, in the first place, to give such information as I have been able to derive from Highland genealogists, and which, for those who have patience to investigate such subjects, really contains some curious information concerning the history of the Isles. In the second place, I shall offer a few remarks upon the rules of succession at that period, without pretending to decide their bearing upon the question at issue, which must depend upon evidence which I have had no opportunity to examine.

"Angus Og," says an ancient manuscript translated from the Gaelic, "son of Angus Mor, son of Donald, son of Ronald, son of Somerled, high chief and superior Lord of Innisgall, (or the Isles of the Gael, the general name given to the Hebrides,) he married a daughter of Cunbui, namely, Cathan; she was mother to John, son of Angus, and with her came an unusual portion from Ireland, viz. twenty-four clans, of whom twenty-four families in Scotland are descended. Angus had another son, namely, young John Fraoch, whose descendants are called Clan-Ean of Glencoe, and the M'Donalds of Fraoch. This Angus Og died in Isla, where his body was interred. His son John succeeded to the inheritance of Innisgall. He had good descendants, namely, three sons procreate of Ann, daughter of Roderic, high chief of Lorn, and one daughter, Mary, married to John Maclean, Laird of Duart, and Lauchlan, his brother, Laird of Coll; she was interred in the church of the Black Nuns. The eldest sons of John were Ronald Godfrey, and Angus. . . . . He gave Ronald a great inheritance. These were the lands which he gave him, viz. from Kilcumin in Abertarf to the river Seil, and from thence to Beilli, north of Eig and Rum, and the two Uists, and from thence to the foot of the river Glaichan, and threescore long ships. John married afterwards Margaret Stewart, daughter to Robert Stewart, King of Scotland, called John Fernyear; she bore him three good sons, Donald of the Isles, the heir, John the Tainister, (i. e. Thane,) the second son, and Alexander Carrach. John had another son called Marcus, of whom the clan Macdonald of Cnoc, in Tirowen, are descended. This John lived long, and made donations to Icolumkill; he covered the chapel of Eorsay-Elan, the chapel of Finlagam, and the chapel of the Isle of Tsuibhne, and gave the proper furniture for the service of God, upholding the clergy and monks; he built or repaired the church of the Holy Cross immediately before his death. He died at his own castle of Ardtorinish, many priests and monks took the sacrament at his funeral, and they embalmed the body of this dear man, and brought it to Icolumkill; the abbot, monks, and vicar, came as they ought to meet the King of Fiongal,[1] and out of great respect to his memory mourned eight days and nights over it, and laid it in the same grave with his father, in the church of Oran, 1380.

[1] Western Isles and adjacent coast.

" Ronald, son of John, was chief ruler of the Isles in his father's lifetime, and was old in the government at his father's death.

" He assembled the gentry of the Isles, brought the sceptre from Kildonan in Eig, and delivered it to his brother Donald, who was thereupon called M'Donald, and Donald Lord of the Isles,[1] contrary to the opinion of the men of the Isles.

" Ronald, son of John, son of Angus Og, was a great supporter of the church and clergy ; his descendants are called Clanronald. He gave the lands of Tiruma, in Uist, to the minister of it for ever, for the honour of God and Columkill ; he was proprietor of all the lands of the north along the coast and the isles ; he died in the year of Christ 1386, in his own mansion of Castle Tirim, leaving five children. Donald of the Isles, son of John, son of Angus Og, the brother of Ronald, took possession of Innisgall by the consent of his brother and the gentry thereof; they were all obedient to him : he married Mary Lesley, daughter to the Earl of Ross, and by her came the earldom of Ross to the M'Donalds. After his succession to that earldom, he was called M'Donald, Lord of the Isles and Earl of Ross. There are many things written of him in other places.

" He fought the battle of Garioch (i. e. Harlaw) against Duke Murdoch, the governor, the Earl of Mar commanded the army, in support of his claim to the earldom of Ross : which was ceded to him by King James the First, after his release from the King of England, and Duke Murdoch, his two sons and retainers, were beheaded : he gave lands in Mull and Isla to the minister of Hi, and every privilege which the minister of Iona had formerly, besides vessels of gold and silver to Columkill for the monastery, and became himself one of the fraternity. He left issue, a lawful heir to Innisgall and Ross, namely, Alexander, the son of Donald : he died in Isla, and his body was interred in the south side of the temple of Oran. Alexander, called John of the Isles, son of Alexander of the Isles, son of Donald of the Isles. Angus, the third son of John, son of Angus Og, married the daughter of John, the son of Allan, which connexion caused some disagreement betwixt the two families about their marches and division of lands,

[1] Innisgall.

the one party adhering to Angus, and the other to John : the dif-
ferences increased so much, that John obtained from Allan all the
lands betwixt *Abhan Fakda* (*i. e.* the long river) and *old na sion-
nach* (*i. e.* the fox-burn brook), in the upper part of Cantyre.
Allan went to the king to complain of his son-in-law ; in a short
time thereafter, there happened to be a great meeting about this
young Angus's lands to the north of Inverness, where he was murdered by his own harper Mac-Cairbre, by cutting his throat with
a long knife. He[1] lived a year thereafter, and many of those con-
cerned were delivered up to the king. Angus's wife was pregnant
at the time of his murder, and she bore him a son who was named
Donald, and called Donald Du. He was kept in confinement until he was thirty years of age, when he was released by the men
of Glencoe, by the strong hand. After this enlargement, he came
to the Isles, and convened the gentry thereof. There happened
great feuds betwixt these families while Donald Du was in confinement, insomuch that Mac-Cean of Ardnamurchan destroyed
the greatest part of the posterity of John Mor of the Isles and Cantyre. For John Cathanach, son of John, son of Donald Balloch,
son of John Mor, son of John, son of Angus Og (the chief of the
descendants of John Mor), and John Mor, son of John Cathanach,
and young John, son of John Cathanach, and young Donald Balloch, son of John Cathanach, were treacherously taken by Mac-
Cean in the island of Finlagan, in Isla, and carried to Edinburgh,
where he got them hanged at the Burrow-muir, and their bodies
were buried in the church of St Anthony, called the New Church.
There were none left alive at that time of the children of John
Cathanach, except Alexander, the son of John Cathanach, and
Agnes Flach, who concealed themselves in the glens of Ireland.
Mac-Cean, hearing of their hiding-places, went to cut down the
woods of these glens, in order to destroy Alexander, and extirpate
the whole race. At length M'Cean and Alexander met, were
reconciled, and a marriage alliance took place ; Alexander married
Mac-Cean's daughter, and she brought him good children. The
Mac-Donalds of the north had also descendants ; for, after the
death of John, Lord of the Isles, and Earl of Ross, and the mur-

---

[1] The murderer, I presume, not the man who was murdered.

der of Angus, Alexander, the son of Archibald, the son of Alexander of the Isles, took possession, and John was in possession of the earldom of Ross, and the north bordering country; he married a daughter of the Earl of Moray, of whom some of the men of the north had descended. The Mac-Kenzies rose against Alexander, and fought the battle called *Blar na Puire.* Alexander had only a few of the men of Ross at the battle. He went after that battle to take possession of the Isles, and sailed in a ship to the south to see if he could find any of the posterity of John Mor alive, to rise along with him; but Mac-Cean of Ardnamurchan watched him as he sailed past, followed him to Oransay and Colonsay, went to the house where he was, and he and Alexander, son of John Cathanach, murdered him there.

"A good while after these things fell out, Donald Galda, son of Alexander, son of Archibald, became major; he, with the advice and direction of the Earl of Moray, came to the Isles, and Mac-Leod of the Lewis, and many of the gentry of the Isles, rose with him: they went by the promontory of Ardnamurchan, where they met Alexander, the son of John Cathanach, were reconciled to him, he joined his men with theirs against Mac-Cean of Ardnamurchan, came upon him at a place called the Silver Craig, where he and his three sons, and a great number of his people, were killed, and Donald Galda was immediately declared Mac-Donald: And, after the affair of Ardnamurchan, all the men of the Isles yielded to him, but he did not live above seven or eight weeks after it: he died at Carnaborg, in Mull, without issue. He had three sisters' daughters of Alexander, son of Archibald, who were portioned in the north upon the continent, but the earldom of Ross was kept for them. Alexander, the son of Archibald, had a natural son, called John Cam, of whom is descended Achnacoichan, in Ramoeh, and Donald Gorm, son of Ronald, son of Alexander Duson, of John Cam. Donald Du, son of Angus, son of John of the Isles, son of Alexander of the Isles, son of Donald of the Isles, son of John of the Isles, son of Angus Og, namely, the true heir of the Isles and Ross, came after his release from captivity to the Isles, and convened the men thereof, and he and the Earl of Lennox agreed to raise a great army for the purpose of taking possession, and a ship came from England with a supply of money to carry on the war, which landed at Mull, and the money was given to Mac-Lean of Duart to be distributed among the commanders of the army, which they not receiving in proportion as it should have been distributed among them, caused the army to disperse, which, when the Earl of Lennox heard, he disbanded his own men, and made it up with the King. Mac-Donald went to Ireland to raise men, but he died on his way to Dublin, at Drogheda, of a fever, without issue of either sons or daughters."

In this history may be traced, though the Bard, or Seannachie, touches such a delicate discussion with a gentle hand, the point of difference between the three principal septs descended from the Lords of the Isles. The first question, and one of no easy solution, where so little evidence is produced, respects the nature of the connexion of John, called by the Archdean of the Isles " the Good John of Ila," and " the last Lord of the Isles," with Anne, daughter of Roderick Mac-Dougal, high-chief of Lorn. In the absence of positive evidence, presumptive must be resorted to, and I own it appears to render it in the highest degree improbable that this connexion was otherwise than legitimate. In the wars between David II. and Edward Baliol, John of the Isles espoused the Baliol interest, to which he was probably determined by his alliance with Roderick of Lorn, who was, from every family predilection, friendly to Baliol and hostile to Bruce. It seems absurd to suppose, that between two chiefs of the same descent, and nearly equal power and rank, (though the Mac-Dougals had been much crushed by Robert Bruce,) such a connexion should have been that of concubinage; and it appears more likely that the tempting offer of an alliance with the Bruce family, when they had obtained the decided superiority in Scotland, induced " the good John of Ila " to disinherit, to a certain extent, his eldest son Ronald, who came of a stock so unpopular as the Mac-Dougals, and to call to his succession his younger family, born of Margaret Stuart, daughter of Robert, afterwards King of Scotland. The setting aside of this elder branch of his family, was most probably a condition of his new alliance, and his being received into favour with the dynasty he had always opposed. Nor were the laws of succession at this early period so

clearly understood as to bar such transactions. The numerous
and strange claims set up to the crown of Scotland, when vacant
by the death of Alexander III., make it manifest how very little
the indefeasible hereditary right of primogeniture was valued at
that period. In fact, the title of the Bruces themselves to the
crown, though justly the most popular, when assumed with the
determination of asserting the independence of Scotland, was, upon
pure principle, greatly inferior to that of Baliol. For Bruce, the
competitor, claimed as son of Isabella, *second* daughter of David,
Earl of Huntingdon; and John Baliol, as grandson of Margaret,
the elder daughter of that same earl. So that the plea of Bruce
was founded upon the very loose idea, that as the great grandson
of David I., King of Scotland, and the nearest collateral relation
of Alexander III., he was entitled to succeed in exclusion of
the great great grandson of the same David, though by an elder
daughter. This maxim savoured of the ancient practice of Scotland, which often called a brother to succeed to the crown as
nearer in blood than a grand-child, or even a son of a deceased
monarch. But, in truth, the maxims of inheritance in Scotland
were sometimes departed from at periods when they were much
more distinctly understood. Such a transposition took place in
the family of Hamilton, in 1513, when the descendants of James,
third Lord, by Lady Janet Home, were set aside, with an appanage
of great value indeed, in order to call to the succession those which
he had by a subsequent marriage with Janet Beatoun. In short,
many other examples might be quoted to shew that the question
of legitimacy is not always determined by the fact of succession:
and there seems reason to believe that Ronald, descendant of
"John of Ila," by Ann of Lorn, was legitimate, and therefore
Lord of the Isles *de jure*, though *de facto* his younger half-brother
Donald, son of his father's second marriage with the Princess
of Scotland, superseded him in his right, and apparently by his
own consent. From this Donald so preferred is descended the
family of Sleat, now Lords Mac-Donald. On the other hand,
from Ronald, the excluded heir, upon whom a very large appanage
was settled, descended the chiefs of Glengary and Clanronald,
each of whom had large possessions, and a numerous vassalage,

and boasted a long descent of warlike ancestry. Their common
ancestor Ronald was murdered by the Earl of Ross, at the Monastery of Elcho, A.D. 1346. I believe it has been subject of fierce
dispute, whether Donald, who carried on the line of Glengary,
or Allan of Moidart, the ancestor of the captains of Clanronald,
was the eldest son of Ronald, the son of John of Isla. A humble
Lowlander may be permitted to waive the discussion, since a
Sennachie of no small note, who wrote in the sixteenth century,
expresses himself upon this delicate topic in the following words:—

" I have now given you an account of every thing you can ex-
pect of the descendants of the clan Colla, (*i. e.* the Mac-Donalds,)
to the death of Donald Du at Drogheda, namely, the true line of
those who possessed the Isles, Ross, and the mountainous coun-
tries of Scotland. It was Donald, the son of Angus, that was killed
at Inverness, by his (own harper Mac-i'Cairbre,) son of John of
the Isles, son of Alexander, son of Donald, son of John, son of
Angus Og. And I know not which of his kindred or relations is
the true heir, except of these five sons of John, the son of Angus
Og, whom I here set down for you, namely, Ronald and Godfrey,
the two sons of the daughter of Mac Donald of Lorn. and Donald
and John Mor, and Alexander Carrach, the three sons of Margaret Stewart, daughter of Robert Stewart, King of Scotland."—
Leabhar Dearg.

Note D.

——*The House of Lorn.*—P. 33.

The House of Lorn, as we observed in a former note, was, like
the Lord of the Isles, descended from a son of Somerled, slain at
Renfrew in 1164. This son obtained the succession of his mainland territories, comprehending the greater part of the three dis-
tricts of Lorn, in Argyleshire, and of course might rather be considered as petty princes than feudal barons. They assumed the patro-
nymic appellation of Mac-Dougal, by which they are distinguished
in the history of the middle ages. The Lord of Lorn, who flourished

during the wars of Bruce, was Allaster (or Alexander) Mac-Dougal, called Allaster of Argyle. He had married the third daughter of John, called the Red Comyn,[1] who was slain by Bruce in the Dominican Church at Dumfries, and hence he was a mortal enemy of that prince, and more than once reduced him to great straits during the early and distressed period of his reign, as we shall have repeated occasion to notice. Bruce, when he began to obtain an ascendancy in Scotland, took the first opportunity in his power to requite these injuries. He marched into Argyleshire to lay waste the country. John of Lorn, son of the chieftain, was posted with his followers in the formidable pass between Dalmally and Bunawe. It is a narrow path along the verge of the huge and precipitous mountain, called Cruachan-Ben, and guarded on the other side by a precipice overhanging Loch Awe. The pass seems to the eye of a soldier as strong, as it is wild and romantic to that of an ordinary traveller. But the skill of Bruce had anticipated this difficulty. While his main body, engaged in a skirmish with the men of Lorn, detained their attention to the front of their position, James of Douglas, with Sir Alexander Fraser, Sir William Wiseman, and Sir Andrew Grey, ascended the mountain with a select body of archery, and obtained possession of the heights which commanded the pass. A volley of arrows descending upon them directly warned the Argyleshire men of their perilous situation, and their resistance, which had hitherto been bold and manly, was changed into a precipitate flight. The deep and rapid river of Awe was then (we learn the fact from Barbour with some surprise) crossed by a bridge. This bridge the mountaineers attempted to demolish, but Bruce's followers were too close upon

---

[1] The aunt, according to Lord Hailes. But the genealogy is distinctly given by Wyntoun :—

> " The thryd douchtyr of Red Cwmyn,
> Alysawndyr of Argayle syne
> Tuk, and weddyt til hys wyf,
> And on hyr he gat in-til hys lyfe
> Jhon of Lorne, the quhilk gat
> Ewyn of Lorne eftyr that."

WYNTOUN's *Chronicle*, Book viii. Chap. vi. line 34.

their rear; they were, therefore, without refuge and defence, and were dispersed with great slaughter.   John of Lorn, suspicious of the event, had early betaken himself to the galleys which he had upon the lake; but the feelings which Barbour assigns to him, while witnessing the rout and slaughter of his followers, exculpate him from the charge of cowardice.

> " To Jhone off Lorne it suld displese
> I trow, quhen he his men mycht se,
> Owte off his schippis fra the se.
> Be slayne and chassyt in the hill,
> That he mycht set na help thar till.
> Bot it angrys als gretumly,
> To gud hartis that ar worthi,
> To se thair fayis fulfill thair will
> As to thaim selff to thole the ill."—B. vii. v. 391.

After this decisive engagement, Bruce laid waste Argyleshire, and besieged Dunstaffnage Castle, on the western shore of Lorn, compelled it to surrender, and placed in that principal stronghold of the Mac-Dougals a garrison and governor of his own.   The elder Mac-Dougal, now wearied with the contest, submitted to the victor; but his son, "rebellious," says Barbour, " as he wont to be," fled to England by sea.   When the wars between the Bruce and Baliol factions again broke out in the reign of David II., the Lords of Lorn were again found upon the losing side, owing to their hereditary enmity to the house of Bruce.   Accordingly, upon the issue of that contest, they were deprived by David II. and his successor of by far the greater part of their extensive territories, which were conferred upon Stewart, called the knight of Lorn.   The house of Mac-Dougal continued, however, to survive the loss of power, and affords a very rare, if not a unique, instance of a family of such unlimited power, and so distinguished during the middle ages, surviving the decay of their grandeur, and flourishing in a private station.   The Castle of Dunolly, near Oban, with its dependencies, was the principal part of what remained to them, with their right of chieftainship over the families of their name and blood.   These they continued to enjoy until the year 1715, when the representative incurred the penalty of forfeiture, for his accession to the in-

surrection of that period : thus losing the remains of his inheritance, to replace upon the throne the descendants of those princes,
whose accession his ancestors had opposed at the expense of their
feudal grandeur.   The estate was, however, restored about 1745,
to the father of the present proprietor, whom family experience
had taught the hazard of interfering with the established government, and who remained quiet upon that occasion.   He therefore
regained his property when many Highland chiefs lost theirs.

Nothing can be more wildly beautiful than the situation of
Dunolly.   The ruins are situated upon a bold and precipitous promontory, overhanging Loch Etive, and distant about a mile from
the village and port of Oban.   The principal part which remains
is the donjon or keep ; but fragments of other buildings, overgrown
with ivy, attest that it had been once a place of importance, as
large apparently as Artornish or Dunstaffnage.   These fragments
enclose a courtyard, of which the keep probably formed one side ;
the entrance being by a steep ascent from the neck of the isthmus,
formerly cut across by a moat, and defended doubtless by outworks
and a drawbridge.   Beneath the castle stands the present mansion
of the family, having on the one hand Loch Etive, with its islands
and mountains, on the other two romantic eminences tufted with
copsewood.   There are other accompaniments suited to the scene ;
in particular, a huge upright pillar, or detached fragment of that
sort of rock called plum-pudding stone, upon the shore, about a
quarter of a mile from the castle.   It is called *Clachna-cau*, or the
Dog's Pillar, because Fingal is said to have used it as a stake to
which he bound his celebrated dog Bran.   Others say, that when
the Lord of the Isles came upon a visit to the Lord of Lorn, the
dogs brought for his sport were kept beside this pillar.   Upon the
whole, a more delightful and romantic spot can scarce be conceived ; and it receives a moral interest from the considerations
attached to the residence of a family once powerful enough to con-
front and defeat Robert Bruce, and now sunk into the shade of
private life.   It is at present possessed by Patrick Mac-Dougal,
Esq., the lineal and undisputed representative of the ancient Lords
of Lorn.   The heir of Dunolly fell lately in Spain, fighting under
the Duke of Wellington,—a death well becoming his ancestry.

NOTE E.

" Fill me the mighty cup," he said,
" Erst own'd by royal Somerled."—P. 58.

A Hebridean drinking cup, of the most ancient and curious workmanship, has been long preserved in the Castle of Dunvegan, in Skye, the romantic seat of Mac-Leod of Mac-Leod, the chief of that ancient and powerful clan.   The horn of Rorie More, preserved in the same family, and recorded by Dr Johnson, is not to be compared with this piece of antiquity, which is one of the greatest curiosities in Scotland.   The following is a pretty accurate description of its shape and dimensions, but cannot, I fear, be perfectly understood without a drawing.

This very curious piece of antiquity is nine inches and three quarters in inside depth, and ten and a half in height on the outside, the extreme measure over the lips being four inches and a half.   The cup is divided into two parts by a wrought ledge, beautifully ornamented, about three-fourths of an inch in breadth. Beneath this ledge the shape of the cup is rounded off, and terminates in a flat circle, like that of a tea-cup ; four short feet support the whole.   Above the projecting ledge the shape of the cup is nearly square, projecting outward at the brim.   The cup is made of wood, (oak to all appearance,) but most curiously wrought and embossed with silver work, which projects from the vessel. There are a number of regular projecting sockets, which appear to have been set with stones ; two or three of them still hold pieces of coral, the rest are empty.   At the four corners of the projecting ledge, or cornice, are four sockets, much larger, probably for pebbles or precious stones.   The workmanship of the silver is extremely elegant, and appears to have been highly gilded.   The ledge brim, and legs of the cup, are of silver.   The family tradition bears that it was the property of Neil Ghlune-dhu, or Black-knee.   But who this Neil was, no one pretends to say.   Around the edge of the cup is a legend, perfectly legible, in the Saxon black-letter, which seems to run thus :

Ufo: Johis: Mich: || Mgn: Pncipis: De: ||
Hr: Manae: Vich: || Liahia: Magryneil: ||
Et: Spat: Do: Jhu: Da: || Clea: Jllora: Jpa: ||
Fecit: Ano: Di: Jr: 930 Onili: Oimi: ||

The Inscription may run thus at length: *Ufo Johanis Mich Magni Principis de Hr Manae Vich Liahia Magryneil et sperat Domino Ihesu dari clementiam illorum opera. Fecit Anno Domini 998 Onili Oimi.* Which may run in English: Ufo, the son of John, the son of Magnus, Prince of Man, the grandson of Liahia Macgryneil, trust in the Lord Jesus that their works (*i. e.* his own and those of his ancestors) will obtain mercy. Oneil Oimi made this in the year of God nine hundred and ninety-three.

But this version does not include the puzzling letters HR before the word Manae. Within the mouth of the cup the letters Jhs. (Jesus) are repeated four times. From this and other circumstances it would seem to have been a chalice. This circumstance may perhaps account for the use of the two Arabic numerals 93. These figures were introduced by Pope Sylvester, A D. 991, and might be used in a vessel formed for church service so early as 993. The workmanship of the whole cup is extremely elegant, and resembles, I am told, antiques of the same nature preserved in Ireland.

The cups, thus elegantly formed, and highly valued, were by no means utensils of mere show. Martin gives the following account of the festivals of his time, and I have heard similar instances of brutality in the Lowlands at no very distant period.

" The manner of drinking used by the chief men of the Isles is called in their language Streah, *i. e.* a Round; for the company sat in a circle, the cup-bearer fill'd the drink round to them, and all was drank out, whatever the liquor was, whether strong or weak; they continued drinking sometimes twenty-four, sometimes forty-eight hours: It was reckoned a piece of manhood to drink until they became drunk, and there were two men with a barrow attending punctually on such occasions. They stood at the door until some became drunk, and they carry'd them upon the barrow to bed, and returned again to their post as long as any continued fresh, and so carried off the whole company, one by one, as they became drunk. Several of my acquaintance have been witnesses to this custom of drinking, but it is now abolished."

This savage custom was not entirely done away within this last generation. I have heard of a gentleman who happened to be a water-drinker, and was permitted to abstain from the strong potations of the company. The bearers carried away one man after another, till no one was left but this Scottish Mirglip. They then came to do him the same good office, which, however, he declined as unnecessary, and proposed to walk to his bedroom. It was a permission he could not obtain. Never such a thing had happened, they said, in the castle! that it was impossible but he must require their assistance, at any rate he must submit to receive it; and carried him off in the barrow accordingly. A classical penalty was sometimes imposed on those who baulked the rules of good fellowship by evading their share of the banquet. The same author continues:—

"Among persons of distinction it was reckoned an affront put upon any company to broach a piece of wine, ale, or aquavitæ, and not to see it all drank out at one meeting. If any man chance to go out from the company, though but for a few minutes, he is obliged, upon his return, and before he take his seat, to make an apology for his absence in rhyme; which if he cannot perform, he is liable to such a share of the reckoning as the company thinks fit to impose: which custom obtains in many places still, and is called Biauchiz Bard, which, in their language, signifies the poet's congratulating the company."

Few cups were better, at least more actively employed in the rude hospitality of the period, than those of Dunvegan; one of which we have just described. There is in the Leabhar Dearg, a song, intimating the overflowing gratitude of a bard of Clan-Ronald, after the exuberance of a Hebridean festival at the patriarchal fortress of Mac-Leod. The translation being obviously very literal, has greatly flattened, as I am informed, the enthusiastic gratitude of the ancient bard; and it must be owned that the works of Homer or Virgil, to say nothing of Mac-Vuirich, might have suffered by their transfusion through such a medium. It is pretty plain, that when the tribute of poetical praise was bestowed, the horn of Rorie More had not been inactive.

Upon Sir Roderic Mor Macleod, by Niall Mor Mac Vuirich.

" The six nights I remained in the Dunvegan, it was not a show of hospitality I met with there, but a plentiful feast in thy fair hall among thy numerous host of heroes.

" The family placed all around under the protection of their great chief, raised by his prosperity and respect for his warlike feats, now enjoying the company of his friends at the feast,—Amidst the sound of harps, overflowing cups, and happy youth unaccustomed to guile, or feud, partaking of the generous fare by a flaming fire.

" Mighty Chief, liberal to all in your princely mansion, filled with your numerous warlike host, whose generous wine would overcome the hardiest heroes, yet we continued to enjoy the feast, so happy our host, so generous our fare."—*Translated by D. MacIntosh.*

It would be unpardonable in a modern bard, who has experienced the hospitality of Dunvegan Castle in the present day, to omit paying his own tribute of gratitude for a reception more elegant indeed, but not less kindly sincere, than Sir Roderick More himself could have afforded. But Johnson has already described a similar scene in the same ancient patriarchal residence of the Lords of Mac-Leod:—" Whatever is imaged in the wildest tales, if giants, dragons, and enchantment be excepted, would be felt by him, who, wandering in the mountains without a guide, or upon the sea without a pilot, should be carried, amidst his terror and uncertainty, to the hospitality and elegance of Raasay or Dunvegan."

NOTE F.

The Broach of Lorn.—P. 66.

It has been generally mentioned in the preceding notes, that Robert Bruce, after his defeat at Methven, being hard pressed by the English, endeavoured, with the dispirited remnant of his followers, to escape from Breadalbane and the mountains of Perth-shire into the Argyleshire Highlands. But he was encountered and repulsed, after a very severe engagement, by the Lord of Lorn. Bruce's personal strength and courage were never displayed to greater advantage than in this conflict. There is a tradition in the family of the Mac-Dougals of Lorn, that their chieftain engaged in personal battle with Bruce himself, while the latter was employed in protecting the retreat of his men; that Mac-Dougal was struck down by the king, whose strength of body was equal to his vigour of mind, and would have been slain on the spot, had not two of Lorn's vassals, a father and son, whom tradition terms M'Keoch, rescued him, by seizing the mantle of the monarch, and dragging him from above his adversary. Bruce rid himself of these foes by two blows of his redoubted battle-axe, but was so closely pressed by the other followers of Lorn, that he was forced to abandon the mantle, and broach which fastened it, clasped in the dying grasp of the Mac-Keochs. A studded broach, said to have been that which King Robert lost upon this occasion, was long preserved in the family of Mac-Dougal, and was lost in a fire which consumed their temporary residence.

The metrical history of Barbour throws an air of credibility upon the tradition, although it does not entirely coincide either in the names or number of the vassals by whom Bruce was assailed, and makes no mention of the personal danger of Lorn, or of the loss of Bruce's mantle. The last circumstance, indeed, might be warrantably omitted.

According to Barbour, the King, with his handful of followers, not amounting probably to three hundred men, encountered Lorn with about a thousand Argyleshire men, in Glen-Douchart, at the head of Breadalbane, near Teyndrum. The place of action is still called Dalry or the King's Field. The field of battle was unfavourable to Bruce's adherents, who where chiefly men-at-arms. Many of the horses were slain by the long pole-axes, of which the Argyleshire Scottish had learned the use from the Norwegians. At length Bruce commanded a retreat up a narrow and difficult pass, he himself bringing up the rear, and repeatedly turning and

driving back the more venturous assailants.   Lorn, observing the
skill and valour used by his enemy in protecting the retreat of his
followers, "Methinks, Murthockson," said he, addressing one of
his followers, "he resembles Gol Mak-morn, protecting his followers from Fingal."—"A most unworthy comparison," observes
the Archdeacon of Aberdeen, unsuspicious of the future fame of
these names; "he might with more propriety have compared the
King to Sir Gaudefer de Layrs, protecting the foragers of Gadyrs
against the attacks of Alexander."[1]   Two brothers, the strongest
among Lorn's followers, whose names Barbour calls Mackyn-
Drosser, (interpreted Durward, or Porterson,) resolved to rid their
chief of this formidable foe.   A third person (perhaps the Mac-
Keoch of the family tradition) associated himself with them for this
purpose.   They watched their opportunity until Bruce's party had
entered a pass between a lake (Loch Dochart probably) and a precipice, where the King, who was the last of the party, had scarce
room to manage his steed.   Here his three foes sprung upon him
at once.   One seized his bridle, but received a wound which hewed
of his arm; a second grasped Bruce by the stirrup and leg, and
endeavoured to dismount him, but the King, putting spurs to his
horse, threw him down, still holding by the stirrup.   The third,
taking advantage of an acclivity, sprung up behind him upon
his horse.   Bruce, however, whose personal strength is uniformly
mentioned as exceeding that of most men, extricated himself from
his grasp, threw him to the ground, and cleft his skull with his
sword.   By similar exertion he drew the stirrup from his grasp
whom he had overthrown, and killed him also with his sword as
he lay among the horse's feet.   The story seems romantic, but
this was the age of romantic exploit; and it must be remembered
that Bruce was armed cap-a-pie, and the assailants were half-clad

[1] " This is a very curious passage, and has been often quoted in the Ossianic
controversy. That it refers to ancient Celtic tradition, there can be no doubt,
and as little that it refers to no incident in the poems published by Mr Macpherson
as from the Gaelic. The hero of romance, whom Barbour thinks a more proper
prototype for the Bruce, occurs in the romance of Alexander, of which there is a
unique translation into Scottish verse, in the library of the Honourable Mr
Maule of Panmure."—See WEBER's *Romances*, vol. L Appendix to Introduction
p. lxxiii.

mountaineers.   Barbour adds the following circumstance, highly
characteristic of the sentiments of chivalry.   Mac-Naughton, a
Baron of Cowal, pointed out to the Lord of Lorn the deeds of
valour which Bruce performed in this memorable retreat, with
the highest expressions of admiration.   " It seems to give thee
pleasure," said Lorn, "that he makes such havoc among our
friends."   " Not so, by my faith," replied Mac-Naughton ; "but
be he friend or foe who achieves high deeds of chivalry, men
should bear faithful witness to his valour; and never have I
heard of one, who, by his knightly feats, has extricated himself
from such dangers as have this day surrounded Bruce."

Note G.

Vain Kirkpatrick's bloody dirk,
Making sure of murder's work.—P. 68.

Every reader must recollect that the proximate cause of Bruce's
asserting his right to the crown of Scotland, was the death of John,
called the Red Comyn.   The causes of this act of violence, equally
extraordinary from the high rank both of the perpetrator and suf-
ferer, and from the place where the slaughter was committed, are
variously related by the Scottish and English historians, and cannot now be ascertained.   The fact that they met at the high altar
of the Minorites, or Greyfriars Church in Dumfries, that their difference broke out into high and insulting language, and that Bruce
drew his dagger and stabbed Comyn, is certain.   Rushing to the
door of the church, Bruce met two powerful barons, Kirkpatrick
of Closeburn, and James de Lindsay, who eagerly asked him what
tidings ? " Bad tidings," answered Bruce, " I doubt I have slain
Comyn."—" Doubtest thou ? " said Kirkpatrick ; " I make sicker," (*i. e.* sure.)   With these words, he and Lindsay rushed into
the church, and despatched the wounded Comyn.   The Kirkpa-
tricks of Closeburn assumed, in memory of this deed, a hand holding a dagger, with the memorable words, " I make sicker."   Some

doubt having been started by the late Lord Hailes as to the identity of the Kirkpatrick who completed this day's work with Sir Roger, then representative of the ancient family of Closeburn, my kind and ingenious friend, Mr Charles Kirkpatricke Sharpe, has furnished me with the following memorandum, which appears to fix the deed with his ancestor:

" The circumstances of the Regent Cummin's murder, from which the family of Kirkpatrick, in Nithsdale, is said to have derived its crest and motto, are well known to all conversant with Scottish history; but Lord Hailes has started a doubt as to the authenticity of this tradition, when recording the murder of Roger Kirkpatrick, in his own Castle of Caerlaverock, by Sir James Lindsay. ' Fordun,' says his Lordship, ' remarks that Lindsay and Kirkpatrick were the heirs of the two men who accompanied Robert Brus at the fatal conference with Comyn. If Fordun was rightly informed as to this particular, an argument arises, in support of a notion which I have long entertained, that the person who struck his dagger in Comyn's heart, was *not* the representative of the honourable family of Kirkpatrick in Nithsdale. Roger de K. was made prisoner at the battle of Durham, in 1346. Roger de Kirkpatrick was alive on the 6th of August, 1357; for, on that day, Humphry, the son and heir of Roger de K., is proposed as one of the young gentlemen who were to be hostages for David Bruce. Roger de K. Miles was present at the Parliament held at Edinburgh, 25th September, 1357, and he is mentioned as alive 3d October, 1357, (*Fœdera ;*) it follows, of necessary consequence, that Rodger de K., murdered in June, 1357, must have been a different person.'—*Annals of Scotland,* vol. ii. p. 242.

" To this it may be answered, that at the period of the regent's murder, there were only *two* families of the name of Kirkpatrick (nearly allied to each other) in existence—Stephen Kirkpatrick, styled in the chartulary of Kelso (1278) *Dominus villæ de Closeburn, Filius et hæres Domini Ade de Kirkpatrick, Militis,* (whose father, Ivone de Kirkpatrick, witnesses a charter of Robert Brus, Lord of Annandale, before the year 1141,) had two sons, Sir Roger, who carried on the line of Closeburn, and Duncan, who married Isobel, daughter and heiress of Sir David Torthorwald of that

Ilk; they had a charter of the lands of Torthorwald from King
Robert Brus, dated 10th August, the year being omitted—
Umphray the son of Duncan and Isobel, got a charter of Torthorwald from the king, 16th July, 1322—his son, Roger of Torthorwald, got a charter from John the Grahame, son of Sir John
Grahame of Mosskessen, of an annual rent of 40 shillings, out of
the lands of Overdryft, 1355—his son, William Kirkpatrick, grants
a charter to John of Garroch, of the twa merk land of Glengip and
Garvellgill, within the tenement of Wamphray, 22d April, 1372.
From this, it appears that the Torthorwald branch was not con-
cerned in the affair of Comyn's murder, and the inflictions of Pro-
vidence which ensued : Duncan Kirkpatrick, if we are to believe
the Blind Minstrel, was the firm friend of Wallace, to whom he
was related ; —

> ' Ane Kyrk Patrick, that cruel was and keyne,
> In Eadaill wod that half yer he had beyne ;
> With Inglise men he couth nocht weyll accord.
> Off Torthorowald he Barron was and Lord,
> Off kyn he was, and Wallace modyr ner ;—&c.
>
> B. v., v. 920.

But this Baron seems to have had no share in the adventures of
King Robert; the crest of his family, as it still remains on a
carved stone built into a cottage wall, in the village of Torthorwald, bears some resemblance, says Grose, to a rose.

" Universal tradition, and all our later historians, have attributed the regent's death-blow to Sir Roger K. of Closeburn. The
author of the MS. History of the Presbytery of Penpont, in the
Advocates' Library, affirms, that the crest and motto were given
by the king on that occasion ; and proceeds to relate some circumstances respecting a grant to a cottager and his wife in the vicinity
of Closeburn Castle, which are certainly authentic, and strongly
vouch for the truth of the other report.—' The steep hill,' (says
he,) ' called the Dune of Tynron, of a considerable height, upon
the top of which there hath been some habitation or fort. There
have been in ancient times, on all hands of it, very thick woods,
and great about that place, which made it the more inaccessible,
into which K. Ro. Bruce is said to have been conducted by Roger

Kirkpatrick of Closeburn, after they had killed the Cumin at
Dumfriess, which is nine miles from this place, whereabout it is
probable that he did abide for some time thereafter; and it is reported, that during his abode there, he did often divert to a poor
man's cottage, named Brownrig, situate in a small parcel of stoney
ground, incompassed with thick woods, where he was content
sometimes with such mean accommodation as the place could afford. The poor man's wife being advised to petition the king for
somewhat, was so modest in her desires, that she sought no more
but security for the croft in her husband's possession, and a liberty of pasturage for a very few cattle of different kinds on the hill,
and the rest of the bounds. Of which priviledge that ancient family, by the injury of time, hath a long time been, and is, deprived : but the croft continues in the possession of the heirs and
successours lineally descended of this Brownrig and his wife; so
that this family, being more ancient than rich, doth yet continue
in the name, and, as they say, retains the old charter."—*MS.
History of the Presbytery of Penpont, in the Advocates' Library
of Edinburgh.*

Note H.

*Where's Nigel Bruce ? and De la Haye,
And valiant Seton—where are they ?
Where Somerville, the kind and free ?
And Fraser, flower of chivalry ?*—P. 84.

When these lines were written, the author was remote from
the means of correcting his indistinct recollection concerning the
individual fate of Bruce's followers, after the battle of Methven.
Hugh de la Haye, and Thomas Somerville of Lintoun and Cow-
dally, ancestor of Lord Somerville, were both made prisoners at
that defeat, but neither was executed.

Sir Nigel Bruce was the younger brother of Robert, to whom
he committed the charge of his wife and daughter, Marjorie, and
the defence of his strong castle of Kildrummie, near the head of
the Don, in Aberdeenshire. Kildrummie long resisted the arms

of the Earls of Lancaster and Hereford, until the magazine was treacherously burnt. The garrison was then compelled to surrender at discretion, and Nigel Bruce, a youth remarkable for personal beauty, as well as for gallantry, fell into the hands of the unrelenting Edward. He was tried by a special commission at Berwick, was condemned, and executed.

Christopher Seatoun shared the same unfortunate fate. He also was distinguished by personal valour, and signalized himself in the fatal battle of Methven. Robert Bruce adventured his person in that battle like a knight of romance. He dismounted Aymer de Valence, Earl of Pembroke, but was in his turn dismounted by Sir Philip Mowbray. In this emergence Seatoun came to his aid, and remounted him. Langtoft mentions, that in this battle the Scottish wore white surplices, or shirts, over their armour, that those of rank might not be known. In this manner both Bruce and Seatoun escaped. But the latter was afterwards betrayed to the English, through means, according to Barbour, of one MacNab, "a disciple of Judas," in whom the unfortunate knight reposed entire confidence. There was some peculiarity respecting his punishment; because, according to Matthew of Westminster, he was considered not as a Scottish subject, but an Englishman. He was therefore taken to Dumfries, where he was tried, condemned, and executed, for the murder of a soldier slain by him. His brother, John de Seton, had the same fate at Newcastle; both were considered as accomplices in the slaughter of Comyn; but in what manner they were particularly accessary to that deed does not appear.

The fate of Sir Simon Fraser, or Frizel, ancestor of the family of Lovat, is dwelt upon at great length, and with savage exultation, by the English historians. This knight, who was renowned for personal gallantry, and high deeds of chivalry, was also made prisoner, after a gallant defence, in the battle of Methven. Some stanzas of a ballad of the times, which, for the sake of rendering it intelligible, I have translated out of its rude orthography, give minute particulars of his fate. It was written immediately at the period, for it mentions the Earl of Athole as not yet in custody It was first published by the indefatigable Mr Ritson, but with so

many contractions and peculiarities of character, as to render it
illegible, excepting by antiquaries.

> " This was before Saint Bartholomew's mass,
> That Frizel was y-taken, were it more other less,
> To Sir Thomas of Multon, gentil baron and free.
> And to Sir Johan Jose be-take tho was he
> > To hand
> > He was y-fettered wele
> > Both with iron and with steel
> > > To bringen of Scotland.

> " Soon thereafter the tiding to the king come,
> He sent him to London, with mony armed groom,
> He came in at Newgate, I tell you it on a-plight,
> A garland of leaves on his head y-dight
> > Of green,
> > For he should be y-know
> > Both of high and of low,
> > > For traitour I ween.

> " Y-fettered were his legs under his horse's wombe,
> Both with iron and with steel mancled were his hond,
> A garland of pervynk [1] set upon his heved, [2]
> Much was the power that him was bereved.
> > In land.
> > So God me amend,
> > Little he ween'd
> > > So to be brought in hand.

> " This was upon our lady's even, forsooth I understand,
> The justices sate for the knights of Scotland.
> Sir Thomas of Multon, an kinde knyght and wise,
> And Sir Ralph of Sandwich that mickle is told in price,
> > And Sir Johan Abel,
> > Moe I might tell my tale
> > Both of great and of small
> > > Ye know sooth well.

---

[1] Periwinckle.   [2] Head.

" Then said the justice, that gentil is and free,
Sir Simond Frizel the king's traiter hast thou be ;
In water and in land that mony mighten see,
What sayst thou thereto, how will thou quite thee,
                    Do say.
            So foul he him wist,
            Nede war on trust
                        For to say nay.

" With fetters and with gives¹ y-hot he was to-draw
From the Tower of London that many men might know,
In a kirtle of burel, a selcouth wise,
And a garland on his head of the new guise.
                        Through Cheape
            Many men of England
            For to see Symond
                        Thitherward can leap.

" Though he cam to the gallows first he was on hung,
All quick beheaded that him thought long ;
Then he was y-opened, his bowels y-brend,²
The heved to London-bridge was send
                            To shende.
            So evermore mote I the,
            Some while weened he
                        Thus little to stand.³

" He rideth through the city, as I tell may,
With gamen and with solace that was their play,
To London-bridge he took the way,
Mony was the wives child that thereon lacketh a day,⁴
                        And said, alas !
            That he was y-born
            And so vilely forlorn,
                        So fair man he was.⁵

" Now standeth the heved above the tu-brigge,
Fast by Wallace sooth for to segge ;

¹ He was condemned to be drawn.—² Burned.—³ Meaning, at one time he little
thought to stand thus.—⁴ viz. Saith Lack-a-day.—⁵ The gallant knight, like
others in the same situation, was pitied by the female spectators as " a proper
young man."

After succoour of Scotland long may he pry,
And after help of France what halt it to lie,
I ween,
Better him were in Scotland,
With his axe in his hand,
To play on the green," &c.

The preceding stanzas contain probably as minute an account as can be found of the trial and execution of state criminals of the period. Superstition mingled its horrors with those of a ferocious state policy, as appears from the following singular narrative.

"The Friday next, before the assumption of Our Lady, King Edward met Robert the Bruce at St Johnstoune, in Scotland, and with his company, of which company King Edward qðelde seven thousand. When Robert the Bruce saw this mischief, and gan to flee, and hov'd him that men might not him find; but S. Simond Frisell pursued was so sore, so that he turned again and abode bataille, for he was a worthy knight and a bolde of bodye, and the Englishmen pursued him sore on every side, and quelde the steed that Sir Simon Frisell rode upon, and then toke him and led him to the host. And S. Symond began for to flatter and speke fair, and saide, Lordys, I shall give you four thousand markes of silver, and myne horse and harness, and all my armoure and income. Tho' answered Thobaude of Pevenes, that was the kinge's archer, Now, God me so helpe, it is for nought that thou speakest, for all the gold of England I would not let thee go without commandment of King Edward. And tho' he was led to the King, and the King would not see him, but commanded to lead him away to his doom in London, on Our Lady's even nativity. And he was hung and drawn, and his head smitten off, and hanged again with chains of iron upon the gallows, and his head was set at London-bridge upon a spear, and against Christmas the body was burnt, for encheson (*reason*) that the men that keeped the body saw many devils ramping with iron crooks, running upon the gallows, and horribly tormenting the body. And many that them saw, anon thereafter, died for dread, or waxen mad, or sore sickness they had."—*MS. Chronicle in the British Museum, quoted by Ritson.*

Note I.

I feel within mine aged breast
A power that will not be repress'd.—P. 91.

Bruce, like other heroes, observed omens, and one is recorded by tradition. After he had retreated to one of the miserable places of shelter, in which he could venture to take some repose after his disasters, he lay stretched upon a handful of straw, and abandoned himself to his melancholy meditations. He had now been defeated four times, and was upon the point of resolving to abandon all hope's of further opposition to his fate, and to go to the Holy Land. It chanced his eye, while he was thus pondering, was attracted by the exertions of a spider, who, in order to fix his web, endeavoured to swing himself from one beam to another above his head. Involuntarily he became interested in the pertinacity with which the insect renewed his exertions, after failing six times; and it occurred to him that he would decide his own course according to the success or failure of the spider. At the seventh effort the insect gained his object; and Bruce, in like manner, persevered and carried his own. Hence it has been held unlucky or ungrateful, or both, in one of the name of Bruce to kill a spider.

The archdeacon of Aberdeen, instead of the abbot of this tale, introduces an Irish Pythoness, who not only predicted his good fortune as he left the island of Rachrin, but sent her two sons along with him, to ensure her own family a share in it.

> " Then in schort time men mycht thaim se
> Schute all thair galayis to the se,
> And ber to see baith ayr and ster'
> And othyr thingis that mystir[1] wer.
> And as the king apon the sand
> Wes gangand wp and doun, bidand[2]
> Till that his menye redy war,
> His ost come rycht till him thar.
> And quhen that scho him halyst had,
> And priwé spek till him scho made ;

[1] Need.   [2] Abiding.

Aud said, ' Takis gud kep till my saw :
For or ye pass I sall yow schaw,
Off your fortoun a gret party
Bot our all speceally
A wyttring her I sall yow ma,
Quhat end that your purposs sall ta.
For in this land is nane trew
Wate thingis to cum sa weill as I.
Ye pass now furth on your wiage,
To wenge the harme, and the owtrag,
That Ingliss men has to yow done :
Bot ye wat nocht quhatkyne forton
Ye mon droy in your werraying.
Bot wyt ye weill, with outyn lesing,
That fra ye now haiff takyn land,
Nane sa mychty, na sa strenth thi of hand,
Sall ger yow pass owt of your countré
Till all to yow abandownyt be.
With in schort tyme ye sall be king,
And haiff the land at your liking.
And ourcum your fayis all.
Bot fele anoyis thole ye sall,
Or that your purposs end haiff tane :
Bot ye sall thaim ourdryve ilkane.
And, that ye trow this sekyrly,
My twa sonnys with yow sall I
Send to tak part of your trawaill ;
For I wate weill thai sall nocht faill
To be rewardyt weill at rycht,
Quhen ye ar heyit to yowr mycht.' "

BARBOUR's Bruce, Book III. v. 866.

NOTE K.

A hunted wanderer on the wild,
On foreign shores a man exiled.—P. 91.

This is not metaphorical.   The echoes of Scotland did actually

—— " ring
With the bloodhounds that bayed for her fugitive king."

A very curious and romantic tale is told by Barbour upon this
subject, which may be abridged as follows : —

When Bruce had again got footing in Scotland in the spring of
1306, he continued to be in a very weak and precarious condition,
gaining, indeed, occasional advantages, but obliged to fly before
his enemies whenever they assembled in force.   Upon one occasion, while he was lying with a small party in the wilds of Cum-
nock, in Ayrshire, Aymer de Valence, Earl of Pembroke, with
his inveterate foe John of Lorn, came against him suddenly with
eight hundred Highlanders, besides a large body of men-at-arms.
They brought with them a slough-dog, or bloodhound, which,
some say, had been once a favourite with the Bruce himself, and
therefore was least likely to lose the trace.

Bruce, whose force was under four hundred men, continued to
make head against the cavalry, till the men of Lorn had nearly cut
off his retreat.   Perceiving the danger of his situation, he acted as
the celebrated and ill-requited Mina is said to have done in similar
circumstances.   He divided his force into three parts, appointed a
place of rendezvous, and commanded them to retreat by different
routes.   But when John of Lorn arrived at the spot where they
divided, he caused the hound to be put upon the trace, which immediately directed him to the pursuit of that party which Bruce
headed.   This, therefore, Lorn pursued with his whole force, paying no attention to the others.   The king again subdivided his small
body into three parts, and with the same result, for the pursuers
attached themselves exclusively to that which he led in person.
He then caused his followers to disperse, and retained only his
foster-brother in his company.   The slough-dog followed the trace,
and, neglecting the others, attached himself and his attendants to
pursuit of the king.   Lorn became convinced that his enemy was
nearly in his power, and detached five of his most active attendants
to follow him, and interrupt his flight.   They did so with all the
agility of mountaineers.   "What aid wilt thou make?" said
Bruce to his single attendant, when he saw the five men gain
ground on him.   "The best I can," replied his foster-brother.
"Then," said Bruce, "here I make my stand."   The five pursuers came up fast.   The king took three to himself, leaving the

other two to his foster-brother. He slew the first who encountered him; but observing his foster-brother hard pressed, he sprung to his assistance, and despatched one of his assailants. Leaving him to deal with the survivor, he returned upon the other two, both of whom he slew before his foster-brother had despatched his single antagonist. When this hard encounter was over, with a courtesy, which in the whole work marks Bruce's character, he thanked his foster-brother for his aid. "It likes you to say so," answered his follower; "but you yourself slew four of the five." —"True," said the king, "but only because I had better opportunity than you. They were not apprehensive of me when they saw me encounter three, so I had a moment's time to spring to thy aid, and to return equally unexpectedly upon my own opponents."

In the meanwhile Lorn's party approached rapidly, and the king and his foster-brother betook themselves to a neighbouring wood. Here they sat down, for Bruce was exhausted by fatigue, until the cry of the slough-hound came so near, that his foster-brother entreated Bruce to provide for his safety by retreating further. "I have heard," answered the king, "that whosoever will wade a bow-shot length down a running stream, shall make the slough-hound lose scent.—Let us try the experiment, for were yon devilish hound silenced, I should care little for the rest."

Lorn in the meanwhile advanced, and found the bodies of his slain vassals, over whom he made his moan, and threatened the most deadly vengeance. Then he followed the hound to the side of the brook, down which the king had waded a great way. Here the hound was at fault, and John of Lorn, after long attempting in vain to recover Bruce's trace, relinquished the pursuit.

"Others," says Barbour, "affirm, that upon this occasion the king's life was saved by an excellent archer who accompanied him, and who perceiving they would be finally taken by means of the blood-hound, hid himself in a thicket, and shot him with an arrow. In which way," adds the metrical biographer, "this escape happened, I am uncertain, but at that brook the king escaped from his pursuers."

> "Quhen the chasseris relyit war,
> And Jhon of Lorn had met thaim thar,

He tauld Schyr Aymer all the cass
How that the king eschapyt wass;
And how that he his five men slew,
And syne to the wode him drew.
Quhen Schyr Aymer herd this, in hy
He sanyt him for the ferly;
And said; ' He is gretly to pryss;
For I knaw nane that liffand is,
That at myscheyff gan help him swa.
I trow he suld be hard to sla.
And he war bodyn ¹ ewynly.'
On this wiss spak Schyr Aymery."

BARBOUR's *Bruce*, Book v. v. 391.

The English historians agree with Barbour as to the mode in
which the English pursued Bruce and his followers, and the dexterity with which he evaded them.   The following is the testimony of Harding, a great enemy to the Scottish nation:—

" The King Edward with hoost hym sought full sore,
But ay he fled into woodes and strayte forest,
And slewe his men at staytes and daungers thore,
 And at marreys and mires was ay full prest
Englyshmen to kyll withoutyn any rest;
In the mountaynes and cragges he slew ay where,
And in the nyght his foes he frayed full sere;

" The King Edward with hornes and houndes him soght,
With menne on fote, through marris, mosse, and myre,
Through wodes also, and mountens (wher thei fought,)
And euer the Kyng Edward hight men greate hyre,
Hym for to take and by myght conquere;
But thei might hym not gette by force ne by train,
He satte by the fyre when thei went in the rain."

HARDYNG's *Chronicle*, p. 303-4.

Peter Langtoft has also a passage concerning the extremities to
which King Robert was reduced, which he entitles

De Roberto Brus et fuga circum circa fit.

" And wele I understode that the Kyng Robyn
Has drunken of that blode the drink of Dan Waryn.

¹ Matched.

Dan Waryn he les iounes that he held,
With wron ghe mad a res, and misberyng of scheld,
Sithen into the forest he yede naked and wode,
Als a wild beast, ete of the gres that stode,
Thus of Dan Waryn in his boke men rede,
God gyf the King Robyn, that alle his kynde so spede,
Sir Robynet the Brus he durst noure abide,
That thei mad him reatus, both in more and wod-side,
To while he mad this train, and did umwhile outrage." &c.

PETER LANGTOFT's Chronicle. vol. ii. p. 335,
8vo, London, 1810.

NOTE L.

These are the savage wilds that lie,
North of Strathnardill and Dunskye.—P. 108.

The extraordinary piece of scenery which I have here attempted to describe, is, I think, unparalleled in any part of Scotland, at least in any which I have happened to visit. It lies just upon the frontier of the Laird of MacLeod's country, which is thereabouts divided from the estate of Mr Maccallister of Strath-Aird, called Strathnardill by the Dean of the Isles. The following account of it is extracted from a journal [1] kept during a tour through the Scottish islands :—

"The western coast of Skye is highly romantic, and at the same time displays a richness of vegetation in the lower grounds to which we have hitherto been strangers. We passed three salt-water lochs, or deep embayments, called Loch Bracadale, Loch Einort, and Loch ——, and about 11 o'clock opened Loch Slavig. We were now under the western termination of the high ridge of mountains called Cuillen, or Quillin, or Coolin, whose weather-beaten and serrated peaks we had admired at a distance from Dunvegan. They sunk here upon the sea, but with the same bold and peremptory aspect which their distant appearance indicated. They appeared to consist of precipitous sheets of naked rock, down which the torrents were leaping in a hundred lines of foam. The

---

[1] [This is the Poet's own journal.—ED.]

tops of the ridge, apparently inaccessible to human foot, were rent and split into the most tremendous pinnacles. Towards the base of these bare and precipitous crags, the ground, enriched by the soil washed down from them, is comparatively verdant and productive. Where we passed within the small isle of Soa, we entered Loch Slavig, under the shoulder of one of these grisly mountains, and observed that the opposite side of the loch was of a milder character, the mountains being softened down into steep green declivities. From the bottom of the bay advanced a headland of high rocks, which divided its depth into two recesses, from each of which a brook issued. Here it had been intimated to us we would find some romantic scenery; but we were uncertain up which inlet we should proceed in search of it. We chose, against our better judgment, the southerly dip of the bay, where we saw a house which might afford us information. We found, upon enquiry, that there is a lake adjoining to each branch of the bay; and walked a couple of miles to see that near the farm-house, merely because the honest highlander seemed jealous of the honour of his own loch, though we were speedily convinced it was not that which we were recommended to examine. It had no particular merit, excepting from its neighbourhood to a very high cliff, or precipitous mountain, otherwise the sheet of water had nothing differing from any ordinary low-country lake. We returned and re-embarked in our boat, for our guide shook his head at our proposal to climb over the peninsula, or rocky headland which divided the two lakes. In rowing round the headland, we were surprised at the infinite number of sea-fowl, then busy apparently with a shoal of fish.

"Arrived at the depth of the bay, we found that the discharge from this second lake forms a sort of waterfall, or rather a rapid stream, which rushes down to the sea with great fury and precipitation. Round this place were assembled hundreds of trouts and salmon, struggling to get up into the fresh water: with a net we might have had twenty salmon at a haul; and a sailor, with no better hook than a crooked pin, caught a dish of trouts during our absence. Advancing up this huddling and riotous brook, we found ourselves in a most extraordinary scene; we lost sight of the sea almost immediately after we had climbed over a low ridge of crags, and were surrounded by mountains of naked rock, of the boldest and most precipitous character. The ground on which we walked was the margin of a lake, which seemed to have sustained the constant ravage of torrents from these rude neighbours. The shores consisted of huge strata of naked granite, here and there intermixed with bogs, and heaps of gravel and sand piled in the empty water-courses. Vegetation there was little or none; and the mountains rose so perpendicularly from the water edge, that Borrowdale, or even Glencoe, is a jest to them. We proceeded a mile and a half up this deep, dark, and solitary lake, which was about two miles long, half a mile broad, and is, as we learned, of extreme depth. The murky vapours which enveloped the mountain ridges, obliged us by assuming a thousand varied shapes, changing their drapery into all sorts of forms, and sometimes clearing off altogether. It is true, the mist made us pay the penalty by some heavy and downright showers, from the frequency of which a Highland boy, whom we brought from the farm, told us the lake was popularly called the Water-kettle. The proper name is Loch Corriskin, from the deep corrie, or hollow, in the mountains of Cuillen, which affords the basin for this wonderful sheet of water. It is as exquisite a savage scene as Loch Katrine is a scene of romantic beauty. After having penetrated so far as distinctly to observe the termination of the lake under an immense precipice, which rises abruptly from the water, we returned, and often stopped to admire the ravages which storms must have made in these recesses, where all human witnesses were driven to places of more shelter and security. Stones, or rather large masses and fragments of rocks, of a composite kind, perfectly different from the strata of the lake, were scattered upon the bare rocky beach, in the strangest and most precarious situations, as if abandoned by the torrents which had borne them down from above. Some lay loose and tottering upon the ledges of the natural rock, with so little security, that the slightest push moved them, though their weight might exceed many tons. These detached rocks, or stones, were chiefly what is called plum-pudding stones. The bare rocks, which formed the shore of the lakes, were a species

of granite.   The opposite side of the lake seemed quite pathless
and inaccessible, as a huge mountain, one of the detached ridges
of the Cuillen hills, sinks in a profound and perpendicular precipice down to the water.   On the left-handside, which we traversed, rose a higher and equally inaccessible mountain, the top
of which strongly resembled the shivered crater of an exhausted
volcano.   I never saw a spot in which there was less appearance
of vegetation of any kind.   The eye rested on nothing but barren
and naked crags, and the rocks on which we walked by the side
of the loch, were as bare as the pavements of Cheapside.   There
are one or two small islets in the loch, which seemed to bear ju-
niper, or some such low bushy shrub.   Upon the whole, though
I have seen many scenes of more extensive desolation, I never
witnessed any in which it pressed more deeply upon the eye and
the heart than at Loch Corriskin ; at the same time that its
grandeur elevated and redeemed it from the wild and dreary
character of utter barrenness."   •

Note M.

Men were they all of evil mien,
Down-look'd, unwilling to be seen.—P. 115.

The story of Bruce's meeting the banditti is copied, with such
alterations as the fictitious narrative rendered necessary, from a
striking incident in the monarch's history, told by Barbour, and
which I shall give in the words of the hero's biographer.   It is the
sequel to the adventure of the bloodhound, narrated in Note K.
It will be remembered that the narrative broke off, leaving the
Bruce escaped from his pursuers, but worn out with fatigue, and
having no other attendant but his foster-brother.

> " And the gud king held forth his way,
> Betuix him and his man, qubill thai
> Passyt owt throw the forest war ;
> Syne in the more thai entryt thar.
> It wes bathe hey, and lang, and braid ;
> And or thai balff it passyt had,

Thai saw on syd three men cummand,
Lik to lycht men and wauerand.
Swerdis thai had, and axys als;
And ane off thaim, apon his hals,[1]
A mekill boundyn wethir bar.
Thai met the king, and halist[2] him thar:
And the king thaim thar hailsing yauld;[3]
An askyt them quethir thai wauld.
Thai said, Robert the Bruyss thai soucht;
For mete with him giff that thai moucht,
Thar duelling with him wauld thai ma.[4]
The king said, 'Giff that ye will swa,
Haldys furth your way with me,
And I sall ger yow sone him se.'

  " Thai persawyt, be his speking,
That he wes the selwyn Robert king.
And chaungyt contenance and late;[5]
And held nocht in the fyrst state.
For thai war fayis to the king;
And thoucht to cum in to sculking.
And duell with him, quhill that thai saw
Thar poynt, and bryng him than off daw.[6]
Thai grantyt till his spek forthi.[7]
Bot the king, that wes witty,
Persawyt weill, by thair hawing,
That thai luffyt him na thing;
And said, 'Falowis, ye mon, all thre,
Forthir aqwent till that we be,
All be your selwyn furth ga;
And, on the samyn wyss, we twa
Sall folow behind weill ner.'
Quoth thai, 'Schyr, it is na myster[8]
To trow in ws ony ill.'
'Nane do I,' said he; 'bot I will,
That yhe ga fourth thus, quhill we
Better with othyr knawin be.'
'We grant,' thai said, 'sen ye will swa;'
And furth apon thair gate gan ga.

  "Thus yeid thai till the nycht wes ner.
And than the formast cummyn wer

---

[1] Neck.—[2] Saluted.—[3] Returned their salute.—[4] Make.—[5] Gestre or manner.—
[6] Kill him.—[7] Therefore.—[8] There is no need.

Till a waist housband houss; [1] and thar
Thai slew the wethir that thi bar:
And slew fyr for to rost thar mete;
And askyt the king giff he wald ete,
And rest him till the mete war dycht.
The king, that hungry was, Ik hycht,
Assentyt till thair spek in by.
Bot he said, he wald anerly [2]
At a fyr; and thai all thre
On na wyss with thaim till gyddre be.
In the end off the houss thai suld ma
Ane othyr fyr: and thai did swa.
Thai drew thaim in the houss end,
And halff the wethir till him send.
And thai rostyt in hy thair mete;
And fell rycht freschly for till ete.
For the king weill lang fastyt had;
And had rycht mekill trawaill mad:
Tharfor he eyt full egrely.
And quhen he had etyn hastily,
He had to slep sa mekill will,
That he moucht set na let thar till.
For quhen the wanys [3] fillyt ar,
Men worthys [4] hewy euirmar;
And to slepe drawys hewynes.
The king, that all fortrawaillyt [5] wes,
Saw that him worthyt slep nedwayis.
Till his fostyr-brodyr he sayis;
' May I traist in the, me to walk,
Till Ik a litill sleping tak?'
' Ya, Schyr,' he said, ' till I may drey.' [6]
The king then wynkyt a litill wey;
And slepyt nocht full encrely;
Bot gliffuyt wp oft sodanly.
For he had dreid off thai thre men,
That at the tothyr fyr war then,
That thai his fais war he wyst;
Tharfor he slepyt as foule on twyst. [7]

     " The king slepyt bot a litill than;
Quhen sic slep fell on his man,

---

[1] Husbandman's house, cottage.—[2] Alone.—[3] Bellics.—[4] Becomes.—[5] Fatigued,
—[6] Endure.—[7] Bird on bough.

That he mycht nocht hald wp his ey,
Bot fell in slep, and rowtyt hey.
Now is the king in gret perile:
For slep he swa a littil quhile,
He sall be ded, for owtyn dreid.
For the thre tratouris tuk gud held,
That he on slep wes, and his man.
In full gret hy thai rais wp than,
And drew thair suerdis hastily;
And went towart the king in hy,
Quhen that thai saw him sleip swa.
And slepand thoucht thai wald him sla.
The king wp blenkit hastily,
And saw his man slepand him by;
And saw cummand the tothyr thre.
Deliuerly on fute gat he;
And drew his suerd owt, and thaim mete.
And, as he yude, his fute be set
Apon his man, weill hewyly.
He waknyt, and rais disily:
For the slep maistryt hym sway,
That or he gat wp, ane off thai,
That com for to sla the king,
Gaiff hym a strak in his rysing,
Swa that he mycht help him no mar.
The king sa straitly stad [1] wes thar,
That he wes neuir yeyt sa stad.
Ne war the armyng [2] that he had,
He had bene dede, for owtyn wer.
But nocht for thi [3] on sic maner
He helpyt him, in that bargayne, [4]
That thai thre tratowris he has slain.
Throw Goddis grace, and his manheid.
His fostyr-brothyr thar wes dede.
Then wes he wondre will of wayn, [5]
Quhen he saw him left allane.
His fostyr-brodyr menyt he;
And waryit [6] all the tothyr thre.
And syne hys way tuk him allane,
And rycht towart his tryst [7] is gane."

The Bruce, Book v. v. 405.

---

[1] So dangerously situated.—[2] Had it not been for the armour he wore —
[3] Nevertheless.—[4] Fray, or dispute.—[5] Much afflicted.—[6] Cursed.—[7] The place
of rendezvous appointed for his soldiers.

NOTE N.

Such hate was his on Solway's strand,
When vengeance clench'd his palsied hand,
That pointed yet to Scotland's land.—P.139.

To establish his dominion in Scotland had been a favourite object of Edward's ambition, and nothing could exceed the pertinacity with which he pursued it, unless his inveterate resentment against the insurgents, who so frequently broke the English yoke when he deemed it most firmly riveted. After the battles of Falkirk and Methven, and the dreadful examples which he had made of Wallace and other champions of national independence, he probably concluded every chance of insurrection was completely annihilated. This was in 1306, when Bruce, as we have seen, was utterly expelled from Scotland : yet, in the conclusion of the same year, Bruce was again in arms and formidable; and in 1307, Edward, though exhausted by a long and wasting malady, put himself at the head of the army destined to destroy him utterly. This was, perhaps, partly in consequence of a vow which he had taken upon him, with all the pomp of chivalry, upon the day in which he dubbed his son a knight, for which see a subsequent note. But even his spirit of vengeance was unable to restore his exhausted strength. He reached Burgh-upon-Sands, a petty village of Cumberland, on the shores of the Solway Firth, and there, 6th July, 1307, expired in sight of the detested and devoted country of Scotland. His dying injunctions to his son required him to continue the Scottish war, and never to recall Gaveston. Edward II. disobeyed both charges. Yet, more to mark his animosity, the dying monarch ordered his bones to be carried with the invading army. Froissart, who probably had the authority of eyewitnesses, has given us the following account of this remarkable charge :—

"In the said forest, the old King Robert of Scotland dyd kepe hymselfe, whan King Edward the Fyrst conquered nygh all Scotland ;. for he was so often chased, that none durst loge him in castell, nor fortresse, for feare of the said Kyng.

" And ever whan the King was returned into Ingland, than he
would gather together agayn his people, and conquere townes,
castells, and fortresses, iuste to Berwick, some by battle, and some
by fair speech and love: and when the said King Edward heard
thereof, than would he assemble his power, and wyn the realme of
Scotland again; thus the chance went between these two foresaid
Kings. It was showed me, how that this King Robert wan and
lost his realme v. times. So this continued till the said King Edward died at Berwick: and when he saw that he should die, he
called before him his eldest son, who was King after him, and
there, before all the barones, he caused him to swear, that as soon
as he were dead, that he should take his body, and boyle it in a
cauldron, till the flesh departed clean from the bones, and than to
bury the flesh, and keep still the bones; and that as often as the
Scotts should rebell against him, he should assemble the people
against them, and carry with him the bones of his father; for he
believed verily, that if they had his bones with them, that the Scotts
should never attain any victory against them. The which thing
was not accomplished, for when the King died his son carried him
to London."—BERNERS' FROISSART's *Chronicle*, London, 1812,
pp. 39, 40.

Edward's commands were not obeyed, for he was interred in
Westminster Abbey, with the appropriate inscription:—

" EDWARDUS PRIMUS SCOTORUM MALLEUS HIC EST.

PACTUM SERVA."

Yet some steps seem to have been taken towards rendering his
body capable of occasional transportation, for it was exquisitely
embalmed, as was ascertained when his tomb was opened some
years ago. Edward II. judged wisely in not carrying the dead
body of his father into Scotland, since he would not obey his living counsels.

It ought to be observed, that though the order of the incidents
is reversed in the poem, yet, in point of historical accuracy, Bruce
had landed in Scotland, and obtained some successes of consequence, before the death of Edward I.

NOTE O.

On Scoorcigg next a warning light
Summon'd her warriors to the fight ;
A numerous race, ere stern Macleod
O'er their bleak shores in vengeance strode. —P. 146.

These, and the following lines of the stanza, refer to a dreadful tale of feudal vengeance, of which unfortunately there are relics that still attest the truth. Scoor-Eigg is a high peak in the centre of the small Isle of Eigg, or Egg. It is well known to mineralogists, as affording many interesting specimens, and to others whom chance or curiosity may lead to the island, for the astonishing view of the mainland and neighbouring isles, which it commands. I shall again avail myself of the journal I have quoted [1]

"26th *August*, 1814.—At seven this morning we were in the Sound which divides the Isle of Rum from that of Egg. The latter, although hilly and rocky, and traversed by a remarkably high and barren ridge, called Scoor-Rigg, has, in point of soil, a much more promising appearance. Southward of both lies the Isle of Muich, or Muck, a low and fertile island, and though the least, yet probably the most valuable of the three. We manned the boat, and rowed along the shore of Egg in quest of a cavern, which had been the memorable scene of a horrid feudal vengeance. We had rounded more than half the island, admiring the entrance of many a bold natural cave, which its rocks exhibited, without finding that which we sought, until we procured a guide. Nor, indeed, was it surprising that it should have escaped the search of strangers, as there are no outward indications more than might distinguish the entrance of a fox-earth. This noted cave has a very narrow opening, through which one can hardly creep on his knees and hands. It rises steep and lofty within, and runs into the bowels of the rock to the depth of 255 measured feet ; the height at the entrance may be about three feet, but rises within to eighteen or twenty, and the breadth may vary in the same proportion. The rude and stony bottom of this cave is strewed with the bones of men, women, and

---

[1] [See note to p. 313, *ante*.]

children, the sad relics of the ancient inhabitants of the island, 200
in number, who were slain on the following occasion :—The Mac-
Donalds of the Isle of Egg, a people dependent on Clan-Ranald, had
done some injury to the Laird of Mac-Leod. The tradition of the
isle says, that it was by a personal attack on the chieftain, in which
his back was broken. But that of the other isles bears, more probably, that the injury was offered to two or three of the Mac-
Leods, who, landing upon Eigg, and using some freedom with the
young women, were seized by the islanders, bound hand and foot,
and turned adrift in a boat, which the winds and waves safely conducted to Skye. To avenge the offence given, Mac-Leod sailed
with such a body of men as rendered resistance hopeless. The
natives, fearing his vengeance, concealed themselves in this cavern,
and, after a strict search, the Mac-Leods went on board their galleys, after doing what mischief they could, concluding the inhabitants had left the isle, and betaken themselves to the Long Island,
or some of Clan-Ranald's other possessions. But next morning
they espied from the vessels a man upon the island, and immediately landing again, they traced his retreat by the marks of his
footsteps, a light snow being unhappily on the ground. Mac-
Leod then surrounded the cavern, summoned the subterranean garrison, and demanded that the individuals who had offended him
should be delivered up to him. This was peremptorily refused.
The chieftain then caused his people to divert the course of a rill
of water, which, falling over the entrance of the cave, would have
prevented his purposed vengeance. He then kindled at the entrance of the cavern a huge fire, composed of turf and fern, and
maintained it with unrelenting assiduity, until all within were destroyed by suffocation. The date of this dreadful deed must have
been recent, if one may judge from the fresh appearance of those
relics. I brought off, in spite of the prejudice of our sailors, a skull
from among the numerous specimens of mortality which the cavern
afforded. Before re-embarking we visited another cave, opening
to the sea, but of a character entirely different, being a large open
vault as high as that of a cathedral, and running back a great way
into the rock at the same height. The height and width of the
opening give ample light to the whole. Here, after 1745, when

the Catholic priests were scarcely tolerated, the priest of Eigg used to perform the Roman Catholic service, most of the islanders being of that persuasion. A huge ledge of rocks rising about half-way up one side of the vault, served for altar and pulpit; and the appearance of a priest and Highland congregation in such an extraordinary place of worship, might have engaged the pencil of Salvator."

NOTE P.

Up Tarbat's western lake they bore,
Then dragg'd their bark the isthmus o'er.—P. 151.

The peninsula of Cantire is joined to South Knapdale by a very narrow isthmus, formed by the western and eastern Loch of Tarbat. These two saltwater lakes, or bays, encroach so far upon the land, and the extremities come so near to each other, that there is not above a mile of land to divide them.

"It is not long," says Pennant, "since vessels of nine or ten tons were drawn by horses out of the west loch into that of the east, to avoid the dangers of the Mull of Cantyre, so dreaded and so little known was the navigation round that promontory. It is the opinion of many, that these little isthmuses, so frequently styled Tarbat in North Britain, took their name from the above circumstance; Tarruing, signifying to draw, and Bata, a boat. This too might be called, by way of preeminence, the Tarbat, from a very singular circumstance related by Torfœus. When Magnus, the barefooted King of Norway, obtained from Donald-bane of Scotland the cession of the Western Isles, or all those places that could be surrounded in a boat, he added to them the peninsula of Cantyre by this fraud: he placed himself in the stern of a boat, held the rudder, was drawn over this narrow track, and by this species of navigation wrested the country from his brother monarch."—PENNANT's *Scotland, London,* 1790, p. 190.

But that Bruce also made this passage, although at a period two or three years later than in the poem, appears from the evidence

of Barbour, who mentions also the effect produced upon the minds
of the Highlanders, from the prophecies current amongst them —

" Bot to King Robert will we gang,
That we haff left wnspokyn of lang,
Quhen he had conwoyit to the se
His brodyr Eduuard, and his menye,
And othyr men off gret noblay,
To Tarbart thai held thair way,
In galayis ordanyt for thair far.
Bot thaim worthyt [1] draw thair schippis thar
And a myle wes betuix the seys ;
Bot that wes lompnyt [2] all with treis.
The King his schippis thar gert [3] draw,
And for the wynd couth [4] stoutly blaw
Apon thair bak, as thai wald ga,
He gert men rapys and mastis ta,
And set thaim in the schippis hey,
And sayllis to the toppis tey ;
And gert men gang thar by drawand.
The wynd thaim helpyt, that was blawand ;
Swa that, in a litill space,
Thair flote all our drawin was.

" And quhen thai, that in the Ilis war,
Hard tell how the gud King had thar
Gert hys schippis with saillis ga
Owt our betuix [the] Tarbart [is] twa,
Thai war abaysit [5] sa wtrely.
For thai wyst, throw auld prophecy,
That he that suld ger [6] schippis sua
Betuix thai seis with saillis ga,
Suld wyne the Ilis sua till hand,
That nane with strenth suld him withstand.
Tharfor thai come all to the King,
Wes nane withstud his bidding,
Owtakyn [7] Jhone of Lorne allayne.
Bot weill sone eftre wes he tayne ;
And present rycht to the King,
And thai that war of his leding.

[1] Were obliged to.—[2] Laid with trees.—[3] Caused.—[4] Could.—[5] Confounded.—
[6] Make.—[7] Excepting.

That till the King had brokyn fay,[1]
War all dede, and destroyit away."

BARBOUR's *Bruce*, Book x. v. 431.

NOTE Q.

For, see! the ruddy signal made,
That Clifford, with his merry-men all,
Guards carelessly our father's hall.—P. 187.

The remarkable circumstances by which Bruce was induced to
enter Scotland, under the false idea that a signal-fire was lighted
upon the shore near his maternal castle of Turnberry—the disappointment which he met with, and the train of success which arose
out of that very disappointment, are too curious to be passed over
unnoticed. The following is the narrative of Barbour. The introduction is a favourable specimen of his style, which seems to be
in some degree the model for that of Gawain Douglas:—

> " This wes in ver,[2] quhen wynter tid,
> With his blastis hidwyss to bid,
> Was our drywn ; and byrdis smale,
> As turturis and the nychtyngale.
> Begouth[3] rycht sariely[4] to syng ;
> And for to mak in thair singyng
> Swete notis, and sownys ser,[5]
> And melodys plesand to her.
> And the treis begouth to ma[6]
> Burgeans,[7] and brycht blomys alsua,
> To wyn the helyng[8] off thair hewid,
> That wykkyt wyntir had thaim rewid.[9]
> And all gressys beguth to spryng.
> In to that tyme the nobill king,
> With his flote, and a few menye[10],
> Thre hundyr I trow that mycht be,
> Is to the se, owte off Arane
> A litill forouth,[11] ewyn gane.

[1] Faith.—[2] Spring.—[3] Began.—[4] Loftily.—[5] Several.—[6] Make.—[7] Buds.—[8] Cover-
ing.—[9] Bereaved.—[10] Men.—[11] Before.

" Thai rowit fast, with all thair mycht,
Till that apon thaim fell the nycht,
That woux myrk [1] apon gret maner.
Swa that thai wyst nocht quhar thei wer.
For thai na nedill had, na stane ;
Bot rowyt alwayis in till ane,
Sterand all tyme apon the fyr,
That thai saw brynnand lycht and schyr. [2]
It wes bot auentur [3] thaim led :
And thai in schort tyme sa thaim sped,
That at the fyr arywyt thai ;
And went to land bot mar delay.
And Cuthbert, that has sene the fyr,
Was full of angyr, and off ire ;
For he durst nocht do it away ;
And wes alsua dowtand ay
That his lord suld pass to se.
Tharfor thair commyn waytit he ;
And met thaim at thair arywing.
He wes wele sone broucht to the King,
That speryt at him how he had done.
And he with sar hart tauld him sone.
How that he fand nane weill luffand ;
Bot all war fayis, that he fand ;
And that the lord the Persy,
With ner thre hundre in cumpany,
Was in the castell thar besid,
Fullfillyt off dispyt and prid.
Bot ma than twa partis off his rowt
War herberyt in the toune without ;
' And dyspytyt yow mar, Schir King,
Than men may dispyt ony thing.'
Than said the King, in full gret ire ;
' Tratour, quhy maid thow than the fyr ?'
' A ! Schyr,' said he, ' sa God me se !
The fyr wes newyr maid for me.
Na, or the nycht, I wyst it nocht ;
Bot fra I wyst it, weill I thocht
That ye, and haly your menye,
In hy [4] suld put yow to the se.
For thi I cum to mete yow her,
To tell perellys that may aper.'

[1] Dark.—[2] Clear.—[3] Adventure.—[4] Haste.

" The King wes off his spek angry,
And askyt his prywé men, in hy,
Quhat at thaim thoucht wes best to do.
Schyr Edward fryst answert thar to,
Hys brodyr that wes swa hardy,
And said; ' I say yow sekyrly
Thar sall na perell, that may be,
Dryve me eftsonys [1] to the se.
Myne auentur her tak will I,
Quhethir it be esfull or angry.'
' Brothyr,' he said, ' sen thou will sua,
It is gud that we samyn ta
Dissese or ese, or payne or play,
Eftyr as God will we purway, [2]
And sen men sayis that the Persy
Myn heretage will occupy ;
And his menye sa ner ws lyis,
That ws dispytis mony wyss ;
Ga we and wenge [3] sum off the dispyte
And that may we haiff done alss tite ; [4]
For thai ly traistly, [5] but dreding
Off ws, or off our her cummyng.
And thoucht we slepand slew thaim al!,
Repruff tharof na man sall.
For werrayour na fors suld ma,
Quhethir he mycht ourcom his fa
Throw strenth, or throw sutelté ;
Bot that gud faith ay haldyn be.' "

BARBOUR's Bruce, Book iv. v. 1.

NOTE R.

The Bruce hath won his father's hall!—P. 214.

I have followed the flattering and pleasing tradition, that the Bruce, after his descent upon the coast of Ayrshire, actually gained possession of his maternal castle. But the tradition is not accurate. The fact is, that he was only strong enough to alarm and drive in the outposts of the English garrison, then commanded, not

---

[*] Soon after.—[2] Prepare.—[3] Avenge.—[4] Quickly.—[5] Confidently.

by Clifford, as assumed in the text, but by Percy. Neither was
Clifford slain upon this occasion, though he had several skirmishes
with Bruce. He fell afterwards in the battle of Bannockburn.
Bruce, after alarming the castle of Turnberry, and surprising some
part of the garrison, who were quartered without the walls of the
fortress, retreated into the mountainous part of Carrick, and there
made himself so strong, that the English were obliged to evacuate
Turnberry, and at length the Castle of Ayr. Many of his bene-
factions and royal gifts attest his attachment to the hereditary followers of his house, in this part of the country.

It is generally known that Bruce, in consequence of his distresses
after the battle of Methven, was affected by a scorbutic disorder,
which was then called a leprosy. It is said he experienced benefit
from the use of a medicinal spring, about a mile north of the town
of Ayr, called from that circumstance King's Ease.[1] The following is the tradition of the country, collected by Mr Train :—"After
Robert ascended the throne, he founded the priory of Dominican
monks, every one of whom was under the obligation of putting up
to Heaven a prayer once every week-day, and twice in holydays,
for the recovery of the king; and, after his death, these masses
were continued for the saving of his soul. The ruins of this old
monastery are now nearly level with the ground. Robert likewise
caused houses to be built round the well of King's Ease, for eight
lepers, and allowed eight bolls of oatmeal, and 28l. Scotch money,
per annum, to each person. These donations were laid upon the
lands of Fullarton, and are now payable by the Duke of Portland.
The farm of Shiels, in the neighbourhood of Ayr, has to give, if
required, a certain quantity of straw for the lepers' beds, and so
much to thatch their houses annually. Each leprous person had a
drinking-horn provided him by the king, which continued to be
hereditary in the house to which it was first granted. One of those
identical horns, of very curious workmanship, was in the possession of the late Colonel Fullarton of that Ilk."

---

[1] [Sir Walter Scott had misread Mr Train's MS., which gave not *King's Ease*,
but *King's Case*, i. e. *Casa Regis*, the name of the royal foundation described below. Mr Train's kindness enables the Editor to make this correction. 1833.]

My correspondent proceeds to mention some curious remnants
of antiquity respecting this foundation. "In compliment to Sir
William Wallace, the great deliverer of his country, King Robert
Bruce invested the descendants of that hero with the right of
placing all the lepers upon the establishment of King's Case. This
patronage continued in the family of Craigie, till it was sold along
with the lands of the late Sir Thomas Wallace. The burgh of Ayr
then purchased the right of applying the donations of King's Case
to the support of the poor-house of Ayr. The lepers' charter-stone
was a basaltic block, exactly the shape of a sheep's kidney, and
weighing an Ayrshire boll of meal. The surface of this stone being
as smooth as glass, there was not any other way of lifting it than
by turning the hollow to the ground, there extending the arms
along each side of the stone, and clasping the hands in the cavity.
Young lads were always considered as deserving to be ranked
among men, when they could lift the blue stone of King's Case. It
always lay beside the well, till a few years ago, when some English
dragoons encamped at that place wantonly broke it, since which the
fragments have been kept by the freemen of Prestwick in a place
of security. There is one of these charter-stones at the village of
Old Daily, in Carrick, which has become more celebrated by the
following event, which happened only a very few years ago :— The
village of New Daily being now larger than the old place of the
same name, the inhabitants insisted that the charter-stone should
be removed from the old town to the new, but the people of Old
Daily were unwilling to part with their ancient right. Demands
and remonstrances were made on each side without effect, till at
last man, woman, and child, of both villages, marched out, and by
one desperate engagement put an end to a war, the commencement
of which no person then living remembered. Justice and victory,
in this instance, being of the same party, the villagers of the old
town of Daily now enjoy the pleasure of keeping the *blue-stane*
unmolested. Ideal privileges are often attached to some of these
stones. In Girvan, if a man can set his back against one of the
above description, he is supposed not liable to be arrested for debt,
nor can cattle, it is imagined, be poinded as long as they are fastened to the same stone. That stones were often used as symbols

to denote the right of possessing land, before the use of written
documents became general in Scotland, is, I think, exceedingly
probable.   The charter-stone of Inverness is still kept with great
care, set in a frame, and hooped with iron, at the market-place of
that town.   It is called by the inhabitants of that district Clack
na Couddin.   I think it is very likely that Carey has mentioned
this stone in his poem of Craig Phaderick.   This is only a conjecture, as I have never seen that work.   While the famous marble
chair was allowed to remain at Scoon, it was considered as the
charter-stone of the kingdom of Scotland."

Note S.

" Bring here," he said, " the mazers four,
My noble fathers loved of yore."—P. 215.

These mazers were large drinking-cups, or goblets.   Mention
of them occurs in a curious inventory of the treasure and jewels
of James III., which will be published, with other curious documents of antiquity, by my friend, Mr Thomas Thomson, D. Register of Scotland, under the title of "A Collection of Inventories,
and other Records of the Royal Wardrobe, Jewel-House," &c.
I copy the passage, in which mention is made of the mazers, and
also of a habiliment, called " King Robert Bruce's serk," i. e.
shirt, meaning, perhaps, his shirt of mail; although no other arms
are mentioned in the inventory.   It might have been a relic of
more sanctified description, a penance shirt perhaps.

*Extract from " Inventare of ane Parte of the Gold and Silver
conyeit and unconyeit, Jowellis, and uther Stuff perteining to
Umquhile oure Soverane Lords Fader, that he had in Depois
the Tyme of his Deceis, and that come to the Handis of oure
Soverane Lord that now is,* M.CCCC.LXXXVIII."

" Memorandum fundin in a bandit kist like a gardeviant,[1] in the
fyrst the grete chenye[2] of gold, contenand sevin score sex linkis.

---

[1] Gard-vin, or wine-cooler.—[2] Chain.

Item, thre platis of silver.

Item, tuelf salfatis.[1]

Item, fyftene discheis[2] ouregilt.

Item, a grete gilt plate.

Item, twa grete bassingis[3] ouregilt.

Item, FOUR MASARIS, CALLED KING ROBERT THE BROCIS, with a cover.

Item, a grete cok maid of silver.

Item, the hede of silver of ane of the coveris of masar.

Item, a fare dialle.[4]

Item, twa kasis of knyffis.[5]

Item, a pare of auld kniffis.

Item, takin be the smyth that opinnit the lokkis, in gold fourty demyis.

Item, in Inglys grotis[6] - - - - - - - - - xxiiii li, and the said silver given again to the takaris of hym.

Item, ressavit in the cloissat of Davidis tour, ane haly water-fat of silver, twa boxis, a cageat tume, a glas with rois-water, a dosoune of torchis, KING ROBERT BRUCIS SERK."

The real use of the antiquarian's studies, is to bring the minute information which he collects to bear upon points of history. For example, in the inventory I have just quoted, there is given the contents of the *black kist*, or chest, belonging to James III., which was his strong box, and contained a quantity of treasure, in money and jewels, surpassing what might have been at the period expected of "poor Scotland's gear." This illustrates and authenticates a striking passage in the history of the house of Douglas, by Hume of Godscroft. The last Earl of Douglas (of the elder branch) had been reduced to monastic seclusion in the Abbey of Lindores, by James II. James III., in his distresses, would willingly have recalled him to public life, and made him his lieutenant. "But he," says Godscroft, "laden with years and old age, and weary of troubles, refused, saying, Sir, you have kept mee, and your *black*

---

[1] Salt-cellars, anciently the object of much curious workmanship.—[2] Dishes.—[3] Basins.—[4] Dial.—[5] Cases of knives.—[6] English groats.

coffer in Sterling, too long, neither of us can doe you any good : I, because my friends have forsaken me, and my followers and dependers are fallen from me, betaking themselves to other masters ; and your black trunk is too farre from you, and your enemies are between you and it: or (as others say) because there was in it a sort of black coyne, that the king had caused to be coyned by the advice of his courtiers ; which moneyes (saith he) sir, if you had put out at the first, the people would have taken it ; and if you had employed mee in due time I might have done you service. But now there is none that will take notice of me, nor meddle with your money."—HUME's *History of the House of Douglas*, fol. Edin. 1644, p. 206.

NOTE T.

When English blood oft delug'd Douglas-dale.—P. 222.

The " good Lord James of Douglas," during these commotions, often took from the English his own castle of Douglas, but being unable to garrison it, contented himself with destroying the fortifications, and retiring into the mountains. As a reward to his patriotism, it is said to have been prophesied, that how often soever Douglas Castle should be destroyed, it should always again arise more magnificent from its ruins. Upon one of these occasions he used fearful cruelty, causing all the store of provisions, which the English had laid up in his castle, to be heaped together, bursting the wine and beer casks among the wheat and flour, slaughtering the cattle upon the same spot, and upon the top of the whole cutting the throats of the English prisoners. This pleasantry of " the good Lord James" is commemorated under the name of the *Douglas's Larder.* A more pleasing tale of chivalry is recorded by Godscroft. " By this means, and such other exploits, he so affrighted the enemy, that it was counted a matter of great jeopardie to keep this castle, which began to be called the *adventurous* (or hazardous) *Castle of Douglas ;* whereupon Sir John Walton being in suit of an English lady, she wrote to him, that when he had kept the adventurous Castle of Douglas seven years, then he might think himself worthy to be a suitor to her. Upon this occasion Walton took upon him the keeping of it, and succeeded to Thruswall, but he ran the same fortune with the rest that were before him. For Sir James, having first dressed an ambuscade near unto the place, he made fourteen of his men take so many sacks, and fill them with grass, as though it had been corn, which they carried in the way to Lanark, the chief market-town in that county : so hoping to draw forth the captain by that bait, and either to take him or the castle, or both. Neither was this expectation frustrated, for the captain did bite, and came forth to have taken this victual (as he supposed). But ere he could reach these carriers, Sir James, with his company, had gotten between the castle and him ; and these disguised carriers, seeing the captain following after them, did quickly cast off their sacks, mounted themselves on horseback, and met the captain with a sharp encounter, being so much the more amazed, as it was unlooked for : wherefore, when he saw these carriers meta-morphosed into warriors, and ready to assault him, fearing that which was, that there was some train laid for them, he turned about to have retired to his castle, but there he also met with his enemies : between which two companies he and his whole follow-ers were slain, so that none escaped : the captain afterwards being searched, they found (as it is reported) his mistress's letter about him."—HUME's *History of the House of Douglas*, fol. pp. 29, 30. [1]

NOTE U.

And Connoght pour'd from waste and wood
Her hundred tribes, whose sceptre rude
Dark Eth O'Connor sway'd.—P. 228.

There is in the Fœdera an invitation to Eth O'Connor, chief of the Irish of Connaught, setting forth that the king was about

[1] This is the foundation of the Author's last romance. *Castle Dangerous.*—ED.

to move against his Scottish rebels, and therefore requesting the attendance of all the force he could muster, either commanded by himself in person, or by some nobleman of his race. These auxiliaries were to be commanded by Richard de Burgh, Earl of Ulster. Similar mandates were issued to the following Irish chiefs, whose names may astonish the unlearned, and amuse the antiquary.

" Eth O Donnuld, Duci Hibernicorum de Tyconil;
Demod O Kahan, Duci Hibernicorum de Fernetrew;
Doneval O Neel, Duci Hibernicorum de Tryowyn;
Neel Macbreen, Duci Hibernicorum de Kynallewan;
Eth. Offyn, Duci Hibernicorum de Turtery;
Admely Mac Anegus, Duci Hibernicorum de Onehagh;
Neel O Hanlan, Duci Hibernicorum de Erthere;
Bien Mac Mahun, Duci Hibernicorum de Uriel;
Lauercagh Mac Wyr, Duci Hibernicorum de Lougherin;
Gillys O Railly, Duci Hibernicorum de Bresfeny;
Geffrey O Fergy, Duci Hibernicorum de Montiragwil;
Felyn O Honughur, Duci Hibernicorum de Connach;
Donethuth O Bien, Duci Hibernicorum de Tothmund;
Dermod Mac Arthy, Duci Hibernicorum de Dessemound;
Denenol Carbragh;
Maur. Kenenagh Mac Murgh;
Murghugh O Bryn;
David O Tothvill;
Dermod O Tonoghur, Doffaly;
Fyn O Dymsy;
Souethuth Mac Gillephatrick;
Leyssagh O Morth;
Gilbertus Ekelly, Duci Hibernicorum de Omany;
Mac Ethelau;
Omalan Helyn, Duci Hibernicorum Midie."

RYMER's *Fœdera*, vol. iii. pp. 176. 477.

NOTE V.

In battles four beneath their eye,
The forces of King Robert lie.—P. 234.

The arrangements adopted by King Robert for the decisive
battle of Bannockburn, are given very distinctly by Barbour, and
form an edifying lesson to tacticians. Yet, till commented upon
by Lord Hailes, this important passage of history has been generally and strangely misunderstood by historians. I will here en-
deavour to detail it fully.

Two days before the battle, Bruce selected the field of action,
and took post there with his army, consisting of about 30,000
disciplined men, and about half the number of disorderly attendants upon the camp. The ground was called the New Park of
Stirling; it was partly open, and partly broken by copses of
wood and marshy ground. He divided his regular forces into four
divisions. Three of these occupied a front line, separated from
each other, yet sufficiently near for the purposes of communication. The fourth division formed a reserve. The line extended
in a north-easterly direction from the brook of Bannock, which
was so rugged and broken as to cover the right flank effectually, ·
to the village of Saint Ninian's, probably in the line of the present
road from Stirling to Kilsyth. Edward Bruce commanded the
right wing, which was strengthened by a strong body of cavalry
under Keith, the Mareschal of Scotland, to whom was committed
the important charge of attacking the English archers; Douglas,
and the young Steward of Scotland, led the central wing; and
Thomas Randolph, Earl of Moray, the left wing. The King himself commanded the fourth division, which lay in reserve behind
the others. The royal standard was pitched, according to tradition, in a stone, having a round hole for its reception, and thence
called the Bore-stone. It is still shewn on the top of a small
eminence, called Brock's-brae, to the south-west of St Ninian's.
His main body thus disposed, King Robert sent the followers of
the camp, fifteen thousand and upwards in number, to the emi-

nence in rear of his army, called from that circumstance the *Gillies'* (*i. e.* the servants') *Hill.*

The military advantages of this position were obvious. The Scottish left flank, protected by the brook of Bannock, could not be turned: or, if that attempt were made, a movement by the reserve might have covered it. Again, the English could not pass the Scottish army, and move towards Stirling, without exposing their flank to be attacked while in march.

If, on the other hand, the Scottish line had been drawn up east and west, and facing to the southward, as affirmed by Buchanan, and adopted by Mr Nimmo, the author of the History of Sirlingshire, there appears nothing to have prevented the English approaching upon the carse, or level ground, from Falkirk, either from turning the Scottish left flank, or from passing their position, if they preferred it, without coming to an action, and moving on to the relief of Stirling. And the Gillies' Hill, if this less probable hypothesis be adopted, would be situated, not in the rear, as allowed by all the historians, but upon the left flank of Bruce's army. The only objection to the hypothesis above laid down, is that the left flank of Bruce's army was thereby exposed to a sally from the garrison of Stirling. But, 1st, the garrison were bound to neutrality by terms of Mowbray's treaty; and Barbour even seems to censure, as a breach of faith, some secret assistance which they rendered their countrymen upon the eve of battle, in placing temporary bridges of doors and spars over the pools of water in the carse, to enable them to advance to the charge.[1] 2dly, Had this not been the case, the strength of the garrison was probably not sufficient to excite apprehension. 3dly, The adverse hypothesis leaves the rear of the Scottish army as much exposed to the Stirling garrison, as the left flank would be in the case supposed.

It only remains to notice the nature of the ground in front of Bruce's line of battle. Being part of a park, or chase, it was considerably interrupted with trees; and an extensive marsh, still

---

[1] An assistance which (by the way) could not have been rendered, had not the English approached from the south-east; since, had their march been due north, the whole Scottish army must have been between them and the garrison.

visible, in some places rendered it inaccessible, and in all of difficult approach. More to the northward, where the natural impediments were fewer, Bruce fortified his position against cavalry, by digging a number of pits so close together, says Barbour, as to resemble the cells in a honey-comb. They were a foot in breadth, and between two and three feet deep, many rows of them being placed one behind the other. They were slightly covered with brushwood and green sods, so as not to be obvious to an impetuous enemy.

All the Scottish army were on foot, excepting a select body of cavalry stationed with Edward Bruce on the right wing, under the immediate command of Sir Robert Keith, the Marshal of Scotland, who were destined for the important service of charging and dispersing the English archers.

Thus judiciously posted, in a situation fortified both by art and nature, Bruce awaited the attack of the English.

Note W.

With these the valiant of the Isles
Beneath their chieftains rank'd their files.—P. 235.

The men of Argyle, the islanders, and the Highlanders in general, were ranked in the rear. They must have been numerous, for Bruce had reconciled himself with almost all their chieftains, excepting the obnoxious MacDougals of Lorn. The following deed, containing the submission of the potent Earl of Ross to the King, was never before published. It is dated in the third year of Robert's reign, that is, 1309.

" OBLIGACIO COMITIS ROSSENSIS PER HOMAGIUM FIDELITATEM
ET SCRIPTUM.

" Universis christi fidelibus ad quorum noticiam presentes litere peruenerint Willielmus Comes de Ross salutem in domino sempiternam. Quia magnificus princeps Dominus Robertus dei gracia

Rex Scottorum Dominus meus ex innata sibi bonitate, inspirataque clemencia, et gracia speciali remisit michi pure rancorem animi sui, et ralaxauit ac condonauit michi omnimodas transgressiones seu offensas contra ipsum et suos per me et meos vsque ad confeccionem literarum presencium perpetratas : Et terras meas et tenementa mea omnia graciose concessit. Et me nichilominus de terra de Dingwal et ferncroskry infra comitatum de Suthyrland de benigna liberalitate sua heriditarie infeodare curauit. Ego tantam principis beneuolenciam efficaciter attendens, et pro tot graciis michi factis, vicem sibi gratitudinis meis pro viribus de cetero digne - - - - - - - - - - - - - - vite cupiens exhibere, subicio et obligo me et heredes meos et homines meos vniuersos dicto Domino meo Regi per omnia - - - - - - - - - - - - - erga suam regiam dignitatem, quod erimus de cetero fideles sibi et heredibus suis et fidele sibi seruicium auxilium et concilium - - - - - - - - - - - contra omnes homines et feminas qui vivere poterint aut mori, et super h - - - Ego Willielmus pro me - - - - - - - - - - - - - - hominibus meis vniuersis dicto domino meo Regi - - - - - - - - - - manibus homagium sponte feci et super dei ewangelia sacramentum prestiti - - - - - - - - - - - - In quorum omnium testimonium sigillum meum, et sigilla Hugonis filii et heredis et Johannis filii mei vna cum sigillis venerabilium patrum Dominorum Dauid et Thome Moraviensis et Rossensis dei gracia episcoporum presentibus literis sunt appensa. Acta scripta et data apud Aldern in Morauia vltimo die mensis Octobris, Anno Regni dicti domini nostri Regis Roberti Tertio. Testibus venerabilibus patribus supradictis, Domino Bernardo Cancellario Regis. Dominis Willielmo de Haya, Johanne de Striuelyn, Willielmo Wysman, Johanne de Ffenton, Dauid de Berkeley, et Waltero de Berkeley militibus, magistro Waltero Heroc, Decano ecclesie Morauie, magistro Willielmo de Creswel eiusdem ecclesie precentore et multis aliis nobilibus clericis et laicis dictis die et loco congregatis."

The copy of this curious document was supplied by my friend, Mr Thomson, Deputy Register of Scotland, whose researches into our ancient records are daily throwing new and important light upon the history of the country.

NOTE X.

The Monarch rode along the van.—P. 237.

The English vanguard, commanded by the Earls of Gloucester
and Hereford, came in sight of the Scottish army upon the evening of the 23d of June.   Bruce was then riding upon a little palfrey, in front of his foremost line, putting his host in order.   It
was then that the personal encounter took place betwixt him and
Sir Henry de Bohun, a gallant English knight, the issue of which
had a great effect upon the spirits of both armies.   It is thus recorded by BARBOUR :—

> " Aud quhen Glosyster and Herfurd war
> With thair batalll, approchand ner,
> Befor thaim all thar come rydand,
> With helm on heid, and sper in hand.
> Schyr Henry the Boune, the worthi,
> That wes a wycht knycht, and a hardy ;
> And to the Erle off Herfurd cusyne ;
> Armyt in armys gud and fyne ;
> Come on a sted, a bow schote ner,
> Befor all othyr that thar wer ;
> And knew the King, for that he saw
> Him swa rang his men on raw ;
> And by the croune, that wes set
> Alsua apon his bassynet,
> And towart him he went in hy.
> And [quhen] the King sua apertly
> Saw him cum forouth all his feris,[1]
> In hy[2] till him the hors he steris.
> And quhen Schyr Henry saw the King
> Cum on, for owtyn abaysing,[3]
> Till him he raid in full gret hy.
> He thoucht that he suld weill lychtly
> Wyn him, and haf him at his will,
> Sen he him horsyt saw sa ill.
> Sprent[4] thai samyn in till a ling.[5]
> Schyr Henry myssit the noble king.

[1] Comrades.—[2] Haste.—[3] Without shrinking.—[4] Spurred.—[5] Line.

And he, that in his sterapys stud,
With the ax that wes hard and gud,
With sa gret mayne[1] raucht him a dynt,
That nothyr hat, na helm, mycht stynt
The hewy[2] dusche[3] that he him gave,
That ner the held till the harnys clave.
The hand ax schaft fruschit[4] in twa ;
And he doune to the erd gan ga
All flatlynys,[5] for him faillyt mycht.
This wes the fryst strak off the fycht."

BARBOCA's Bruce, Book viii. v. 684.

The Scottish leaders remonstrated with the King upon his temerity. He only answered, " I have broken my good battle-axe."— The English vanguard retreated after witnessing this single combat. Probably their generals did not think it advisable to hazard an attack, while its unfavourable issue remained upon their minds.

Note Y.

What train of dust, with trumpet-sound.
And glimmering spears, is wheeling round
Our leftward flank ?———P. 243.

While the van of the English army advanced, a detached body attempted to relieve Stirling. Lord Hailes gives the following account of this manœuvre and the result, which is accompanied by circumstances highly characteristic of the chivalrous manners of the age, and displays that generosity which reconciles us even to their ferocity upon other occasions.

Bruce had enjoined Randolph, who commanded the left wing of his army, to be vigilant in preventing any advanced parties of the English from throwing succours into the castle of Stirling.

" Eight hundred horsemen, commanded by Sir Robert Clifford, were detached from the English army ; they made a circuit by the low grounds to the east, and approached the castle. The king perceived their motions, and coming up to Randolph, angrily exclaim-

---

1 Strength, or force.—2 Heavy.—3 Clash.—4 Broke.—5 Flat.

ed, 'Thoughtless man! you have suffered the enemy to pass.' Randolph hasted to repair his fault, or perish. As he advanced, the
English cavalry wheeled to attack him. Randolph drew up his
troops in a circular form, with their spears resting on the ground,
and protended on every side. At the first onset, Sir William
Daynecourt, an English commander of distinguished note, was
slain. The enemy, far superior in numbers to Randolph, environed
him, and pressed hard on his little band. Douglas saw his jeo-
pardy, and requested the king's permission to go and succour him.
'You shall not move from your ground,' cried the king; 'let
Randolph extricate himself as he best may. I will not alter my
order of battle, and lose the advantage of my position.'—'In
truth,' replied Douglas, 'I cannot stand by and see Randolph
perish; and, therefore, with your leave, I must aid him.' The
king unwillingly consented, and Douglas flew to the assistance
of his friend. While approaching, he perceived that the English
were falling into disorder, and that the perseverance of Randolph
had prevailed over their impetuous courage. 'Halt,' cried Douglas, 'those brave men have repulsed the enemy; let us not di-
minish their glory by sharing it.'"—DALRYMPLE's *Annals of
Scotland*, 4to, Edinburgh, 1779, pp. 44, 45.

Two large stones erected at the north end of the village of Newhouse, about a quarter of a mile from the south part of Stirling,
ascertain the place of this memorable skirmish. The circumstance
tends, were confirmation necessary, to support the opinion of Lord
Hailes, that the Scottish line had Stirling on its left flank. It will
be remembered, that Randolph commanded infantry, Daynecourt
cavalry. Supposing, therefore, according to the vulgar hypothesis, that the Scottish line was drawn up, facing to the south, in the
line of the brook of Bannock, and consequently that Randolph
was stationed with his left flank resting upon Milntown bog, it is
morally impossible that his infantry, moving from that position,
with whatever celerity, could cut off from Stirling a body of
cavalry who had already passed St Ninians,[1] or, in other words,

---

[1] Barbour says expressly, they avoided the New Park, (where Bruce's army
lay,) and held " well neath the Kirk," which can only mean St Ninian's.

were already between them and the town. Whereas, supposing Randolph's left to have approached St Ninian's, the short movement to Newhouse could easily be executed, so as to intercept the English in the manner described.

NOTE Z.

Forth, Marshal, on the peasant foe !
We'll tame the terrors of their bow,
* And cut the bow-string loose !—*P. 251.

The English archers commenced the attack with their usual bravery and dexterity. But against a force, whose importance he had learned by fatal experience, Bruce was provided. A small but select body of cavalry were detached from the right, under command of Sir Robert Keith. They rounded, as I conceive, the marsh called Milntown bog, and, keeping the firm ground, charged the left flank and rear of the English archers. As the bowmen had no spears, nor long weapons, fit to defend themselves against horse, they were instantly thrown into disorder, and spread through the whole English army a confusion, from which they never fairly recovered.

> " The Inglis archeris schot sa fast,
> That mycht thair schot haff ony last,
> It had bene hard to Scottis men.
> Bot King Robert, that wele gan ken[1]
> That thair archeris war peralouss,
> And thair schot rycht hard and grewouss,
> Ordanyt, forouth[2] the assemblé.
> Hys marschell with a gret menye,
> Fyve hundre armyt in to stele,
> That on lycht horss war horsyt welle,
> For to pryk[3] amang the archeris ;
> And swa assaile thaim with thair speris,
> That thai na layser haiff to schute.
> This marschell that Ik of mute,[4]
> Tha Schyr Robert of Keyth was cauld,
> As Ik befor her has yow tauld,

[1] Know.—[2] Disjoined from the main body.—[3] Spur.—[4] That I speak of.

Quhen he saw the batalllis sua
Assembill, and to gidder ga,
And saw the archeris schoyt stoutly ;
With all thaim off his cumpany,
In hy apon thaim gan he rid ;
And our tuk thaim at a sid ;[1]
And ruschyt amang thaim sa rudly,
Stekand thaim sa dispitously,
And in sic fusoun[2] berand doun,
And slayand thaim, for owtyn ransoun ;[3]
That thai thaim scalyt[4] euirilkane.[5]
And fra that tyme furth thar wes nane
That assemblyt schot to ma.[6]
Quhen Scottis archeris saw that thai sua
War rebutyt,[7] thai woux hardy,
And with all thair mycht schot egrely
Amang the horss men, that thar raid ;
And woundis wid to thaim thai maid ;
And slew of thaim a full gret dele."

BARBOUR's Bruce. Book ix. v. 228.

Although the success of this manœuvre was evident, it is very remarkable that the Scottish generals do not appear to have profited by the lesson. Almost every subsequent battle which they lost against England, was decided by the archers, to whom the close and compact array of the Scottish phalanx afforded an exposed and unresisting mark. The bloody battle of Halidoun-hill, fought scarce twenty years afterwards, was so completely gained by the archers, that the English are said to have lost only one knight, one esquire, and a few foot-soldiers. At the battle of Neville's Cross, in 1346, where David II. was defeated and made prisoner, John de Graham, observing the loss which the Scots sustained from the English bowmen, offered to charge and disperse them, if a hundred men-at-arms were put under his command. "*But,* to confess the truth," says Fordun, "he could not procure a single horseman for the service proposed." Of such little use is experience in war, where its results are opposed by habit or prejudice.

[1] Set upon their flank.—[2] Numbers.—[3] Ransom.—[4] Dispersed.—[5] Every one.—

NOTE A 2.

To arms they flew,—axe, club, or spear,—
And mimic ensigns high they rear.—P. 261.

The followers of the Scottish camp observed, from the Gillies'
Hill in the rear, the impression produced upon the English army
by the bringing up of the Scottish reserve, and prompted by the
enthusiasm of the moment, or the desire of plunder, assumed, in a
tumultuary manner, such arms as they found nearest, fastened
sheets to tent-poles and lances, and shewed themselves like a new
army advancing to battle.

> " Yomen, and swanys,[1] and pitaill,[2]
> That in the Park yemyt wictaill,[3]
> War left ; quhen thai wyst but lesing,[4]
> That thair lordis, with fell fechtyng,
> On thair fayis assemblyt wer ;
> Ane off thaim selwyn[5] that war thar
> Capitane of thaim all thai maid.
> And schetis. that war sumedele[6] brad,
> Thai festnyt in steid off baneris,
> Apon lang treys and speris :
> And said that thai wald se the fycht ;
> And help thair lordis at thair mycht,
> Quhen her till all assentyt wer,
> In a rout assemblit er ;[7]
> Fyftene thowsand thai war, er ma.
> And than in gret hy gan thai ga,
> With thair baneris, all in a rout,
> As thai had men bene styth[8] and stout,
> Thai come, with all that assemblé,
> Rycht quhill thai mycht the bataill se ;
> Than all at anys thai gave a cry,
> ' Sla ! Sla! Apon thaim hastily !' "
>
> BARBOUR's *Bruce*, Book ix. v. 410.

The unexpected apparition, of what seemed a new army, completed the confusion which already prevailed among the English,

---

[1] Swains.—[2] Rabble.—[3] Kept the provisions.—[4] Lying.—[5] Selves.—[6] Somewhat
—[7] Are.—[8] Stiff.

who fled in every direction, and were pursued with immense slaughter. The brook of Bannock, according to Barbour, was so choked with the bodies of men and horses, that it might have been passed dry-shod. The followers of the Scottish camp fell upon the disheartened fugitives, and added to the confusion and slaughter. Many were driven into the Forth, and perished there, which, by the way, could hardly have happened, had the armies been drawn up east and west, since, in that case, to get at the river, the English fugitives must have fled through the victorious army. About a short mile from the field of battle is a place called the Bloody Folds. Here the Earl of Gloucester is said to have made a stand, and died gallantly at the head of his own military tenants and vassals. He was much regretted by both sides; and it is said the Scottish would gladly have saved his life, but, neglecting to wear his surcoat with armorial bearings over his armour, he fell unknown, after his horse had been stabbed with spears.

Sir Marmaduke Twenge, an English knight, contrived to conceal himself during the fury of the pursuit, and when it was somewhat slackened, approached King Robert. "Whose prisoner are you, Sir Marmaduke?" said Bruce, to whom he was personally known. "Yours, sir," answered the knight. "I receive you," answered the king, and, treating him with the utmost courtesy, loaded him with gifts, and dismissed him without ransom. The other prisoners were all well treated. There might be policy in this, as Bruce would naturally wish to acquire the good opinion of the English barons, who were at this time at great variance with their king. But it also well accords with his high chivalrous character.

Note B 2.

O! give their hapless prince his due.—P. 262.

Edward II., according to the best authorities, shewed, in the fatal field of Bannockburn, personal gallantry not unworthy of his great sire and greater son. He remained on the field till forced

away by the Earl of Pembroke, when all was lost.   He then rode
to the Castle of Stirling, and demanded admittance ; but the governor, remonstrating upon the imprudence of shutting himself up
in that fortress, which must so soon surrender, he assembled
around his person five hundred men-at-arms, and, avoiding the
field of battle and the victorious army, fled towards Linlithgow,
pursued by Douglas with about sixty horse.   They were augmented by Sir Lawrence Abernethy with twenty more, whom
Douglas met in the Torwood upon their way to join the English
army, and whom he easily persuaded to desert the defeated monarch, and to assist in the pursuit.   They hung upon Edward's
flight as far as Dunbar, too few in number to assail him with
effect, but enough to harass his retreat so constantly, that whoever
fell an instant behind, was instantly slain, or made prisoner.
Edward's ignominious flight terminated at Dunbar, where the
Earl of March, who still professed allegiance to him, " received
him full gently."   From thence, the monarch of so great an empire, and the late commander of so gallant and numerous an army,
escaped to Bamborough in a fishing vessel.

Bruce, as will appear from the following . document, lost no
time in directing the thunders of parliamentary censure against
such part of his subjects as did not return to their natural allegiance after the battle of Bannockburn.

.

APUD MONASTERIUM DE CAMBUSKENNETH,

VI DIE NOVEMBRIS, M,CCC,XIV.

Judicium Reditum apud Kambuskinet contra omnes illos qui
tunc fuerunt contra fidem et pacem Domini Regis.

Anno gracie millesimo tricentisimo quarto decimo sexto die
Novembris tenente parliamentum suum Excellentissimo principe
Domino Roberto Dei gracia Rege Scottorum Illustri in monasterio
de Cambuskyneth concordatum fuit finaliter Judicatum [ac super]
hoc statutum de Concilio et Assensu Episcoporum et ceterorum

Prelatorum Comitum Baronum et aliorum nobilium regni Scocie nec non et tocius communitatis regni predicti quod omnes qui contra fidem et pacem dicti domini regis in bello seu alibi mortui sunt [vel qui dic] to die ad pacem ejus et fidem non venerant licet sepius vocati et legitime expectati fuissent de terris et tenementis et omni alio statu infra regnum Scocie perpetuo sint exheredati et habeantur, de cetero tanquam inimici Regis et Regni ab omni vendicacione juris hereditarii vel juris alterius cujuscunque in posterum pro se et heredibus suis in perpetuum privati Ad perpetuam igitur rei memoriam et evidentem probacionem hujus Judicii et Statuti sigilla Episcoporum et aliorum Prelatorum nec non et comitum Baronum ac ceterorum nobilium dicti Regni presenti ordinacioni Judicio et statuto sunt appensa.

     Sigillum Domini Regis

     Sigillum Willelmi Episcopi Sancti Andree

     Sigillum Roberti Episcopi Glascuensis

     Sigillum Willelmi Episcopi Dunkeldensis

     . . . Episcopi . . . .

     . . . Episcopi . . . .

     . . . Episcopi . . . .

     Sigillum Alani Episcopi Sodorensis

     Sigillum Johannis Episcopi Brechynensis

     Sigillum Andree Episcopi Ergadiensis

     Sigillum Frechardi Episcopi Cathanensis

     Sigillum Abbatis de Scona

     Sigillum Abbatis de Calco

     Sigillum Abbatis de Abirbrothok

     Sigillum Abbatis de Sancta Cruce

     Sigillum Abbatis de Londoris

     Sigillum Abbatis de Newbotill

     Sigillum Abbatis de Cupro

     Sigillum Abbatis de Paslet

     Sigillum Abbatis de Dunfermelyn

     Sigillum Abbatis de Lincluden

     Sigillum Abbatis de Insula Missarum

     Sigillum Abbatis de Sancto Columba

     Sigillum Abbatis de Deer

Sigillum Abbatis de Dulce Corde
Sigillum Prioris de Coldinghame
Sigillum Prioris de Rostynot
Sigillum Prioris Sancte Andree
Sigillum Prioris de Pettinwem
Sigillum Prioris de Insula de Lochlevin
Sigillum Senescalli Scocie
Sigillum Willelmi Comitis de Ros

. . . .

. . . .

. . . .

Sigillum Gilberti de la Haya Constabularii Scocie
Sigillum Roberti de Keth Mariscalli Scocie
Sigillum Hugonis de Ros
Sigillum Jacobi de Duglas
Sigillum Johannis de Sancto Claro
Sigillum Thome de Ros
Sigillum Alexandri de Settone
Sigillum Walteri Haliburtone
Sigillum Davidis de Balfour
Sigillum Duncani de Wallays
Sigillum Thome de Dischingtone
Sigillum Andree de Moravia
Sigillum Archibaldi de Betun
Sigillum Ranulphi de Lyill
Sigillum Malcomi de Balfour
Sigillum Normanni de Lesley
Sigillum Nigelli de Campo bello
Sigillum Morni de Musco Campo

. . . .

. . . .

Note C 2.

Nor for De Argentine alone,
Through Ninian's church these torches shone,
And rose the death-prayer's awful tone.—P. 265.

The remarkable circumstances attending the death of De Argentine have been already noticed (p. 57.)   Besides this renowned warrior, there fell many representatives of the noblest houses in England, which never sustained a more bloody and disastrous defeat.   Barbour says that two hundred pairs of gilded spurs were taken from the field of battle; and that some were left the author can bear witness, who has in his possession a curious antique spur, dug up in the morass, not long since.

> " It wes forsuth a gret ferly,
> To se samyn ¹ sa fele dede lie.
> Twa hundre payr of spuris reid,²
> War tane of knichtis that war deid."

I am now to take my leave of Barbour, not without a sincere wish that the public may encourage the undertaking of my friend Dr Jamieson, who has issued proposals for publishing an accurate edition of his poem and of Blind Harry's Wallace.*   The only good edition of The Bruce was published by Mr Pinkerton, in 3 vols., in 1790; and, the learned editor having had no personal access to consult the manuscript, it is not without errors ; and it has besides become scarce.   Of Wallace there is no tolerable edition ; yet these two poems do no small honour to the early state of Scottish poetry, and The Bruce is justly regarded as containing authentic historical facts.

The following list of the slain at Bannockburn, extracted from the continuator of Trivet's Annals, will shew the extent of the national calamity.

¹ Together.—² Red, or gilded.

* [The extracts from Barbour in this edition of Sir Walter Scott's poems have been uniformly corrected by the text of Dr Jamieson's Bruce, published, along with Blind Harry's Wallace, Edin. 1820, 2 vols. 4to.—Ed.]

LIST OF THE SLAIN.

Barons and Knights Bannerets.
Gilbert de Clare, Earl of Glou-
 cester,
Robert de Clifford,
Payan Tybetot,
William Le Mareschal,
John Comyn,
William de Vescey,
John de Montfort,
Nicolas de Hasteleigh,
William Dayncourt,
Ægidius de Argenteyne,
Edmond Comyn,
John Lovel, (the rich,)
Edmund de Hastynge,
Milo de Stapleton,
Simon Ward,

Robert de Felton,
Michael Poyning,
Edmund Maulley.

Knights.
Henry de Boun,
Thomas de Ufford,
John de Elsingfelde,
John de Harcourt,
Walter de Hakelut,
Philip de Courtenay,
Hugo de Scales,
Radulph de Beauchamp,
John de Penbrigge,
With thirty-three others of
 the same rank, not named.

PRISONERS.

Barons and Baronets.
Henry de Boun, Earl of Hereford,
Lord John Giffard,
William de Latimer,
Maurice de Berkley,
Ingelram de Umfraville,
Marmaduke de Twenge,
John de Wyletone,
Robert de Maulee,
Henry Fitz-Hugh,
Thomas de Gray,
Walter de Beauchamp,
Richard de Charon,
John de Wevelmton,
Robert de Nevil,

John de Segrave,
Gilbert Peeche.
John de Clavering,
Antony de Lucy,
Radulph de Camys,
John de Evere,
Andrew de Abremhyn.
Knights.
Thomas de Berkeley,
The son of Roger Tyrrel,
Anselm de Mareschal,
Giles de Beauchamp,
John de Cyfrewast,
John Bluwet,
Roger Corbet,

Gilbert de Boun,
Bartholomew de Enefeld,
Thomas de Ferrers,
Radulph and Thomas Bottetort,
John and Nicholas de Kingstone,
(brothers,)
William Lovel,
Henry de Wileton,
Baldwin de Frevill,
John de Clivedon,[1]
Adomar la Zouche,

John de Merewode,
John Maufe,[2]
Thomas and Odo Lele Er-
cedekene,
Robert Beaupel, (the son,)
John Mautravers, (the son,)
William and William Giff-
ard, and thirty-four other
knights, not named by the
historian.

And in sum there were there slain, along witn the Earl of Gloucester, forty-two barons and bannerets. The number of earls,
barons, and bannerets made captive, was twenty-two, and sixty-
eight knights. Many clerks and esquires were also there slain
or taken. Roger de Northburge, keeper of the king's signet,
(*Custos Targiæ Domini Regis*) was made prisoner with his two
clerks, Roger de Wakenfelde and Thomas de Switon, upon which
the king caused a seal to be made, and entitled it his *privy seal*,
to distinguish the same from the signet so lost. The Earl of
Hereford was exchanged against Bruce's queen, who had been
detained in captivity ever since the year 1306. The *Targia*, or
signet, was restored to England through the intercession of Ralph
de Monthermer, ancestor of Lord Moira, who is said to have
found favour in the eyes of the Scottish king.—*Continuation of*
TRIVET's *Annals, Hall's edit. Oxford*, 1712, vol. ii. p. 14.

Such were the immediate consequences of the field of Bannockburn. Its more remote effects in completely establishing the national independence of Scotland, afford a boundless field for specu-
lation.

[1] **Supposed Clinton.**   [2] **Maule.**

END OF NOTES TO THE LORD OF THE ISLES.

OCCASIONAL PIECES,

NOT CONTAINED IN ANY FORMER EDITION OF

SIR WALTER SCOTT'S POETICAL WORKS.

z

PHAROS LOQUITUR.*

FAR in the bosom of the deep,
O'er these wild shelves my watch I keep;
A ruddy gem of changeful light,
Bound on the dusky brow of night,
The seaman bids my lustre hail,
And scorns to strike his timorous sail.

* ["On the 30th of July, 1814, Mr Hamilton,[1] Mr Erskine,[2] and Mr Duff,[3] Commissioners, along with Mr (now Sir) Walter Scott, and the writer, visited the Lighthouse; the Commissioners being then on one of their voyages of inspection, noticed in the Introduction. They breakfasted in the Library, when Sir Walter, at the entreaty of the party, upon inscribing his name in the Album, added these interesting lines."—STEVENSON'S *Account of the Bell-Rock Lighthouse.* 1824.]

[1] The late Robert Hamilton, Esq. Advocate, long Sheriff-Depute of Lanarkshire, and afterwards one of the Principal Clerks of Session in Scotland—died in 1831.
[2] Afterwards Lord Kinnedder.
[3] Adam Duff, Esq. Sheriff-Depute of the county of Edinburgh.

LINES,[1]

ADDRESSED TO

RANALD MACDONALD, ESQ. OF STAFFA.

STAFFA, sprung from high Macdonald,
Worthy branch of old Clan Ranald!
Staffa! king of all kind fellows!
Well befall thy hills and valleys,
Lakes and inlets, deeps and shallows—
Cliffs of darkness, caves of wonder,
Echoing the Atlantic thunder;
Mountains which the grey mist covers,
Where the Chieftain spirit hovers,
Pausing while his pinions quiver,
Stretch'd to quit our land for ever!
Each kind influence reign above thee!
Warmer heart, 'twixt this and Staffa
Beats not, than in heart of Staffa!

[1] [These lines were written in the Album, kept at the Sound
of Ulva Inn, in the month of August, 1814.]

THE BOLD DRAGOON;[1]

OR,

THE PLAIN OF BADAJOS.

~~~~~~~~~

'Twas a Maréchal of France, and he fain would hon-
    our gain,
And he long'd to take a passing glance at Portugal
    from Spain ;
    With his flying guns this gallant gay,
    And boasted corps d'armée—
O he fear'd not our dragoons, with their long swords,
    boldly riding,
    Whack, fal de ral, &c.

To Campo Mayor come, he had quietly sat down,
Just a fricassee to pick, while his soldiers sack'd the
    town,

[1] [This song was written shortly after the battle of Badajos,
(April, 1812,) for a Yeomanry Cavalry dinner. It was first printed in Mr George Thomson's Collection of Select Melodies, and
stands in vol. vi. of the last edition of that work.]

When, 'twas peste ! morbleu ! mon General,
Hear the English bugle call !
And behold the light dragoons, with their long swords,
     boldly riding,
Whack, fal de ral, &c.

Right about went horse and foot, artillery and all,
And as the devil leaves the house they tumbled through
     the wall ;[1]
    They took no time to seek the door,
    But best foot set before—
O they ran from our dragoons, with their long swords,
     boldly riding,
Whack, fal de ral, &c.

Those valiant men' of France they had scarcely fled
     a mile,
When on their flank there sous'd at once the British
     rank and file ;
    For Long, De Grey, and Otway, then
    Ne'er minded one to ten,
But came on like light dragoons, with their long
     swords, boldly riding,
Whack, fal de ral, &c.

Three hundred British lads they made three thousand
     reel,

---

[1] In their hasty evacuation of Campo Mayor, the French pulled down a part of the rampart, and marched out over the glacis.

Their hearts were made of English oak, their swords
>of Sheffield steel,
>Their horses were in Yorkshire bred,
>And Beresford them led ;
So huzza for brave dragoons, with their long swords,
>boldly riding,
>Whack, fal de ral, &c.

Then here's a health to Wellington, to Beresford, to
>Long,
And a single word of Bonaparte before I close my
>song :
>The eagles that to fight he brings
>Should serve his men with wings,
When they meet the bold dragoons, with their long
>swords, boldly riding,
>Whack, fal de ral, &c.

FOR A' THAT AN' A' THAT.[1]

A NEW SONG TO AN OLD TUNE.

~~~~~~~~~

Though right be aft put down by strength,
　As mony a day we saw that,
The true and leilfu' cause at length
　Shall bear the grie for a' that!
For a' that an' a' that,
　Guns, guillotines, and a' that,
The Fleur-de-lis, that lost her right,
　Is queen again for a' that!

We'll twine her in a friendly knot
　With England's Rose, and a' that;
The Shamrock shall not be forgot,
　For Wellington made bra' that.
The Thistle, though her leaf be rude,
　Yet faith we'll no misca' that,

[1] [Sung at the first meeting of the Pitt Club of Scotland; and published in the Scots Magazine for July, 1814.]

She shelter'd in her solitude
   The Fleur-de-lis, for a' that.

The Austrian Vine, the Prussian Pine
   (For Blucher's sake, hurra that,)
The Spanish Olive, too, shall join,
   And bloom in peace for a' that.
Stout Russia's hemp, so surely twined
   Around our wreath we'll draw that,
And he that would the cord unbind,
   Shall have it for his gra-vat!

Or, if to choke sae puir a sot,
   Your pity scorn to thraw that,
The Devil's elbo' be his lot,
   Where he may sit and claw that.
In spite of slight, in spite of might,
   In spite of brags and a' that,
The lads that battled for the right,
   Have won the day and a' that!

There's ae bit spot I had forgot
   America they ca' that!
A coward plot her rats had got
   Their father's flag to gnaw that:
Now see it fly top-gallant high,
   Atlantic winds shall blaw that,
And Yankee loon, beware your croun,
   There's kames in hand to claw that!

For on the land, or on the sea,
 Where'er the breezes blaw that,
The British Flag shall bear the grie,
 And win the day for a' that!

LINES,

ADDRESSED TO MONSIEUR ALEXANDRE,[1] THE CELEBRATED
VENTRILOQUIST.

OF yore, in old England, it was not thought good
To carry two visages under one hood;
What should folk say to you? who have faces such
    plenty,
That from under one hood, you last night show'd us
    twenty!
Stand forth, arch-deceiver, and tell us in truth,
Are you handsome or ugly, in age or in youth?

[1] [" *When Monsieur Alexandre, the celebrated ventriloquist, was
in Scotland, in 1824, he paid a visit to Abbotsford, where he entertained his distinguished host, and the other visitors, with his un-
rivalled imitations. Next morning, when he was about to depart,
Sir Walter felt a good deal embarrassed, as to the sort of acknow-
ledgment he should offer; but at length, resolving that it would probably be most agreeable to the young foreigner to be paid in pro-
fessional coin, if in any, he stepped aside for a few minutes, and,
on returning, presented him with this epigram. The reader need
hardly be reminded, that Sir Walter Scott held the office of Sheriff
of the county of Selkirk.*"—Scotch Newspaper, 1830.]

Man, woman, or child—a dog or a mouse?
Or are you, at once, each live thing in the house?
Each live thing, did I ask?—each dead implement,
    too,
A work-shop in your person,—saw, chisel, and screw!
Above all, are you one individual? I know
You must be at least Alexandre and Co.
But I think you're a troop—an assemblage—a mob,
And that I as the Sheriff, should take up the job;
And instead of rehearsing your wonders in verse,
Must read you the Riot-Act, and bid you disperse.

ABBOTSFORD, 23d *April.*[1]

[1] [The lines, with this date, appeared in the Edinburgh Annual Register of 1824.]

VERSES,

COMPOSED FOR THE OCCASION, ADAPTED TO HAYDN'S AIR,

" *God Save the Emperor Francis,*"

AND SUNG BY A SELECT BAND AFTER THE DINNER GIVEN BY
THE LORD PROVOST OF EDINBURGH TO THE

GRAND-DUKE NICHOLAS OF RUSSIA,

AND HIS SUITE, 19th DECEMBER 1816.

GOD protect brave ALEXANDER,
Heaven defend the noble Czar,
Mighty Russia's high Commander,
First in Europe's banded war ;
For the realms he did deliver
From the tyrant overthrown,
Thou, of every good the Giver,
Grant him long to bless his own !
Bless him, 'mid his land's disaster,
For her rights who battled brave,
Of the land of foemen master,
Bless him who their wrongs forgave.

O'er his just resentment victor,
Victor over Europe's foes,
Late and long supreme director,
Grant in peace his reign may close.
Hail ! then, hail ! illustrious Stranger !
Welcome to our mountain strand ;
Mutual interests, hopes, and danger,
Link us with thy native land.
Freemen's force, or false beguiling,
Shall that union ne'er divide,
Hand in hand while peace is smiling,
And in battle side by side.[1]

[1] [Mr, afterwards Sir William Arbuthnot, the Lord Provost of Edinburgh, who had the honour to entertain the Grand-Duke, now Emperor of Russia, was a personal friend of Sir Walter Scott's; and these *Verses*, with their heading, are now given from the newspapers of 1816.]

LINES,[1]

WRITTEN FOR MISS SMITH.

WHEN the lone pilgrim views afar
The shrine that is his guiding star,
With awe his footsteps print the road
Which the loved saint of yore has trod.
As near he draws, and yet more near,
His dim eye sparkles with a tear;
The Gothic fane's unwonted show,
The choral hymn, the tapers' glow,
Oppress his soul; while they delight
And chasten rapture with affright.

---

[1] [These lines were first printed in ".The Forget-Me-Not, for
1834." They were written for recitation by the distinguished
actress, Miss Smith, now Mrs Bartley, on the night of her benefit at the Edinburgh Theatre, in 1817; but reached her too late
for her purpose. In a letter which enclosed them, the poet intimated that they were written on the morning of the day on
which they were sent—that he thought the idea better than the
execution, and forwarded them with the hope of their adding
perhaps " a little salt to the bill."]

No longer dare he think his toil
Can merit aught his patron's smile ;
Too light appears the distant way,
The chilly eve, the sultry day—
All these endured no favour c aim,
But murmuring forth the sainted name,
He lays his little offering down,
And only deprecates a frown.

We too, who ply the Thespian art,
Oft feel such bodings of the heart,
And, when our utmost powers are strain'd,
Dare hardly hope your favour gain'd.
She, who from sister climes has sought
The ancient land where Wallace fought ;—
Land long renown'd for arms and arts,
And conquering eyes and dauntless hearts ;—[1]
She, as the flutterings *here* avow,
Feels all the pilgrim's terrors *now ;*
Yet sure on Caledonian plain
The stranger never sued in vain.
'Tis yours the hospitable task
To give the applause she dare not ask ;
And they who bid the pilgrim speed,
The pilgrim's blessing be their meed.

---

[1] ["O favour'd land ! renown'd for arts and arms,
For manly talent, and for female charms."
              Lines written for Mr J. Kemble]

CARLE, NOW THE KING'S COME![1]

BEING NEW WORDS TO AN AULD SPRING.

~~~~~~~~~~~~~~

THE news has flown frae mouth to mouth,
The North for ance has bang'd the South;
The deil a Scotsman's die o' drouth,
   Carle, now the King's come !

CHORUS.

 Carle, now the King's come !
 Carle, now the King's come !
 Thou shalt dance, and I will sing,
   Carle, now the King's come !

Auld England held him lang and fast;
And Ireland had a joyfu' cast;
But Scotland's turn is come at last—
   Carle, now the King's come !

---

[1] [This imitation of an old Jacobite ditty was written on the appearance, in the Frith of Forth, of the fleet which conveyed his Majesty King George the Fourth to Scotland, in August, 1822, and was published as a broadside.]

Auld Reekie, in her rokelay gray,
Thought never to have seen the day ;
He's been a weary time away—
        But, Carle, now the King's come !

She's skirling frae the Castle-hill ;
The Carline's voice is grown sae shrill,
Ye'll hear her at the Canon-mill—
        Carle, now the King's come !

" Up, bairns !" she cries, " baith grit and sma',
And busk ye for the weapon-shaw !—
Stand by me, and we'll bang them a'—
        Carle, now the King's come !

" Come from Newbattle's ancient spires,
Bauld Lothian, with your knights and squires,
And match the mettle of your sires—
        Carle, now the King's come !

" You're welcome hame, my Montagu !
Bring in your hand the young Buccleuch ;—
I'm missing some that I may rue—
        Carle, now the King's come ;[1]

" Come, Haddington, the kind and gay,
You've graced my causeway mony a day ;

1 [Lord Montagu, uncle and guardian to the young Duke of
Buccleuch, placed his Grace's residence of Dalkeith at his Majesty's disposal during his visit to Scotland.]

I'll weep the cause if you should stay—
    Carle, now the King's come ! [1]

" Come, premier duke,[2] and carry doun
Frae yonder craig[3] his ancient croun ;
It's had a lang sleep and a soun'—
    But, Carle, now the King's come !

" Come, Athole, from the hill and wood,
Bring down your clansmen like a cloud ;
Come, Morton, show the Douglas' blood,—[4]
    Carle, now the King's come !

" Come, Tweeddale, true as sword to sheath ;
Come, Hopetoun, fear'd on fields of death ;
Come, Clerk,[5] and give your bugle breath ;
    Carle, now the King's come !

---

[1] [Charles, the tenth Earl of Haddington, died in 1828.]

[2] [The Duke of Hamilton, as Earl of Angus, carried the ancient royal crown of Scotland on horseback in King George's procession, from Holyrood to the Castle, Edinburgh, August. 1822.]

[3] The Castle.

[4] [MS.—" Come, Athole, from your hills and woods,
    Bring down your Hielandmen in cluds,
    With bannet, brogue, and tartan duds."]

[5] Sir George Clerk of Pennycuik, Bart. The Baron of Pennycuik is bound by his tenure, whenever the King comes to Edinburgh, to receive him at the Harestone, (in which the standard of James IV. was erected when his army encamped on the Boroughmuir, before his fatal expedition to England,) now built into the park-wall at the end of Tipperlin Lone, near the Boroughmuirhead ; and, standing thereon, to give three blasts on a horn.

" Come, Wemyss, who modest merit aids;
Come, Rosebery, from Dalmeny shades;
Breadalbane, bring your belted plaids;
  . Carle, now the King's come!

" Come, stately Niddrie, auld and true,
Girt with the sword that Minden knew;
We have ower few such lairds as you—
   Carle, now the King's come!

" King Arthur's grown a common crier,
He's heard in Fife and far Cantire,—
' Fie, lads, behold my crest of fire!' [1]
   Carle, now the King's come!

" Saint Abb roars out, ' I see him pass,
Between Tantallon and the Bass!'
Calton, get out your keeking-glass,
   Carle, now the King's come!"

The Carline stopp'd; and, sure I am,
For very glee had ta'en a dwam,
But Oman[2] help'd her to a dram.—
   Cogie, now the King's come!

[1] [MS.—" Brave Arthur's Seat's a story higher;
  Saint Abbe is shouting to Kintire,—
  ' You lion, light up a crest of fire.'"
As seen from the west, the ridge of Arthur's Seat bears a marked
resemblance to a lion couchant.]
[2] [Mr Oman, landlord of the Waterloo Hotel.]

Cogie, now the King's come !
Cogie, now the King's come !
I'se be fou', and ye's be toom,[1]
          Cogie, now the King's come !

[1] Empty.

CARLE, NOW THE KING'S COME!

PART SECOND

~~~~~~~~

A HAWICK gill of mountain dew,
Heised up Auld Reekie's heart, I trow,
It minded her of Waterloo—
   Carle, now the King's come!

Again I heard her summons swell,
For, sic a dirdum and a yell,
It drown'd Saint Giles's jowing bell—
   Carle, now the King's come!

"My trusty Provost, tried and tight,
Stand forward for the Good Town's right,
There's waur than you been made a knight—[1]
   Carle, now the King's come!

[1] [The Lord Provost had the agreeable surprise to hear his health proposed, at the civic banquet given to George IV. in the Parliament-House, as "Sir William Arbuthnot, Bart."]

" My reverend Clergy, look ye say
The best of thanksgivings ye ha'e,
And warstle for a sunny day—
  Carle, now the King's come !

" My Doctors, look that you agree,
Cure a' the town without a fee ;
My Lawyers, dinna pike a plea—
  Carle, now the King's come !

" Come forth each sturdy Burgher's bairn,
That dints on wood or clanks on airn,
That fires the o'en, or winds the pirn—
  Carle, now the King's come !

" Come forward with the Blanket Blue,[1]
Your sires were loyal men and true,
As Scotland's foemen oft might rue—
  Carle, now the King's come !

[1] [The Blue Blanket is the standard of the incorporated trades
of Edinburgh, and is kept by their convener, " at whose appearance therewith," observes Maitland, " 'tis said, that not only the
artificers of Edinburgh are obliged to repair to it, but all the artificers or craftsmen within Scotland are bound to follow it, and
fight under the convener of Edinburgh, as aforesaid." According to an old tradition, this standard was used in the Holy Wars
by a body of crusading citizens of Edinburgh, and was the first
that was planted on the walls of Jerusalem, when that city was
stormed by the Christian army under the famous Godfrey. But
the real history of it seems to be this :—James III., a prince who
had virtues which the rude age in which he lived could not ap-

" Scots downa loup, and rin and rave,
We're steady folks and something grave,
·We'll keep the causeway firm and brave—
    Carle, now the King's come!

" Sir Thomas,[1] thunder from your rock,[2]
Till Pentland dinnles wi' the shock,
And lace wi' fire my snood o' smoke—
    Carle, now the King's come!

" Melville, bring out your bands of blue,
A' Louden lads, baith stout and true,
With Elcho, Hope, and Cockburn, too—[3]
    Carle, now the King's come!

" And you, who on yon bluidy braes
Compell'd the vanquish'd Despot's praise,

preciate, having been detained for nine months in the Castle of
Edinburgh by his factious nobles, was relieved by the citizens of
Edinburgh, who assaulted the castle and took it by surprise; on
which occasion, James presented the citizens with this banner,
"with a power to display the same in defence of their King,
country, and their own rights."—*Note to this stanza in the
"Account of the King's Visit,"* &c. 8vo. 1822.]

[1] [Sir Thomas Bradford, then Commander of the Forces in
Scotland.]

[2] Edinburgh Castle.

[3] [Lord Melville was Colonel of the Mid-Lothian Yeomanry
Cavalry; Sir John Hope of Pinkie, Bart., Major; and Robert
Cockburn, Esq., and Lord Elcho, were Captains in the same
corps, to which Sir Walter Scott had formerly belonged.]

Rank out—rank out—my gallant Greys—[1]
    Carle, now the King's come!

"Cock of the North, my Huntly bra',
Where are you with the Forty-twa?[2]
Ah! waes my heart that ye're awa'—
    Carle, now the King's come!

"But yonder come my canty Celts,
With durk and pistols at their belts,
Thank God, we've still some plaids and kilts—
    Carle, now the King's come!

"Lord, how the pibrochs groan and yell!
Macdonell's[3] ta'en the field himsell,
Macleod comes branking o'er the fell—
    Carle, now the King's come!

"Bend up your bow each Archer spark,
For you're to guard him light and dark;
Faith, lads, for ance ye've hit the mark—
    Carle, now the King's come!

---

[1] [The Scots Greys, headed by their gallant Colonel, General Sir James Steuart of Coltness, Bart., were on duty at Edinburgh during the King's visit. Bonaparte's exclamation at Waterloo is well known: "Ces beaux chevaux gris, comme ils travaillent!"

[2] Marquis of Huntly, now Duke of Gordon, Colonel of the 42d regiment.

[3] [The late Colonel Ronaldson Macdonell of Glengarry—who died in January, 1828.]

" Young Errol,[1] take the sword of state,
The sceptre, Panie-Morarchate ;[2]
Knight Mareschal,[3] see ye clear the gate—
     Carle, now the King's come !

" Kind cummer, Leith, ye've been mis-set,
But dinna be upon the fret—
Ye'se hae the handsel of him yet,
     Carle, now the King's come !

" My daughters, come with een sae blue,
Your garlands weave, your blossoms strew ;

[1] [The Earl of Errol is hereditary Lord High-Constable of Scotland.]

[2] [In more correct Gaelic orthography *Banamhorar-Chat*, or the Great Lady, (literally *Female Lord*) *of the Chatte:* the Celtic title of the Countess of Sutherland. " Evin unto this day, the countrey of Sutherland is yet called Cattey, the inhabitants Catteigh, and the Erle of Southerland, Morweir Cattey, in old Scottish or Irish ; which language the inhabitants of this countrey doe still use."—GORDON's *Genealogical History of the Earls of Sutherland*, p. 18. It was determined by his Majesty, that the right of carrying the sceptre lay with this noble family; and Lord Francis Leveson Gower, second son of the Countess (now Duchess) of Sutherland, was permitted to act as deputy for his mother in that honourable office. After obtaining his Majesty's permission to depart for Dunrobin Castle, his place was supplied by the Honourable John M. Stuart, second son of the Earl of Moray.]

[3] [The Author's friend and relation, the late Sir Alexander Keith, of Dunottar and Ravelstone.]

He ne'er saw fairer flowers than you—
    Carle, now the King's come!

" What shall we do for the propine——
We used to offer something fine,
But ne'er a groat's in pouch of mine—
    Carle, now the King's come!

" Deil care—for that I'se never start,
We'll welcome him with Highland heart;
Whate'er we have he's get a part—
    Carle, now the King's come!

" I'll show him mason-work this day—
Nane of your bricks of Babel clay,
But towers shall stand till time's away—
    Carle, now the King's come!

" I'll show him wit, I'll show him lair,
And gallant lads and lasses fair,
And what wad kind heart wish for mair?
    Carle, now the King's come!

" Step out, Sir John,[1] of projects rife,
Come win the thanks of an auld wife,

---

[1] [MS.—" Rise up, Sir John, of projects rife,
    And wuss him health and length of life,
    And win the thanks of an auld wife."]
The Right Honourable Sir John Sinclair of Ulbster, Bart., author

And bring him health and length of life—
Carle, now the King's come !

of "The Code of Health and Longevity," &c. &c.,—the well-
known patron and projector of national and patriotic plans and
improvements innumerable during a lifetime of now about four-
score years.   1833.]

END OF VOLUME TENTH.

www.ingramcontent.com/pod-product-compliance
Lightning Source LLC
Chambersburg PA
CBHW021712110726
47902CB00005B/1156